THE SANTANGELOS

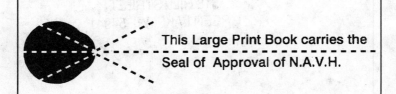

This Large Print Book carries the
Seal of Approval of N.A.V.H.

THE SANTANGELOS

JACKIE COLLINS

THORNDIKE PRESS
A part of Gale, Cengage Learning

GALE
CENGAGE Learning®

Farmington Hills, Mich • San Francisco • New York • Waterville, Maine
Meriden, Conn • Mason, Ohio • Chicago

LIBRARY OF CONGRESS CATALOGING-IN-PUBLICATION DATA

Collins, Jackie.
  The Santangelos / Jackie Collins. — Large print edition.
    pages cm. — (Thorndike Press large print core)
    ISBN 978-1-4104-7737-8 (hardback) — ISBN 1-4104-7737-1 (hardcover)
    1. Matriarchy—Fiction. 2. Italian American families—Fiction. 3. Large type books. I. Title.
  PR6053.O425S26 2015b
  823'.914—dc23   2015017020

Published in 2015 by arrangement with St. Martin's Press, LLC
Printed in the United States of America

Printed in the United States of America
1 2 3 4 5 6 7 19 18 17 16 15

To my many loyal and wonderful readers
who have faithfully followed the
Santangelo family for years.
I wish you nothing but love and peace.
Oh yes, and remember —
never fuck with a Santangelo!

PROLOGUE

The king of Akramshar — a small but wealthy Middle Eastern country located between Syria and Lebanon — ruled his oil-rich country with an iron fist. And although King Emir Amin Mohamed Jordan embraced many old-fashioned values and traditions, he also implemented his own rules, and they were harsh.

The king had countless wives and more than thirty children. In his mind, they were all useless. Women were good for only two things: giving birth and being at his sexual beck and call. As for his offspring — some of them grown men — they were all disappointments. The only son who'd given him any pleasure at all was his dear departed son Armand, a worthy successor to the king's coveted crown. And Armand was gone. Murdered by the American infidels. A bullet to the head in a degenerate American city called Las Vegas.

The king's fury was boundless. How could this have happened? And why?

King Emir had given Armand a royal funeral

fit for his favorite son. His people had lined the streets, heads bowed, showing their respect as they should. Several of his many sons carried the solid gold casket on their shoulders. Peggy, Armand's American mother; his widow, Soraya; and Armand's four children walked solemnly behind. The women, including Peggy, wore traditional robes covering their entire bodies. The king rode on a white stallion, resplendent in a gold-trimmed uniform, waving to his people.

King Emir was a man who believed in revenge. And who exactly was to blame for the unfortunate demise of his favorite son, shot to death like a dog?

King Emir had his own ideas. Armand had been trying to buy the very hotel he was murdered in — the Keys — a hotel owned by a woman. That a woman could actually own a hotel was ridiculous, but even more ridiculous — according to Peggy — the woman had refused to sell her property to Armand, and on top of that she had insulted him to his face, and the king had no doubt that it was she who had arranged for Armand's brutal murder.

King Emir simmered with fury, while dark thoughts of revenge filled his head. Justice had to be done.

But how?

Kill the woman? Take her life exactly as she had taken Armand's?

No. That was not punishment enough. The

10

woman had to suffer, and her family had to suffer.

This was a given.

For almost a year, King Emir had been busy putting plans in place — for his rage would rain down on the offensive American mongrels. And they too would feel the pain of a terrible loss.

The woman's name was Lucky Santangelo.

BOOK ONE

CHAPTER ONE:
LUCKY

The Keys was Lucky Santangelo Golden's dream hotel, but sometimes one can dream bigger, and Lucky had decided that she should create something even more special. She was at a place in her life where she felt ready for a new challenge. Everything was running smoothly; her kids were all doing well. Bobby, with his chain of successful clubs. Max, busy making a name for herself in London as an up-and-coming model. Young Gino Junior and Leo (Lennie's son, whom she'd adopted) were ensconced in summer camp, while her father, Gino, was happily living out his days in Palm Springs with his fourth wife, Paige.

So Lucky had decided it was time to shake things up, and she'd come up with the idea of building a hotel/casino/apartment complex plus a movie studio. This was something nobody had done before. Why not? It was a brilliant idea.

When she'd told her filmmaker husband,

Lennie, he'd thought it was a crazy concept, although certainly doable. The movie community would love it. Everything in one place. And it wasn't as if Lucky was a newcomer to making movies — she'd owned and run Panther Studios for several years. She *was* the Lady Boss. Lucky Santangelo could do anything she chose to do.

Today she was lunching with a team of architects that she was considering hiring. One of her favorite moves was testing people, observing their strengths and weaknesses, deciding if working with them would be calm or stressful.

Danny, her trusty assistant, accompanied her on the way to the Asian, an elegant Chinese restaurant located in her hotel.

Danny was one of the few privy to the fact that she was plotting and planning on building yet another fantastic Vegas complex. Danny got it. He understood that the Keys — a truly amazing combination of grand hotel, luxurious apartments, and one of the best casinos in Vegas — was simply not enough for her. As usual, his dynamic boss wanted more.

The moment Lucky entered the restaurant, conversation stopped and people stared. They couldn't help themselves. Lucky had a magnetic, charismatic quality about her. She radiated beauty, power, passion, and strength. A lethal combination.

Danny relished every minute of the way people reacted when they saw Lucky. She deserved the attention. She was a true star, an incredibly smart businesswoman who could achieve anything she set her mind to. The thing about Lucky was that she needed to be collaborative, but she also needed to be in control. Nobody told Lucky Santangelo what to do. Her motto was "If I'm going to fail, I'll fail on my own mistakes, not on someone else's." Her other motto was "Never fuck with a Santangelo."

Danny had both mottos engraved on two coffee mugs that sat in the kitchen of his L.A. apartment along with his somewhat mangy cat, Ethel.

They were lunching at the Asian because although most meetings took place in the boardroom, at other times Lucky liked to see for herself how efficiently everything was running. Danny could just imagine the panic taking place in the kitchen. *Ms. Santangelo is in the house. Everything has to be perfect.*

Lucky strode through the restaurant, unaware of the buzz of excitement she was causing. The two men and one woman she was meeting with jumped to their feet as she approached. Danny detected much nervous tension.

Lucky immediately put them all at ease. "How's everyone today?" she asked, flashing them a dazzling smile.

Everything about Lucky was dazzling — from her wild mass of long dark curls to her deep olive skin and her black-as-night eyes. Lucky was ageless, and she exuded sex appeal; she always had.

"All the better for seeing you," one of the men managed. He was balding and nervous, a trait many people exhibited when meeting Lucky for the first time.

Directing her attention to the female of the group, an attractive black woman in her early forties, Lucky said, "You must be Nina. I've heard many positive things about your work. In fact, I should tell you that you're the main reason I requested this meeting."

Danny watched the men shrivel. He knew what they were thinking: Nina worked *for* them, not alongside them. She was a junior partner in their firm, but Lucky had insisted they bring Nina to the meeting. Ah yes, Lucky was all about female power — it pleased her to see other women succeed.

Nina blossomed. She was full of ideas that Lucky seemed to be into, and the meeting went well once the two men realized that Nina could turn out to be an asset, not a threat.

"If we get together on this," Lucky announced at the conclusion of lunch, "then I expect Nina to head up your team. How do you feel about that?"

The men nodded. This could be an enormous project, and if Lucky Santangelo wanted Nina, that's exactly who she'd get.

Danny escorted Lucky out of the restaurant, reminding her of the agenda for the rest of the day. She had more meetings; a drink with her superstar friend Venus, who was currently shooting a movie in Vegas; then a late-night flight back to her other home in L.A.

Lucky divided her time between her Vegas penthouse and her Malibu beach house. In Vegas it was mostly work. In Malibu she could sit back and relax — especially when Lennie was home, which wasn't always the case. Like his wife, Lennie was a workaholic. Once a stand-up comedian and then a movie star, his current passion was writing, producing, and directing his own independent movies.

Lennie spent a lot of time on location.

Lucky spent a lot of time in Vegas.

Time apart boded well for their marriage. They had never been happier — for when they were in the same place, things were as steamy as the first time they'd gotten together. It helped that Lennie was a master of tantric sex, and that Lucky had always maintained a wild streak in the bedroom. It amused her when married people complained about their sex life being boring. Didn't they realize that it wasn't their sex life, it was them — allowing themselves to fall into a state of lethargy and disinterest? Nothing like disinterest to put the brakes on adventures in the bedroom.

After more meetings, Lucky felt in need of a drink. She was looking forward to seeing Venus. Once so close, over the last year they'd kind of lost touch. Lucky understood why. First of all, Venus had abandoned her latest boy toy and hooked up with Hugo Santos, a Venezuelan avant-garde filmmaker who obviously saw the platinum-blond superstar as much more than a luscious world-famous sex symbol. He'd moved in on Venus big-time and taken over her career. She was currently playing a drugged-out whore in his gritty movie *Woman.*

Venus viewed Hugo Santos as her intellectual savior, while Lucky considered him to be a grasping opportunist who saw Venus as his ticket to conquer Hollywood.

The second reason they'd drifted apart was Max, and her fleeting thing with Billy Melina — Venus's ex-husband. Max making out with her best friend's ex was more than awkward.

Lucky had never discussed it with Venus, and fortunately, the burgeoning romance between Billy and Max had fizzled — with a little help from Lennie, who'd visited Billy and told him in no uncertain terms to stay away from his teenage daughter or there'd be major repercussions. Faced with pressure from his team of advisers as well, Billy had complied, and Max had taken off to London,

20

where she now resided. Lucky missed her, although not as much as Lennie did. Lennie was way too protective, while Lucky knew it was good for Max to be out on her own experiencing independence.

Lucky waited for Venus on a secluded terrace overlooking the golf course. Usually Venus liked to make an entrance, but today she'd requested that they meet somewhere quiet. Lucky had agreed, and now she was sitting on the terrace sipping a Campari and orange juice. Closing her eyes for a moment, she imagined the new hotel complex she was planning. A hotel attached to a movie studio. How fantastic! How innovative! And even though it would take at least two or three years to build, she was excited. It occurred to her that maybe she'd even start producing movies again. She'd always enjoyed the process, and it could be fun, another challenge. Perhaps she and Lennie could work on something together. Although if they did that, they'd probably kill each other.

She smiled at the thought of two incredibly stubborn people working side by side. No. It was never going to happen.

A woman was walking toward her. A dark-haired woman wearing frumpy clothes and old-fashioned horn-rimmed glasses. There was something vaguely familiar about her, but Lucky wasn't sure what it was until the woman pulled out a chair and sat down opposite her.

Oh my God, Lucky thought, her mind spinning. *It's Venus!*

CHAPTER TWO:
BOBBY

It pissed Bobby Santangelo Stanislopoulos off that his live-in girlfriend, Denver Jones, was never available to travel with him. Even with texting, sexting, and Skype, long separations were no damn good. Oh sure, he understood that Denver was fixated on her job as a high-powered deputy district attorney, but surely just sometimes she could put him first?

Lately she'd been so into the drug case she was working on that even when he was home at their house in L.A., he barely saw her. She was intent to prosecute; he'd never seen her so determined.

This too shall pass, he told himself. *And when it's over, I will finally give her the seven-carat Tiffany diamond engagement ring I purchased months ago, and ask her to marry me.*

He had to tread carefully with Denver. She wasn't like the other girls he'd been with.

She was exceptionally smart, beautiful, and a self-achiever. She didn't want anything from him other than his love, and that suited him just fine, because as the heir to a great shipping fortune, he knew that most women looked at him with dollar signs flashing in their eyes.

Bobby Santangelo Stanislopoulos, son of the infamous Lucky Santangelo and the late Greek shipping tycoon Dimitri Stanislopoulos. Drop-dead handsome with longish dark hair, intense eyes, and olive skin — all inherited from the Santangelo side of the family. Six foot three, with his father's strong features and steely business acumen, plus Lucky's street smarts. An interesting mix.

Without touching his massive inheritance, Bobby had gone into business for himself. He and his partner, M.J., had opened a chain of highly successful nightclubs called Mood. From New York to Las Vegas, Mood was the place to see and be seen.

Currently they were in the process of opening Mood in Chicago, which meant Bobby had a full agenda.

Pacing up and down in his Chicago hotel room, he missed Denver, although at the same time, he was also kind of mad at her. In the course of pursuing a notorious drug cartel, she'd been part of a sting operation that had ended with the arrest of Frankie Romano.

Poor old Frankie — who happened to be a longtime pal of Bobby's. Unfortunately, Frankie had gotten himself caught up in the so-called glamour of the Hollywood high life. A druggie who'd once been Annabelle Falcon's boyfriend, Frankie had partnered in a sleazy Hollywood club with the son of a Colombian drug lord, then gotten himself taken down for illegally peddling drugs. The charges against him were distribution and possession — charges that could get him a twenty-year prison sentence. It seemed his operation was connected to a notorious Colombian drug cartel, and Denver was making it her business to find out exactly how. She was relentless in her pursuit.

Bobby had tried his best to persuade her to go easy on Frankie. It hadn't worked; she'd refused to listen to him. Deep down he'd known she was right. Frankie had been a bad boy, and he deserved to be punished. But such a long jail term? Couldn't Denver fix it so that Frankie was put on probation for co-operating with the investigation? She had the inside track — why not do it as a favor for him? It was a situation he was not happy with.

M.J. called up from the lobby. "You on your way down?" he asked.

"Be right there," Bobby answered, checking his watch and realizing that he was running late.

They were headed for the opening night of Mood Chicago. The club was not yet open to the public; this evening was by invite only. VIPs, local celebrities, attention grabbers.

Bobby placed a call to Denver on her cell, but it went straight to voice mail. Grabbing his jacket, he headed downstairs. M.J. was waiting in the lobby.

M.J. was African American, short of stature, handsome — with a shaved head and an endless enthusiasm for all their projects. More outgoing than Bobby, he was the perfect business partner.

Tonight M.J. was all hyped up, looking his usual cool self in a black Armani suit. "It's gonna be a full house," he announced when Bobby appeared. "We got all the right faces comin'. The PR we hired has done a fine job."

Bobby nodded. Their club was looking stellar. And so it should, since they'd spent the last week in Chicago making sure everything was perfect, testing food, drinks, waiters, bartenders, and the couple of hosts who were all set to run the place when they weren't there.

M.J. had a car and driver waiting outside the hotel. Bobby elected to take his rental car in case he chose to leave earlier.

M.J. shrugged. "Gotta get back to check in with your girl," he said, his tone lightly mocking. "Man, Denver's got your ass well whipped. I remember when —"

"Gimme a break," Bobby interrupted with a friendly grin. "You *wish* you had someone to check in with."

Since divorcing his pretty but overly ambitious wife, Cassie, M.J. had turned into the perennial bachelor, sampling a parade of random girls at an alarming rate. Bobby realized that it was all bravado. The truth was that M.J. missed Cassie, only he would never admit it.

"Someone, anyone — as if I give a fast fuck," M.J. said. "Y'see, me, I got it all figured. Variety is where it's at, an' you, my man, are missin' out."

By the time Bobby arrived at the club, it was already packed. Word was out that Mood was about to be *the* place, and the movers in town were determined to mark their territory, making sure they got the right table and the attention they imagined they deserved.

M.J. was already doing the rounds, stopping by tables, buying drinks, turning on the M.J. charm. He had the knack.

Bobby hovered near the bar. He was in no way as social as M.J.; he was more into the design and financial aspect of the business. But he was well aware that a few personal greetings went a long way, so after one quick shot of vodka, he forced himself into host mode and stopped by a few tables to say hello.

Bobby's particular brand of charm worked well with both men and women. The women loved getting attention from such an attractive man, while the men related to him because he could talk sports, cars, and cigars, plus he bought every table he stopped by a bottle of champagne. Lucky had taught him that the two golden rules of owning a successful club were remembering the customers' names, and buying them a drink.

Soon he was into the rhythm of the place, feeling that certain rush he got when everything was moving in the right direction. Mood was set to take over Chicago nightlife — the same way it had in Vegas and New York.

Nursing another vodka, he settled into a corner booth, observing the action and wondering if he should call Denver again.

No. He'd left her a message; it was her turn to call him.

M.J. loped over. "Looks like we got ourselves another winner," he announced, sitting down next to Bobby. "We're takin' over Chicago, man. Bet on it."

Bobby laughed, and as he did so he caught sight of a young woman descending the staircase into the club. She wasn't just any woman, she was a Latina version of Michelle Pfeiffer making her entrance in the movie *Scarface.* The woman was a showstopper. A stone-cold beauty in a body-hugging red dress.

M.J. noticed her too. "Are you seein' what I'm seein'?" he gulped.

"Yeah, I'm seeing it," Bobby said, attempting not to stare.

"Who the fuck is she?"

"Like *I* would know."

"Hey, man," M.J. said, jumping to his feet. "Got me a feelin' it's time to find out."

"Go for it."

"That's my main plan."

Bobby observed as M.J. launched into action, greeting the exotic woman and her escort, a short Latino man with bland features, a scraggly beard, and hard eyes. They did not look like a couple — they looked all wrong together.

M.J. led them to a premier table, ordered them a bottle of champagne, then backed off.

"Who are they?" Bobby asked when M.J. returned to the booth.

M.J. shrugged. "They're not on the list. I asked our PR, and she doesn't know them either. But hey, who gives a shit? They can stay. Man, the woman's a freakin' ten plus."

"I can see that. The guy with her — husband? Boyfriend?"

"Dude's her cousin, an' that works for me, 'cause I got major plans on movin' right back in."

"Sure you do," Bobby said with a knowing smile.

"Oh yeah," M.J. said, nodding to himself. "Gonna cool it for now. Make my move later. Watch an' learn, my man. You'll see how it's done."

Bobby felt his phone vibrate and reached

for it. It was about time Denver called him back.

Suddenly the Latina Michelle Pfeiffer clone was merely a distant memory.

CHAPTER THREE:
MAX

"More?" Athena Hyton-Smythe inquired, leaning over to her friend Max Santangelo Golden. Athena was tall and ultra skinny — six feet *without* her five-inch Louboutins. She had frizzed-out flame-colored hair, cut-glass cheekbones, cat eyes, and a permanent super-sexy scowl. At twenty, Athena was the current "It" girl of the modeling world, and Max was her sidekick, and on the way to making a name for herself as well. The London gossip columns had nicknamed them the Terrible Two. They had a reputation for all-night partying and always being the leaders of the pack.

"More what?" Max replied, sucking a tall mojito through a straw.

"Whatever turns you on," Athena said with a casual shrug of her glistening bare shoulders randomly scattered with gold glitter. "Coke, grass, tequila shots, Molly, pills, you name it." She indicated a heavyset man sitting in their booth downing shots of straight vodka.

"This Russian dude is like a freakin' pharmacy. He's offering, so we should take advantage while we can. You know I don't get off on paying for my drugs."

Max leaned back on the plush leather banquette in the London club and considered her options. She was a very pretty girl with full, pouty lips, emerald-green eyes, and long dark hair. Tonight she wore a cutoff top, multiple gold chains, ridiculous heels, and tight black leather pants.

Max was just nineteen, and delighted that in London she could get away with drinking in clubs. Her brother Bobby, who owned a string of successful nightclubs around the world, wouldn't allow her to drink in his Vegas and New York clubs. "You're underage," he'd informed her. "Go get someone else's license pulled."

"Screw you, Bobby," she'd responded.

The truth was that since moving to London, she really missed Bobby — along with the rest of her family. Mom Lucky. Dad Lennie. Little bro Gino Junior, half brother Leo, and grandpa Gino. What a family. What a close-knit group. She loved them all, but she'd had to get away after everything that had taken place with the whole Billy situation.

Athena was pushing her for an answer. Drake was pounding it over the sound system.

"What?" Max said irritably. "You go for it,

'cause I'm like so not in the mood for getting high."

Athena widened her eyes as if she couldn't quite believe anyone would be dumb enough to turn down free drugs. "Oh *please,*" she said impatiently. "Make a decision."

"Actually, I'm about to head out," Max announced, reaching for her phone and texting for an Uber cab to pick her up.

"You're leaving me?" Athena said with a put-upon frown.

"You're a big girl. You'll manage," Max said, sliding out of the booth past the heavyset man and several other rich men only too happy to pick up the check for two delectable young females.

Max and Athena had first met through Athena's older brother, Tim, in the South of France, where Lucky and Lennie had taken Max on vacation to recover from her short but sweet affair with hot movie star Billy Melina. *Short* was the operative word. Everything between her and Billy had ground to a shattering halt when they'd both been witnesses to a violent robbery where Billy had gotten his cheek slashed defending her while the murder of businessman Armand Jordan had been taking place. This had all happened at Lucky's hotel complex, the Keys. Billy's minders had distanced him from Max immediately, whisking him off to the best plastic surgeon in town. And even though Billy had

assured Max that they would get back together soon, it had never happened.

Eventually he'd called and told her that his
PR team and manager had suggested that
they cool it for a while. "You're so damn
young, Green Eyes," he'd said. "And I'm getting over my divorce from Venus, so you and
I being together right now isn't cool for either
of us."

"I get it," she'd said. Although she was
totally heartbroken, she'd been determined
not to crumble.

After that she couldn't get in touch with
him, and he certainly hadn't reached out to
her. Finally, she'd realized that it was definitely over.

Depression overcame her. Wasn't eighteen
too young to experience a broken heart?

Apparently not, for she'd experienced it, all
right, and it was extremely painful.

The South of France vacation helped.
She'd hooked up with a twenty-two-year-old
French guy who turned out to be nothing
more than a vacation fling. Her second sexual
foray.

He wasn't Billy.

Nobody was Billy.

After a couple of miserable months back in
L.A. lurking around doing nothing, she'd run
into Athena at a party, and Athena had
invited her to come stay with her in London.

"Endless fun and games," Athena promised.

"We can do anything we want."

"I'm on it," Max enthused. "Can't wait."

The next morning she'd informed Lucky and Lennie that she was thinking of moving to London for a while. They couldn't stop her; she was eighteen. Lucky encouraged her to go do her own thing. Lucky was all into girls being strong and independent. Lennie — not so much. In his mind, Max was still his little girl, and he wasn't sure he wanted her roaming the world. But Max was determined, so off she went.

Now it was nine months later and she'd made a life for herself away from L.A. and all memories of Billy. Except that this morning, while idly browsing the Internet, she'd come across an item about Billy making his next movie in Europe. The locations where he would be shooting included Paris, London, and Rome.

This was majorly annoying. Wasn't it enough that she had to see his photo in magazines accompanied by a parade of stunning young actresses hanging on to his arm? Now he was about to encroach on *her* territory. It simply wasn't fair.

Several paparazzi were hovering outside the club when she exited. As soon as they spotted her, they jumped to attention. "Where's your sexy girlfriend?" one of them asked with a knowing smirk, his camera flashing in her face. "You two haven't split up, have you?"

Everyone salivated over the thought that she and Athena *might* be gay. They weren't, but it amused them to keep people guessing. They called each other "Sweet Eyes," and sometimes fake kissed for the cameras, putting on an outrageous act.

Max got off on the attention, often wondering if Billy ever saw her photo on the gossip sites or in the magazines. Probably not, because although Athena was red-hot in Europe, well known as a happening "It" girl, her particular brand of fame had not yet crossed over to America.

Max was full of anticipation the following week. She had an important photo shoot for a well-known jeans company. The ads, her agency had assured her, would break internationally, and that meant that Billy was certain to see them.

Ha! Billy Melina. Big movie star. Would he even remember her?

Of course he would, she told herself. After all, they'd shared something really special. Billy was the first man she'd gone all the way with, and that had to count for something.

Her Uber cab arrived and she got in, still thinking about Billy. Would he ever make his way out of her mind?

Probably not.

"Wait!" Athena yelled, tottering out of the club on her five-inch heels and flinging open the door of the cab, oblivious to the flashing cameras. "I'm coming too. Who cares about free drugs?"

Max shifted to make room for her friend.

"You little minx!" Athena exclaimed, flopping next to Max on the backseat of the cab. "Leaving me with those boring old men. I hate you!"

"We've got to find a new group to hang with," Max said, pulling at a red string bracelet wrapped around her wrist. "I'm so over the London club scene."

"Me too," Athena agreed, licking her gold-glossed lips. "Here's what we should do, after our weekend at the Abbey — we should take off and go cause chaos somewhere different."

Max wrinkled her nose. "Where?"

"Not to worry. I'll come up with an amazingly fun place," Athena responded. "Don't I always?"

Max nodded. This was true. Athena had a knack for sniffing out the best locations, and quite frankly she couldn't wait.

CHAPTER FOUR: DENVER

"Long-distance relationships suck," Denver Jones complained to her friend Carolyn Henderson as they sat out on the back patio of Carolyn's small house in West Hollywood eating breakfast. Carolyn's infant son, Andy, slept nearby in a wicker bassinet.

"Then maybe you should break up with him," Carolyn responded with a casual shrug, tearing at a warm croissant and smothering it in butter.

"I didn't *say* I wanted to break up with him," Denver said, throwing her a stony look, wondering why Carolyn was always so negative. "I'm merely bitching about Bobby traveling all over the place while I'm stuck in L.A. 'cause of my job."

"Ah, but it's a job that you live, breathe, and totally love," Carolyn pointed out.

"Oh, yeah," Denver drawled sarcastically. "I so *love* trying to nail sleazebags who sell drugs to children and murder people when they get in their way. It's *so* rewarding, not to mention majorly exciting."

"Although, as a very competent deputy DA, you *do* love it when you hear the magic word: *guilty,*" Carolyn said matter-of-factly. "You're the one who gets to lock the bad guys away."

"And how often does *that* happen?" Denver said, reflecting on how screwed up the justice system could be. Nothing was ever a sure thing. "These guys hire the most expensive and canny lawyers, men in five-thousand-dollar suits who are paid fortunes to get those criminal assholes off the hook. And most times they succeed."

"Unfortunately, that's the system," Carolyn said, adding jam to her croissant.

"Yeah," Denver said glumly. "The system blows, and I should know since I was once part of it. I am *so* much happier being on the other side."

"I can tell," Carolyn said. "And you *did* get Frankie Romano arrested and thrown into jail."

"True," Denver said thoughtfully. "In spite of Bobby urging me to go easy on him."

"Bobby gave you a hard time, right?"

"He certainly did, Frankie being an old friend of his. I mean, what did he *expect* me to do? It's my *job,* for God's sake. There's no way I can call in favors. Frankie's apartment was drug city. *And* he was dealing big-time."

Since leaving the law firm of Saunders, Fields, Simmons and Johnson, where she had been one of their youngest defense attorneys, Denver was thrilled that she no longer had to defend scuzzy celebrities who were obviously guilty — including action-movie star Ralph Maestro. It was all a big relief. She was so glad she'd switched sides to become a deputy DA. She was currently part of a drug task force — a tight-knit group of people, all with the same endgame in mind: to stop the endless flow of illegal drugs into America. The stories that she saw and heard devastated her. Babies born addicted to crack; teenagers overdosing at parties; young girls forced into addiction and prostitution. And who profited from all this misery? The dealers, of course. From the kids on the street who peddled pot and pills to the drug lords like Pablo Fernandez Diego, an unprincipled Colombian who funneled drugs from his country into the United States at an alarming rate. The Diego cartel was notorious for supplying large shipments of cocaine, marijuana, heroin, and methamphetamine. It seemed Pablo's drug operation was unstoppable, and although it would be more or less impossible to nail him in Colombia, if they could nab his lowlife son, Alejandro, it would be a major coup. Alejandro owned Club Luna, a Hollywood hangout that everyone knew was merely a front for laundering drug money — but so far, nothing could be proved. Arresting Frankie Romano was a positive, and Denver had high hopes that soon Frankie would start hemorrhaging information, for as Alejandro's former close friend and minor partner in the club, he had to know plenty. Getting him to talk was the key to maybe indicting Alejandro. So far Frankie had refused to cooperate.

"Have you ever thought that Bobby might fool around on you?" Carolyn asked.

"Are you kidding me?" Denver said, surprised that Carolyn would even suggest it. "Why would you say that?"

"It's never crossed your mind that he could cheat?"

"No, it never has."

"Then you're more naive than I thought," Carolyn said, taking a gulp of hot coffee. "*All* men cheat."

"And since when did *you* become such an expert on men?"

"Oh, *please,*" Carolyn sighed. "Try waking up to the real world. Your boyfriend is Bobby Santangelo Stanislopoulos, a total catch. Rich, handsome, charming. *And* he owns a bunch of hot clubs, which means he's exposed to all the best-looking girls — and you can bet they come on to him. Single girls hitting the club scene are ruthless. They'll go after a guy big-time. Especially a guy like Bobby."

"So what?" Denver said, narrowing her eyes. "It's not as if I'm exactly a dog. Men come on to me too. Besides, Bobby and I are in a secure relationship. We trust each other."

"Okay, okay," Carolyn said, thinking that it was true, Denver *was* a knockout, with her shiny auburn hair, curvy body, and wide-spaced hazel eyes. However, relationships were always at risk when there were long separations involved. "You're not getting the big picture," Carolyn added. "You should keep an eye on him, not give him so much freedom."

"For God's sake," Denver said, an exasperated frown covering her face. "Ever since you decided to play for the other team, you have absolutely no respect for men."

"Respect?" Carolyn said, raising a cynical eyebrow. "Surely you kid. Men are horny all the time, and let's not forget, you're here and he's there."

"Thanks," Denver said drily. "It's great to have such supportive friends."

"What?" Carolyn said. "You really think he doesn't play around? I'm merely the teller of truths."

"Then may I suggest you go tell them to someone else," Denver said, getting to her feet. "I'm out of here. Thanks for breakfast. As for the lecture — no thanks."

"Have fun catching criminals."

"I wish you wouldn't say that," Denver responded, still frowning. "How many times do I have to tell you — my job is not fun."

"Whatever . . ."

Denver shook her head. There were times that Carolyn got on her nerves, and today was one of them. She had too much on her mind to worry about Carolyn putting thoughts of Bobby cheating in her head. Besides, Bobby wasn't the cheating type. He was one of the good guys, and yes, she did trust him, just as he trusted her. They'd been living together in a house in the Hollywood Hills for almost a year, and so far everything was cool.

"Don't forget tomorrow night," Carolyn said as Denver headed inside. "Special dinner at the Falcons'. I'll pick you up."

"Not a plan," Denver replied, moving through the house toward the front door.

"Why not?" Carolyn asked, following her inside.

" 'Cause I might be working late," Denver said, opening the door and briskly walking outside to her car, which was parked on the street. "Do not depend on me."

"You can't miss dinner," Carolyn called out. "You know what Annabelle is like. She'll throw one of her diva fits."

"You think I care *what* Annabelle does?" Denver called back, getting behind the wheel of her car. " 'Cause I don't."

"Well, you should," Carolyn shouted. "She can be a real pain in the ass."

Ignoring her, Denver started the engine and drove off.

Annabelle Falcon, née Maestro, and Carolyn Henderson were her two former college roommates. Over the years, the three of them had remained friends in spite of several full-on dramas, and although they both drove her a little bit crazy, they still shared a close bond.

Annabelle was less of a problem since she'd married agent Eddie Falcon and settled into the spoiled daily routine of a Hollywood wife. Pilates, spinning, yoga, daily sessions with a life coach and a shrink, weekly visits to a dermatologist. And of course the Hollywood Wife basics — shopping, lunches, putting together exclusive dinner parties. Denver was in awe of how busy Annabelle was at achieving absolutely nothing.

Carolyn, on the other hand, had suffered big problems. An illicit affair with the very much married Senator Gregory Stoneman in Washington had ended in a horrific kidnapping, after which Carolyn had fled back to L.A., without revealing to her married lover that she was still pregnant. The senator was under the impression she'd lost the baby.

She hadn't.

Back in L.A., well away from Washington, she'd given birth to a son, Andy, then announced to her friends that she was now a lesbian and wanted nothing more to do with men. It was all very complicated, and even though Denver had tried to convince her that

44

she should tell the senator about Andy and at least receive child support, Carolyn had stubbornly refused to entertain the thought.

As Denver drove toward her office, she attempted to concentrate on the big picture. Getting Frankie Romano to talk was number one on her agenda. She was sure he knew plenty about Alejandro's activities, and if it meant a lighter sentence, then surely he'd be prepared to spill? Frankie — who happened to be an ex-boyfriend of Annabelle's — was a weasel. Why wouldn't he give Alejandro up? After all, he was Frankie Romano — wouldn't he do anything to save his skinny ass from languishing in jail?

Arriving at the office, she was greeted by Leon, a fellow member of the task force. Leon was carrying a bag of donuts and two cups of coffee. "You look kinda tired," he said, placing one of the cups on her desk.

"Thanks," she said caustically. "That's exactly what a girl wants to hear."

In his mid-thirties and black, Leon had a kind of chill Will Smith vibe going for him. He changed girlfriends as often as he changed his pants, always leaving them with a smile on their face. A likable guy, he was one of Denver's best friends, even though he was always teasing her, saying that if she weren't living with Mr. Rich Pants — his nickname for Bobby — they would make a happening couple.

"Happening in what way?" she always asked with an amused smile.

Leon came up with the same answer every time. "Sex, baby," he assured her. "Bed-breakin' sex."

It was a running joke between them.

She dove into the bag of donuts and selected one. "Is this raspberry cream?" she asked.

"What do you think?" Leon said with a big grin. "I know your taste buds like I know my own."

"That sounds vaguely rude."

"It's meant to," he said with a jaunty wink. "Hard night?"

"Bobby's away, so I was home," she said, biting into the donut.

"You should've called me. I would've come right over."

"Somehow I'm not sure staying home is quite your style."

"Hey — I'm always stylin'."

"Anyway, I had company. Reruns of *Scandal.* Nothing better."

"How's your foxy friend Carolyn?"

"How many times do I have to tell you?" Denver said, exasperated. "Carolyn does *not* play on your side of the fence, *and* she has a girlfriend, so isn't it about time you stopped lusting after her?"

"Y'know," Leon said, perching on the edge of her desk, "I could turn that girl around

46

anytime you gimme the word. I got a magic wand that works every time."

"Such confidence!" Denver said, smiling, as she wiped a dab of raspberry cream off her chin.

"If you got it, use it," Leon boasted. "An' I happen t' have all the right moves."

"Then I suggest you take some of those moves and arrange another get-together with Frankie Romano and his douche-bag lawyer. I'm sure Frankie's not loving spending time in prison. I sense a deal in our future, don't you?"

"I'm right on it," Leon said, taking off.

Denver took another bite of her donut and thought about what Carolyn had said, that all men — if given the opportunity — cheated.

Bobby's different, she assured herself.

Or is he?

Suddenly she was full of doubt.

Chapter Five:
Alejandro

"That fuckin' DA is a fuckin' bitch cunt," Alejandro Diego fumed, pacing up and down the polished white marble floor of his luxury penthouse located on the Wilshire Corridor in L.A. "I got people telling me she's putting on the pressure trying to get Frankie Romano to talk shit on me. You know what my father would say? That they both got to be dealt with, an' my *papi,* he's always right."

"Pablo's not here," Rafael, Alejandro's right-hand man, pointed out. "Pablo's in Colombia."

Alejandro's nostrils flared, indicating his sour anger. "You think I don't know that?" he steamed. "You think I'm a fool?"

"You never should have become involved with Frankie," Rafael said in his best I-told-you-so voice. "I tried to warn you he was a loser. The problem is that you never listen to me."

"Shut the fuck up," Alejandro spat. "Frankie's the one who got me to buy the club. And how come you're always the voice of doom? What is it with you?"

"Your lawyer says you're safe for now," Rafael said, remaining calm, even though he had an urge to smash Alejandro in his dumbass face.

"Horace Bendon doesn't know shit," Alejandro muttered. "It's *my* opinion that matters, and *I* say that Frankie needs to get warned about what will happen to him if he opens his big mouth. As for that DA *puta* — you *know* she's trying to get me indicted, so why aren't you doing something?"

"I am," Rafael said quietly. "I'm taking her mind off you. I have put a plan in motion."

Alejandro turned on Rafael with a vicious expression. "It better be good," he threatened.

"It will be."

Alejandro was the privileged son of Pablo Fernandez Diego, a feared Colombian drug lord who ruled an empire. Rafael was the lowly son of Eugenia, Pablo's housekeeper. The two men had grown up together.

Eugenia, a comely woman, had cared for both boys as if they were brothers, and many people suspected that they were, for Eugenia had no husband or significant other. The only man in her life was Pablo, whom she doted on.

Pablo Fernandez Diego was not only a major drug lord, he was also a notorious womanizer. Married three times to a trio of beauty queens, he entertained an endless parade of mistresses. After business, sex was his favorite pastime.

Alejandro's mother had died in a tragic car accident when he was a baby, so the only mother figure he'd known was Eugenia. He had no siblings — maybe Rafael, although neither Eugenia nor Pablo would admit that Rafael *was* his actual brother, which suited him fine. Alejandro took pride in the fact that *he* was the chosen one who would eventually inherit Pablo's huge drug empire. Rafael had no inheritance rights.

At twenty-nine, the two of them were a month apart in age — Rafael being older. They'd attended school together, hung out together, screwed the same girls, and finally completed their education at UCLA in California, where Rafael had spent most of his time cleaning up Alejandro's messes. Over time there were many — from several girls Alejandro had gotten pregnant to a major cheating scandal.

Alejandro had fallen in love with the American way of life, and after returning to Pablo's ranch in Bogotá for a couple of years, working in the family business, he'd persuaded his father that there was more money to be made if Pablo put him in charge of trafficking cocaine and other illegal shipments to California.

"I already have people in place who are taking care of that," Pablo had informed him. "Everything's running smoothly."

"I know," Alejandro had replied, working on Pablo as only he could. "But do not forget, Papi, that *I* am family, so who better to trust?"

After a while, Pablo had agreed that it wasn't such a terrible idea. If his son wanted power, perhaps it would be prudent to give him a small taste. Eventually he'd arranged for Alejandro to make the move to the United States — as long as Rafael accompanied him and the two of them worked with the people Pablo already had there.

Rafael had balked at the thought of leaving. He had a young girlfriend, Elizabetta, who'd recently given birth to a baby boy, and he had no wish to leave them. However, Pablo insisted — and when Pablo insisted, nobody dared to argue, not if they valued their life.

Before they headed back to L.A., Pablo had summoned Rafael into his private sanctum, his face a stern mask. "You will *always* have Alejandro's back," he'd decreed. "If anything happens to my son, it will be on your head. *You* will be to blame, nobody else. You must protect him at all times. Do you understand me, Rafael?"

Rafael understood him, all right. Rafael understood everything. He was locked in a steel trap, under the control of Pablo Fernandez Diego — a ruthless man who would never claim him as his rightful son, a man who

51

always expected him to be around.

This had come to pass because he was way smarter than Alejandro, and Pablo was well aware of this. Therefore, Pablo had decided that Rafael's fate in life was to be Alejandro's watchdog.

In California, the Diego cartel had several legitimate businesses where they could hide their drug money and make it legitimate. Among them was a discount pharmacy chain and a low-end canned-goods company. Neither of these businesses suited Alejandro. He'd wanted more. He'd wanted Hollywood glamour.

Soon he'd begun hanging out at River, a dubious low-level club, where he became asshole buddies with Hollywood player Frankie Romano. Frankie, who had a stake in River — and his own small-time drug business on the side — eventually persuaded Alejandro that it might not be a bad idea for him to buy River and make it his own. Alejandro thought this was an excellent plan, and he'd gone ahead and purchased River, changed the name to Club Luna, and, against Rafael's advice, made Frankie a minority partner.

Club Luna had turned out to be the perfect front. It was a legitimate business that suited Alejandro's lifestyle, for he was a major playboy, into fast cars and boats, beautiful women, and recreational drugs. A smooth operator, he was swarthy, his long hair greased and gelled, his suits handmade, and his attitude arrogant. He strode around as if he owned the world, sleeping with as many women as he could.

Rafael, on the other hand, was more low-key. He drove a Prius, was comfortable wearing nondescript sports jackets and pants. His dark brown hair was cropped short, he kept his beard well trimmed, and his eyes were always watchful and alert.

The two men were opposites, joined together because Pablo insisted it be that way. Rafael had never wanted to be part of the drug cartel, but his fate in life was that he'd been given no choice. The alternative to *not* being part of Pablo's world was unthinkable for him and his family. Pablo Diego was a vengeful man, and his word was law. Pablo controlled everything, and that was that.

Rafael understood that there was no reasonable out, so he'd applied himself. He'd moved to L.A. with Alejandro, and now he ran the financial side of their operation. Their big problem was Frankie, an American asshole who'd eventually gotten caught with an apartment full of everything from heroin to coke. Recently he'd been arrested for dealing and possession, and Rafael's fear was that Frankie would start running his mouth, implicating Alejandro, making him a further target of the deputy DA — and she was one determined hard-ass.

Did Alejandro expect him to do something drastic about Frankie *and* the deputy DA? Probably, and he'd be wise to do it before Alejandro ran crying to Pablo.

Frankie was an easy target. He had no balls, and if he was threatened in prison, surely that would persuade him to keep his mouth shut? As for the deputy DA, Rafael had set a plan in motion that would take her mind off the Diego family for a while, giving Alejandro time to think about making it back to the safety of his homeland before he found himself arraigned and thrown into jail. For if Alejandro was smart (which he wasn't), that's what he had to do — get his dumb ass out of America before he was indicted.

Rafael would happily accompany him. Safely back in Colombia, he would put together another plan — this time an escape plan for himself, Elizabetta, and his son. His mother too if she wanted to come with them.

Rafael had had enough of playing watchdog to the shallow and stupid Alejandro.

Hopefully the time was not too far off when he could get out.

CHAPTER SIX

"What the hell happened to you?" Lucky exclaimed, staring in shock at the once exquisite, sexy, talented platinum-blond superstar who now resembled a shadow of her former self.

"Excuse me?" Venus said, removing her glasses and placing them carefully on the table. "In case you're interested, I'm playing a highly dramatic role in Hugo's latest film, a role that Hugo says could very well bring me an Oscar nomination."

"Well, Oscar nomination or not, you look like shit," Lucky said.

"Thanks a lot. For your information, that's exactly how I'm *supposed* to look."

"When you're working," Lucky pointed out.

"I *am* working," Venus said, throwing her friend a haughty glare. "We're on location here. I've been shooting all day."

"Okay — sorry," Lucky said, then, pausing for a moment, she added, "It's just that —"

"I know, I know," Venus sighed. "You're

55

used to seeing me all sparkly and glam. But you have to realize that ever since I've been with Hugo, he's taught me that none of that exterior crap matters."

"Has he now?"

"People need to see the *real* me," Venus added with a dramatic wave of her arm. "The woman, not the shallow sexual image the press puts out."

Brainwashing alert, Lucky thought. *This Hugo guy has her under his spell.*

"Okay," Lucky said, deciding to go with it. "How about I order us tea or a drink, whatever you'd like."

"Vodka rocks."

"Vodka it is," Lucky said, signaling for a server.

Venus tapped her fingers impatiently on the table. Lucky noticed that her nails were unkempt and short, the murky green polish peeling off.

Venus caught her looking and muttered, "Don't you get it? It's for my role."

"So," Lucky said. "Does this mean no more singing? No more over-the-top shows? No more Venus the public knows and loves?"

"I'm doing whatever Hugo advises me to do — and I doubt that singing and prancing around a stage in revealing costumes are on his agenda."

"He has an agenda, does he?" Lucky said drily.

"Doesn't everyone?" Venus snapped back.

"If you say so."

"You're just not used to seeing me so happy and fulfilled," Venus said, hunching her shoulders.

Lucky took a long deep breath. "*Are* you?" she asked.

"Am I *what*?"

"Happy and fulfilled."

"Yes, I am," Venus said with a defiant toss of her head.

"You don't look it."

"Oh, for God's sake," Venus said cuttingly. "Are looks all you care about?"

Lucky held her temper in check. Who the hell did Venus think she was talking to? She'd never seen her like this.

"Let me tell you something," she said at last. "I don't think you know me at all, 'cause if you did, you'd understand that the last thing I'm into is looks. Here's what bothers me — it's the expression in your eyes."

"Really?" Venus sniped. "And what expression would that be?"

"Are you high?"

"If I was," Venus answered grandly, "it would be because my role calls for me to be in that state. You seem to forget that I'm playing a drug addict. If there's one thing Hugo demands, it's realism."

"I bet he does."

"Hugo warned me that it would be a mistake to see you," Venus said, picking up her glasses. "He told me not to come, and he was right."

Lucky realized that there was no reasoning with Venus while she was under the great Hugo's spell; there was nothing to be gained from carrying on this conversation.

Venus obviously felt the same way, because she rose to her feet and said abruptly, "I have to go."

Lucky nodded and also got up. "So do I," she said crisply.

They parted awkwardly, Venus all set to run back to her Svengali, Lucky more than ready to catch her flight back to L.A. and Lennie, who was waiting for her.

She was somewhat saddened by the state Venus was in. They'd been friends for a very long time, and she hated to see the way Hugo was taking advantage of her. Venus was not an actress, she was an amazing singer, dancer, and performer. Nobody put on a show like Venus. She outpaced them all — including Beyoncé and Rihanna.

Now Hugo was trying to turn her into a serious actress. Really? Because in Lucky's opinion, Venus was heading for career suicide, and she hated having to bear witness to the disaster that was bound to take place.

Still . . . Venus was a grown woman, and like Lucky, she'd always done things her way, so there was no stopping her. Venus had to figure it out for herself, and when she did, Lucky would be right there to pick up the pieces.

She checked her watch, realizing that it was time to get to the airport and home to Lennie, the love of her life.

Before leaving Vegas, she put in a call to her father, Gino — or Gino the Ram as he was once known. Or Gino the Enemy, because they sure as hell had experienced enough crazy knockdown fights over the years. Memorable ones. However, time and age had turned Gino into an almost mellow man, and she loved him dearly in spite of their rocky past.

"Hey," she said into her cell phone. "It's me, your long-lost daughter."

"Kiddo," he responded affectionately. "What's goin' on?"

"How are you?"

"Breathing."

"I want to see you. I miss you. It's been weeks."

"You miss me, huh?" he said, sounding pleased.

"You know I do. I hate that you're stuck out in the desert."

"Then whyn't you haul your pretty ass to Palm Springs an' come visit, 'cause I'm sittin' here doin' shit."

"I'm *so* not into Palm Springs," she said. "It's way too quiet for me, I don't know how you stand it. Aren't you bored? Everyone's either on their way to being dead or totally gay."

"Well, since I ain't gay, kiddo, I guess that makes me on my way to bein' dead."

"Ha-ha!"

"You've always pushed t' be smack in the middle of the action, ever since you were a little kid."

"Look who's talking."

Gino gave a hearty laugh.

"Okay, let me run this by you," she said enthusiastically. "Why don't *you* haul *your* pretty ass to Vegas next weekend? You're just like me, and I *know* you miss the action. Plus I've got exciting new plans to tell you about."

"How exciting?" he rasped.

"Plenty exciting," she responded.

"I'll think about it."

"C'mon, Gino," she urged. "Don't *think* — *do.* You know you want to."

"Lemme check with Paige."

"Oh come *on*! Since when did you have to check with the wife?"

"Since I got old," he said ruefully.

"You're not old, and Paige doesn't have to come."

"I'll tell her you said so."

"Don't do that," Lucky said quickly. "She'll be pissed. Anyway, is it wrong that I want you all to myself for a change?"

"Okay, kiddo," Gino said, chuckling again.

"You got yourself a date."

"Promise?"

"I'll be there."

Lucky clicked off her phone with a smile on her face. *Gino, Gino, Gino.* There were times she really missed him. They had to get together more often. He was getting older every day; who knew how long he'd be around?

She started thinking about the time — way back — when he'd married her off to boring Craven, Senator Richmond's son, right after her sixteenth birthday. Oh yes, she'd been a wild one, and Gino had thought that was the only way to control her. How wrong was *that*? She'd been a baby, a teenager he'd delivered to a political family for his own gain. But she'd showed everyone a few years later when she'd gotten a divorce and taken over Gino's business while he was out of the country on a tax evasion deal.

Screw getting trapped in a dull marriage. She was a true Santangelo, exactly like Gino. She'd seized her future and run with it.

It was all light-years away, so why was she thinking about it now?

Because she couldn't help herself. Memories — even the bad ones — kept her strong, kept her going.

Oh Gino. You were a tough father, but you made me the woman I am today. And I love you so much.

61

Danny was waiting outside, sitting patiently in the back of a dark blue town car.

"We're off," Lucky said, jumping in next to him. "L.A., here we come."

CHAPTER SEVEN

"Hello," the woman in the red dress murmured in a low, husky voice. "Would it bother you if I sat with you for a moment?"

Bobby glanced up. He was in no mood to be polite and make small talk. However, the young woman standing by his table was the Latina Michelle Pfeiffer clone he'd noticed earlier, so what was he supposed to do?

"Uh . . . hi," he responded.

The woman didn't hesitate. Without waiting for Bobby to invite her, she slid into the booth next to him.

He took a quick look around, searching for M.J., who was nowhere in sight. Then he spotted his partner on the dance floor making out with a girl in tight pink jeans and a backless top. M.J. was obviously busy. No help there.

"Is there something I can do for you?" he inquired, uncomfortable, yet at the same time intrigued. What man wouldn't be?

"I'm sorry to say that it's my cousin," she

said, her accented voice soft and alluring. "He is a very controlling man, always telling me what I can and cannot do."

"That doesn't mean you have to listen, does it?" Bobby said, perplexed.

"I am his cousin. He is a man," she said with a helpless shrug of her bare shoulders. "There is nothing I can do."

"What exactly is he telling you?"

"He warned me that I should not marry my fiancé — the man I love. He insists that I should break up with him."

Bobby frowned. How the fuck had he gotten involved in *this* conversation? The woman might be a beauty, but he wasn't interested in her story. He had Denver, and as work-obsessed and annoying as his girlfriend could be, he still loved her, and he certainly had no plans to be unfaithful — even though after almost two weeks apart, he was horny as hell. Not that this delectable creature seemed to be coming on to him. She was engaged, and she'd just told him that she was in love too. Someone had probably pointed him out as one of the owners of the club, so she'd figured he was safe to talk to.

"Okay, so how can I help?" he asked.

"Nobody can help me," she said with another small, hopeless gesture. "I must learn to stand up for myself, although I know that is not easy." Her soft brown eyes filled with tears. "I am Nadia," she added.

"Bobby," he said, inhaling her musky scent, which he had to admit was intoxicating.

"I know," she said, big brown eyes fixed on his.

"How do you know?"

"Bobby Santangelo Stanislopoulos. Our waiter told us that you own this club."

"That's right," he said, reminding himself to write a stern memo to all staff members about giving out personal information. It pissed him off.

"I didn't mean to bother you . . ." she said softly.

"No bother."

Her eyes stayed on his, holding the gaze a moment too long.

"It's simply that —" she started to say.

"What?"

"Oh, it is nothing. I should go back to my table."

"You sure you're okay?"

"Yes, thank you. My cousin will calm down. Underneath all the macho gesturing, he is a good man. The problem is, he has a bad temper when he doesn't get his own way, especially when he drinks too much."

"As long as he doesn't take it out on you."

"He wouldn't do that," she murmured. "I am his family."

"You're sure?" Bobby said, realizing that there was something about her that was bringing out the protective streak in him.

"Yes, I am sure," she said, sliding out of the booth, a heady combination of demure and seductive, her red dress clinging to every curve. "Thank you for listening to me, Bobby. I should get back to my cousin." Then she was making her way across the club to her table, a vision in red.

M.J. left the dance floor and came rushing over, trailed by the girl in the pink jeans. "What was *that* all about?" he wanted to know.

"Beats me," Bobby said, trying to figure it out for himself.

"She was all over you, man," M.J. pointed out.

"Not really," Bobby answered vaguely.

"I got eyes," M.J. said.

"It was nothing."

"Yeah? Didn't look like nothin' to me."

Before they could get into it further, there was a commotion at Nadia's table. Her surly cousin was standing over her, screaming in Spanish while shaking his fists in her face.

Bobby was instantly on his feet, followed by M.J., who was trailed by the girl in the pink jeans.

Shit! Bobby thought. *The last thing we need is a scene on our opening night.*

He rushed over to her table, quickly grabbing the Latin man's flailing arms. "Cool it," he warned sternly. "You're about to get thrown out on your sorry ass."

The Latin man glared at him, mean eyes glittering with anger, garlic breath filling the air. "You can keep the *puta* here," he snarled. "I'm leaving." Then, hurling a stream of expletives at Nadia, he shook free of Bobby and headed for the staircase.

M.J. went to go after the man. Bobby stopped him. "Don't even bother," he said. "No scenes. Let the asshole go." He turned to Nadia. "What the hell happened?"

Lowering her eyes, she looked away. "I warned you he had a bad temper," she muttered. "He was upset that I was talking to you. He was under the impression that I was flirting."

M.J. threw Bobby a knowing look. "This one's all yours, Bobby," he said, hanging on to the girl in the pink jeans, obviously his captive for the night. "Trouble, trouble, trouble. I don't want no part of it."

"Get lost, then. I'm not asking you to get involved," Bobby said, sitting down beside Nadia.

"Suits me," M.J. said, adding a succinct, "Oh yeah, an' don't forget you got a girlfriend at home."

Bobby threw him a warning look, and M.J. and the girl in pink jeans took off.

"Well," Bobby said to Nadia, "seems like your cousin's a real charmer."

"I'm so sorry," she murmured.

"Not your fault."

"No," she said, quickly agreeing. "It is not my fault."

"Do you live with him?" Bobby asked.

She shook her head, thick hair swirling. "We are in Chicago visiting his mama — *my* mama's sister. He is staying with her. I am at a hotel."

"Okay, this is the deal," Bobby said, deciding that M.J. was right, Nadia was trouble waiting to happen. "I'll put you in a cab, and the two of you can work out your problems in the morning. Sound good?"

"Please," she said, hesitating for a moment. "Can you come with me?"

"That's not possible, Nadia. I'm kinda busy —" he began to say.

"Please," she implored once more, her brown eyes gazing into his. "I would feel so much safer. I am a little afraid of being alone."

He was torn. What was he supposed to do? Nadia was obviously upset, so how could he simply dump her in a cab and leave it at that? Denver would probably want him to make sure the woman got home safely. Denver was all about treating women with respect.

"Okay," he said, a tad reluctantly. "I'd better tell my partner, then I'll drop you at your hotel."

She touched his arm, her eyes wide and grateful. "Thank you so much, Bobby."

M.J. took the news with a cynical laugh.

68

"You're kidding, right?"

"I'll be no more than fifteen minutes."

"Is that how long it takes you to get laid?"

"C'mon, M.J., it's not what you think," Bobby explained. "She's engaged, and she's upset. So I'm playing Good Samaritan. That's all there is to it."

"Yeah," M.J. replied, rolling his eyes. "An' I got property I can sell you in Afghanistan."

"Fuck you."

"Enjoy."

"Double fuck you."

Outside the club, the parking valet brought Bobby's rental car to the front. Nadia climbed in. Bobby noticed a flash of bare thigh, and hurriedly averted his eyes. He thought of Denver and how much he missed her. They'd be reunited soon, and all would be right in the world. He'd call her as soon as he was back at the club.

He got behind the wheel and started the car. "How come the man you're engaged to isn't here with you?" he asked.

"It's a family trip," she replied. "My fiancé lives in New York. He's an architect, a wonderful, kind man. You would like him."

"Seems like a great profession. Why doesn't your cousin approve of him?"

"Because, unfortunately, he is divorced," she sighed. "And divorce is frowned upon in our culture. My cousin is a very proper man. All he wants is the best for me."

"I get it."

"And you?" she asked. "What is your situation? Are you married?"

"Almost. I live with the greatest girl, the love of my life."

"She's a very fortunate woman."

They rode the rest of the way in silence until they reached her hotel. There, a doorman stepped forward and opened the passenger door.

Bobby waited for Nadia to get out. She didn't move.

"Uh, we're here," he said at last. "You'll be okay now. I'll say good night."

"Bobby." Her voice was no more than a whisper.

"Yes?" he said patiently.

"Would you mind coming upstairs with me?"

"Look, I'm sorry," he said, clearing his throat. "The thing is, I'm in a hurry. I've got to get back to the club pronto. It's opening night and they need me. M.J. is waiting."

"It's simply that . . . well, I do not wish to sound like a foolish little girl, but when I was very young, a man molested me in a hotel, and ever since then . . ." She trailed off.

Oh yes! Bobby thought. *She might look like she has it all together, but this is one broken bird. Shit!*

"Maybe you can ask security to escort you," he suggested.

"I can't do that," she said, her lower lip trembling. "It was a security guard who molested me. I was only thirteen at the time, too young to understand what was happening."

"Where was your mom? Wasn't she watching out for you?"

"She was waiting for me in our room. I was molested in the elevator on my way downstairs to buy a candy bar. It was a terrible experience."

"Jesus!" Bobby exclaimed. Beauty on the outside, a frightened little girl within.

"I know," she said softly. "Ever since then . . ."

"Okay, okay," he said. "I'll take you up."

He wasn't pleased, but then again, she was genuinely upset. How in all good conscience could he abandon her?

The valet took his car, and he escorted Nadia to the elevator. She clung to his arm as if they were a couple. And what a couple! Heads turned.

He was getting impatient, yet at the same time he couldn't help noticing the rise of her breasts in the slinky red dress and how enticing she smelled.

Calm down, he told himself. *You're simply being Mr. Good Guy. Nothing's going on here.*

Once they reached the door of her suite, he once again attempted to say good-bye. Nadia was having none of it. "Please, Bobby," she

71

pleaded. "Can you come in for a moment and check out the closet and bathroom? I know I sound crazy, but anyone could be hiding."

"You're kidding?"

"It was a frightening experience, the thing that happened to me — I fear I'll never get over it."

Checking his watch, Bobby realized that it was past eleven. He'd already been gone for half an hour, and if he didn't get back soon, M.J. would definitely accuse him of getting laid. That's all he needed.

Tomorrow morning he'd tell Denver what happened, and how innocent it all was. She'd understand; she always did.

Reluctantly, he entered Nadia's suite, dutifully checking out the bathroom and opening the closet doors. By the time he was finished, she was standing in the living room proffering him a drink.

"What's this?" he asked.

"Vodka," she said boldly. "For luck. For love. For the future of our loved ones. And," she added quietly, "for me to thank you so very much. If my fiancé was here, he would thank you too."

She picked up her own glass and clinked it with his.

One drink. What could it hurt?

CHAPTER EIGHT

Hyton Abbey was Athena's family's ancestral home. Located several miles from Windsor Castle, it was a magnificent if somewhat crumbling country estate. Half of the abbey was open to the public on weekends, while the rest of the time Athena's esteemed parents, Lord and Lady Hyton-Smythe, lived there in solitary splendor. Well, not exactly splendor, because money was extremely tight — currently they were down to employing a measly four servants to take care of the rambling abbey, which boasted fourteen bedrooms, numerous bathrooms, and a couple of random ghosts.

The first time Max visited, she'd had an "encounter," which had totally freaked her out. She was washing her hands in one of the downstairs powder rooms when she'd sensed someone standing behind her while fingertips played tag on her shoulders. Startled, she'd spun around, only to find that there was no one there. Running from the room, she'd bumped straight into Lord Henry Hyton-Smythe, who'd chuckled when she'd told him what had happened.

"No worries, child," he'd boomed with a rakish leer. "We have a couple of resident ghosts here. They'll do you no harm, although I must say, they certainly enjoy frightening our guests."

Max was speechless. Ghosts! Why hadn't Athena warned her?

That evening while they were all sitting in the dining room, the entire Hyton-Smythe family had enjoyed a hearty laugh at her expense.

"I wonder if it was Great-aunt Sephora. Or perhaps it was the stable boy," Athena giggled. "The story is that Sephora stabbed him with a pitchfork back in the eighteen hundreds, and they've both been hanging around ever since."

"I bet it was the stable boy," Tim, Athena's brother, intoned, his thin face lighting up. "Nothing he likes better than watching a pretty girl pee!"

Lady Harriet Hyton-Smythe roused herself from a half-drunken stupor, her dangly silver earrings clinking below her droopy earlobes. "Stop being so disgusting," she slurred. "Max is a guest in our home."

Athena was totally into spending weekends at the abbey with her family. They were an eccentric group — her brother, Tim, was a cross-dresser who refused to admit he was gay. Lady Harriet started drinking in the morning and was never finished until she slumped her way up to bed past midnight. Lord Henry spent most of his time checking out his gun collection, going hunting with his cronies, and ogling the prettiest tourists who visited to take the tour.

Sometimes Max considered not going with Athena for the weekend, instead opting to hang out by herself in the flat they shared in Kensington. But Athena always managed to persuade her to go. The Hyton-Smythes were the closest thing to family Max had in London, so why not spend time with them?

Once a week she called home. No more than once a week, because she didn't want her parents thinking of her as being clingy. Lucky was okay with it. Lennie complained that he'd like to hear from her more often.

Her parents had better get used to it, for she was an independent being, not some little girl constantly whining that she was lonely. Although the truth was that sometimes she *was* lonely. Athena's lifestyle was totally out there, and even though Max tried to keep up, at times it was all too much. Early on, Max had decided to stick it out until she made a real name for herself. Only then would she return to L.A.

Half of Hyton Abbey's extensive grounds were kept in pristine order. The lawns were picture-perfect green and neatly mowed, the numerous rosebushes and banks of colorful flowers blossomed. Tall, stately trees adorned the property. This was all on the public side of Hyton. Behind the scenes, where paying visitors were not allowed to venture, it was a vastly different story. Overgrown, unkempt grass scattered with fast-growing weeds; a stagnant pond filled with water, a slick of green slime floating on the surface; old pool furniture rusting beside an empty, leaf-filled swimming pool.

Whenever the London sun came out — which was rare — Athena and Max laid threadbare crested towels over the rusting pool furniture and sunbathed. Today was one of those days.

"I should have taken advantage of the free drugs last night," Athena ruminated. "Such a damn waste not to."

"Why didn't you?" Max responded, adjusting her bikini top.

" 'Cause *you* ran away, you rotten spoilsport," Athena complained, yanking the top half of her bikini off and throwing it on the ground. "Don't you simply hate feeling confined?"

"I've noticed that you do. Tits on display whenever you feel like it."

"You should take your top off too," Athena suggested. "Free up those luscious boobies."

"No way," Max said, trying not to stare at

Athena's outrageous nipples attached to her almost flat chest.

"Why not?"

" 'Cause your dad might appear. I didn't want to mention it before, but he has a weird habit of creeping up on me."

Athena hooted with laughter. "That old fart," she said derisively. "Henry couldn't get it up if you ran naked into his bedroom. Dear Daddy's all talk and no action."

"Good to know," Max said crisply. "But I have no intention of going anywhere near his bedroom."

"Ha-ha! Mummy and Daddy haven't had sex in yonks," Athena giggled. "I think I was their last hurrah. Mummy told me on one of our spa days. She couldn't wait to inform me that Daddy's dinky is no bigger than his pinky!"

"*Oh my God!* Too much info," Max exclaimed, flashing onto her family's Malibu house with its azure pool overlooking the blue Pacific Ocean. She wouldn't mind being there right now.

Athena rose up, stretching her long lean frame, nipples still erect. "I think I've decided where we'll go," she announced with a grand gesture.

"Where?" asked Max, trying to stop herself from thinking about Billy, because Malibu was where it had all happened. Memories came flooding back. One night she'd thrown a wild party that had gotten so out of control, she'd escaped to the beach below the house, and that's where Billy had found her, and that's where they'd made love for the first time.

Oh, Billy. What happened? Why haven't I heard from you?

"You're not concentrating," Athena admonished.

"Huh?"

"I just told you, silly goat. We're staying at a friend's house in Saint-Trop."

"When?"

"We'll take off tomorrow. Tim knows someone with a plane we can borrow. Commercial is *so* yesterday."

"I can't," Max said. "I have that jeans shoot."

"Blow it off. Something else will come along."

"I'm not you, Athena," Max was quick to point out. "I don't book jobs like the jeans campaign every day. This is important to me."

Athena raised a quizzical eyebrow. "Surely you're not saying no to a divine trip to Saint-Trop?"

"Seems like I am."

"Oh dear me. I think it's time you got your priorities in order, Sweet Eyes."

"They *are* in order," Max said firmly. "I'm staying here and doing the shoot. It's a commitment."

"Well, *I'm* going to Saint-Trop," Athena said with an entitled pout.

"That's great. I'll join you."

"When?" Athena said, throwing Max a penetrating look.

"Uh, I don't know exactly. Probably the next day or so."

"Hmm . . . well, I suppose I could wait. . . ."

"You don't have to," Max said quickly, thinking that there were times Athena could be a little clingy, and a few days apart might be a welcome change. "I'll make my own way there."

"Whatever," Athena said, crossing her arms across her small breasts.

Later there was dinner with the family, a home-cooked meal of leg of lamb, peas, gravy, and roast potatoes. After dinner, Tim drove Athena and Max back to their flat. He was an erratic driver. Max refused to sit in the passenger seat, especially as he was smoking a joint.

"Frightened that I'll pounce on you like old Henry?" Tim teased.

"Do you tell your brother everything?" Max demanded, turning to Athena.

"Tim is my closest confidant," Athena said, plucking the joint from Tim and taking a long deep drag. "He knows how to use information," she added, offering the joint to Max.

Max turned it down. Not that she was into being all goody-goody, but she'd decided not to smoke or drink before the shoot.

Outside their flat, a couple of paparazzi were camped out on the steps, hoping for a weekend sighting.

"Bloody pests," Tim growled, hopping out of the car and immediately mooning them.

"That'll go down well with the old folks," Athena observed as cameras flashed, catching his naked white bottom. Then, grabbing Max, she planted a kiss full on her mouth.

The two photographers leaped into action, thrilled to be earning next month's rent.

Max wiped her hand across her mouth. They both played at being lesbians for the press, only there were times Athena took it a step too far.

"You coming?" Athena called out to Tim.

"No. Just breathing heavily," he said with a wolfish grin.

"For God's sake!" Athena snapped. "You're such a juvenile."

Following them upstairs, Tim headed straight to Athena's closet, where he began trying on her clothes, then parading around their flat, wobbling on dangerously high heels.

"Are you *really* gay or just playing?" Max inquired curiously.

"Gay?" Tim questioned, raising a shocked eyebrow. "Why would you think that?"

" 'Cause you're always dressing up in our clothes," she stated, cocking her head to one side. "Can't you just come out and admit it?"

"No, my dear, because I am certainly *not* gay," Tim said, narrowing his eyes. "So there."

"I've never seen you with a girl," Max accused.

"Or a boy," Athena said, joining in.

"You two lezzies need a thorough spanking," Tim said, quite peeved.

"Oh yes," Athena said with a wild giggle. "And wouldn't we love *that.*"

Unzipping himself out of Athena's Valentino dress, Tim unceremoniously dropped it on the floor. "I've had enough," he said, glaring at them. "Good night, ladies — and trust me, I use the word *ladies* loosely."

"Bye-bye, baby bro," Athena crowed. "See you tomorrow."

For a moment Max missed her half brother, Bobby — along with Gino Junior and even Leo. Bobby was such a major fox. She wondered what he was up to and if he was still with Denver. She decided that come morning, she would definitely phone him and catch up on everything.

"Time for beddy byes," Athena announced. "I'm *totally* exhausted."

"Me too," Max agreed, although once in her room, she couldn't sleep. After half an hour of tossing and turning, she finally grabbed her laptop and googled Billy. She knew she shouldn't submit to such torture, but why not? The only person she was hurting was herself.

There were a few new photos, nothing of interest. Billy standing by the ocean looking beached-blond and tousled and so freaking *hot*!

Too bad.

Yes. Too bad for him. They would've made a great couple.

After a while, she decided to call Cookie, her best girlfriend in L.A. Maybe Cookie would have some more up-to-date news about Billy.

"I got an amazeballs new boyfriend," Cookie announced. "He's a rapper. Dad hates him."

"A name might help."

Cookie stifled a giggle. "Taste Shit."

"Nice."

"The dude is cutting-edge. Harry is *way* into him."

"How *is* Harry?" Max inquired, thinking about her other best friend in L.A.

"Gettin' gayer by the day."

"I miss both of you," Max said wistfully. "And I miss L.A."

"Come home, then," Cookie urged.

"Yeah, maybe soon." After a long meaningful beat, she asked, "Any news on Billy?"

"Oh crap, you're not still thinkin' of *him,* are you? He's just another actor. They're all the same: chasing supermodels, making dumb action movies, and getting high."

"Is Billy chasing a supermodel?" she asked,

filled with alarm.

"Face it, babe, as far as Billy and you are concerned, it's over. You gotta move on."

"I have."

"Yeah, sure."

Max clicked off her phone, depressed. Eventually, she fell asleep, Billy's image firmly embedded in her head.

CHAPTER NINE

Denver was not into Hollywood parties. She found them to be boring and pretentious. Nobody ever seemed to have anything intelligent to say — it was all about movie grosses and endless mindless gossip.

Annabelle fit right in. As the wife of Eddie Falcon, one of the most powerful agents in town, she had finally found her place in the Hollywood hierarchy. A former redhead, Annabelle was now blond and bodacious. She was the daughter of two movie stars, one of them deceased — shot to death in her bed, some said by Annabelle's father, Ralph Maestro. Nothing was ever proven.

Annabelle had led a privileged life. She was the girl who always got what she wanted, and after a wild ride in New York as a would-be madam, with Frankie Romano as her boyfriend, she'd returned to L.A. and hooked up with Eddie, who in Hollywood-speak was a real comer. Right now he was a top agent with a list of superstar clients. But Eddie was moving up — he had all the right connections, and in his future, he saw himself running a major studio. It was a given. And with Annabelle and her famous father in his corner, it shouldn't take too much longer.

Denver had a strong suspicion that if she weren't living with Bobby Santangelo Stanislopoulos, she would be crossed off the guest list, for Annabelle wasn't the most loyal of friends. As for Carolyn — well, Annabelle obviously felt that having a token lesbian at her get-togethers made her look totally cool. After all, lesbians were way in fashion — Ellen, Portia, Rosie, and of course the fabulous Jane Lynch.

Denver looked around at the select group of Hollywood players, and decided that the time had come to start turning down Annabelle's invites. After a few minutes, she spotted Carolyn sitting at the bar and made her way over. "What's the occasion this time?" she asked, for Annabelle always had some kind of announcement to make at her dinners.

"Dunno. Annabelle informed me it was major," Carolyn said with a casual shrug. "And from the faces she's gathered here, I guess it must be."

Denver scanned the room again. She spotted a couple of politicians — friends of Eddie's. A famous late-night talk-show host with a decades-younger actress. Eddie's client, Billy Melina. An aging actress well known for having bedded President Kennedy. Rock star Kris Phoenix. Plus a scattering of directors, producers, and studio heads, along with their wives — three of the wives being Asian.

She wished Bobby were with her, then she thought it was probably just as well that he wasn't, because he too hated Annabelle's gatherings.

"What do *you* think she's coming up with tonight?" Carolyn asked.

"I don't know. I don't care," Denver said, shrugging. "I'm not doing this again."

"Why not?" Carolyn said, downing a mojito. "We're Annabelle's only true friends. We *should* support her."

Really? Denver thought, flashing onto the memory of Annabelle in high school, where she'd practically ignored both of them because they weren't members of the affluent group she hung with. It was only years later when Annabelle had needed them that she'd renewed their friendship.

"Handsome movie stud approaching to your left," Carolyn whispered.

Denver turned around and there stood Billy Melina, all tousled dirty-blond hair and piercing blue eyes.

"Hey. Denver, right?" he said, standing tall.

She'd met him with Bobby in Vegas at Lucky's hotel, and she was well aware of the thing he'd had with Bobby's teenage sister, Max. Bobby had been furious, raging that Max was just a kid. Denver had pointed out that Max was eighteen, making her legal.

"Well, you have a good memory," Denver said, regarding Billy coolly.

"And you have an unusual name," Billy said. "By the way, I gotta say, you look great."

"Thanks."

He leaned against the bar, holding on to a bottle of beer. "How's Bobby doin'?" he asked.

"Working hard," she replied.

Billy let loose a movie-star grin. "Aren't we all."

"I'm sure you are."

After an awkward pause, Billy said, "How about Max. What's up with her?"

"She's living in Europe."

"No shit?" Billy said, attempting to keep it casual. "I'm leaving tomorrow to make a movie. Where is she?"

"London."

"Hey, if I get to London, I'll give her a call."

"I don't think so," Denver said shortly.

"Really?"

"Truth is, Billy, I hardly imagine she needs any more heartbreak."

"Excuse me?" he said, blue eyes blazing. Who the heck did this woman think she was talking to? He was Billy Melina, a goddamn movie star, for crissake. Shouldn't she be showing him a little respect?

"You broke her heart," Denver continued, keeping her voice low. "End of story."

Bobby would be so pleased with her when she gave him a blow-by-blow of their conversation.

"You don't understand. It was complicated —" Billy started to say, only to be interrupted by Annabelle standing in the middle of the room, clinking a glass to get all her guests' attention.

"Hi, everyone," Annabelle trilled. "Eddie and I are so happy you could be with us on this very special night. Eddie," she added coyly, beckoning her husband, "come join me."

Eddie bounced his way over to his wife and stood proudly beside her. He was short and stocky with a clever comb-over and an engaging grin. "I know you all wanna hear about what a hit movie *Cartel* is gonna be," he said. "Box-office gold, folks. You heard it here first. But tonight is not about our movie, tonight is all about my gorgeous, sexy wife."

He turned to Annabelle and they linked arms. Then, as if they'd both rehearsed it, they yelled out the good news in unison.

"We're pregnant!"

CHAPTER TEN

The partying never stopped for Alejandro Diego. Much as Rafael begged him to keep a low profile, Alejandro couldn't care less. Club Luna was his playpen and women were his toys. His womanizing was out of control; his drinking and drugging too.

Everyone knew that Alejandro was a coke whore, sampling the product and sharing it with his dubious group of hangers-on. Rafael realized that any one of them could be working undercover, all the better to trap Alejandro. It was bad enough that Frankie Romano had gotten himself arrested, although that didn't stop Alejandro from doing whatever he felt like.

Rafael was disgusted with Alejandro's carelessness, so much so that he was tempted to call Pablo and beg permission to knock Alejandro out, stash him on a plane, and fly him home. As far as Rafael was concerned, it was the only sane way to deal with the situation.

Unfortunately, he knew that Pablo would never agree to such drastic action, because Pablo had no idea how serious the situation was. If Pablo *was* aware of how inept his son was, he'd surely send for him immediately. And if that happened, somehow or other Pablo would manage to blame Rafael. It was a given.

Once again, Rafael found himself in a no-win position.

Damn Alejandro. His stupidity knew no bounds.

Tonight Alejandro was planning on entertaining, and when Alejandro entertained at home it was always a fuck-fest of girls, drugs, music, and booze.

"You have to be careful," Rafael warned. "You're being watched."

"Not by you," Alejandro cackled. "Tonight I am free of your disapproval."

They were standing in the men's department at Neiman Marcus, where Alejandro was busy purchasing two Brioni suits and a brown leather studded Versace jacket.

"Gangster, huh?" he boasted, parading up and down, before stopping to admire himself in a full-length mirror.

"Not so much," Rafael muttered, willing Alejandro to dial it down a notch. People were staring at him, which is exactly the way Alejandro liked it. In his mind, they were thinking how handsome he was, how rich and privileged.

He winked at a pretty girl in a skimpy orange dress, her bare arms tanned by the sun.

She caught sight of his wink and scurried away.

Alejandro didn't appreciate her response. He supposed she was a lesbian, the only reason a girl would turn away from him. Besides, he was not a big fan of natural. He preferred huge fake breasts and an allover fake tan.

"Time for a cocktail," Alejandro said, gesturing toward the upstairs bar.

"Not for me," Rafael said, tired of being the watchdog to his idiot half brother. Yes, Pablo could deny it all he wanted, but Rafael had no doubt that they *were* brothers.

"How come you're such a tight-ass?" Alejandro mocked. "You act as if you're an old man."

"Not old, merely smart," Rafael replied.

"Smarter than me?" Alejandro sneered. "There is *nobody* smarter than me."

Then, throwing his charge card at the startled salesman, he strutted toward the circular bar.

Rafael followed. As usual, he had no choice.

The music was deafening, the girls plentiful. A few celebrities were scattered here and there, mostly young actors looking to get their rocks off. Alejandro got off on collecting celebrities; they were so easy to please as long as the drugs were plentiful. Naturally, Alejandro made sure that they were. Coke, pills, heroin — if anyone was so inclined. He played on their vices, and had one of his many so-called girlfriends take surreptitious pictures, always useful to lock away for future use.

Tonight he was cozying up to Willow Price, a young actress who covered the waterfront with her sexual activities. This suited Alejandro, for threesomes were his thing.

Willow had never been what one would describe as a girl's girl. She'd always operated in a world filled with men, most of whom wanted to sleep with her or have her suck them off. Willow exuded a girlish sensuality — she was the extremely pretty girl next door who was ready to do anything that was required to forward her career. She was also famous for her record amount of stays in rehab, several DUIs, and her outrageous public behavior. She was into Alejandro because he paid her bills and bailed her out of jail when she needed him to. In return, she indulged his threesome fantasies, and occasionally invited him to accompany her to a premiere or a fancy Hollywood party.

Alejandro got a big kick out of seeing his photo in the magazines alongside Willow, especially when they described him as an affluent businessman. It upped his profile, made him more appealing to women.

Tonight Willow was in a ready-to-party mood. She'd recently split with her latest agent and gotten her third DUI, and since her last movie, in which she'd starred alongside Billy Melina, nothing worthwhile had come her way. It infuriated her that younger actresses were now getting the roles that should be hers. Jennifer Lawrence, Rooney Mara, Kristin Stewart. Fuck 'em. She was more talented than the three of them put together.

Willow had a plan; she always had a plan. She'd discussed it with her friend and sometime lover Frankie Romano before he'd gotten his dumb ass arrested. Frankie had considered it a fine idea. Her plan was to get Alejandro to put up the money for a movie she could star in. After all, he was always boasting about how much money he had, so how about sliding some of it her way?

Falling out of a slinky dress, sans underwear, she decided to get to work on Alejandro, and with that in mind, she'd hired a porno player to help her out. The porno girl was tanned and big-breasted — the best that silicone had to offer. Her professional name was Bee Bee, and Willow knew from past experience that Bee Bee took direction well.

Alejandro had no clue that Bee Bee was getting paid to do anything he so desired. In his mind she was a female, he was a male, and his masculine lure was impossible to resist.

Willow had decided that Bee Bee should do all the heavy lifting. Willow didn't mind sucking Alejandro's cock once in a while, but lately he was into butt-fucking, and that was not her idea of a fun time. He was also into sitting astride her, straddling her tits, and stuffing his member into her mouth while almost suffocating her with his weight.

There were plenty of girls at the party — skanky would-be model/actresses ready to entertain Alejandro in any way he saw fit. Willow's advantage was that none of them had a name like she did. She was a famous, out-of-control bad girl, and Alejandro was a fame whore.

Guns, coke, and endless women — Alejandro was into it all. He kept a Glock in a drawer next to his bed, and an Uzi in his walk-in closet. Oh yes, he was prepared for anything. One night he'd revealed to Willow that his idol was Al Pacino. He'd raved over the way the actor had portrayed drug dealer Tony Montana in *Scarface*. Alejandro considered himself a Pacino/Montana clone, minus the death scene at the end of the movie.

After a while, Willow maneuvered Alejandro, herself, and Bee Bee into the master bedroom — a room dominated by an enormous bed and white leather furniture with heavy gold accents. Loud rap music emanated from several speakers.

Alejandro was coked out of his mind, simultaneously roaring with laughter and screaming that he was the man.

"You sure are, baby," Willow assured him, exposing her breasts and shaking them in his face.

He grabbed her, squeezing her breasts while bending his head to suck greedily on her nipples.

She knew she had great tits, and they were all real too. "We should make a movie," she whispered in his ear, planting the seed.

"Where's the camera?" he demanded. "I wanna see a close-up of your pussy."

"No," she said, breaking away from him. "I'm talking about a legitimate movie, starring me."

"An' me," said Bee Bee, joining in when she wasn't supposed to.

"Get undressed," Willow hissed at her. "And while you're at it, shut your mouth. I'm paying you to fuck, not talk."

"A movie, huh?" mumbled Alejandro, warming to the idea.

"Independent," Willow said, "so we don't have to answer to any studio assholes."

Alejandro chuckled.

"We'll do it my way," Willow continued.

"Doncha mean *our* way?" Alejandro said, watching Bee Bee strip.

Hmm, Willow decided. *He's not as out of it as I thought.*

"Yeah, baby, *our* way," she agreed. "You can be the exec producer. You'll have your name up there on the big screen for everyone to see. How about *that*?"

"I like it," Alejandro said, beckoning Bee Bee to move closer, then tipping a vial of coke onto her big tits and snorting the white powder off her naked skin.

"So," Willow said, cradling his balls the way she knew he liked. "Do we have something? Should I get a deal memo drawn up?" She squeezed his balls hard. "Are we in business?"

He groaned and let out an anguished, "Yeah, let's do it."

Bee Bee leaned over him, smothering his face with her huge breasts. She was a true professional.

Alejandro felt himself coming.

Too soon.

What the fuck. The night was young, and he was just getting started.

CHAPTER ELEVEN

The plane ride to L.A. was quick and un-eventful. Upon arrival, Lucky bid good-bye to Danny at the airport, picked up her Ferrari, and headed straight to Malibu. Using drivers did not appeal to her. Being behind the wheel of a kick-ass car had always been her thing. Besides, she preferred being in control.

Stopping at Malibu Market, she picked up steaks for Lennie to barbecue, a jar of Texas grilling sauce, and a bottle of tequila. Tonight was to be their night. She'd given the house-keepers a couple of days off, so it would be just her and Lennie. The two of them alone at last.

Thinking about Lennie always brought a smile to her face. He was everything she could ever want in a man. Sexy, wry, charis-matic, talented, great in bed, no way a yes-man. In fact, Lennie was the only man who'd ever stood up to her. He was strong and opinionated and they sometimes enjoyed fierce fights. However, the making up was always worth it.

Her thoughts moved on to Venus, and how her friend was possibly ruining her life, not to mention her career. Venus had a habit of becoming the woman she imagined the man she was with expected her to be. During the time she was married to movie star Cooper Turner, she'd glammed it up all the way. Then, while she was married to Billy Melina — who was younger than her — she'd turned into the rock chick of his dreams, riding on the back of his Harley, playing Ping-Pong, going bowling with his rowdy group of friends, even camping because Billy was into it. After her divorce from Billy, she'd sampled a few boy toys, finally settling for Brazilian Jorge. With Jorge, Venus had paid all the bills, while Jorge had lived the life. Then along came Hugo Santos, and Venus had fallen prey to his bullshit *I-can-make-you-into-a-dramatic-actress* spell.

The only consolation was that it wouldn't last. Venus's relationships never did.

Lucky sighed. Venus had to be careful; fans had a way of moving on.

By the time she pulled into the driveway, Lennie was already home.

"Here comes my beautiful wife," he said, greeting her at the door.

"Hey," she responded. "And I bring food too."

"I always knew you were perfect."

"Did you, now?"

"Yes, sweetheart, I always did."

They entered their Malibu retreat, arms entwined.

Five minutes later, their lovemaking was fast and furious. No foreplay, no tender kisses, simply a raw urgency that took them both by surprise.

Lucky fell into it with a fervent passion. Nothing with Lennie was ever predictable, which is why they had such a great and exciting marriage.

"You leave me breathless," she sighed when they were both fully satisfied. "Breathless and extraordinarily happy."

Lennie grinned. He still had an irresistible grin, and an irresistible everything else.

Tracing her fingers across his taut abs, she murmured, "Whatever happened to tantric? You've gone all macho on me."

"Is my lovely wife complaining?"

"Never."

"Well, y'know I like to keep you guessing."

"Really?" she said, her fingers tiptoeing downward.

"If I didn't, you'd be off runnin' around like you were when I first met you."

"You remember, huh?" she said with a soft smile.

"How could I ever forget? There I was, this

lowly stand-up comedian working the lounge in your hotel — only I didn't know it was your hotel — and you invited me up to your suite an' tried to take advantage of me —"

"Oh, *please,*" Lucky interrupted. "If I remember clearly, nobody was taking advantage of anyone. All I wanted was to get laid and you didn't."

"C'mon, Lucky," he said with a lazy grin. "You wouldn't even give me your name."

"How sad," she teased. "No name, no hard-on."

"Then when I wouldn't do it, you had me fired."

"I did?" she said innocently.

"Oh yeah, that was a really classy move. Why'd you do that?"

"Because I could," she said, her fingers still moving downward.

"Jesus, Lucky, you had balls of fire."

"I still do."

"Yeah, and if you ever fucked around on me I'd cut 'em off."

"Technically speaking, Lennie, *you're* the one with balls. So exactly who would be doing the cutting?"

"I'm not risking it."

"You'd better not."

Her hand reached its destination, and she began slowly caressing him. Naturally, he rose to the occasion; there wasn't a time when he didn't.

Once more they made love, this time at a more leisurely pace.

Later, Lennie barbecued steaks out by the pool, while Lucky fixed them strong margaritas. After they finished eating, they sat on loungers facing the ocean.

"This is my favorite kind of evening," Lennie said. "You and me — no housekeepers, no kids."

"Mine too," Lucky agreed.

"I love our kids, only I gotta say that being alone with you is the best."

"I know exactly what you mean," she said, sipping her margarita.

"Talking of kids," he added, "you spoken to Max lately?"

"Not in the last few days. She seems to be having a good time with all her new friends in London."

"Not *too* good, I hope. Not like you when you were her age."

"Oh yeah, eighteen was a really fun time," Lucky said drily. "There I was, trapped in Washington with Craven Richmond, the dullest, most boring husband in the world, and his desperately ambitious political family. Those were the days."

"With a dozen lovers on the side, right?"

"Hey, what else was I going to do?" she said, laughing. "Play tennis?"

"Just as well you didn't. You'd have ripped the ass off any opponent."

"So eloquent."

"That's 'cause I'm a writer."

"Really?" she said, playing with him. "I thought you were a stand-up comedian."

"That was way back, babe, when you were sleeping with anything that moved."

"Oh, and I suppose you weren't?"

That irresistible grin appeared again. "I had my moments."

"Yeah, don't I know it. More girls than hot dinners."

"That, my crazy beautiful wife, is why neither of us is looking to get out of our marriage. We can truthfully say, 'Been there, done that.' "

Lucky got up to refill her glass. "I spoke to Gino earlier," she said. "I've persuaded him to come to Vegas next weekend. I want to get him up to speed on my latest project. Can you make it? It would be so great if we were all there together."

"I'm gonna try."

"Like I said to Gino, don't try — do it," she said, sitting down again.

"We're in post, which means I might have to stay in L.A. Besides, wouldn't it be kinda nice for you and Gino to have some alone time?"

"You *do* know that Gino isn't getting any younger," she pointed out. "We have to take advantage of every moment."

"Trust me, Gino Santangelo will outlive us

all," Lennie assured her with a husky laugh. "He ain't goin' nowhere, babe. Gino is a raging fucking bull."

"That he is," Lucky agreed, once more thinking about her father and their turbulent history. So much hate. So much love. They'd been reconciled for years now, and she loved him with all her heart, although it hadn't been an easy journey.

"By the way — in case I haven't told you lately," Lennie added, "you make me the happiest man in the world."

"I like it! More!"

"The woman wants more," Lennie drawled, shaking his head. "You're insatiable."

"I think you already know that."

"I think I do."

They smiled at each other, totally content.

CHAPTER TWELVE

The Italian photographer was thirtyish and hot, with a cocky attitude and hair tied back in a sleek ponytail. *"Ciao,"* he said.

Athena had warned Max about Italian men. In fact, everyone had warned her about Italian men, even Lady Harriet, who'd one day revealed that as a young girl she'd lived in Rome and had experienced a procession of Italian lovers, all of them untrustworthy, concerned only with the size and performance of their precious members.

"Mummy!" Athena had exclaimed, feigning shock. "I never knew you were so bloody randy!"

"I experimented plenty in my day," Lady Harriet had replied, slurping down even more wine. "And you, my dear, have inherited my adventurous spirit."

So Max was warned. However, Carlo, with his olive skin and sexy eyes, was quite attractive in a bad-boy kind of way, and Max couldn't help wondering if *he* would be the one to take her mind off Billy.

It turned out that he wasn't. He was what Lucky would call an arrogant little prick.

Carlo obviously considered himself the second coming of Mario Testino. He had three assistants, all of whom he treated like crap. Also present were two male representatives from the jeans company, and the usual glam squad of hairstylists, makeup artists, and clothes stylists. Max knew the glam squad through Athena, and they too considered Carlo to be an annoying diva.

"His cock is bigger than his talent," the makeup man confided in a low voice. "And that's not saying much."

Max giggled. She was standing in front of the camera in low-rise jeans and a crop top, her long dark hair piled on top of her head. She radiated sexy teenage spirit.

"Too much trouble for you to concentrate?" Carlo yelled at her across the studio floor. "You look like a donkey with that *stonato* smirk on your face."

What would Athena do? She'd probably tell him to go fuck himself. But Max was nowhere near the dizzying heights of Athena, so she bit down hard on her lower lip and remained silent. These photos had to be good. No, not good — awesome. These photos were her gateway to the big-time.

One of the jeans reps stepped forward and whispered something in Carlo's ear.

Carlo gave a vigorous nod and shouted instructions to Max. "Top off," he commanded as if it was no big deal, and if she were Athena, it wouldn't have been. However, Max had never done topless, nor did she want to.

"Excuse me?" she said, feeling a sudden rush of nervousness.

"*Scusi,*" he said, mimicking her. "Top off, *sticchiu.*"

She didn't understand what *sticchiu* meant, but she sure as hell knew it wasn't nice. "My agent never said anything about nudity," she ventured, standing her ground.

Carlo launched into a stream of Italian. He then grabbed one of his assistants by the arm, a thin girl with a sallow complexion, her hair in braids, and instructed her to translate. The girl was a wreck. But although Carlo had almost twisted her arm off, she still seemed to be in total awe of him.

"Carlo would like you to remove your top and cover your breasts with your hands," the girl said in halting English. "He will not show nipples. Artistically, the covering-your-breasts shot will work for him."

"Oh," Max gulped. She'd seen Athena do the pose a hundred times, so why not? "Okay," she mumbled unsurely. "As long as it's not *too* revealing. I'm like so not into doing nudity."

The gay stylist hurried forward as Carlo

strode around the set, muttering to himself while absentmindedly stroking his manhood as if to reassure himself it was still there. "Let's go, my beauty," the stylist murmured. "We will remove your top in privacy."

"Don't forget to come back," Carlo sneered sarcastically as the stylist escorted her to the dressing room. "We have all the time in the world."

Max threw him a stony look. "Oh, I'll be back," she said, recovering her composure. "And these photos better rock!"

And rock they did, for shedding her top forced Max to shed her inhibitions — helped by the few puffs of a joint the stylist happened to have handy.

She returned to the set full of attitude, determined to make it work.

"Can we have some sounds?" she demanded, feeling herself morphing into Athena, who always expected music to be played at her photo sessions.

Drake flooded the studio — pounding out "Best I Ever Had," followed by CeeLo Green's "Fuck You," and then the incomparable Amy W. refusing to go to rehab.

Max settled into working with the camera lens, channeling an old photo of Janet Jackson on the cover of *Rolling Stone,* her hands covering her boobs. Then she started channeling Rihanna, Lady Gaga, and Katy Perry. They'd all posed seminude. If she wanted to make it as a model, she knew that she had to be bold.

Good-bye, inhibitions.

Hello, freedom.

Carlo was suddenly silent. So was everyone else. Between them they were creating magic, and they both realized it.

Later there were drinks with the glam squad at a nearby pub. All the talk was about how great the photos had turned out, even though Carlo was a major prick.

"Girl, you look wicked amazing," the stylist assured her.

"As did your tits," added the makeup man — also gay.

Max had to admit that the digital images she'd seen were pretty incredible — just racy enough. And even though she'd ended up topless, the images were highly stylized, and the only thing on show above her waist was a glimpse of side boob. Nothing for Lucky or Lennie to go ape-shit about, although Lennie probably would, he was so overprotective.

She couldn't wait for Athena's opinion; Athena's approval meant more than anyone's.

Finally, it was time to go home.

Being in the apartment by herself made for a pleasant change. She took a shower, jumped into bed, and snuggled under the covers, resisting the impulse to google Billy. Soon she fell into a deep sleep.

Hours later she was awakened by the persistent ringing of her doorbell. Groping for her phone, she noted that it was almost three in the morning.

"What the hell . . . ," she muttered, picking up the intercom. "Who's there?"

A male voice mumbled something unintelligible. It was Tim, she was sure of it. He sometimes sought refuge with them when, drunk and stoned, he couldn't make it back to the house he rented in Chelsea. Athena had given him a key to their flat, but of course he'd immediately lost it. Typical Tim behavior.

Max pressed the buzzer to let him in, then dove back under the covers, ready to go back to sleep.

The next thing she knew, Tim was crawling into bed next to her. Only to her horror it wasn't Tim, it was the annoying Italian photographer, Carlo.

Max let out a startled yell and scrambled from her bed, almost tripping over her own feet.

"What's the matter?" Carlo purred, seemingly unperturbed.

"What's the *matter*?" she shrieked, waving her arms in the air. "You're here, in my bed! Get *out,* you pervert!"

Carlo was way drunk. "Ah, *bellissima,*" he crooned. "You *know* you want me. Do not fight it. *Calma, calma.*"

"*You* stay fucking calm!" she shouted, thinking, *What would Athena do?* Probably screw him, *then* throw him out.

What would Lucky do? Well, her mom had a signature move she'd taught Max when she was seven, and that was to kick a man in the balls. It stopped them every time. However, since Carlo was now ensconced in her bed, Lucky's move didn't seem possible.

"Get out," she said through clenched teeth. "I mean it, or I'm calling the police."

"Soon, *cara,* very soon." And with those words Carlo closed his eyes and drifted off into a drunken sleep.

Max was outraged. What was she supposed to do now? Calling the police was not an option. The publicity would be out of control, plus it would make her look like a fool.

Athena was in Saint-Tropez, so no help there.

The only person she could think of to call was Tim.

Okay, Tim. Let's see if you can man up.

Tim arrived half an hour later and bravely attempted to wake Carlo with a timid shove. The Italian photographer did not budge.

"C'*mon,*" Max urged, impatiently jumping up and down. "Move the fucker. Get him out of my bed!"

"He's legless," Tim offered.

"What do you mean, 'legless'?" Max said, livid that she had to deal with such a screwed-up situation.

"Drunker than a skunk," Tim opined.

"Then what the hell am I supposed to do?" Max wailed. "This is *so* not right."

"You could come home with me, camp out on the sofa," Tim suggested. "I wouldn't mind."

"I'm sure you wouldn't," Max sniffed. "Only there's no way I'm leaving my own apartment."

"Then may I suggest that you take Athena's bed and let him sleep it off," Tim said, stifling a yawn. "I'm going home."

"Oh no you're not," Max said adamantly. "You're not leaving me alone with this drunken Italian asshole."

"What makes you think he's an arsehole?"

"I worked with him today, and he's a *total* asshole."

"He obviously likes *you,* dear," Tim said with a knowing smirk.

"Do not call me dear," she said, thoroughly pissed off. "You sound like your freaking father."

"Methinks you have a thing for Lord Henry," Tim said, wagging a bony finger in her face. "You quite fancy him, don't you?"

"Oh *puh-leeze*!" Max exclaimed, rolling her eyes. "That's so gross."

"You American girls always go gaga for titles," Tim stated. "I've seen it before."

"Shut *up,*" she said furiously. "*This* American girl doesn't give a fast crap."

"Ah," Tim said knowingly, "and the truth shall out."

They were having this conversation next to Max's bed, where Carlo was spread out, still fully dressed, snoring like a satisfied bull.

Max was in shock that this was happening. How had Carlo even gotten her address? And why wasn't Athena around to deal with the situation? It was quite apparent that Athena had bigger balls than her useless brother. Tim was such a loser.

"Okay," she said at last. "I'll take Athena's bed, and you can sleep on the pull-out couch."

Tim threw her a frosty look. "I never indicated that I was prepared to stay."

"I'll let you wear my Dolce and Gabbana leopard-print pajamas," Max said, tempting him the only way she knew how.

"They're Athena's."

"She gave them to me," Max lied.

Tim considered the possibilities. He was a fervent fan of designer outfits. Dolce & Gabbana had impeccable flair; even their pajamas were chic.

"Very well," he said, after a moment or two. "And for your information, I shall be expecting a hot breakfast."

"Sure," Max said, although she had no intention of cooking anything. Once Carlo

was out, Tim would follow.
Saint-Tropez, here I come.

CHAPTER THIRTEEN

It was almost noon and Bobby still hadn't called. Denver was inwardly steaming, although she refused to allow it to show. She sat at her desk mulling over the last time they'd spoken. The previous night, Bobby had left her a voice mail. She'd called him back and he'd blurted out a hurried, "Can't talk. Catch you later."

Only he hadn't caught her later, and she'd then left him two messages that he'd failed to return. It wasn't as if she was some needy girlfriend craving his attention. However, not getting back to her was so unlike Bobby.

Before he'd left for Chicago, he'd accused her of being obsessed with the Diego case. Unfortunately, it was true. She didn't feel guilty, because it was her job. Besides, he was equally obsessed with opening his clubs across America, and lately he'd been talking about building a chain of boutique hotels. Great! Something else to take all his time.

Things were not so good. A month ago

she'd lost her beloved dog, Amy Winehouse — named after the legendary singer. Bobby had promised her they would visit the pound and pick out a rescue dog, only so far he'd been too busy. If he *was* in town on the weekend, all he seemed to want to do was sit in front of the TV and watch endless sports.

What was it with men and sports? Why were they so obsessed? Could it be that they were all frustrated ballplayers?

Was their relationship becoming mundane? Had she made a mistake moving in with him? Well, Carolyn certainly hadn't helped matters with her "all men cheat" comments.

Denver made up her mind that if she found out that Bobby *had* cheated on her, she would pack up and move out. No hesitation. It was about time he realized that she was an independent working woman, not a girl he could screw around on.

Apart from the Bobby situation, the news from her boss was hardly what she'd hoped to hear. According to the DA, they needed stone-cold evidence to indict Alejandro. They needed Frankie Romano to start talking.

If that was the case, she'd damn well put a deal on the table that would lure Frankie into talking. As for Alejandro, he wasn't exactly low-key; he was always front and center at his club, always hooking up with different women, and no doubt passing out drugs like candy.

The DA decided that their next move was to put in place a female undercover agent. It sounded like a plan.

And so the chase continued. Only it wasn't a chase, more like a game of cat and mouse.

Her cell buzzed. Bobby?

No. It read "Unknown caller."

She answered anyway with a tentative "Yes?"

"Denver?" said a male voice.

"That's me."

"Guess who?"

Was there anything more tedious than playing guessing games about who was on the other end of the phone?

"Obama," she said drily.

"Close."

"Ryan Gosling."

"You're getting warmer."

"I don't have time for this."

"Busy as always. Surprise, surprise — it's Sam."

Sam Slade. An ex. Well, not really an ex — more like a one-night stand before she'd met Bobby. He'd rescued her when she'd been on a difficult assignment in New York back in her defense attorney days. They'd spent one very pleasant night together. After that she'd hooked up with Bobby, and she and Sam had remained friends, although they hadn't spoken in months.

Sam was a successful screenwriter whose

name had appeared on two hit movies. He was hardworking, self-deprecating, and interesting to hang out with. When she'd first met him, he'd been struggling. Now, in Hollywood-speak, he was red-hot.

Sam Slade. Tall, slightly gawky, with curly hair, brown eyes, and crooked teeth.

She couldn't help wondering if he'd had his teeth fixed. She hoped not, his crooked-toothed smile was one of his most endearing qualities.

"I saw your latest movie," she said, smiling because she was genuinely pleased to hear from him. "Too much violence, although I have to admit it was very entertaining."

"That's the way they like 'em."

"At least it wasn't aimed at teenage boys. Not one fart joke, if I remember correctly."

"Thanks for the compliment. Coming from you it means a lot."

"You know me — I say what I think. I'm not full of crap."

"You never were."

She took a long deep breath. "Okay, Sam," she said. "What exactly can I do for you?"

"You can dump Bobby and move in with me."

His words startled her. "Seriously?"

"I'm joking," he said, laughing. "How's it going with you and Bobby anyway? Married? Pregnant? Still madly in love?"

What did he have, ESP? He was catching

her at a time when she had no answers.

"Everything's great," she lied. "How's *your* love life?"

"Sad."

"Sad?"

"Believe me, it's not easy searching for another you."

"Oh, c'mon . . ." she replied, secretly flattered. "You must be surrounded with gorgeous young starlets dying to jump your body."

"Actresses don't do it for me. They're way too obsessed with projecting the right image. All they want to talk about is themselves, and that gets tired very fast."

"How about actors?" she teased. "You could change tracks."

"Ha-ha. I'm not *that* desperate."

What do you want, Sam? she thought. *Why are you coming back into my life when I'm feeling hurt and vulnerable?*

"Listen, here's the thing," he said, turning all businesslike. "I've been commissioned to write a script about a tough, beautiful female DA, and I was figuring you could supply me with some special inside info."

"Who exactly is going to be playing this tough, beautiful DA?"

"Not cast until I'm done with the script. The powers that be are thinking Scarlett or Jessica Chastain."

"Nice."

"It all comes down to whether they or their agents or managers or whoever makes their decisions like the script. I'm striving for authenticity — which is why I'm coming to you."

"I guess I can help you," she ventured, remembering how much she enjoyed Sam's company. "E-mail me your questions and I'll try to answer them."

"E-mail?" he said. "I was thinking more like lunch."

She was tempted. Bobby was on the missing list. It wasn't as if they were married or anything, and she was hardly planning on jumping into bed with Sam. He was merely a friend, albeit a friend who'd always had a bit of a crush on her. Why *not* have lunch with him?

Glancing at the time on her phone, she noted it was past noon and she was hungry. Starving, actually.

"How about today?" she said crisply, deciding that if Bobby wanted to play games, she could too. "Does that work for you?"

"It certainly does."

"Then where?"

"I could take you somewhere fancy."

"No thanks."

"Fatburger on Santa Monica?"

"Junk food. Exactly what I feel like."

"See you in fifteen."

"You got it." She clicked off and couldn't

help smiling.

Leon approached her desk as she was gathering her things.

"Where're you goin'?" he asked.

"Lunch," she said shortly.

"Want me to tag along?"

"No, thank you."

"Meetin' Bobby? Is he back?"

She felt herself blushing. "No. And it's none of your business who I'm seeing."

Leon rolled his eyes. "I didn't ask. Although the thing is — now you got me all curious."

Collecting her purse, she quickly brushed past him.

"Okay, lady, be like that," Leon said. "Only get your cute ass back here by two. We got a meetin' with the agent who's goin' in under-cover on our boy."

"Alejandro Diego is not a boy," she said sternly. "He's a scumbag. And stop making sexist remarks, or I'll have to report *your* cute ass."

"Understood," he said, grinning.

"See you later, Leon."

She hurried to her car, got in, checked her appearance in the visor mirror, applied a dab of lip gloss, and fluffed out her hair.

Then she felt ridiculous. This was a business meeting, nothing more.

Sam was his usual somewhat scruffy self, a look that suited him. Denver was delighted to note that he had not had his teeth fixed. In fact, he hadn't changed at all, even though he was probably raking in millions. He was sitting at a table outside Fatburger, the smell of burgers wafting in the air. He jumped up as soon as he saw her approaching.

"Here she is, the DA of my dreams," he said, enveloping her in a clumsy embrace.

"Deputy DA," she corrected.

"Whatever. You're still a raving beauty. It's a real drag you're not an actress."

"I'm not, so don't start with me," she said, feeling a slight blush coming on.

"Who's starting?"

"You are."

They grinned at each other.

"Where's my favorite pooch, Amy Winehouse?" he asked. "I thought she went everywhere with you."

"Unfortunately, we lost her."

"Huh?"

"She was having seizures. We were forced to put her down."

"Sorry to hear that."

"Thanks. It was really difficult."

"Did you get another dog?"

"I want to. I will," she said fervently. "Bobby's promised we can pick out a rescue. I can't wait."

"Amy Winehouse," Sam reflected. "She's probably in heaven with the great singer herself."

Denver gave a wan smile. Sam always managed to say the right thing.

"Now," Sam said. "If I remember correctly, the lady likes a double cheeseburger fully loaded, with french fries and an extra-thick chocolate shake. You stay here. I'll go put in our order."

While Sam went inside, Denver checked her phone, which she'd set to go directly to voice mail. Bobby had a jealous streak, especially when it came to Sam, and she didn't want him calling and questioning her, because she was not the greatest liar. Besides, Bobby was on her shit list, and so far it seemed he was making no effort to get off it.

Lunch with Sam sped by. His stories about life on the set of a big Hollywood movie were hilarious. She told him a little about the Diego case, and he couldn't have been more interested. Sam was unusual because he actually *listened* to what she had to say, a rare quality in a man.

By the time she realized that it was past two, Sam was still plying her with questions.

"I've got to go," she said, abruptly getting up. "I'm late for a meeting."

"We're not finished," Sam said, reaching for her hand. "I need more inside info."

"I'll call you," she said quickly.

"No you won't."

"Yes, I will," she said, withdrawing her hand from his.

"Promise?"

"Yes," she said, although she was not sure it was a promise she would keep.

CHAPTER FOURTEEN

Slowly, Bobby opened his eyes, only to find that he was stuck in a thick swirling fog. The fog was in his ears, his nose, his mouth. The fog was suffocating him.

Fuck! What was happening?

It seemed the fog was all around, pulling him down, making him sick to his stomach. He controlled an urge to throw up.

Where the fuck was he?

Certainly not in his bed. Certainly not in a bed at all. He was slumped over the wheel of his rental car feeling as if he'd been hit over the head with a hammer.

Jesus Christ! How had this happened? What the hell . . .

He pulled himself to a sitting position and glanced out the window. The car was parked on a residential street. A kid was riding his bike; a stooped old man was walking his dog. The dog stopped and took a crap, while two joggers in matching spandex outfits pounded the sidewalk next to him.

All was normal.

All was not.

Swallowing hard, he choked up a cough. The fog was slowly lifting. It was being replaced with aching limbs, more nausea, a dry throat, and a raging thirst.

Still coughing, he groped for his phone, only to discover that it was turned off. He quickly activated it and checked his messages, noting that it was eight A.M.

He had three voice mails.

Message one. Denver. *I thought you were calling me back. Don't bother now. I'm going to sleep.*

Message two. Lucky. *I just wanted to wish you luck for tonight. I'm sure it'll be a great success. Love you.*

Message three. M.J. *Thanks a lot. I hope she was worth it.*

M.J. and Denver both sounded pissed.

Bobby attempted to recall what had happened. The opening of their club, everything running smoothly. Then enter the seductive Latina woman in the clingy red dress.

He'd driven her back to her hotel, accompanied her upstairs.

Had he gone to her room?

He couldn't remember.

He *did* remember her telling him a security guard had attacked her and could he look around, and then . . . yes . . . he *had* taken

125

her to her room.

No, not a room, a suite. She'd asked him to check out the closets and bathrooms. He'd done so, and when he was finished, she'd handed him a drink. After that it was all a total blank.

Had she drugged him? Slipped him a roofie or two?

Why would she do that?

His burning mission was to find out.

The doorman at the hotel stared at Bobby blankly.

"Were you on duty last night?" Bobby asked, hot to discover exactly what had taken place.

The man shook his head and started to turn away.

"Maybe you can tell me who was?" Bobby said, his tone aggressive although he still felt like crap.

"If you have a complaint, sir, I suggest you talk to management," the doorman said, waving down a cab for a hotel guest.

Yes. Talk to management. That was an excellent idea. Or even better, talk to Nadia and find out what kind of sick game she was playing.

Entering the hotel, he headed straight for the men's room, where he relieved himself and splashed his face with ice-cold water. He stared at his reflection in the mirror above

A few minutes later, Mr. Goodsun appeared. He was English and uptight. The hotel group he worked for had placed him in this Chicago hotel when his one desire was to return to his native England. His dream was to manage the Savoy Hotel in London.

He approached Bobby with attitude. "Are you a guest here?" he asked, looking down his long thin nose.

"No," Bobby replied. "I'm trying to locate one of your guests."

"And that would be?"

"A woman called Nadia."

"Nadia?"

"Jesus Christ!" Bobby said sharply. "How many times do I have to tell you people?"

"And that would be *Mrs.* Nadia?"

"No," Bobby said, beginning to lose it. "Nadia's her first name. She's a very attractive Latina woman. Last night she had on a red dress. Someone must know who I'm talking about."

Mr. Goodsun gave a discreet cough. He understood the situation. Obviously a call girl had lured this young man up to her room and stiffed him in some way. Not that Mr. Goodsun allowed call girls to operate in his hotel — that was a definite no-no. However, loose women had a way of pretending to be legitimate guests, so what could he do?

"I'm sorry, sir," Mr. Goodsun said, repeating the words of his desk clerk with a little

129

too much relish. "Unless you can give us more details, we are unable to help you."

Realizing that he was getting nowhere fast, Bobby decided he'd better come back later when his head wasn't on fire and his stomach wasn't doing cartwheels. The scrambled eggs had obviously been a big mistake.

Writing down his cell number and name, he thrust it at the manager, then said, "Call me when you find out who this hotel guest is. It's urgent."

Mr. Goodsun managed a fake smirk. "Certainly, sir," he said. As if he was going to spend his time chasing down an anonymous call girl. He had other, more important matters to take care of.

Bobby left the hotel. He'd been taken for some fucking ride, and he was determined to find out why.

CHAPTER FIFTEEN

Alejandro shot up in bed after a night of vivid dreams. He was wide awake and not even hungover. Reaching for a bottle of water, he downed a couple of hefty swigs.

Willow lay asleep in bed beside him, snoring daintily. She didn't usually spend the night, but he was glad that she had.

He studied her for a moment. Willow Price. Legitimate movie star. A troubled girl, whose troubles only got her more headlines. Long, pale red hair draped across his black silk sheets; a perfect heart-shaped face; endless tanned legs; perky breasts — although he would've preferred them to be larger.

Alejandro was sleeping with a star, and she was a beauty. A notorious beauty whose career needed a hefty boost. Recalling the previous night's conversation, it occurred to him that *he* was the man to give it to her.

He contemplated how he would tell Rafael that he was about to become a Hollywood producer. Rafael wouldn't like it; he was always whining about keeping a low profile. Too bad, because Alejandro was sick of the low-profile shit. He desired recognition in the film industry. He *should* be a player, and there was absolutely no reason why he couldn't be. He knew plenty of guys who were major players. They made multimillion-dollar movies backed by big studios, and for kicks they hung out at Club Luna, snorting coke, popping pills, receiving head in the men's room, picking up random girls, and getting shit-faced whenever they felt like it. It didn't matter whether they were married or not; they went for it big-time. They did whatever they wanted.

Alejandro had the hots to be part of the tribe, not just the man who owned a club and was known for giving outrageous parties and supplying primo drugs. Willow had planted the idea firmly in his head, and now he was primed for action. He wished that Frankie Romano were around so he could run shit by him. Frankie knew plenty about the inner workings of Hollywood. Too bad he'd gotten his skinny ass arrested and thrown in jail.

When Willow finally awoke, sex was not on Alejandro's mind, getting things started was.

Willow yawned and stretched like a jungle cat. She was in no way a morning person — and although it was almost noon, she wasn't pleased when Alejandro opened the heavy drapes and she discovered him standing over her like a hawk about to pounce on its prey.

"For crap's sake, no morning sex," she groaned, shielding her eyes from the light, reaching for a cigarette, lighting up, and inhaling deeply. "Y'know it's not my scene."

"No sex," Alejandro said. "We talk."

"About what?" she asked suspiciously, blowing a stream of smoke in his direction.

"Our movie."

Those two words acted like a shot of adrenaline. Willow stubbed out her cigarette and sat up in bed, covering her breasts with the black satin sheet, her long hair tumbling around her shoulders.

"Coffee. I need coffee," she gasped, surprised and yet thrilled that he'd remembered their conversation.

Alejandro buzzed for his maid, a surly Colombian woman who hated him almost as much as she hated her job. Unfortunately, her son worked for Pablo Fernandez Diego in Colombia, and Pablo wanted someone in his son's apartment he could trust, so she was stuck with the job.

"How much?" Alejandro asked Willow after he'd instructed his maid to bring them coffee.

Willow shook her head, desperately attempting to get her thoughts in synch. "How much what?" she asked, thinking that maybe she should snort a line of coke to start the day.

"How much to make our own fucking movie?" Alejandro said, pacing up and down.

"Oh, finances," she murmured vaguely. "We're gonna have to hire a production manager to tell us that. Although I've heard one can make a decent independent movie for maybe fifteen mill."

Alejandro nodded. The fifteen million figure didn't faze him — in fact, it was less than he'd expected.

"What would be our first move?" he asked. "I'd like to see a big announcement in the *Hollywood Reporter.* Front page."

"We gotta get a property first," Willow said, realizing that he was serious. This must be her lucky day, so she'd better get it together fast.

" 'Property'?" Alejandro questioned.

"A book. A script. Something tangible."

"Where do we get that?"

Her mind began working overtime. "There's this screenwriter I met on one of my movies," she said. "He's kind of sweet and I know he likes me. When I met him he was a nonentity, but now he's hot. I kinda remember him telling me about a script he's got stashed away we could use. And he wants to direct, so what could be more perfect?"

"Who is this guy?" Alejandro asked suspiciously.

"I didn't fuck him," Willow offered.

"I don't care," Alejandro said.

"His name's Sam. I'll call him, see if he's interested. I got a hunch he will be."

"You do that. Let's get this thing going," Alejandro said, already imagining himself standing on a podium at the Academy Awards in front of a thousand cameras accepting an Oscar.

Yes, anything was possible.

And the winner is Alejandro Diego for his critically acclaimed movie . . .

It all sounded like he was on the road to mega-fame and success.

There was a time when Willow would disguise her voice and call the paparazzi pretending to be a shopkeeper or a waiter alerting the paps to where they could find Willow Price. Now she didn't have to do that anymore. The paparazzi automatically followed her everywhere, waiting impatiently for her next bad move. It was annoying, for now she always had to try to look her best, otherwise the haters on the Internet and the TMZ watchers would pull her to pieces with their vile comments.

She knew full well that she'd screwed up an extremely promising career, and that it was nobody's fault but her own. Surrounding herself with the wrong people had not helped. Enablers were everywhere.

Want some coke?
Done.
Pills?
Of course.
Smack? Heroin? Speedballs? Molly?
Why not?

Oh God, there wasn't a drug she hadn't tried, and all it got her was nowhere. She'd lost jobs, money, friends. Spent too much time in rehab fucking the wrong male or female. Yet she still looked amazing, with a little help from the right dermatologist. She was only twenty-five, and maybe this movie thing with Alejandro would be her salvation, would put her back on top where she belonged. She was talented, of that there was no doubt.

She had to get a script, and she had to get it fast. Alejandro was full of enthusiasm now, but how long would that last? He was mercurial. He could change his mind, or someone could change it for him.

Oh yes, it was imperative that she act immediately.

She hurried home from Alejandro's to her less luxurious abode — a small house off Fountain that she rented from a gay interior designer who doubled as a drag queen by night. The paparazzi were hanging around outside, as usual. She knew some of them by name, and there were times when she would arrange a setup shot and split the money with

136

the photographer — that's how far she had fallen.

"Hard night out?" one of them yelled. "Same outfit as last night."

Ignoring the pesky pap, she hurried inside her house, took a quick shower, changed clothes, sat at her kitchen counter, and called Sam Slade.

"Sam," she exclaimed, relieved he'd kept the same number. "It's Willow — Willow Price."

"Hey," Sam said slowly. "Willow. Long time no hear from."

She gave a girlish laugh. "I know. Time goes fast when you're having a blast."

They'd worked together on a low-budget movie he'd written. Sam was originally from New York and kind of geeky in a weirdly attractive way. He'd definitely liked her. She hadn't reciprocated; underpaid screenwriters were not her thing. They hadn't spoken in over a year, and now he was a big deal and her star had fallen. It was time to reconnect.

"I have a work proposition I'd like to discuss with you," she said briskly. She could almost hear him groan on the other end of the phone.

"Sorry, Willow. My work card's all jammed up," he said, sounding pleasant, although not exactly ecstatic to hear from her.

"I'm sure." She paused, then said, "Only this is something different and *really* exciting, Sam." She paused again for effect. "Remember that script you told me about, the one you'd written on spec and said that one day you wanted to direct? Well, I might have exactly the deal you're looking for."

CHAPTER SIXTEEN

"You've got to call Denver for me," Bobby informed M.J., confronting him in his hotel room.

"Jeez — don't *you* look like dog shit," M.J. exclaimed, adding a succinct, "Oh yeah, an' thanks for comin' back last night. I coulda really used your help. Like I said on the phone, I hope she was worth it."

"Hey," Bobby said, confused and angry. "Nothing happened."

"Sure," M.J. sneered.

"I think I was drugged," Bobby said, flopping down in a chair, still feeling like shit.

"Jesus!" M.J. said, shaking his head disbelievingly. "I've heard excuses in my time, only you, my man, are takin' it way too far."

"I'm dead serious," Bobby said, realizing how crazy he must sound.

"No, what you *are* is full of crap," M.J. said sharply.

"I want you to listen to me," Bobby said, attempting to keep his cool. "I drove that girl to the hotel, and the next thing I know I'm waking up in my car blocks away, and it's morning."

"I see you've still got your watch," M.J. pointed out. "Your wallet too?"

"It wasn't a robbery," Bobby said flatly. "I don't know what the fuck it was."

"C'mon, man, whyn't you just admit it — you got laid," M.J. said. "An' I'm not the one who's gonna be runnin' to Denver, so chill."

"You're not getting it, are you?" Bobby said, shaking his head.

"Gettin' *what*?" M.J. said, throwing Bobby a skeptical look.

"That for some reason I got slammed, and I have to find out why. But in the meantime you've got to call Denver and tell her I came down with some kind of stomach bug and that I'll call her later."

"What's up with you not callin' or texting her yourself?"

" 'Cause I'm gonna have to explain what happened, and I'm in no shape to do that," Bobby said, wishing that M.J. would simply do what he asked and stop questioning him. "She'll be wondering why she hasn't heard from me, so just do it."

M.J. shrugged. "You really think Denver's gonna believe me? There's no way she'll buy that you were too sick to pick up a phone. No fuckin' way."

"Do it anyway. Convince her," Bobby said,

trying his best to remain calm. " 'Cause I gotta get myself over to the emergency room and try to find out what kind of shit they gave me."

" 'They'? Who the fuck is 'they'?"

"Nadia couldn't've done it by herself," Bobby said, his mind racing with possibilities. "She had to have someone help her. How else could I have ended up dumped in a car, for crissake? It must've been her and that lowlife cousin."

"Jeez, you're really serious."

"You bet your ass I am, 'cause you should know I wouldn't bail on you — not on our opening night."

"Then let's figure this shit out," M.J. said. "If you *were* drugged, there's gotta be a reason."

"You think I don't know that?"

"Whyn't you tell me again what happened."

"After I woke up in the car, I drove back to the hotel and tried to find her. Dead end. All I have is her first name. I gave it to the manager, who looked at me like I was batshit crazy."

"Can't blame him for that."

"For crissake, it happened," Bobby said, fast losing patience. "I'm not hallucinating. This is for real."

"Don't go freakin' out on me. I believe you. Your story's too fucked up to be an excuse."

"Damn right it is."

"Here's the deal," M.J. said, finally on board. "I'll call Denver for you. Then we're headin' straight to the emergency room."

Bobby nodded. "Now, *that* sounds like a plan."

After lunch with Sam, Denver headed back to the office, where she and Leon met with the female undercover agent, Sonia Gonzalez.

Sonia Gonzalez was Puerto Rican and verging on pretty, in a tough "don't fuck with me" kind of way. Leon and she had partnered together before and they seemed to know each other well.

Denver couldn't help wondering if they'd slept together. The vibe in the air was that they had. The two of them had been on an undercover assignment in San Diego two years previously and they'd brought down a major human-trafficking ring. They were obviously tight.

Sonia had long black hair tied back in a ponytail, full lips, and a taut body. Today she was dressed for real life in pants and a denim shirt. Denver could just imagine her in full regalia as a party girl. Sonia would own the role.

They circled around each other, both with their own agendas. Denver wanted to make sure that Sonia knew what she was getting herself into, while Sonia was going for trust.

She only worked with people she was sure had her back.

Later, Leon revealed to Denver that Sonia's older sister had also been an undercover agent, and had gotten shot and killed for her trouble. "Sonia's the best," he assured Denver. "If anyone's gonna nail our boy, it'll be her."

"I wish you'd stop calling Alejandro 'our boy,' " Denver said, her tone sharp. "He's a douche-bag drug dealer who's ruining people's lives."

"Got it."

"Good," Denver said, feeling her phone vibrate. She quickly reached for it and checked out the caller. It was M.J. What the hell did *he* want?

Then it suddenly occurred to her that maybe Bobby had gotten into an accident, and while she was out on a lunch date mildly flirting with an old flame, Bobby was lying in a hospital mortally wounded.

"I have to take this," she said.

"Go ahead," Leon replied, giving her space. "Later."

"M.J.?" she said into the phone as soon as Leon was out of earshot. "Where's Bobby? Is he okay? What the *hell* is going on?"

"Funny you should ask . . ."

"What?" Denver gasped, her imagination launching into overdrive.

"It's nothin' major," M.J. said quickly.

"Your man came down with an attack of the runs. He's gonna call you later."

Before she could get into it, M.J. clicked off, and she was left with the distinct impression that M.J. was covering for Bobby.

Now she was really angry. An attack of the runs indeed. What kind of lame excuse was *that*?

Bobby, Bobby, Bobby, what are you doing? I thought we had something special going on, so why are you trying to sabotage it?

She sat still for a moment, trying to process what had just happened. Then, on a sudden impulse, she called Sam. "I was thinking," she said. "If you really need more info for your script, I guess I can meet up with you later."

"Twice in one day?" Sam said, sounding delighted. "How come I'm getting so lucky?"

"Don't get carried away," she said crisply. "Nobody's getting lucky."

"I knew it was too good to be true."

"We could meet at the Polo Lounge," she suggested.

"I'd prefer somewhere quieter," he said. "How would you feel about coming to my apartment?"

"Sam —"

"Strictly business," he said. "I'll even throw in a dish of pasta with my special sauce. You know you can't resist my culinary skills."

"Maybe not, but I can certainly resist

144

everything else," she said, determined that he know up front that she was not to be tempted.

"I get it," Sam said. "You're well and truly taken. However, that doesn't mean you can't enjoy my pasta. Right?"

"We'll see," she said, and quickly clicked off.

CHAPTER SEVENTEEN

Lucky awoke with a deep sense of foreboding and wondered why. She and Lennie had enjoyed a fantastic evening together — amazing sex, delicious food, a special kind of love and commitment. They were so in tune with each other. Everything was perfect.

Too perfect? There was a vibe in the air, an ominous vibe.

Instinct told her something was wrong.

Instinct told her to check on her family.

She slipped quietly out of bed, leaving Lennie sleeping on his back, his arms stretched above his head.

Her first call was to the camp where Gino Junior and Leo were spending the summer. A camp counselor assured her that both boys were fine.

Next she called Max in London. Max informed her she was off to Saint-Tropez the following day. Nothing wrong there.

Bobby didn't answer his cell, so she called M.J., who told her that Bobby had a stomach bug. Nothing serious.

And finally — Gino.

No answer.

She tried his wife Paige's cell. Straight to voice mail.

She tried the landline at their house in Palm Springs.

Nobody picked up.

A shiver enveloped her, a shiver of fear.

And yet . . . there was nothing to be fearful of. Both Gino and Paige hated cell phones — technology did not interest either of them. As for the house phone, they were probably on their morning walk, and their housekeeper had yet to arrive. At his advanced age, Gino claimed that walking was the key to his longevity.

Sure, Gino. It's your stubborn spirit that's the key — screw walking.

Making her way into the open-plan kitchen overlooking the ocean, she considered what to do next.

Was she being paranoid? Should she start checking further afield? Maybe she should contact her half brother, Steven, who resided in Brazil. Or perhaps Bobby's niece, Brigette, who'd recently moved to Barcelona with her girlfriend.

No way.

Cool it, Santangelo.

Nothing's going on.

She picked up the remote and turned on

147

the TV. The morning news was all about a cheating politician who'd been caught at an orgy with a bevy of hookers. What a surprise! A raging forest fire in Oklahoma. Two vacuous movie stars getting a divorce. Who cared? And a violent home invasion in Calabasas.

Same old, same old. Bad news ruled. How about someone starting a good-news-only channel?

The thought intrigued her. Maybe it was a factor she could incorporate into her new venture. A streaming channel on the Internet featuring nothing but upbeat stories.

Lennie ambled into the kitchen wearing low-slung jeans and not much else. She enveloped him in a tight hug, loving the smell of him. There was something about the way their bodies were in perfect synch.

"What's up with you?" he asked with a lazy half smile. "The sex wasn't enough last night? My beautiful wife wants more?"

"I always want more," she purred, running her fingers across his bare chest. "But only with you."

"My wife — the sex addict," he said, laughing.

"And don't you love it," she countered.

"Gotta admit — I do," he said, kissing her.

His breath was minty fresh. She loved him so much. He was her soul mate, her anchor, the father of two of her children. He was her everything.

"Wanna take a trip back to bed?" he suggested.

"I wouldn't say no," she answered, putting all thoughts of a bad premonition out of her head.

"Such enthusiasm," he teased. "Where's the girl I used to know?"

"Do you realize how much I love you?" she said quietly. "Do you even understand?"

He caught her sense of unrest and leaned toward her. "What's up, sweetheart?" he asked, putting his arms around her. "Something bothering you?"

"It was," she admitted. "Although I'm okay now."

"Anything you want to talk about?"

"I don't know," she said slowly. "It's just that I woke up this morning with a bad feeling."

"About what?"

"If I knew, I'd tell you."

"Knowing you, I'd be the last to find out."

"That's 'cause there's nothing to find out. I called everyone, and they're all fine."

He raised a skeptical eyebrow. "You called everyone?"

"Just to make sure."

"You're something else," he said, shaking his head. "If something was up, don't you think they'd all be calling *you*?"

"You're right," she agreed.

And at that exact moment, the phone rang.

And Lucky knew for sure it could only be bad news.

CHAPTER EIGHTEEN

"You're an extremely fortunate young man," the Indian doctor informed Bobby. He wasn't that old, probably late forties, with prematurely gray hair cut short and a wise expression. He wore a white coat, and had a stethoscope hanging around his neck.

When Bobby and M.J. had arrived at the emergency room and revealed what they were there for, a nurse had whisked Bobby into a curtained-off cubicle, asked him to put on a hospital gown, and taken his temperature and blood pressure. Then another nurse had drawn blood and requested a urine sample.

Now, after a long wait, Dr. Sanjay had appeared.

"Fortunate how?" Bobby asked, feeling ridiculous that he was stuck in a hospital bed like some kind of invalid. It wasn't necessary. All he'd wanted was for them to find out what he'd been drugged with.

"It seems that you were given a very large dose of gammahydroxybutyrate," Dr. Sanjay said, clearing his throat. "Or in layman's terms — GHB."

"I knew it!" Bobby exclaimed, shooting M.J. a triumphant look.

M.J., sitting in a bedside chair, nodded, as if he'd known all along.

"What is it normally used for?" Bobby asked.

"Sometimes a general anesthetic, or to treat alcoholism, clinical depression, and insomnia."

"Jesus!" Bobby said, shaking his head.

"And of course," Dr. Sanjay added, "it's well known as the date rape drug."

"Shit!" Bobby exclaimed.

"You must have a very strong constitution," Dr. Sanjay continued. "For I should warn you that such a large dose of GHB can be lethal."

"It can?" Bobby managed, experiencing a quick shudder of fear.

"Yes. It can cause unconsciousness, respiratory depression, and cardiac arrest," Dr. Sanjay said matter-of-factly. "In other words, it can kill you. And for your further information — if mixed with alcohol, it is even more dangerous. Had you been drinking?"

"A couple of vodkas, that's all."

Dr. Sanjay tapped the side of his nose. "Once again I must say that you are extremely fortunate." After a long pause, he added, "Are you aware of who gave you this drug?"

"No clue," Bobby said, shooting M.J. a warning look not to say a word.

"I should really inform the authorities," Dr. Sanjay mused.

"I'd prefer you didn't," Bobby said, mustering his most persuasive powers. "We own a club here, and last night was our big opening. It wouldn't be good for business if this got out."

"And I am sure that it wouldn't be good for business if something like this happened again and someone died," Dr. Sanjay said curtly, his expression stern.

Bobby wondered if the doctor was bribable, and decided he wasn't.

"Look," he said quickly. "I'll be honest with you. What happened was just a stupid prank my girlfriend played on me. It's something she would never do again."

"An extremely foolish prank indeed."

"I know," Bobby said with a sincere nod. "Believe me — she's mortified."

"As well she should be."

"We were . . . uh . . . experimenting," Bobby said, warming to his story. "Our experiment obviously went too far."

"Yes, it did," Dr. Sanjay said, his thick eyebrows knitting together to signal deep disapproval.

"I'd really like to get out of here," Bobby said. Now that he felt better, he was ready to go back to the hotel with more questions.

Fuck it. He was desperate to know why this had happened to him.

"Very well, then," Dr. Sanjay said, nodding. "I suppose I can allow you to leave without taking this any further."

"Thanks, Doc. I appreciate it."

"Although I must insist that you drink plenty of liquids and rest up. It's possible that you could have a delayed reaction. If you feel anything unusual, you must return here immediately. Do you understand?"

"Got it. I'll be following your orders all the way," Bobby said, still thinking that he couldn't wait to investigate further, find out why he'd been chosen as a victim. A victim who could've died. *Son of a bitch!*

"Think of your body as a finely tuned machine that needs to take time to recover," Dr. Sanjay said. "Also, tell your girlfriend that if the authorities *had* been brought in, she would most likely be under arrest."

"I think she knows that. And, uh . . . maybe I can make a donation to the hospital, or one of your favorite charities?"

"Not necessary," Dr. Sanjay said.

"Okay, then," Bobby said, sliding off the bed. "Thanks for everything." He glanced quickly at M.J. "Well, I guess we're outta here."

CHAPTER NINETEEN

Sleep was impossible, so as soon as light began creeping into the apartment, Max jumped up, hurriedly dressed, and shook Tim awake. He was quite a sight with his lank mousy hair and pale complexion, still clad in Athena's leopard-print Dolce & Gabbana pj's.

"Wake up," she hissed. "We've gotta get him out."

"What time is it?" Tim groaned, opening his eyes.

"Never mind the time," Max said impatiently, brushing a lock of dark hair back from her forehead. "Put on your clothes."

"Oh God!" Tim complained. "I knew it was a mistake staying here. You American girls are so damn bossy."

"I try, only it's not doing me much good," Max lamented, wishing that Athena were around to take care of things. Athena would kick *everyone's* ass. It was her way of getting things done, and it always worked.

155

"What about my hot breakfast?" Tim demanded, reluctantly sitting up.

"As soon as you've removed the problem," Max promised, although she still had no intention of cooking him anything.

Tim threw her an alarmed look. "I'm not becoming involved in anything physical," he warned. "That sort of stuff is not for me."

"You don't have to," Max assured him. "Simply tell him you're my boyfriend. That should be enough to shift his Italian butt."

"Very well," Tim said, acquiescing. "Is he awake?"

"Not yet. We'll catch him off guard. He'll probably be sober and mortified."

By the time they reached Max's bedroom, Carlo was neither of those things. He was lying on top of the bed, eyes open. He stared up at Max and Tim — who was now fully dressed — and gave a pleased smirk. *"Buon giorno, bellissima,"* he said, zeroing in on Max. *"Bene, sì?* We will kill. Yes?"

"What?" Max said, a frown spreading across her pretty face.

"I came here last night to tell you," Carlo offered, raising himself onto one elbow. "Perhaps I maybe overstayed my welcome."

"What welcome?" Max spluttered, thinking that Carlo was totally delusional. Or maybe he was simply an idiot.

Carlo yawned, acting as if everything was totally normal.

If only he wasn't such a dick, Max thought, *he'd be kind of attractive in a down and dirty brooding kind of way.*

She could almost like him. Only almost. He was no Billy Melina.

"You rolled in here last night — pissed out of your mind — and fell into my bed," she informed him, in case he didn't remember. "You told me nothing. So now you can shift your ass and get out."

"Out!" Tim repeated, a frantic tick taking over his left eye.

"Who is *he*?" Carlo asked, favoring Tim with an unfriendly scowl. "Your pet dog?"

"My boyfriend," Max said firmly. "And he wants you out even more than I do, so you'd better move it before he totally loses it."

"You have a boyfriend?" Carlo said, obviously not thrilled with the information.

"Don't sound so surprised," Max answered sharply. "And oh yes — I should tell you that he has a black belt in judo."

Tim took a step back and shot Max a glare — as if to say, *What the hell — I told you no fisticuffs for me, young lady.*

Carlo sat up. Tim took another cautionary step back.

"Too much tequila," Carlo announced. "My weakness. *Scusi.*" He jumped off the bed. "Now I must take a piss."

Before Max could object, Carlo was heading for the bathroom.

She and Tim exchanged looks.

"Judo?" Tim said, quite horrified. "Black belt?"

"It sounds threatening," Max said, defending her words. "I think it made him nervous."

"It certainly made *me* nervous," Tim snorted, a red flush creeping up his neck. "Him — not so much."

"When he stops peeing," Max said, all business, "you'll throw him out."

"I'll do no such thing," Tim objected. "I'm going home. He's all yours."

"You wouldn't leave me," she said, attempting to appeal to Tim's better nature. "You wouldn't do that to me."

"That's *exactly* what I'm doing," Tim stated. And with those words, he made a hurried dash for the front door.

"Thanks a lot," Max yelled after him. "You *suck.*"

Carlo emerged from the bathroom. "Your boyfriend take off?" he asked, scratching his balls.

At least he's fully dressed and sober, Max thought. *And if Tim can't shift him, I certainly can.*

"Yes," she said stiffly. "He took off, and that's exactly what I'd like you to do."

"Ah, but not before I tell you our news, *bella,*" Carlo said, turning on a great deal of Italian charm.

"*Our* news?" she demanded, confronting

158

him, hands on hips.

"We have *bene bene* news."

"We do?"

"Sì, my *piccola bambina."*

"Can you please speak English," she said, quite exasperated. "And while you're at it — stop with the terms of endearment, 'cause for your information, I am not anyone's little baby."

Carlo gave a casual shrug while reaching into his pocket for a cigarette, which he proceeded to light up.

"Last night," he said. "I had *grande* dinner with friends, *importante* people in the industry."

"What industry?" she questioned, trying to avoid the stream of smoke he was busily exhaling in her direction.

"The fashion industry, *cara.*"

"Exactly how does that have anything to do with you crawling into my bed in the middle of the night?"

"I am sure you have heard of the American company Guess?"

"Yes."

"Then I tell you their equivalent in Italy is Dolcezza."

More smoke drifted into her face.

"Last night I show them our photos," Carol continued. "They were mad for them. They want you to be their face, and me to helm their next big advertising campaign."

"Huh?" Max said, quite startled.

"This is huge, *mia carina.*"

"Stop calling me names," she said, attempting to digest this exciting information. Could it mean that she might be the new face of Dolcezza? She needed to get to her iPad immediately and check out Dolcezza, find out if they were indeed the Italian version of Guess.

"Tell your agent, *pronto,*" Carlo instructed. "They make immediate deal. We start shooting next week."

"Is this for real?" she asked, wide-eyed.

"*Sí, bella.* Only now I must leave you. I have work to do. *Scusi* for last night. We meet again very soon in beautiful Italia. Ciao, *cara.*"

And just like Tim, Carlo was heading out the door, leaving Max in a total state of confusion.

CHAPTER TWENTY

"Jesus Christ, you don't know how glad I am to be out of there. I got a deep aversion to hospitals," Bobby said as they headed down the street toward M.J.'s car. He was still feeling shaky, although a lot better than he was before.

"Like the man said," M.J. offered, cheerful as ever, "you're one fortunate son of a bitch."

"You got that right," Bobby agreed, trying not to think about what could've happened.

"An' here's the kicker," M.J. pointed out. "You didn't even get laid for your trouble."

"Don't even go there," Bobby groaned. "I told you — getting laid was never my intention."

"Sure," M.J. drawled.

"Will you quit with that shit, M.J. It's not funny. You heard what the doc said. I could've died."

"Yeah, but you gotta admit she *was* hot."

"Oh, she was hot, all right," Bobby said with a cynical laugh. "One hot criminal psycho bitch. Just my type."

M.J. laughed too.

"Jesus," Bobby said as they reached M.J.'s car. "I should call Denver. She must be goin' nuts."

"Denver's too cool for that."

"You don't know her like I do."

"So call her. Nobody's stopping you."

"I guess it's better if I see her in person. That way I can explain the whole fucked-up story."

"Oh yeah," M.J. remarked with a dry chuckle. "She's gonna love that bit about her slipping you a roofie. That'll really thrill her."

"Maybe I'll skip the part where I told the doc that."

"If you wanna keep your balls intact, that sounds like the way to go," M.J. said, sliding behind the steering wheel.

"My balls are fine, thank you."

"You're sure about that?"

"Fuck you, M.J.," Bobby said, shaking his head. "You're treating this like the joke it's not."

"Okay, okay, so what's the plan?" M.J. asked. "Am I drivin' you to the club or the hotel?"

"How about the airport?" Bobby said. "I hate to dump on you, but I kinda think I need a couple of days in L.A. to get my head around what happened. Can you take care of the club without me? Forty-eight hours and

I'll be back."

"You got it. In another few days we'll both be able to leave the place in the new manager's hands. He did great last night."

"At least we've got that going for us."

"Wanna stop by the hotel an' pick up your stuff?" M.J. asked.

"Don't need to, since I'm coming back. Only, do me a big favor — see if you can find out anything about psycho bitch. Could be someone in the club knew her or the so-called cousin. And maybe you can get the number of a reputable PI 'cause I'm getting way into it when I'm back. She's not walking away, I can promise you that."

M.J. revved his engine. "The airport it is."

With Carlo finally gone, Max couldn't wait to get on the phone and call Athena in Saint-Tropez.

"This place is sublime," Athena crowed. "Nothing but amazing yachts, super-interesting rich people, and nonstop parties. I'm in heaven. Get your pretty butt over here, Sweet Eyes. I'm in dire need of my coconspirator."

Max could hear loud techno music blaring in the background, and the sound of several male voices. "It sounds fun," she said tentatively.

"It *is* fun," Athena said, brimming with enthusiasm. "A ton of action, and you know me — I'm the star of everything."

"I'm sure you are."

"I hope you're keeping up with my selfies. They're amazeballs," Athena boasted.

"I'll be sure to check 'em out."

"You do that. My arse looks divine!"

Max hesitated for a moment. "Uh . . . have you heard of Dolcezza?" she asked.

"Of course," Athena said airily. "*Dolcezza* means *sweetheart*. I took Italian in school, you know. That was before I was thrown out for bashing a girl over the head with a lacrosse stick. The cow deserved it."

"I don't mean the word," Max said patiently. "I'm talking about the Italian fashion line."

"Sure. I was supposed to do a huge campaign for them last year, but shockingly they passed. They even had the nerve to tell my agent I was too heroin chic. Can you imagine? I've never touched heroin *ever*. Their bloody loss."

Oh great, Max thought. *Now Athena's going to be pissed that I'm about to land a job she possibly wanted.*

"Why are you asking?" Athena inquired.

Don't tell her now, before it's all signed, Max thought. *Better to wait.*

"Just curious," she answered vaguely. "Carlo kind of mentioned them."

"Ah, yes — Carlo," Athena said with a knowing chuckle. "I forgot that you were working with that sexy Italian stud. Did you screw him?"

"Certainly not."

"*I* did," Athena admitted with a wild giggle.

This was news to Max. How come Athena hadn't mentioned it before?

"Wow! I didn't know that," she mumbled. "You could've told me."

"It was a one-night thing," Athena said matter-of-factly. "Carlo has the reputation of bedding all his models, especially the young ones. I was sixteen at the time and naive as fuck. I suppose I should have warned you."

Kind of sketchy that you didn't, Max thought. *What's up with that?*

"Anyway," Athena continued. "When will you be here? I have a superhot friend with a helicopter. He'll pick you up from Nice Airport."

"I was thinking of flying in tomorrow," Max said, although she wasn't sure if that would happen now.

"Fab," Athena exclaimed. "Text me the deets. Must go now. Some random rich dude is taking me power-sailing."

Max clicked off and phoned her agent, Melissa Brown, a brisk ex-model in her fifties who called everyone "luvvie." Melissa repped only the best, and Max knew that it was only because of Athena that Melissa had signed her.

Melissa had gotten her the jeans campaign

165

and warned her not to screw it up. Since she hung with Athena — who often arrived at shoots late and was known to be difficult — she had to prove herself. If the whole Dolcezza thing was true, then Melissa would begin to realize that she was indeed a contender.

"Well, well, well," Melissa drawled over the phone. "Somebody's made a big impression. I'm proud of you, luvvie. Dolcezza are hot to trot — they're e-mailing me contracts as we speak."

"They are?" Max gulped, thinking that things were moving really fast.

"Apparently they're mad for Carlo's photos, and they've fallen in love with you," Melissa continued. "This is quite a coup. They've been searching for the face of Dolcezza for months. Apparently you're it."

"Wow! I'm excited."

"As so you should be, luvvie. This could be the start of something really big."

"When would I have to go to Italy?"

"Sooner rather than later. They're planning two days of test shots for makeup, hair, and clothes. A press conference, followed by a ten-day shoot in Rome, Venice, and Capri. You're one very lucky girl, so do not screw it up."

Why was Melissa always telling her that?

Oh yes, it was because of her connection to party-hard Athena.

166

She hoped Athena would be as thrilled as she was. Somehow she had a hunch Athena might not be. After all, Athena was always the star, and she, Max, was always the sidekick. However, if the Dolcezza campaign was a success, things could radically change.

And if they did, Max was more than ready. This was her shot, and she was all over it.

Chapter Twenty-One

"What the fuck is it?" Lennie demanded, his eyes focused on Lucky as she dropped her phone to the ground and fell back into a chair. Her face was ashen, her black-as-night eyes filled with shock and disbelief. "For God's sake, tell me," Lennie urged, knowing that whatever it was, it couldn't be good.

Lucky could barely summon the strength to speak. The room was spinning. She felt as if she were trapped in the middle of a deadly nightmare. A feeling of helplessness overcame her. *Wake up!* her inner voice screamed in her head. *Wake the fuck up and get it together.*

"Is it Max?" Lennie continued, thinking that if anyone had harmed his daughter, he would kill them. "Has something happened to Max?"

Slowly Lucky shook her head. "It's . . . Gino," she managed.

"What, exactly?" Lennie asked, expecting her to tell him that Gino had experienced a heart attack or a stroke. He'd never seen his strong, beautiful wife in such a state.

"Gino's been shot," she muttered, hardly believing her own words. "He was shot in the back of the head, execution-style."

"What?"

"I know," she gasped. "It seems impossible."

"Jesus *Christ*!"

"Who would do this, Lennie?" she implored, shaking her head in disbelief. "Who would do such a thing? The days of Gino having enemies are long past. He was an old man living out his final days in peace. WHO WOULD DO THIS?"

Lennie gave a helpless shrug. He was as shocked as his wife, and he had no idea what to say.

For a moment Lucky was lost, adrift, until she realized that she'd better summon her strength and do something. "Call Danny and tell him to arrange a helicopter," she said, her throat dry and raw. "We have to get to Palm Springs immediately."

"I'm doing it now," Lennie said, hurrying from the room.

Lucky buried her head in her hands, her mind overflowing with deadly memories. She pictured her mother's body covered in blood floating on a raft in the family swimming pool. Then she thought of her brother, Dario, tossed from a car like a piece of garbage. And finally Marco — the love of her life before

Lennie — gunned down in the parking lot of the Magiriano.

Violence had always been part of her life. Now this.

Oh God. Not Gino.

Yes. Gino.

She began thinking . . . thinking . . . going through a list of Gino's enemies from his nefarious past. Her head began filling with names — most of the men were deceased. She'd personally taken care of Gino's biggest enemy of all: her godfather, Enzio Bonnatti, the man responsible for the brutal murders of her beloved family. She'd shot the son of a bitch, claiming it was self-defense, that he'd been attempting to rape her. She'd gotten away with it, and she'd never regretted what she'd done, not for one single moment.

It was karma.

Never fuck with a Santangelo.

Unfortunately, there were many other members of the Bonnatti clan. There was also a slew of business associates who could be harboring grudges against Gino from way back.

Oh my God, she thought. *So many vengeful people who might have felt they'd been wronged. So many faceless enemies.*

Over the years, the Santangelos had seen more than their share of murder and mayhem.

Desperately, she attempted to gather her

thoughts. Gino had not been involved in any business ventures for years. His life with Paige in Palm Springs consisted of an occasional dinner out with friends, poker night with old cronies, and watching classic movies on TV. Every so often he made the trip to Vegas, which as far as Lucky was concerned was not often enough.

Gino Santangelo.

Gino the Ram.

Stern father who'd married her off at sixteen.

Loving father who'd finally come to terms with the fact that she, his daughter, could do anything she set her mind to.

Gino was proud of all her achievements; he'd often told her she was the ballsiest woman he'd ever known. When he was feeling nostalgic, he called her his little Italian Princess — the nickname he'd used when she was a child, before Maria's murder, before he'd locked her and Dario away in an enormous Bel Air mansion to protect them.

Childhood memories overwhelmed her, mostly memories of family time with her gentle mother, and her younger brother, Dario. Gino was so happy then — not the stern father he'd turned into after Maria's murder.

Goddamn it! How could this happen to an old man who loved his grandkids, and possessed such a zest for life? *I'm gonna live t' be*

171

one hundred an' three, he'd often boasted. *Then they can finally bury my fine ass in the city I love.*

Las Vegas. Gino had always had a thing for Vegas. His favorite hotel was the Magiriano — a combination of his name and Maria's. A special place with special memories.

Her uncle Costa had often regaled her with tales of Gino's misspent youth — racketeering, loan-sharking, owning a fancy speakeasy during prohibition, a lengthy stint in jail, countless women, then finally Vegas, where he'd turned things around and become a legitimate businessman building hotels and creating an empire.

It's impossible, Lucky thought. *Gino cannot be gone. Not like this.*

"You'd better get dressed," Lennie said, coming back into the room, interrupting her thoughts. "Danny's organizing everything."

She shook her head, clearing the cobwebs, wondering if this was indeed a devastating nightmare, and if she would wake up soon and everything would be fine.

Palm Springs was hot and balmy. *Too damn hot,* Lucky thought. *Why did Gino choose to live in the fucking desert?*

Oh yes, she knew why. Because Paige wanted to. Because Paige hated Vegas. She said it was too flashy and not a place to grow

172

old. Gino had gone along with whatever Paige wanted, although he'd have been so much safer if he'd stayed in Vegas.

"I have to call Bobby, Steven, Max, and —" Lucky began.

"Don't even think about it," Lennie interrupted as a black sedan sped them from the helicopter pad toward Gino's house. "The deal is we should find out exactly what happened, then you call the kids."

Lucky threw him a furious look. "We *know* what happened," she said bitterly. "My father got shot in the fucking head. Isn't that enough?"

Danny sat silently next to the driver. He didn't know what to do or say, he only knew he had to be there for Lucky at all times.

"He should've kept his security guards," Lucky said, drumming her fingers on the leather seat. "I told him to, but as usual, he wouldn't listen."

"Gino refused to live like that," Lennie reminded her. "He was always talking about how much he enjoyed his freedom. No worries. No responsibilities. No shit. Just an old man living out his final days in Palm Springs."

"A *stubborn* old man," Lucky fumed, her anger mixing with the tears she was desperately trying to hold back. "I fucking *hate* him. He should've known better."

"You don't mean that," Lennie said.

"Yes. I do." After a long beat, she added a

173

shaky, "No. I don't. Of course I don't. I loved him with all my heart."

"C'mon, Lucky. You've got to keep it together," Lennie said, taking her hand. "We're almost there."

"How am I supposed to know what to do?" she said sadly, once again feeling helpless because she knew there was nothing she *could* do.

Gino is dead.

My father is gone.

How can I carry on?

Because you're a goddamn Santangelo, a voice in her head said. It was Gino's voice. He was talking to her; she could hear him clearly.

She took a deep breath. *Never fuck with a Santangelo.*

Well, someone had. And they would pay for it. Oh yes, she would make sure of that.

The next few hours were a blur of activity. Homicide detectives were on the scene; police crime investigators were going door-to-door talking to the neighbors.

Paige was hysterical. Darlene, a friend of hers who lived nearby, had arrived at the house and was consoling her.

Lucky insisted on viewing Gino's body — which was still lying on the sidewalk.

Detective Allan, the lead detective assigned to the case, escorted her outside. Seeing her

174

beloved father's lifeless body slumped on the sidewalk in his jogging outfit was simply too much. She felt a lump form in her throat and a gaping emptiness within. This couldn't be happening. Yet it was.

Gino, the invincible.

Shot. In the back of the head.

Dead.

How was this possible?

She curbed the urge to throw herself on top of his body and hug him close.

Finally, Detective Allan led her gently away. "We're very sorry, Ms. Santangelo," he said. "Everyone knew your father. He was a generous man — we could always depend on him to support all our events. Gino Santangelo was quite a character. He'll be missed."

Don't be sorry, she'd wanted to scream. *Find out who the fuck did it. Do that, and I'll take care of the rest.* "I know," she murmured.

It wasn't long before random people started bringing flowers and laying them on the ground next to the police tapes that surrounded the area where Gino had been gunned down. Bad news travels like lightning. TV cameras and their crews were also arriving on the scene — talking to neighbors, trying to blow the story up. Everyone was hungry for more.

After viewing Gino's body, Lucky took refuge in the house with Lennie by her side and Danny ready to do her bidding. Paige was now locked in the master bedroom with Darlene.

Lucky questioned Detective Allan. He informed her that so far Paige was their only witness. She'd made a statement that a man had jogged toward them, passing them as they walked along their usual path, then once he'd gone by, he'd apparently turned around and shot Gino in the back of the head. One bullet was all it took.

Paige's description of the man was sketchy. According to Paige he was dressed all in black, with a baseball cap pulled so low that it partially obscured his face, and dark sunglasses. Paige had gotten the vague impression that he could be in his thirties, but that was all she could come up with.

"Now's the time to call the kids," Lennie said, after Lucky had finished talking to Detective Allan. "Want me to take care of it?"

"It can wait," she said, shaking her head.

"No, it can't," Lennie insisted. "This is going to be all over the Internet. It's probably already up on Twitter. Besides, in the car, you said you *wanted* to call them."

"Not now, Lennie."

"Does that mean that you think it's a better idea for them to find out about it online?" he said.

"I can call," Danny volunteered, sensing tension.

Again Lucky shook her head. "No, Danny. What you *can* do is fix me a drink. Jack on the rocks. Then I'll call them."

"Since when did you start drinking Jack —" Lennie began.

"It was Gino's drink," Lucky interrupted sharply. "I'm having it for him."

Lennie understood his wife enough to know when to leave her alone. She had to process this tragedy in her own way, and it would take time.

"The celebration of Gino's life will be in Vegas," Lucky said to no one in particular. "Gino's wishes. He told me over and over exactly what he wanted when the time came." She turned to Danny. "Make sure the family knows this. Everyone will attend."

Danny had a slew of questions, only now was not the right time to ask them.

"Lennie," Lucky said, turning to her husband. "I'm going to stay here tonight. You should go back to L.A."

"Sweetheart," he said firmly, "there's no way I'm leaving you."

"You've got to do this for me," she insisted. "I have to talk to Paige, and after that I need to be alone."

"How about security?" Lennie asked, thinking that whoever had targeted Gino could come after Lucky.

"You think I can't protect myself?" she said, throwing him a fierce look.

177

"I know you can."

Her voice softened. "Then please do this for me."

Lennie knew there was no arguing with Lucky Santangelo. She might be his wife, but she was also a woman who always did things her way.

Today was no exception.

CHAPTER TWENTY-TWO

Concepción Abascal was almost late for work, and this was bad, for Martha Crabstone, the surly housekeeper who was in charge of the hotel floor she worked on, had threatened to dismiss her if Concepción was late one more time.

Unfortunately, the early evening traffic was not good, nor was her old car — a 1970s Buick that probably should have been laid to rest years ago. However, it was all Concepción had to get around in, and with three young children to ferry back and forth to school, and an out-of-work disabled husband to care for, she depended on her car.

Fortunately, she made it just in time. Out of breath and flushed, she rushed into the room where all the hotel maids kept lockers and changed into her uniform.

Martha Crabstone stood guard. She was a formidable-looking woman with badly dyed black hair and hardly any forehead. This did not seem to faze her, for she wore scarlet lipstick and plenty of badly applied eye makeup. She was big and stout and usually in a vile mood.

"Nice of you to join us, Concepción," Martha said with a sarcastic snarl. She tapped her watch — a cheap Gucci copy — and added, "Two more minutes and you would have found yourself out of a job."

"Sorry, Miss Crabstone," Concepción muttered. "The traffic, it was bad."

"Then leave home earlier," Martha said sternly. "Your excuses are becoming ridiculous."

"So sorry," Concepción said, lowering her eyes, for she could hardly stand to look at the horrible woman who always talked down to her as if she were dirt on the street.

"Anyway," Martha continued, with a brisk clap of her hands, "there is work to get done. Suite 701 has had the Do Not Disturb sign on since last night. Use your passkey and go in there."

"But if the Do Not Disturb sign is on the door —"

"Take fresh towels and get yourself in there," Martha interrupted. "You know my policy: if a sign is on longer than fifteen hours, we should see what's going on."

Concepción gave a reluctant nod. The last time she'd entered a room with a Do Not Disturb sign, she'd been confronted with two naked men having sex on the floor. She shud-

180

dered at the memory.

"Very well, then," Martha said, clapping her large hands together again. "Get moving. I don't have all night to stand here telling you what to do."

Martha left the room. Concepción had already worked her daytime job, and now she had another eight hours ahead of her. She'd be lucky if she got home by two A.M., and then she had to be up at six to fix her children breakfast and get them off to school.

She was tired and depressed and often wondered how her life had turned out to be such sheer drudgery. Once she'd been voted the prettiest girl in her high school. Now, ten years later, she was probably the ugliest. Or at least, that's the way she saw it.

After making sure everything she needed was on her cart, she slipped a bar of soap and a small container of bubble bath into a secret compartment in her purse, and set off to clean her quota of rooms.

Suite 701 still had the Do Not Disturb sign on. Concepción listened at the door and heard nothing. She hesitated before inserting her passkey, then opened the door a crack. Still no sounds.

Perhaps the occupant or occupants had gone out and forgotten to remove the sign. Or maybe they were asleep or — God forbid — having sex in the bedroom.

Concepción entered slowly. The living room

was empty.

Warily, she checked out the guest toilet, then headed for the bedroom. The door was closed. She knocked — not too hard — and called out, "Maid service. Clean towels."

Nothing.

Martha Crabstone would expect her to investigate further, but surely hotel guests were entitled to their privacy?

Not according to Martha. She had strict rules, and everyone was expected to obey them. To not do so would bring the wrath of Martha full upon them, and nobody wanted that.

Very carefully, Concepción pushed open the bedroom door and peered inside.

Again, nothing.

The large double bed was neatly made; everything was in place.

Concepción was pleased. One less chore to take care of.

Idly, she wondered what it would be like to have someone do everything for you — make your bed, clean your toilet, cook your food — or to order room service if you were lucky enough to stay in a luxury hotel.

It suddenly struck her that the room looked unused. There were no personal items on display, no messy newspapers and magazines lying around, no jars of face cream or half-full plastic bottles of water on the bedside table.

She moved over to the closet and gingerly pushed it open.

No clothes. Just a row of empty hangers and a courtesy tray offering dry-cleaner bags, slippers, and a hotel hair dryer.

It occurred to Concepción that the hotel guests of suite 701 were no longer in residence. They'd probably done a midnight flit and not paid their bill.

Concepción couldn't help smiling to herself. Martha Crabstone would be one angry woman — she'd take it personally that it had happened on her floor.

Before leaving the suite, Concepción decided she should check the bathroom to see if perhaps they'd left a tip for maid service. It was highly unlikely, but just in case . . . She opened the bathroom door and froze.

Her scream of terror reverberated against the marble walls.

Then she fainted.

CHAPTER TWENTY-THREE

The day passed and Denver did not hear another word from Bobby. It was enough already; she was frustrated and angry. Reaching for her cell, she called Sam and told him she was on her way over. Why not? Bobby was obviously having his own kind of fun.

Arriving outside Sam's apartment, she didn't feel guilty at all. Why should she? Her boyfriend was in Chicago screwing around. She was upset, and rightfully so.

There were times she wished she'd never gotten involved with Bobby. She'd had a crush on him since high school — where she'd watched him from afar. He was the most popular and handsome senior and all the girls had lusted after him.

Bobby Santangelo Stanislopoulos.

Now here they were, years later, living together.

The question was — were they right for each other?

It was a question she kept asking herself.

She could smell the pasta sauce before Sam opened the door. The delicious aroma lingered in the air, tempting her inside.

Sam greeted her warmly with a kiss on both cheeks. "Here she is, my favorite muse," he said, wearing a nonsensical *I Ate the Sheriff* apron over his clothes.

She remembered the first time she'd run into him in New York. He'd been leaving the apartment building where Annabelle and Frankie lived. As Annabelle's father's lawyer, she was in town with orders to bring them back to L.A. Sam was all wrapped up against the icy cold in a striped scarf, knit hat, and long khaki army coat, whereas she was freezing her ass off, having forgotten to bring warm clothes. As an L.A. native, she didn't even own any. They'd exchanged a word or two before he'd headed down the block to a local coffee shop — where later she'd bumped into him again. This time he was hunched over his laptop, and after a while, they'd got to talking. Before long she'd told him who she was looking for and that they weren't around. To help her out, Sam had googled Frankie and gotten her his cell number. She'd called Frankie and he'd informed her that he and Annabelle would not be available to fly back to L.A. with her until the next morning. Sam had once again helped out and suggested that she spend the night at his place.

So she had, and one thing had led to an-

185

other. . . .

This had all taken place before Bobby. It didn't matter; Sam would always have a special place in her heart. She still had the striped scarf and knit hat he'd given her on that fateful day in New York.

Sam's apartment was like Sam himself: low-key, comfortable, and welcoming. There were books piled everywhere, along with DVDs and stacks of cooking magazines.

"Nice place," she said, looking around.

"It'll do," Sam said, casual as ever. "It has that famous L.A. view and a cozy guest room, which means that if you and Bobby ever get into a fight, you know where to come."

"We're not fighting," she said quickly.

"Never thought you were," Sam replied. "Where is he, by the way?"

"On a business trip," she said shortly, not about to fill him in.

"The club business, right?"

"That's what he does."

"Y'know, Denver, if you and I were together, I'd never leave you for a second," Sam said, opening a bottle of wine.

"Hmm. That sounds really . . . suffocating," she said, trying to make a joke of it.

"Ah, but think of all the meals you'd enjoy," Sam said, a wicked gleam in his eyes. "You know I'm a master in the kitchen."

I shouldn't have come here, she thought. *I should have gone over to Carolyn's and bitched to her about Bobby.*

Although that would not have been the best of plans either. Carolyn would probably have riled her up even further with one of her "all men are dogs" speeches.

"Sit down, relax," Sam said, handing her a glass of red wine. "I'm sure you've had a busy day."

"I can't stay long," she stated. "So if you have questions about your script, you'd better start asking now."

"What's your rush?" he asked, clinking glasses with her. "I thought you mentioned Bobby was away."

"He is," she said, becoming flustered. "But I have a killer workload to go over, so like I said — I can't stay long."

"All work and no fun."

"Bobby and I have plenty of fun," she stated defiantly.

"Drink up, lady. You're about to taste the best sauce outside of Little Italy."

Two hours later she was still there, delightfully satisfied after a dish of Sam's delicious pasta smothered with his special Bolognese sauce, accompanied by three glasses of excellent red wine.

"You haven't changed a bit," he said, giving her a long meaningful look as he settled on the couch next to her.

"Nor have you," she replied, wishing she'd gone a little easier on the wine. He'd removed his offending apron, and he was looking pretty good in a long-sleeved shirt and casual pants. Not dazzling like Bobby, but extremely attractive in his own particular quirky way. She remembered their time in New York, and how good it had been. Comfortable and warm. Sam made her feel good and very secure. Nothing wrong with that.

"Maybe I should be going," she murmured.

"Maybe you shouldn't," he responded.

"But —"

"But what, Denver?"

And before she knew it, he was leaning toward her and they were kissing — long blissful kisses.

For once all thoughts of Bobby and his apparent bad behavior drifted away.

There was something about Sam. . . .

Fifteen million dollars. How was he supposed to slide a cool fifteen million past Rafael?

Alejandro began plotting and planning. He knew that Rafael considered him to be nothing more than a joke — a playboy only out to have a good time. However, when Alejandro wanted something, he could be a sly fox, and Alejandro was determined to make a movie. Therefore, nobody was going to stop him — especially Rafael.

He decided that he had two choices to raise the money for his movie.

Choice one: call his father in Colombia and

tell him that he'd found his calling in life and that he was on track to produce a movie, that all he needed was the financing.

Choice two: go behind his father's back and make a deal with one of Pablo's rivals to import their wares into Los Angeles. They'd jump at the opportunity to screw Pablo Fernandez Diego — especially if the screwing involved his son.

After thinking it through, he realized that it was not such a smart idea. Crossing Pablo could only lead to major trouble. Besides, he, Alejandro, was the heir to everything, which meant that choice one was his only option. Besides, fifteen mil would mean nothing to Pablo Fernandez Diego. His drug business brought in billions. Why would he refuse his son the chance to make his own millions?

Alejandro continued thinking. What if he promised his father an executive producer credit? Then tempted him with stories of all the beautiful and available actresses Pablo could meet and make love to. Pablo enjoyed female company, so surely a string of women, a change of scene, and his name on a Hollywood movie would be lure enough. How could Pablo possibly resist?

First Alejandro realized that he would have to deal with Rafael, convince him that making a movie was a lucrative business. Rafael had Pablo's ear, so with him on board it would be easier to obtain Pablo's approval.

The problem was that Rafael was an uptight snake who watched over Alejandro's every business move, and strongly disapproved of his freewheeling lifestyle. Plus Rafael was desperate to get home to his girlfriend and son back in Colombia.

It occurred to Alejandro that it was time to bring Rafael in from the cold, soften him up, make him forget his annoying girlfriend, give him a taste of what he was missing out on. And who was the perfect person to do that?

Willow Price, of course.

Willow was Alejandro's secret weapon.

CHAPTER TWENTY-FOUR

Driving like a madman was M.J.'s signature style. Why stop for a red light when nothing is coming in the opposite direction? As for pedestrians — they took their life in their hands when crossing in front of M.J.'s vehicle. He'd gotten countless tickets, although fortunately for him, nothing ever stuck. He always had a ready excuse, and for some reason or other most cops seemed cool with him.

They made it to the airport in record time. Upon arrival, M.J. was all about parking the car and escorting Bobby into the airport.

Bobby quickly assured him it wasn't necessary. "Get your ass back to the club," he insisted. "It's more important that you check on the receipts for last night, find out how we did. Stop worrying about me. I'm feeling fine now. I'll call you when I get to L.A."

"You do that," M.J. said. "Meanwhile, I'll be doin' some investigatin' of my own."

"Thanks, bro," Bobby said, jumping out of

the car. "Much appreciated."

The airport was crowded, long lines of people everywhere. Bobby joined the line for the next American Airlines flight to L.A. and bought a ticket.

The plump girl stationed behind the desk flirted with him. "What an unusual name," she said, fluttering over-mascaraed eyes. "Santangelo Stanislopoulos. Where are you from?"

"America," he said shortly, wishing she would hurry up issuing him the ticket. He was fed up with dealing with people. All he wanted was to get home to L.A.

The girl offered up what she considered a beguiling smile. "Me too," she simpered. "Syracuse originally. Moved to the Windy City when I was five."

Who cares? Bobby thought. He'd just gotten a text from Denver asking where he was. This was a good sign, because at least she was communicating with him, even though he knew she must be majorly pissed because of his silence.

The girl handed him his ticket. Since the flight was not due to take off for another hour, he made his way through security and found a quiet corner to wait in until his flight was called. He contemplated texting Denver back before deciding it would be easier to explain everything when he got home.

There were texts on his phone to be read,

but he wasn't in the mood to open them. The whole being drugged scene was beginning to freak him out.

Jesus Christ! What if he'd *died*? The doc had said that there was a strong possibility that it could've been fatal.

What if they'd stolen an organ from him? He'd read about that happening to innocent people.

Shit! What the *fuck.*

He couldn't stop his mind from racing. Who the hell was Nadia and what was her damn motive?

Had she targeted him specifically?

Yes. It seemed as if she had.

Why? That was the question.

Max took a quick glance at her phone. There was a message from her mom, and two from her agent.

Hmm . . . whom to answer? Her agent, of course. Lucky could wait.

Like all teenage girls, Max had a love/hate relationship with her parents. While Lucky was constantly encouraging her to have a plan career-wise, Lennie was more into lecturing her about boys and how they only wanted one thing.

Duh! Yes, Daddy. That's a well-known fact.

Lucky was always after her to pursue an interesting and fulfilling career. But how could she ever hope to compete with her dynamic mother? Lucky had done so many things, all of them successful. No way could Max ever hope to reach such dizzying heights. Business wasn't her thing. She had no interest in building hotels or running a movie studio — she was no mirror image of her mom. Besides, there were other paths to success, and modeling was one of them. Athena made a ton of money *and* she was famous as the current European "It" girl. Max realized that if the Dolcezza campaign was a hit, she too could become a force in the modeling industry. After all, Gisele, Cindy, and Kate hadn't done too badly. And they were old now, but still going full speed ahead.

Full of excitement, she called Melissa, who told her to grab her passport, pack a bag, and come in to the office immediately. According to Melissa, the contracts had arrived and the Dolcezza people were anxious to get Max on the next plane to Italy.

Talk about things happening fast. She could barely breathe.

It was unexpected and crazy, but she was on for the ride all the way.

Closing his eyes, Bobby found himself nodding off in the departure area — the result of being drugged, not to mention the extreme stress of the situation he'd been trapped in. When he opened his eyes, it was in time to see the American Airlines girl who'd issued him his ticket heading in his direction. She was accompanied by two uniformed cops, and a heavyset man in a brown sports jacket. She looked nervous.

Bobby frowned. He had a gut feeling that something was up.

The group stopped a few feet away. The girl pointed at him before scuttling off, while the cops and sports jacket guy continued toward him.

Bobby got to his feet just as the men reached him.

"Bobby Santangelo Stanislopoulos?" the burly one barked, glaring at him with hard eyes.

"Yeah, that's me," he said, glancing around. "Is there a problem?"

"You're under arrest for the murder of Nadia Sharai Gómez," the burly one said in a flat monotone. "You have the right to remain silent. Anything you say . . ."

Suddenly everything took off like a blaze of fireworks in his head. This wasn't happening. This *couldn't* be happening. It was all some insane nightmare from which he would eventually awaken.

Arrest . . . murder . . . Were they fucking *kidding*?

The detective continued to drone on in an emotionless voice. ". . . you have the right to consult an attorney before speaking to the police and to have . . ."

Bobby tuned out. He was spiraling into shock. He heard Lucky's voice clearly in his head — *You need a lawyer. I'll get you the best. Understand me. Do not say anything.*

He felt dizzy and nauseated. People were staring. Strangers, their mouths hanging open. Everyone was watching him.

Was it possible that in his drugged-out state he'd *killed* the psycho in the red dress?

No. No. NO. It wasn't possible.

Next he was being handcuffed, his arms pulled roughly behind him, and with a feeling of dread, he knew that his life would never be the same.

CHAPTER TWENTY-FIVE

"I thought you told me this Sam guy was a sure thing?" Alejandro complained, not happy when things didn't go his way.

"He is," Willow replied.

"Then how come this asshole isn't jumpin' up an' down to see you today?" Alejandro added, fixing her with a baleful glare.

"Oh," she replied, determined that nothing was going to screw up her big opportunity to coproduce a movie and maybe even star in it, "you gotta realize that creative types are majorly flaky. They have to get their head around what's going on before they're ready to commit. Besides, when I talked to Sam on the phone he was *way* into the idea of directing his own project, which means that when I meet with him tomorrow morning and he realizes the potential of what we're offering, he'll be all over me."

"Maybe *I* should come to the meeting," Alejandro suggested with a creepy smile. "I have ways of being *very* persuasive. Does he have a family?"

No way! Willow thought. *One look at Alejandro and Sam will run for the hills.*

"Don't worry," she said tartly. "I've got it covered."

"You're *sure?*"

"I'm very sure."

Alejandro ran his tongue across his lips. The thought of producing a movie was making him horny. "Blow me," he said, his voice thickening along with his cock.

"Excuse me?" Willow said.

"Blow me, my little movie star, then I'll take you to Tiffany's and buy you something nice."

"*How* nice?" she demanded, immediately tempted, although she would've sooner he'd offered to pay her massive late tax bill.

"I'll allow you to choose whatever you want," Alejandro said, unzipping his pants.

Launching into action, she decided that some offers were too good to turn down.

Blowing Alejandro involved plenty of tongue play and much cradling of his small, tight balls. She knew exactly what he liked. And what he liked was spreading his legs, leaning back, and reveling in her ministrations. Alejandro enjoyed nothing more than taking his time getting off. The upside for Willow was that as soon as he was done, he was into spending money.

Later they had lunch on the patio of the Polo Lounge — where on her way to the ladies' room, Willow ran into Billy Melina, who was sitting outside with her former agent, Eddie Falcon.

This is meant to be, Willow thought as she sauntered past their table. "What are you two handsome men plotting and planning?" she cooed flirtatiously.

Billy flashed her a smile. "Wouldn't *you* like to know," he said.

"Yes, I would," Willow replied.

"You'll read all about it on *Deadline Hollywood,*" Eddie said, barely glancing up.

"How exciting. I can't wait!" Willow exclaimed, blowing Billy a kiss before returning to her table and Alejandro, who was guzzling a vodka martini.

"Who was that?" Alejandro asked.

"Only one of the most important agents in town. And Billy Melina — *movie* star Billy Melina. I made a movie with him, you know."

"Yeah?" Alejandro said. "Didja fuck him?"

"No," Willow replied. "His loss. He was married to Venus at the time, and boringly faithful."

Alejandro beckoned for the waitress and ordered another drink.

Willow's mind was abuzz. Surely if she told Eddie about her project, he'd want to get involved? Maybe he could even persuade Billy to commit. How great would *that* be? She could just imagine the movie posters and how insane they'd look together. Billy Melina and Willow Price. A dynamite combination.

Ah yes, Willow Price is on her way back to the top, exactly where I belong.

An hour later she was prancing around Tiffany's searching for something *really* expensive, finally settling on a pair of forty-thousand-dollar diamond earrings.

Her purchase did not faze Alejandro at all. He threw down his black AmEx and the earrings were hers.

She'd already made up her mind to wear them once before selling them and putting the money toward her tax bill. Or maybe she should pay her lawyer, to whom she owed thousands on account of several DUIs.

"Y'know," she said to Alejandro, climbing into the passenger seat of his illegally parked Maserati, purposefully flashing her pantyless crotch at the pack of paparazzi who'd materialized out of nowhere, "we should have start-up money. Cash we can use to bring the best people aboard."

A couple of passing tourists recognized Willow. They began waving excitedly and calling out her name.

"What people?" Alejandro said, revving the engine of his powerful car.

Ignoring her fans, Willow said, "A cinematographer, a production manager. I can reach out to those people. If we put a hold on their services, they can't accept other jobs."

"Sounds like a smart idea."

"We should start with Sam," Willow said, full of enthusiasm. "We'll pay him cash for his script. Nobody can resist cash."

"How much?"

Willow thought for a second or two. "A million should do it," she said guilelessly. "With more to come when he signs up."

Alejandro nodded. He knew nothing about the movie business, which in his mind was okay, because Willow had been working in it since she was eight and she obviously had it all down.

"I'll put it together," he said, realizing that now was the time to get Rafael on his side.

Willow smiled and shivered with anticipation.

"First," Alejandro added, "there's a little something I wish you to do for me."

Willow's smile faded. Not another blow job. Surely one a day was enough. It wasn't that she *minded* blowing him, although having his cock shoved down her throat wasn't exactly her favorite pastime. Once their movie was up and running, she'd have more important matters to take care of, such as hiring a top publicist and getting her name out there again as a *serious* actress, not some fucked-up party girl with a penchant for coke.

"What?" she asked sweetly.

"Rafael," Alejandro said.

"What about Rafael?"

"I want you to fuck him," Alejandro announced. "And I want you to leave him begging for more."

"I thought he had a girlfriend back in Colombia," she said, chewing on her lower lip.

"He does," Alejandro said, carelessly running a stop sign.

"So . . ."

"So what?" Alejandro said sharply. "He's a man, isn't he? And you're a very skillful girl."

Sometimes a setback or two got in the way. It didn't faze her. She was prepared for anything, because soon she'd be a star again. And when she was, she could tell them all to go take a hike.

Screwing Rafael was a small price to pay.

Alejandro was not a patient man. When he wanted something done, he wanted it done immediately. After dropping Willow at her house, he'd informed her that tonight they would dine with Rafael at Club Luna, and that after dinner she was to seduce Rafael.

Willow laughed to herself as she stalked around her house wearing nothing but sky-high Louboutins, a purple thong, and her new diamond earrings. *Seduce!* Alejandro had actually used the word *seduce*. Where the hell had he come up with such an old-fashioned word?

Was Rafael even vaguely seduceable? She barely knew him, and the few times they'd met he'd seemed extremely uptight. Although as Alejandro had said, he was a man, wasn't he? He had a penis, didn't he? And most men were ruled by their dicks.

Was Rafael any different?

Hmm. . . . she'd never met a man she couldn't seduce.

Her cell rang and she picked it up without checking who it was.

Bad move, for it was her mother, Pammy, who lived in Palm Desert and only called when she needed money.

"Hi, Mom," she said, experiencing that familiar trapped feeling.

"I'm broke," Pammy whined, not a woman to make polite conversation. "You gotta send me a check, an' make it fast, 'cause they're gonna turn off my electricity."

"I sent you a check last month," Willow said tightly.

"It wasn't enough."

It was never enough. Ever since Willow had fired her mother as her manager, Pammy was always after more money. Willow often wondered what Pammy had done with all the money Willow had made as a child actress. When she'd asked, years ago, Pammy had claimed it had all gotten eaten up by taxes and living expenses.

Willow knew this was a blatant lie. It had all gotten eaten up by her mother's various loser drug addict boyfriends over the years. Willow's dad had taken a hike when she was two. She couldn't blame him; her mom was a nightmare.

Thank God she'd had the smarts to dump Pammy as her manager and take control of her money and her life when she reached eighteen. At least now when she blew a paycheck, it was all hers to blow.

"How much do you need?" she sighed.

"Ten thousand," Pammy said briskly, as if it was nothing.

"No *way*," Willow said, frowning.

"Why not?" Pammy said, reverting to her whiney voice. "You owe me big-time. If it wasn't for me, you'd have no career."

"If it wasn't for you, I'd have savings in the bank," Willow snapped back. "You spent all my money back in the day when I was too young to know what was going on. I made millions, and you blew through it all."

"Jesus, why're you moanin' 'bout that again?" Pammy grumbled. "I told you — it all went to the tax man, an' he's a greedy son of a bitch."

"Tax man my ass," Willow muttered.

"Wash out your mouth. I didn't teach you no bad language."

"Oh, *please*!" Willow said, rolling her eyes.

"I'm your mother. You should have more respect."

"Leave me alone, *Mother*. I'm not a frigging bank."

Silence. Then, "I've had an offer to sell my story."

"*What* story?"

"The one about you."

So . . . the veiled threat. Pammy was an expert at veiled threats.

"Okay, okay. I can send you a thousand," Willow said, eager to get off the phone. "That's *it,* though. I'm not exactly rolling in money right now."

"FedEx me two thousand, and I won't take the offer from the magazine that wants to know all about your teenage years."

"Oh for God's sake," Willow said bitterly. "I'll send you the damn check, and that's it."

The last thing she needed was her stoned mother revealing all her past indiscretions. And she had a few. More than a few. A quickie marriage at fifteen, which was annulled. Two abortions. An affair with a powerful married man decades older than her. No, this was not the time for Pammy to be selling stories. Not when her career was all set to rise again.

Well. . . . almost. If everything went according to plan, then she could pay off her mom for good.

CHAPTER TWENTY-SIX

Reaching everyone in the family was not easy, but as Lennie had pointed out, the news was more palatable coming from her than from the Internet, so even though she didn't feel like talking to anyone, Lucky steeled herself and called her half brother, Steven, in Brazil.

Steven was devastated, especially since he hadn't seen Gino in two years, although he'd been planning a trip to California. "God-damn it, I loved that man," Steven said, his voice breaking with emotion.

"I know," Lucky answered softly, feeling his pain.

"It's hard to believe," Steven said flatly. "Gino was *the* man." After a long beat, he added, "Who did this to him?"

"I wish I knew, but you can bet that I'm sure as hell going to find out."

"Knowing you, it won't be a problem."

"No it won't, Steven. 'Cause when I find who did this, they'll wish they were dead, and then they will be."

"Hard words."

"True words."

"What can *I* do?"

"You can fly here and be with the family. The funeral service is going to be in Vegas. He always said that's where he wanted to spend his last day, so that's what's happening."

"I get it," Steven said. "Vegas has special memories for all of us."

"It sure does," Lucky agreed, aware that like her, Steven was reflecting on their colorful past. New York, Vegas, L.A. It had taken years before she'd found out that Steven was her half brother — the result of a one-night stand Gino had had with a beautiful black woman, Carrie. And when they'd discovered they were half siblings, they'd bonded as if they'd always known. She loved Steven dearly.

"My assistant, Danny, will make all the hotel and flight arrangements," she said. "It won't be a funeral, it'll be an amazing celebration of Gino's life, 'cause here's the deal — first we have a very special service, then later we party."

"Sounds like exactly what Gino would've wanted."

As soon as she'd finished speaking with Steven, Lucky called Max, then Bobby. Neither of them picked up their phones. It seemed nobody ever did anymore — it was all about texting. She left them both a terse message to call her back.

Meanwhile, Danny was busy contacting the head of Gino Junior and Leo's summer camp. He told the man in charge that he'd be sending a car to pick the boys up. "I'd appreciate it if you can keep them away from any news stories," Danny requested, although he knew it was a futile request, since the boys were bound to find out.

Later, Lucky bid good-bye to Lennie. He was reluctant to leave her, although he understood. Lennie always understood, which is why she loved him so much.

With Lennie on his way back to L.A., she went into Gino's study feeling a strong urge to be alone. Detective Allan and his partner were still around, waiting to question Paige further when the widow emerged from her bedroom. Lucky had already sussed out that they had nothing. No clues. No eyewitnesses. No shit. She wasn't surprised. Whoever had done this was a professional.

Shutting the study door, she settled into Gino's well-worn leather chair behind his desk and took a deep breath. She noted that the room smelled of her father's favorite cigars — Cubans, of course. Only the best for Gino Santangelo. The aroma still lingered in the air, while the stub of a cigar rested in a marble ashtray next to Gino's usual drink — a Jack and Coke — the glass almost empty.

For a brief moment she closed her eyes,

trying to picture Gino the night before, sitting at his desk, smoking his cigar, nursing his drink, never imagining the unspeakable violence that would take place the following morning.

Violent death never gives you a warning, it simply takes you — just like that.

Thank God she'd spoken to him the previous day. He'd promised to come see her in Vegas without bringing Paige. Time alone with Gino was precious.

She'd been so revved up about sharing her plans for the new hotel with him. She could just imagine what he would've said. He would've told her she was crazy — what did she need it for? *The Keys is spectacular,* he'd have said with an affectionate chuckle. *My daughter — the overachiever.* Then he would've gotten into it, going over every detail of what she planned to create.

Since he was a big fan of movies, he would've really loved the idea of incorporating a movie studio. Anything with Pacino, De Niro, or Nicholson and he was there. He'd always harbored a big crush on Sharon Stone and often commented that Sandra Bullock reminded him of Maria.

Ah, Maria, Lucky's beautiful, gentle mother. . . . Lucky still missed her so very much. She often daydreamed about how different her life might have been if Maria had lived.

There was a solitary silver photo frame on Gino's desk containing a photo of her father and mother on their wedding day, arms entwined, the two of them so happy and in love.

Lucky wondered how Paige felt about *that.*

Then she started wondering if perhaps Paige had any motive for wanting Gino dead.

It was a wild thought. Still . . . always expect the unexpected, as Gino often said.

She knew her father had taken care of Paige in his will. However, she also knew that by no means did Paige inherit everything. According to Gino, he'd left Paige a few million dollars plus the Palm Springs house. The rest of his estate — and it was substantial — was in trust for his grandchildren. Or at least that's what he'd told her.

Maybe Paige had persuaded him to change his will. It was possible. Anything was possible. Gino might have been old, but he certainly hadn't been senile; he'd remained as sharp as ever.

Paige would not have been able to get anything past him.

Or would she?

Lucky wasn't at all sure. Right now she trusted no one.

When Paige finally emerged, Lucky immediately noticed that her stepmother had applied fresh makeup, styled her hair, and put on a pencil skirt, a fancy silk blouse, and high heels.

Is this what grief looks like? Lucky thought, her suspicions building.

Paige Wheeler. Gino's fourth wife. A short, tough redhead with a pocket-Venus body. Years ago, Gino had caught Paige in bed with his previous wife, Susan Martino, and after that it had been all systems go. He'd divorced Susan and married Paige. Lucky had never really warmed to her.

"You're still here," Paige exclaimed, finding Lucky in Gino's study.

"Why wouldn't I be?" Lucky responded, picking up an engraved silver paper opener and transferring it from hand to hand. "I thought you'd want to talk about what happened."

"Of course, dear. However, first I must speak with the detectives," Paige said, seemingly calm and in control, unlike the hysterical wreck from earlier. "I've already told them everything I know, but it seems they would like me to go over every single detail one more time."

Hmm. From hysterical wreck to lady of the manor, Lucky thought. *What's that about?*

"Sure," Lucky said. "I'll be around. I've decided to stay the night."

"Oh," Paige said, raising a surprised eyebrow. "I must tell the housekeeper to make sure the guest room is ready for a visitor."

Lucky glowered. *A visitor! Was she fucking kidding? A fucking visitor indeed!*

I'm not a visitor, she felt like yelling. *I'm Gino's daughter.*

However, controlling her emotions in times of stress was something else Gino had taught her, among many other things.

Gino is dead.

Murdered.

Shot.

Assassinated.

Too bad for whoever did it. Too bad, for she would make sure that they burned in hell.

Paige trotted off to speak with the detectives, while Lucky stayed put. It occurred to her that it might be a smart move to check out the drawers in Gino's desk, try to find out if anything was going on that he hadn't mentioned to her. He was supposed to have given up all business dealings ten years ago, only knowing Gino, it was probably not the case. He was always involved in something — whether it was helping old friends or investing in a project that interested him. Gino was an easy touch; he'd always had compassion for friends in need. Nothing wrong with that, although he'd lent money as if it were going out of style.

The desk drawers were jammed with miscellaneous papers, bills, and receipts. Organization had never been his thing.

She started a methodical search, stacking the papers she took from the drawers on the desktop, trying to sort them into piles. Somebody had to do it, and it might as well be her, for she didn't want a stranger going through Gino's private papers, and Paige would never have the patience.

There was nothing of real interest. A stack of IOU's. No surprise. When Gino lent money, he never expected to get it back. She had no doubt that he'd want her to tear them up, so she did so, placing the torn pieces of paper in her purse. If Paige got hold of them, she might insist that the debts be paid.

The lower-right-hand drawer was locked. Gino, a creature of habit, always kept his keys in a hidden compartment located at the bottom of his maple-wood cigar humidifier. Sure enough, the key was there, along with the keys to a couple of safe-deposit boxes only she and Gino had access to.

"Anythin' ever happens t' me, kiddo," he'd told her many times, "you go to the bank an' clear out those boxes. Just you, nobody else. Got it?"

Yes. She got it.

The locked drawer contained a Glock, a small hand pistol, and several boxes of bullets. Probably both guns were unlicensed. Best to get them out of here.

She dropped them into her oversized purse. There were also stacks of hundred-dollar bills held together with elastic bands. Gino had always kept plenty of cash on hand. Finally, she came across an envelope addressed to Gino Santangelo and family. The envelope was pale beige and there was no postmark or return address. It had obviously been hand delivered.

Lucky felt a sudden chill. Was this the clue she'd been looking for?

She slipped the expensive note card edged in gold from the envelope and quickly scanned the one-word message.

It was printed.

And it read VENGEANCE.

CHAPTER TWENTY-SEVEN

All dressed up and ready for anything, Willow joined Alejandro in his penthouse, where he was busy snorting mounds of coke off a glass-topped coffee table before they set off for Club Luna.

"Come join me, my little rabbit," he sang. "We get happy before dinner."

She didn't need to be asked twice. Cocaine was her drug of choice — it filled her with a warm, cozy feeling of total confidence. On a coke-fueled high, she could rule the world. Besides, she needed something to forget about the conversation with her damn mother. The woman was a blood-sucking leech. Why couldn't she just leave her alone?

Alejandro threw Willow a snakelike grin. "You ready for tonight?"

"Of course," she said, bending down and snorting a line. "Are *you* ready to be a major Hollywood producer?"

"I will be the best," Alejandro boasted, a flurry of white powder decorating his nose.

Willow snorted another line. "I know," she murmured, savoring the moment. "Together we will rule this fucking town."

Rafael was a reluctant dinner guest. He had no idea why Alejandro had been so insistent that he join him tonight. They didn't usually socialize, which suited Rafael, because he had no interest in hanging out with Alejandro unless it was business related.

Earlier, he'd met with Alejandro and informed him what had gone down in Chicago, and how the deputy DA would now have other, more pressing things on her mind. Alejandro had not seemed as grateful as Rafael had thought he would be. He, Rafael, had executed an elaborate plan to stop the DA in her tracks, although he had not ordered it to end in the girl's death. She was supposed to be beaten, not killed. Collateral damage. Rafael would not use that contact again.

Unfortunately, it was what it was, so surely this was the perfect opportunity for Alejandro to think about returning to Colombia while he could?

But no, Alejandro was settled in L.A. and he had no intention of going back to his homeland.

Rafael decided to raise the subject again at dinner.

However, this was not to be, for Alejandro

arrived accompanied by one of his whores. Rafael considered most American girls to be whores. The way they flaunted their bodies in almost nonexistent outfits, while drinking too much liquor and falling about drunk, disgusted him.

This one clinging to Alejandro's arm was no different. Clad in a skimpy purple dress that almost exposed her breasts, she had long pale red hair and a pretty face.

Willow greeted him with a widemouthed smile. Perfect teeth and pouty lips. "Hi, Rafael," she cooed. "It's so nice that we get to spend some time together. Usually you're all business. Tonight it's all about fun."

Rafael was startled. Alejandro's girls *never* acknowledged him, and this one actually knew his name. Then he realized that this was the famous one — the girl Alejandro enjoyed accompanying to premieres and Hollywood events. The girl with the bad reputation.

Rafael did not care about fame; it failed to impress him. Whereas Alejandro enjoyed seeing his photo on the Internet and splashed all over the trashy magazines.

"Tonight we celebrate," Alejandro roared, waving over the table hostess, a sleek Asian girl clad in silver satin shorts and a matching halter top. "Champagne, my dear, and tequila shots all round."

The Asian girl allowed herself a thin smile;

she knew a good tipper when she saw one.

"What are we celebrating?" Rafael inquired, quite uncomfortable.

Alejandro thought for a moment, then it came to him. "Chicago, of course," he said, throwing his arm around Rafael's shoulder. "You protect me as if you were my brother. And for that, my friend, you deserve a big reward."

Three hours later, Willow and Rafael were finally alone together in a guest bedroom in Alejandro's penthouse. As far as Willow was concerned, it had not been an easy ride. First off, Rafael had refused to drink, and she'd had to use all her persuasive powers to convince him that not toasting Alejandro with a glass of champagne was unlucky.

So . . . one glass of champagne had led to another. After which came the tequila shots, followed by more champagne.

Gradually Rafael had loosened up, helped by Willow turning on the flattery big-time. She was an expert at making men feel good about themselves, and after a lot of work, Rafael was no exception.

By the time the three of them left the club, Rafael was no longer the man who was always in control. He was about as drunk as he'd ever been, unaware that Alejandro had dropped a quaalude into his final drink.

"Gotta go home," he'd mumbled, outside

the club. "Don' feel so good."

"No, sweetie," Willow had said, hanging on to his arm. "There's something I wanna show you at Alejandro's apartment."

"What? What you wanna show me?" he'd said, stumbling against her.

At which point she'd shoved him into the back of Alejandro's Bentley — one of his many cars. "You'll see," she'd purred, jumping into the front passenger seat next to Alejandro.

Once they'd reached Alejandro's apartment, she'd steered Rafael into the guest bedroom, where, unsteady on his feet, he'd fallen on top of the oversized bed with the faux fur cover, still mumbling to himself.

Willow had him exactly where she wanted him.

She glanced at the clock above the TV facing the bed. The tiny red light was flashing in the concealed camera Alejandro had set up.

Time for . . .

ACTION.

Very slowly, she began stripping off her clothes in the most sensuous way possible. She'd perfected the routine, and it always impressed.

First one shoulder strap, then the second. Slowly . . . slowly . . .

Taking her time was the key. Never rushing it. Making it last.

"What're you doing?" Rafael slurred, trying

to sit up, but failing to make it.

"Showing you something I know you're dying to see," Willow murmured, using her best husky voice while revealing one breast, nipple erect. It was a magnificent breast with no enhancements. Proud and perky. Tempting and luscious.

Rafael let out an involuntary groan. The groan encouraged Willow. She hadn't even touched him, yet she knew he was ready. She could *see* he was ready, his erection quite obvious.

Allowing her slip of a dress to fall to the ground, she approached the bed wearing what she'd had on earlier while getting ready — a barely there purple thong, her Tiffany diamond earrings, and her sky-high Louboutins. This was her sex outfit. It never failed. *She* never failed.

Rafael put up no objections when she crawled on top of him, straddled his waist, and began loosening his belt, her breasts dangling tantalizingly close to his mouth.

"How would you like to suck my nipples?" she whispered, working on removing his pants and shorts, startled to notice how big he was. He was way bigger than Alejandro, a fact that she knew would not please Alejandro.

"*Sí,* Elizabetta," Rafael muttered.

Willow fumed. Who was Elizabetta? A man should not be thinking of another woman while he was with her. It was disrespectful.

She pushed her nipple into his mouth to shut him up.

He sucked on it like a baby, unlike most men, who were inclined to be fast and rough. No, Rafael sucked as if he meant it.

Unexpectedly, she felt herself warming up, especially when he started with a certain amount of tongue play.

Don't start enjoying this, she warned herself. *You've got a job to do. Now get on with it.*

Reaching down, she grabbed his erection, guiding it between her legs. Her thought was that she'd stay on top, ride him like a pony, then he'd climax really fast and she'd be on her way.

As it turned out this was not to be, for Rafael suddenly seemed to come alive. He flipped her over so that she was flat on her back and before she could object, he began thrusting inside her with long deep strokes, all the while muttering, "Elizabetta, Elizabetta" and a whole lot of other things in his mother tongue that she didn't understand.

This was not the ride Willow had expected. This was a man who might be drunk and out of it, but he sure knew what he was doing. He wasn't just fucking her, he was making love to her as if she actually was this Elizabetta woman, whom Willow figured must be the girlfriend Alejandro had told her about, the one back in Colombia who'd given birth to Rafael's son.

Alejandro never made love to her like this. Alejandro was into blow jobs, anal, and threesomes, and if he *did* decide to fuck her, it was never more than a couple of quick jabs, and that was the sum of it.

Oh my God, she thought. *I'm actually enjoying this. Rafael is taking his time and it feels amazing.*

It helped that he was extremely well-endowed and had a fit, strong body. Alejandro was inclined to flab around his middle and an unruly mass of body hair that he never thought of grooming.

Who'd have thought that out of the two of them, Rafael would turn out to be the better lover? Uptight Rafael was leading her all the way to an incredible climax — the kind she'd only ever experienced with the help of her trusty vibrator.

His hands reached up to fondle her breasts, while his cock kept up the deep thrusting she never wanted to end.

Willow let out a gasp of pure pleasure as she felt herself coming. At the same time, Rafael shuddered to a halt with another shout of "Elizabetta." Then he rolled off her and fell into a restless half sleep, groaning to himself.

Willow jumped off the bed, grabbed her clothes, and made a fast exit. It wouldn't do for Alejandro to realize that she'd actually

number one, and she might not be thrilled that Max was about to score such a big opportunity.

After leaving Melissa's office, she took an Uber cab to the airport, and had to dash to make her flight. It was all exciting stuff, even more so when she discovered she'd been booked into first class on the luxurious Airbus A380. The Dolcezza people obviously meant business.

A friendly steward offered her a glass of champagne, which she happily accepted.

I'm on my own, she thought, *and I'm loving it! No powerful mom for everyone to kiss up to. No movie-star dad. No Athena — full of attitude and demands. I'm me, and I'm getting the star treatment.*

For a brief moment her mind wandered toward Billy Melina, and how he would feel if she became famous.

Would he even remember her?

Of course he would. They'd shared such a traumatic experience in Vegas — something he couldn't possibly forget.

She'd spoken to him once since then. Only one time. And that was that. No more Billy.

But there was no forgetting the fact that he was the first man she'd gone all the way with; there was no moving on.

He lingered in her head. Billy Melina. Her first.

Bobby stared at the detective, and Detective Cole — he of the burly build, bulbous nose, bushy unkempt eyebrows, and grayish brush cut hair — stared right back at him. The detective was chewing on a piece of gum, masticating loudly.

The two of them sat facing each other in a stripped-down interrogation room, a scratched-up wooden table separating them.

"Well," Detective Cole said, placing his large palms flat on the table. "If you got any chance of this goin' easy for you, I suggest you'd better start making a full confession."

Bobby said nothing. He was still in shock that this was actually happening to him. Up until now he'd led a charmed life, full of privilege. How the fuck had he gotten himself caught in this nightmare of a situation?

Detective Cole gave a guttural cough. "You do know that we got enough evidence to toss you in jail an' throw away the key, which means if you're smart you're gonna start talkin'."

"When do I get my phone call and a lawyer?" Bobby asked, attempting to focus, although his mind was all over the place.

"Ah, he speaks," Detective Cole sighed, bulbous nose twitching.

"When?" Bobby repeated, determined to

stay strong.

Detective Cole clenched his teeth. He hated it when they knew their rights.

"Soon," he muttered.

Desperately trying to get his head around what was going on, Bobby realized that one thing was obvious: he'd been well and truly set up.

Only why? That was the big question.

From the moment the detective had arrested him, he'd kept his mouth shut. After one of the uniformed cops had slapped handcuffs on him, the three of them — two cops and the detective — had marched him through the terminal to a waiting squad car, whereupon they'd shoved him in the back of the car, one of them clamping a not too gentle hand on his head. There followed a short ride to the precinct.

That's when he'd started to realize the full severity of his situation — sitting in the back of a squad car on his way to jail. *Jail! Fucking jail!* Accused of a murder there was no way he could've committed. And nobody knew this was happening to him. He was completely alone.

One thing he was sure of: he'd stay silent until he had a lawyer sitting beside him.

At the precinct, he'd been fingerprinted, photographed, and relieved of his watch, wallet, cell phone, belt, and shoelaces, then thrown into a holding cell. His companions were an unruly drunk with a loud burping problem, and a six-foot-four black man dressed in shocking-pink hot pants and a purple tank top.

Now here he was in the interrogation room, and he was damn sure that by this time he should've been allowed a phone call.

"Guess you're not plannin' on cooperatin'," Detective Cole said, a scowl covering his sallow face. "Guess you think you can get away with murderin' a pretty little thing 'cause you got plenty of money to hire yourself some big fancy lawyer."

Bobby was dying to answer him and tell his story, because once they found out he'd been drugged, he knew he would be absolved of all blame.

Or would he?

Yes. There was no way he could be involved.

And yet . . . he'd been seen at the hotel with her . . . he'd gone up to her suite . . . he'd accepted a drink. Then nothing, until he'd woken up in his rental car blocks away.

Nadia. He didn't even know *how* she'd been killed, and he wasn't about to ask.

Had she been lying to him?

Of course she had.

And somebody must have put her up to telling him stories, luring him up to her suite, then drugging him. Yes, he'd been set up bigtime.

Jesus Christ! Nadia was dead. He'd never

get any answers from her.

He thought about her so-called cousin, the swarthy-looking man. Better start remembering what the son of a bitch looked like. Better remember every single detail. His life was on the line; it was time to start thinking straight.

By the time Max arrived in Rome, she was more tired and apprehensive than excited. Suddenly the adventure she'd always yearned for was happening, and she had no one to share it with. Maybe she should've told Athena. They always had exciting times together. Then she reminded herself that this wasn't about having fun, this was the opportunity she'd been hoping for, and she'd better take it seriously and put all her energy into making it happen. No more farting around with Athena; it was time to concentrate.

A driver stood at the gate holding up a sign with her name on it. Next to him stood a bespectacled young man with sharp features. He was very thin and extremely fashionable in a tight brown suit and pointy-toed crocodile shoes.

"Signorina Max," the young man said, stepping forward and proffering a formal handshake. "I am Lorenzo, your assistant."

Assistant! Was he kidding?

"I am to escort you to your hotel," Lorenzo

said in perfect English, with hardly any trace of an accent. "Once we are there, we will go over your itinerary for tomorrow. It is a busy day for you. I hope it will not be too much."

Max was in shock. She had her own assistant! This was insane!

"Sounds good," she gulped.

"It is very good," Lorenzo said. "And may I say that you are even more lovely than your photos. Welcome to beautiful Roma."

Oh yes, she thought, *I am going to enjoy every minute of this.*

Detective Cole led Bobby down a bleak hallway, at the end of which was a pay phone attached to the wall.

"One call," the detective warned him. "That's it."

Yes, Bobby thought. *One call. Better make it a good one.*

He debated whether to call M.J. or the real estate lawyer in Chicago who'd sold them the property for Mood. Or maybe he should reach out to Denver, who had her own connections? Or Lucky?

No contest. Lucky would know what to do; she always did.

He picked up the phone feeling like a little kid running to his mommy for help.

Hey, he thought ruefully. *That's exactly what I'm doing.*

"Hurry it up," Detective Cole snarled, watching him as if he were about to make a sudden run for it.

Bobby did not need to be asked twice. This had been the longest day of his life.

Chapter Twenty-Nine

Watching Paige, Lucky soon reached the conclusion that in no way was the woman behaving like a bereaved widow. Paige seemed to be everywhere in her tight skirt and high heels, a pocket-Venus pain in the ass — it was almost as if she were *enjoying* the attention.

It occurred to Lucky that she'd put up with her stepmother for years only because of Gino. The truth was that she actually couldn't stand her.

After speaking with the detectives, Paige sauntered back into Gino's study and announced that several friends and acquaintances would be stopping by later to pay their respects.

Lucky was outraged. Paige couldn't wait a day? This was ridiculous. Gino had been shot that very morning, and now his grieving widow was about to entertain. What a fucking *bitch*!

"You're kidding me, right?" Lucky said,

glaring at her. "Surely you don't want people over tonight?"

"Ah, but I do," Paige sighed. "Company will soothe my nerves."

Her fucking nerves? What about Gino lying dead in the morgue? Didn't she *care*?

This situation was out of control, and Lucky's anger was building.

"May I ask what you're still doing in here, dear?" Paige said, planting herself in front of Gino's desk.

No, you may not. Back off. And stop asking dumb questions.

"I'm trying to find any indication of who might've done this," Lucky said, remaining calm. "We have nothing to go on, yet someone was obviously holding a grudge."

"You think so?"

"No," Lucky drawled sarcastically. "Someone shot Gino just for the fun of it."

"Not to worry," Paige said, a tad impatiently. "The detectives are in charge now, and I really don't think you should be going through Gino's desk."

"You don't, huh?" Lucky said, her black eyes glittering dangerously.

"No, dear," Paige said, pursing her thin lips. "It's simply not appropriate. The lawyers would not approve."

Lawyers? What fucking lawyers? Lucky thought, overcome with even more anger. Anger and grief mixed together was a lethal

233

combination.

Paige didn't see it. She stood there in her high heels and fresh makeup, probably already planning her next husband, already spending the money she would inherit. It was as if she hadn't watched her husband get gunned down that very morning.

"You know what — screw you, Paige," Lucky suddenly exploded. "Just who exactly do you think you are?"

"Excuse me?" Paige said with a haughty toss of her head.

"C'*mon,*" Lucky said, seething. "I *know* who you are. You're nothing but Gino's fourth wife, a companion he pulled out of a lesbian tryst to amuse himself with in his old age. And let me tell you this: he *never* loved you like he loved my mother, Maria. No woman *ever* measured up to her, so get over yourself."

"How *dare* you," Paige spluttered.

"How dare I what?" Lucky challenged. "Gino was my father, and if I want to go through his things I'll do so without any interference from you. You know Gino's motto — 'Never fuck with a Santangelo' — and *I* am a true Santangelo. So unless you want big problems, stay out of what I do."

Paige took a step back, trying to decide whether to retaliate or not.

Or not seemed to be the correct answer.

She turned to leave the room.

"As soon as they release Gino's body, I'm taking him to be buried in Vegas at the family mausoleum," Lucky said, her black eyes still afire. "After the funeral service there'll be a big party — a celebration of his life. You can attend or not, I'll leave that to you. But I'm warning you — do *not* fuck with me, or you'll live to regret it."

Paige was silent. Lucky on a rant was not a woman to be confrontational with.

"Of course I'll be there," she muttered before fleeing the room.

Paige was not kidding when she'd said that people would be stopping by the house to pay their respects. Lucky found it interesting observing the parade and the way everyone spoke so highly of Gino. It seemed he was a very popular Palm Springs figure — loved and admired by men and women alike. And why not? Gino had always been one of a kind. A true macho man.

As she looked around, she wondered if any of them were the author of the note she'd found. One word. Printed. VENGEANCE.

Why hadn't Gino mentioned the note to her? Why hadn't he stepped up his security?

Damn Gino. He'd always been such a stubborn man.

Oh yes, he was stubborn, all right, but how she'd loved him, and how she'd fought with him over the years. They'd had such a complicated relationship, and now he was gone, and she knew that she would miss him forever. Gino Santangelo, her beloved father, would always be a part of her.

Famous people soon began dropping by. Al King, the soul singer, and his stunning wife, Dallas. They lived in a mansion nearby and were devastated by the news.

Nick Angel, the edgy movie star who couldn't wait to inform Lucky that Gino had helped him research his role in a recent gangster movie he'd been nominated for. "Gotta tell you — Gino was such a character," Nick enthused. "He knew it all. I could've listened to him an' his crazy stories for hours. I wanted to make a movie of his life. We were gonna talk about it, figure out some kinda option deal."

Yes, Gino would've loved having a movie made about him, especially one starring Nick Angel. She could just imagine him telling Nick his story, embellishing every detail.

She nodded, her watchful eyes checking out the room, wondering how many of the gathered guests had borrowed money from her generous father — money they'd conveniently forgotten to pay back.

A well-preserved Gina Germaine, sex symbol supreme, undulated around the open-plan living room, all bountiful bosoms and fluffy blond hair.

"Can I confess how much I loved your

daddy," Gina confided, pulling Lucky over to a corner. Then with a knowing wink and a soft whispery voice, she added, "Believe me, he loved me back. And how!"

An affair? Probably. Why not? Her father wasn't known as Gino the Ram for nothing.

After a while, Lucky decided that there was no point in staying the night. She had a sudden urge to fly back to L.A. and Lennie. There was nothing more for her to do here.

Besides, she had to be with Lennie. He was her lifeline, and right now she needed him desperately.

Lennie was asleep when she finally arrived at their house.

Without waking him, she threw off her clothes and slid into bed beside him.

He groaned, imagining that he was dreaming.

She rubbed her breasts against his back, her nipples hard.

Within seconds he was fully awake and fully erect. "You're home," he mumbled. "How did *that* happen?"

"I want you to make love to me," she urged. "I want you to fuck me like you've never fucked me before."

Lennie didn't need to be asked twice. He knew exactly what his wife wanted. She was out to validate her existence, to reassure herself that life went on.

Lucky craved wild, crazy, unfiltered sex. And Lennie was ready to oblige.

■ ■ ■ ■

BOOK TWO

■ ■ ■ ■

The king of Akramshar traveled with an extremely large entourage on his own plane. Accompanying him was his most trusted confidant,
Faisal, and a slew of bodyguards, assistants,
wives, nannies, children, grown sons, drivers,
and chefs.

Arriving in Las Vegas, the king took over the
entire vast penthouse floors of the Magiriano
hotel. Money was no object. Akramshar was an
oil-rich country with an endless supply of product.

The king traveled often; it amused him. Only
this time, the trip was not to entertain him or his
wives. This trip was to avenge his most revered
son's untimely death.

It had taken time and meticulous planning to
put everything in place, plenty of money and
the loyalty of the citizens of Akramshar, who
obeyed his every command. Plus a few dedicated men who would do anything for their king.
Everything he desired was now in place.

King Emir was satisfied that vengeance would

finally be his. And when it was done, he would return to Akramshar and throw a public celebration for all of his loyal citizens to know that Armand's death had been avenged a thousand-fold.

The guilty would be punished and fall as they so deserved. King Emir had organized himself a front-row seat for the chaos that was to come.

The spectacle would soon begin. He was in no rush.

CHAPTER THIRTY

Willow Price met Sam for breakfast dressed to impress. She wore extra-short denim cutoffs, a clinging white tank top, and gold sandals to match her gold earrings. Her pale red hair was pulled back into a girlish ponytail, and she had carefully applied natural-looking makeup. After her night with Rafael, she was feeling kind of wrecked. What a surprise *he'd* turned out to be, a first-class lover with moves she was not about to forget — even if he *had* imagined she was his damn girlfriend back in Colombia. However, this meeting with Sam was extremely important, and she was well aware that she had plenty of convincing to do.

When they'd been making the movie Sam had written, she'd gone out of her way to ignore him. At the time, he was nothing more than a lowly screenwriter with no important credits; plus she was screwing her costar. Now Sam was a big deal, and she desperately needed him to make Alejandro's movie happen.

She greeted him with an all-enveloping hug, making sure she pressed her breasts firmly against him, nipples slightly erect as always. Men got off on her nipples; in full bloom, they were quite spectacular.

"Hello, handsome," she crooned. "Fantastic to see you again."

Sam took a step back. *Hello, handsome! Fantastic to see him!* Was this the girl who'd studiously pretended he'd barely existed when they'd worked together? Now she was calling him handsome and saying it was fantastic to see him. Talk about transparent. He was unimpressed.

"What's up, Willow?" he asked, as the two of them followed the hostess to a window table.

"Like I told you on the phone, plenty," she said excitedly, wriggling into a fake leather booth. "Can't wait to fill you in."

Sam sat down and observed her across the table, studying her lips. She'd obviously had work done. What did they call it in Hollywood? Ah yes, a trout pout. It didn't suit her, like it didn't suit most women. What was up with this obsession with plastic surgery? Even men were at it, getting eye jobs that looked so wrong on their craggy aging faces.

Damn it, his mind was wandering. Willow was waffling on and he hadn't taken in a word. Why would he be interested in anything she had to say? Breakfast with Willow was a mistake.

A tall thin waitress with a weary expression stood by their table, pad in hand. "What can I get for you folks?" she asked, summoning a tired smile.

"Green tea," Willow said grandly. "Decaffeinated. And a wheat muffin with organic blueberry jam. Oh, and a glass of chilled coconut milk."

Their waitress seemed perplexed. "Don't have none of that, dear. How about a nice stack of pancakes with butter and syrup?"

Willow threw her a disgusted glare. "Water, thank you. Bottled, not tap."

"I'll have coffee and the pancakes," Sam said, once again wondering why he'd agreed to meet with this spoiled Hollywood starlet when his mind was all about Denver and whether there was a way he could win her over. Last night was a start; he definitely had plans for their future.

"This place sucks," Willow said in a loud voice, causing a couple of customers to stare at her. "Can you *imagine* not having green tea?"

"We're in a diner," Sam said drily. "What did you expect?"

"Well, *you* chose it," Willow said, then, realizing that she might be sounding petulant, she hurriedly changed her attitude. "Actually, maybe I will have the pancakes."

Sam nodded. "Excellent choice."

Willow couldn't help herself. "Unhealthy choice," she pointed out, making a face. "All that sugar."

"You smoke, don't you?" he said.

"Only socially," she answered vaguely.

"You do know there's nothing cool about smoking," Sam said, fixing her with a stern look. "It makes your clothes stink, not to mention your hair, until it eventually kills you."

"That's cheerful."

"Just giving you the truth," he said, deciding that although Willow was very pretty, she was still as obnoxious as ever, and he couldn't wait to leave.

"Anyway," Willow said, hurriedly moving on while she had his attention. "What do you think?"

"About what?" he countered.

"About what I was telling you," she said, hiding her aggravation behind a forced smile. Sam might be in the money and a happening screenwriter, but he was still a dick.

"Tell me again," Sam said, wondering how soon he could make a fast exit.

And so she began her pitch once more. This time she hoped he was listening.

"Hey," Leon said, leaning over Denver's desk,

iPad in hand. "Isn't this dude Bobby's grand-dad?"

"What?" Denver said impatiently. She was mad at herself for letting things go too far with Sam the night before. Not that they had gone any further than kissing — although she knew that he would certainly have liked to take it all the way. Kissing was bad enough. She was suffused with guilt in spite of Bobby's continued silence.

"Take a look," Leon said, thrusting the iPad in her face.

She glanced at the story quickly — and with a sudden jolt she realized that the news *was* all about Bobby's grandfather, the once infamous Gino Santangelo.

"Oh my God!" she gasped, reading about his execution in Palm Springs. "This is ter-rible. When did it happen?"

"Yesterday," Leon said. "Read on," he encouraged. "They're hinting it could be a mob hit."

"Now, that's crazy," Denver said, a frown creasing her forehead. "Gino is in his nine-ties. Who's going to go after an old man? It doesn't make any sense."

"Gotta say that most things don't," Leon said with a wise nod. "Didya know him?"

Of course she knew him. Bobby and Gino had always been close, and she was well aware of how much Bobby loved and admired his grandfather. He must be going out of his mind.

Was this the reason she hadn't heard from him?

No. The timing was off.

It was all too confusing. The only thing she knew for sure was that she had to reach Bobby immediately, even though she had no idea where he was. The shooting had taken place the previous day. Had he left Chicago and gone straight to Palm Springs? Why hadn't he called her? What the hell was going on?

Feeling totally in the dark, she grabbed her purse, stood up, and headed for the door.

"Where're you goin'?" Leon asked, startled. "We got work to do. You know we're meetin' with Romano and his lawyer today."

"You'll have to take the meeting without me," she said. "Right now I've got to find Bobby. He shouldn't be alone at a time like this."

"Thought he was in Chicago."

"He's hardly likely to stay there now this has happened."

"Hey, how about nailin' Alejandro?" Leon persisted. "We're gettin' real close, an' you're runnin' off? What's the deal with that?"

"You can handle it."

"Jeez, Denver . . . Sonia's comin' in today, and there's a shitload of stuff goin' on. You're really gonna bail on me?"

"I'm sorry," she said abruptly. "Keep working on everything. I promise I'll be back as soon as I can."

And even though she knew Leon was pissed, she felt she had no choice but to take off.

CHAPTER THIRTY-ONE

Rolling over in bed, Max opened her eyes and gazed blankly at the ceiling. For a moment she couldn't remember where she was. L.A.? New York? London?

Ah yes . . . beautiful *Roma.*

She couldn't help smiling as she pushed away the covers and sat up in bed, taking in her hotel bedroom with its glorious view of the city. She was still psyched that this was happening to her.

Last night Lorenzo had escorted her to this luxurious hotel suite, where he had produced what he referred to as her itinerary. It encompassed a long list of things she had to do the following day. First off she was to meet with a makeup artist, hair person, and stylist. When she was ready, she was to be introduced to the Dolcezza team of executives, followed by more makeup tests and a photo session for PR purposes. Later there would be dinner with the executives, then bed so she'd be ready for the following day's press conference and announcement that she was to be the new face of Dolcezza. After that the real work would begin. It was a daunting schedule.

Lorenzo had thrown her a concerned look. "This is fine?" he'd questioned, hovering. "Not too much?"

"I guess I'm going to be busy," she'd replied.

"I will pick you up at eight-thirty in the morning," he'd said. "Is there anything else you might need tonight?"

She'd shaken her head. "No thanks. I'm kind of tired. I see nothing but sleep in my future."

"Then I will leave now."

As soon as Lorenzo was gone, she'd made a quick tour of her surroundings before falling into bed, exhausted.

Now it was morning and she was about to get ready to rock and roll. All systems go. Seize the opportunity she'd been presented with and kick some ass.

I sound like my mom, she thought, giggling to herself as she headed for the shower. *Girls can do anything.*

Right on!

After showering, she pulled on her favorite ripped jeans and an oversized cashmere sweater, dug out her cell phone from her purse, and finally checked her messages. There were quite a few, several of them from

Lucky, which was unusual, for her mom never called her more than once a week, claiming she was giving her daughter plenty of space to do her own thing.

And now I am, Max thought. *And how!*

Because of the time difference it was too early to call Lucky back. Max promised herself that she would definitely do so later, get both of her parents on a conference call and tell them her amazing news. Hopefully they'd be thrilled for her.

She was tempted to call Athena, then decided not to — even though Athena had sent her several texts demanding to know when she was coming to the South of France. Not to mention dozens of selfies showing off her bronzed and buff ass.

Too bad, girl, Max thought. *You're on your own with your fine ass, your yachts, and your rich guys. I'm busy making a name for myself.*

Lorenzo appeared on time, immaculate in a gray pin-striped jacket and pale pink shirt paired with narrow-legged black jeans and pointy-toed black and white shoes.

She wondered if he was gay.

Yes, no doubt about it. What straight man would be such a snappy dresser? Nobody *she* could think of.

"You slept well?" Lorenzo inquired.

"I certainly did."

"Are you hungry?"

"Starving."

"There will be food at the studio."

"Can't wait."

"Then we shall be on our way."

A night in jail was an experience Bobby never wished to repeat. Detective Cole was a sadistic son of a bitch who'd taken great pleasure in the fact that Bobby's one phone call had gotten him nothing except Lucky's voice mail. He'd left a terse message and hoped that she'd pick it up soon.

Apparently not soon enough, for he'd spent the night locked in a cell, trying to sleep on a hard wooden bench, getting up to pee in a bucket, while keeping a wary eye on his cellmate, the drunk with the burping problem who never stopped pacing around, muttering obscenities between burps.

By the time morning came, he was royally pissed. Surely Lucky should've gotten his message by now? It was imperative that he hire a lawyer. And fast.

He moved to the front of the cell. "I need to make a phone call," he called out to the cop on desk duty.

The cop got up and strolled over, stood by the bars, and threw him a dirty look. "Not up to me," he said gruffly.

"Then who the fuck *is* it up to?" Bobby demanded.

"Maybe you should ask the woman you murdered," the cop sneered, walking back to his desk.

Bobby attempted to clear his head. This wasn't happening. This couldn't be happening.

"Nobody's gonna help you," the burping drunk offered, leaning unsteadily against the wall of the cell. Verging on sober, the man was morose and red-eyed. "*You* wanna make a phone call. *I* wanna get a drink. Guess that means we're both shit outta luck. Tough times, buddy."

Bobby ignored him. He was in no mood to make new friends.

"You really murder someone?" the drunk inquired, lurching off the wall and moving in close. " 'Cause if that's the business you're in, I got a cunt of a wife you can take care of. An' I'll pay you plenty of big bucks t' do the job. I'm not as broke as I look."

Bobby backed away from the man's rancid breath.

Was this what his life had come to?

So many people. So many smartly clad men, along with several chic women all perfectly coiffed and made up. Everyone was pulling and prodding at Max while wildly gesticulating and speaking in Italian — a language she wished she knew, because *ciao* and *prego* simply didn't cut it.

A razor-thin man zeroed in on her hair, clucking his tongue, while a woman in a

254

tightly belted zebra-print coat studied her face, makeup brushes ready for action.

Thank goodness for Lorenzo. "Don't leave me," she whispered, clutching desperately on to his arm as a hard-faced blonde attacked her with a tape measure, touching every inch of her body as if they were lovers.

The blonde indicated that she wanted Max to do something and stood back, waiting.

Max threw Lorenzo a questioning look.

"She would like you to remove your top," Lorenzo said, slightly embarrassed.

"My top? You mean my sweater?" Max gulped.

"Yes, and your jeans. If you wish, I can leave the room."

"No way. You're the only sane person here. Besides, you're gay, aren't you?"

Lorenzo recoiled in horror. "Me? Gay?" he said. "Why would you think that?"

Flustered, Max didn't know what to say. "Well . . ." she managed. "I just thought . . ." She trailed off, while the hard-faced blonde tapped her foot impatiently.

"Sorry if I disappoint you," Lorenzo sniffed. "I will wait outside while Lucia finishes taking your measurements."

"Please don't," Max pleaded. "I can't understand a word anyone says."

Lorenzo shrugged. It was obvious she'd offended him, but hopefully he'd get over it. "As you wish," he said, still uptight.

Stripping down to my underwear is no big deal, Max assured herself. *I'm a model. They're all professionals. Everyone in this room has seen it all before.*

However, that didn't stop her from feeling like a piece of meat. She hated them all. And she especially hated the result when they'd all finished their jobs.

"We go now," Lorenzo informed her.

"Where?" she asked.

"To meet the executives."

As soon as they left the little room of horrors, as Max had christened it, she informed Lorenzo that she needed to use the restroom.

"Very well," he said. "I will wait outside."

Gazing at her image in the mirror, she was horrified. She didn't look like herself at all. Is this how they wanted her to look? Teased hair and an abundance of makeup? Plus the stylist had chosen a shiny pink jumpsuit that was a size too big, and flashy gold jewelry that was more suited to a forty-something socialite. *I look like a freaking clown,* she thought, totally mortified.

What to do? That was the question.

Hurriedly digging into her purse, she grabbed a brush and attacked her hair, brushing out the teasing until it was almost back to normal. Then she took a Kleenex and quickly wiped off most of the heavy makeup. Unfortunately, there was nothing she could do about the horrible pink outfit.

Gritting her teeth, she joined Lorenzo, who was patiently waiting for her. He gave her a startled look but said nothing.

Then they were off to meet the Dolcezza executives.

Max tried to convince herself that she'd gained a little bit of control. She was a Santangelo, after all, and that had to count for something.

CHAPTER THIRTY-TWO

There was no sign of Bobby at the house. Denver had imagined that he might miraculously appear, but no such luck.

She'd raced home, and now she was suffused with guilt about her job. She shouldn't have left, but honestly, what else could she do? Her heart had won over her head. Bobby came first.

Should she call Lucky or not? The problem was that she had no wish to intrude, yet at the same time she was desperate to connect with her elusive boyfriend and find out what was going on.

Damn him! Bobby could be such an asshole, but she loved him anyway.

She tried to imagine what Lucky must be going through.

She *should* call her.

No. She shouldn't.

There were times Lucky could be quite intimidating. Besides, she was never quite sure whether Bobby's mom thought she was

258

good enough for her number one son.

Bobby Santangelo Stanislopoulos.

Heir to a massive shipping fortune.

Handsome beyond.

Charming.

A sensational lover.

Was she good enough for him? Sometimes her insecurities took over and drove her crazy. Wouldn't she be better off with a man like Sam? A down-to-earth, talented, regular guy.

"Damn it," she muttered under her breath. This wasn't the time to be thinking such thoughts. She should be concentrating on Bobby and what he was going through. Gino had always been his hero, and no way could Bobby ever have expected his grandfather's life to end in such a violent and brutal fashion. He must be inconsolable.

She tried calling him again. Her call went straight to voice mail.

Then the doorbell rang, and hoping it was him, she rushed to answer it.

But it was not Bobby, it was Sam, standing on the threshold carrying a large cardboard box.

"What are *you* doing here?" she exclaimed, not thrilled to see him.

Sam grinned, all crooked teeth and rumpled clothes. "Delivering a package," he announced, thrusting the box at her.

"H-how did you know I was home?" she stammered.

"I stopped by your office. Some guy told me you had a family emergency. Anything I can do to help?"

Yes, she thought. *You can go away.* And while she was thinking this, something began moving inside the box she was holding.

Leaning forward, Sam obligingly removed the lid. "Meet Lady Gaga," he said, still grinning as he scooped a golden puppy out of the box and thrust it at her. "She's a Malti-poo rescue and desperate for a new home."

Denver was speechless.

"There's no *way* I can take care of a dog," she said at last as the small puppy wriggled in her arms.

"Sure you can," Sam said cheerily. "You took care of Winehouse. Face it, D., you're a dog person."

"No, I'm not," she said stiffly.

"Yes," he teased, not realizing that she was pissed. "You are."

"Well, maybe I am," she allowed. "Only now is not the time for me to be getting one."

"No?"

"No," she answered firmly. "I appreciate the gesture, but I cannot accept."

The puppy licked her face, forcing her to admit to herself that the little dog was adorable, but she wasn't about to weaken.

"Is everything all right?" Sam inquired. "I was under the impression that last night was —"

"Was *what*?" she interrupted, still filled with guilt. "As far as I'm concerned, last night was a big mistake."

Sam looked crestfallen. He'd been sure they'd forged a connection, but now Denver was acting as if nothing had happened between them.

"Did I do something to offend you?" he asked.

She shook her head, thinking how impossible this situation was. Sam, on her doorstep, gifting her with a puppy. It wasn't right, and it was all her fault. Like an idiot she'd encouraged him, and now here he was, all ready for her to take it a step further, something she had no intention of doing.

"Look," she said quietly. "Last night should never have happened. I was upset 'cause I hadn't heard from Bobby, and I guess I drank too much wine. What went on with you and me . . . well, like I said, it shouldn't have."

"Is that how you really feel?"

"Yes, Sam, it is."

Breakfast with Willow, followed by this put-down. Apparently it wasn't his day.

What the heck was he supposed to do with a puppy? He had a meeting in San Francisco, and he couldn't take the puppy with him.

Willow came to mind. She had to be useful for something.

"Okay, then," he said, finally realizing that he was getting nowhere. "If you change your

261

mind, you know where to find me."

Denver nodded. She knew where to find him, all right, although she had no intention of ever doing so.

Sam was her past.

Bobby was her future.

And that's the way it had to be.

Waking up with the Malibu morning light flooding their bedroom and the sound of the waves breaking outside, Lucky lay very still.

Gino is dead.

My beloved father is gone.

Goddamn it, Gino. How could you do this to me?

Or perhaps it was all some horrible nightmare and everything would soon be back to normal.

No. It wasn't a nightmare. Sadly, it was the truth.

Tears stung her eyes and rolled silently down her cheeks. Yesterday she hadn't cried. Today she'd allow herself the luxury of doing so, although only for a few minutes. She refused to weaken; it was imperative that she stay strong.

We must celebrate Gino's life, not mourn his death. That's what he would want.

Of course, she'd known this day would come. Gino was old. She'd imagined he'd go to bed one night and pass peacefully in his sleep. Unfortunately, that was not to be. Gino had been violently gunned down execution-style, and whoever was responsible would pay the price. The Santangelo price.

Never fuck with a Santangelo.

Lennie came into the room carrying a mug of strong black coffee. "Mornin', beautiful," he said, handing her the mug. "How'd you sleep?"

Quickly she wiped away her tears and sat up.

"That's okay, sweetheart. I've seen you cry before," he said, sitting on the side of the bed.

"I'm not crying," she insisted, taking a sip of the hot coffee. "It's just an allergy."

"Sure," he said, reaching for her free hand.

"Don't baby me, Lennie," she said, pulling her hand away. "I need to be strong for the family."

"You *are* strong," he assured her. "Never let it be said that Lucky Santangelo isn't a warrior."

"A warrior, huh?" she said, summoning a weak smile. "I like it."

"You want to tell me what happened yesterday after I left?" he said.

"It wasn't great," she sighed. "Paige started acting like the queen of Palm Springs."

"Nice."

"Can you imagine, she actually invited people over to the house."

"You're kidding?"

"No, I'm not. The heartbroken widow couldn't even wait a day."

"Sounds pretty cold to me."

"Oh, she's cold, all right," Lucky said, experiencing a flash of righteous anger. "She's turned into the calculating bitch I always suspected she was."

"Yeah," Lennie said slowly. "None of us ever warmed to her."

"*I* tolerated her for Gino's sake, although I always had the feeling she was in it for the perks. She got off on being Mrs. Gino Santangelo. The title suited her, and she basked in the attention. You should've seen her last night, surrounded by celebrities and loving every moment of it."

"More important, what's going on with the case?"

"The detectives have nothing except Paige's description of the shooter."

"Is that it?"

"Apparently so," Lucky said, finishing her coffee. "They had a slew of cops canvassing the nearby houses. It seems nobody saw anything, and I'm not surprised 'cause everybody lives behind fucking iron gates."

"So nothing, huh?"

"A dead end." She paused for a moment. "After you left, I went through Gino's desk."

"Good thinking. Did you find anything useful?"

"I don't know if it means anything or not,

but I did discover some kind of threatening note."

"Trust you to come across something. What did the note say?"

"Short and to the point. One printed word — *vengeance.*"

"I guess you handed it over to the detective on the case, right?"

"What do *you* think?" she said, throwing him a disparaging look.

He raised a cynical eyebrow. "If I had to make an educated guess, I'd say you didn't."

"That's because I'll be taking care of it myself."

"Of course you will."

"Yes, Lennie, of course I will."

He took a long silent beat before getting into it with her. "You *do* know that you shouldn't get involved," he said.

"You know what? Don't even go there," she replied, narrowing her dark eyes. "Whoever did this to Gino will pay for it, you can bet on that."

"Here's the thing, sweetheart," he said, making what he knew was a futile attempt to convince her. "You could be putting not only yourself in danger, but the rest of the family too."

"What exactly do you *expect* me to do, Lennie?" she said fiercely, brushing back a lock of jet-black hair. "The detectives are coming up with nothing. *Nada.* Believe me

— this is personal."

"For you, yes."

She fixed him with a long steady gaze. "For all of us."

"Yeah, yeah, I know," he said, giving way a little. "Only you've got to be careful. Whoever did this to Gino could have you in his sights next."

"You think?"

"It's possible."

"You're being dramatic."

"Dramatic or not, what we should do is hire security for the whole family."

"There's no way I'm running scared, you know that."

"Jesus Christ," he said, shaking his head. "You're just like Gino — fucking stubborn."

"And you're not?" she countered. "You're the most stubborn man I know."

Lennie decided that right now it was time to back off. Maybe later he could reason with her. "Have you spoken to the kids?" he asked.

"I left messages. Still haven't heard back from Max or Bobby."

"Typical — which brings me to my thoughts on Max."

"What *are* your thoughts on Max?"

"We should be keeping a more diligent eye on her. She's over in London doing her own thing, doesn't have to answer to anyone, and I gotta say, I don't like it at all."

"Max is nineteen. We can't tell her what to

do," Lucky said, fully aware that Lennie still regarded Max as his precious little girl whom he needed to protect.

"I don't give a crap how old she is," he said irritably. "She's still a kid."

"A kid who's learning to be independent," Lucky said, willing herself to remain patient, because this was not the time to start a fight. "I mean, that's what we want for her, isn't it?"

"That's what *you* want for her," Lennie said, wondering why Lucky wasn't more concerned about their daughter. "*I* want her back in America where she belongs, especially now."

"Spoken like a true chauvinist," Lucky exclaimed. "You know something — it's you who's beginning to sound exactly like Gino."

"Not such a bad thing," Lennie said. "He was a smart one. I'm sure as hell gonna miss that old guy."

"We all are," Lucky said, reaching for her cell phone and clicking on her messages. "Let's see if Max or Bobby have texted me."

There was nothing from Max. One voice mail from Bobby. He sounded panicked and shaken.

She listened intently to his voice.

Bobby.

Her son.

Arrested in Chicago for murder.

Lucky launched into action.

267

CHAPTER THIRTY-THREE

"Your lawyer's here," the duty cop announced, unlocking the cell door.

Bobby quickly jumped up from the hard wooden bench where he'd spent a restless night. Lucky must've finally received his frantic message and hired someone. Thank Christ for that, because it was imperative that he get out of this hellhole before he lost it. He brushed a hand through his dark hair, thinking how crappy he must look. Disheveled and tired, he was more than ready to get out of jail and resume life as he knew it. Being locked up was no fucking joke.

Even though his mind was all over the place, one thing he was sure of — drugged or not, he had nothing to do with the girl in the red dress's murder.

He followed the cop down a long narrow corridor, up some stone stairs, and into what he presumed was an interview room, similar to the one where he'd been interrogated by the burly gum-chewing detective. He sat down on one side of an oblong wooden table and waited. After a few minutes, an attractive black woman entered the room. She was in her late forties, well dressed in a smart blue suit. Her hair was cut short in a sleek bob, and she wore tinted glasses.

Turning to the cop, she said a brisk "I need time alone with my client. I'll call you when we're finished."

The cop threw Bobby a surly look and left the room.

"Beverly Villiers," she said, proffering her hand to Bobby. "I'm an old friend of your mother's, and I'm sure you'll be glad to know that I'm one helluva lawyer."

He immediately liked her style, but who was she? Lucky had never mentioned a Beverly Villiers, but then again there were many things about his mom he didn't know. Lucky had led some life, and she wasn't one to dwell on her past.

"All I can say is thank Christ you're here," he muttered, swallowing hard.

"My intent is to get you out of here as fast as possible," Beverly said, sitting down opposite him.

"Then you should know that this is all some big fucked-up mistake," he said, rubbing his chin.

"I'm listening," Beverly said, removing a weathered crocodile-skin notebook from her purse. "I'm old-school," she said with a wry smile. "So . . . I suggest you tell me everything — and I do mean everything."

"I will. I want to."

"Good, so let's start off with: Did you do it?"

"No way," he said, fervently shaking his head. "I don't even know how the girl died. The last time I saw her she was alive and well."

He flashed onto Nadia offering him a drink, handing him a glass, and saying, *Vodka. For luck. For love. For the future of our loved ones.* That was all he could remember until he'd woken up slumped over the steering wheel of his rental car.

"Miss Gómez was discovered naked in the hotel bathtub," Beverly said, lowering her glasses and watching him closely. "Her throat was slit with a hunting knife." She paused. "Your prints were on the weapon."

Once again, Bobby swallowed hard, feeling a sickening pit in his stomach. "I . . . I told you, I didn't do it," he stammered, images of the beautiful vibrant girl in the red dress once again flashing before his eyes. "It wasn't me."

"Then start talking," Beverly said calmly. "And please keep in mind that no detail is too trivial for me to hear. The more details you can come up with, the better. Do you understand?"

Bobby understood. And so he began his story.

■ ■ ■ ■

Sitting in the back of a chauffeur-driven car on the way to meet with the Dolcezza group of executives, Lorenzo gave Max a brief rundown. Alfredo Agnelli owned the company. His two sisters, Marcella and Gabriella, ran it, while Alfredo's daughter, Natalia, and his son, Dante, were both creative consultants. They were twins.

"It is a family business," Lorenzo explained. "Very successful for many years. The face of Dolcezza changes every eighteen months. Now — if all goes well — that face will be you."

Max didn't like the sound of "if all goes well." What did *that* mean? Surely she was the chosen one? Her agent had assured her that the Dolcezza people loved her. She'd signed a contract. Oh crap! What if it all went wrong? What if they sent her back to London? That would really suck.

"I hate this stupid outfit," she said, turning up her nose. "I look like a joke."

"You are a very lovely girl," Lorenzo said, his thin face sincere. "They will adore you."

"You think?" she asked hopefully.

Lorenzo took a furtive glance around as if someone might be listening to their conversation. "Be careful of Dante," he warned. "He will try to use his position to get you into

271

bed. Do not succumb."

"I haven't even met the dude," Max said, frowning. "What makes you think he's gonna jump me?"

"Dante has a reputation . . . that's all I will say."

"Oh, come *on,*" Max insisted. "Don't throw me crumbs. You gotta fill me in."

Lorenzo shook his head. "We are here now," he said as the car pulled up in front of an impressive old building. "This is the Dolcezza headquarters."

Max got out of the car and followed him into the building, feeling like an idiot in her oversized pink jumpsuit. Some way to make a first impression. At least she'd managed to tame her hair and wipe off most of the heavy makeup.

Alfredo Agnelli greeted her with a bear hug and kisses on both cheeks. He was a distinguished-looking man, very tall, with a face carved out of rock, extra-large teeth, a deep suntan, and a strident voice. His English was limited, and Max couldn't understand a word he was saying. Lorenzo translated. "Signor Dolcezza welcomes you to the house of Dolcezza, and says they are delighted to see you."

Hmm . . . delighted to see her. A good sign.

"May I present Signora Marcella and Signora Gabriella, my dear sisters," Alfredo boomed, gesturing toward the two women in the room.

His dear sisters couldn't have been more different. Marcella was as tall as Alfredo, with sharp features, heavy makeup, long straight blond hair, and a pained expression. Gabriella was short and plump, with rosy cheeks, a twinkle in her eye, and spiky red hair. Max figured that they were both in their fifties.

More cheek kisses were exchanged.

They were meeting in a large room that looked more like a well-appointed living room than an office. Antiques and comfortable leather couches abounded, and right in the center of the room stood an enormous desk, its surface covered in silver frames — all of them filled with photos of smiling, suntanned children doing everything from waterskiing to riding horses.

Alfredo noticed her checking out the frames. "My family," he said with an expansive wave of his hand.

"Wow!" Max exclaimed. "You have a huge family."

"And now you are a part of it," Gabriella said, joining in with a jolly smile.

Things are definitely improving, Max thought. *Pink jumpsuit or not, I am about to become part of the Dolcezza family.*

An hour and a half later, Beverly Villiers had made copious notes and talked on her cell phone several times. She was now preparing to leave.

"What do you think?" Bobby asked anxiously, his stomach churning as he leaned forward.

"Truth or bullshit?" Beverly said, putting away her notebook.

"You believe me, don't you?"

"Yes, I do," she said, then, after pausing for a moment, she said, "Although, Bobby, surely you should've been able to spot a setup when it was coming at you full force? After all, you're Lucky's son. Gino's grandson." After another, thoughtful pause, she added, "By the way, I was extremely sorry to hear about Gino."

"Huh?"

"I knew him back in the day," Beverly continued. "He was a great man."

"What are you talking about?" Bobby said, alarm sweeping over him. "Has something happened to Gino?"

For a few moments, Beverly almost lost her composure as it occurred to her that Bobby was unaware of the tragedy that had taken place. "He was . . . uh . . . shot," she said at last. "I thought you knew."

"Gino was *shot*?" Bobby said feverishly. "How the hell would *I* know? I've been locked up here all night."

"I was under the impression that you'd spoken to Lucky. Surely she must have told you?"

"No," he said, the knot in his stomach becoming unbearable. "I haven't spoken to anyone. They only allowed me one phone call. All I got was Lucky's voice mail, so I left a message."

"I see," Beverly said.

"Tell me about Gino," Bobby said urgently. "Is he doing okay? Where was he shot? How serious is it?"

"He's gone, Bobby," Beverly said quietly, lowering her voice. "I'm so very, very sorry."

Realization dawned. Was this woman telling him that Gino was *dead*?

It wasn't possible. It couldn't be. Gino was a survivor — an unstoppable force of nature.

"How did it happen?" he asked, choking back his emotions. "Who did it?"

"Lucky thinks it was a hit. An assailant shot him execution-style while he was out walking with his wife. It was no accident."

"Jesus *Christ!*" Bobby exclaimed as a black rage overcame him. Here he was stuck in jail for a murder he hadn't committed. Now Gino was *dead*? *Assassinated.* Was this a conspiracy against the Santangelos? It sure as hell seemed like it was. And he was trapped in jail, unable to do anything.

"You've got to get me out of here," he said forcefully. "My family needs me."

"I'm on it," Beverly said, nodding. "I've already set up a meeting with the DA, and after the story you've told me, I'm almost sure I can get the charges dropped, or at least get you out on bail."

"When?" he demanded, grief and frustration mixed with a hard cold anger.

"Soon."

"Soon's not soon enough," he said, the words sticking in his throat as he imagined what Lucky must be going through.

"Unfortunately, there are hoops to jump through," Beverly explained. "The positive news is that I'm tight with the ringmaster, so let's see if I can speed up the process. Going to the emergency room and getting tested for drugs was the best thing you could've done. I'll be back this afternoon. Hang in there, Bobby. You know that's what Lucky would want."

Beverly was right: Lucky would expect him to stay strong.

He thought about Denver. Did she know about any of this? And Max, his kid sister, where was she? Still in Europe? Or had Lucky summoned her home? And how about his two younger brothers. Where were they?

Jesus Christ! So much to deal with, and here he was languishing in jail, unable to do anything.

For the first time in his life, he felt powerless. All the money in the world and yet he couldn't buy himself out of this one.

He had to believe in Beverly Villiers. He had to get the fuck out.

CHAPTER THIRTY-FOUR

Sam was standing on her doorstep, surprising Willow, because even though she'd given him her cell number, she hadn't given him her address, so how had he found her?

Not that she minded. Sam turning up at her house was an excellent omen. It meant that he was indeed interested in her proposal that he write and direct his own movie. Well, not really *his* movie — more like *her* movie. Although what was his movie about anyway? When they'd worked together, she'd had a vague recollection of him telling her it was the story of a young man's journey toward career and love. Hmm . . . maybe he could change it to a young woman's story and she would star alongside Billy Melina.

She'd already placed a call to Eddie Falcon. He'd agreed to meet with her later. This was a good sign, since Eddie was one of the hottest agents in town. During the time he'd represented her, they'd shared many an intimate moment. That is, until he'd informed her he could no longer be her agent due to her latest brush with the law — a stupid incident when, high on drugs and tequila, she'd run over a paparazzo with her car, smashed the asshole's camera, and spat at the cops when they'd arrived on the scene. It had not been her finest moment.

Anyway, that was back during her days of *really* bad behavior. Now she was clean and sober. Well, kind of sober — not exactly, because life without booze would be boring beyond.

"What's up?" she asked Sam. "Are you here to tell me that you've made a decision?"

"Not exactly," he said. "Thought you might do me a favor."

A favor. Oh yes, she'd do him a favor all right, if it meant him getting on board with her project.

"Okay," she said, spotting a lone paparazzo taking shots from a distance. "You'd better move your ass inside before we're all over the tabloids."

Sam quickly made his way into her small, cluttered house. The last thing he needed was to be pictured in the tabloids alongside Willow Price.

Her house was a mess. There were empty wine bottles, trashy magazines, piles of shoes, and random clothes thrown everywhere. There were dirty dishes on the coffee table, and an orchid plant by the window that had seen better days. Worst of all, there was a dead fish floating in a glass bowl full of murky water.

It didn't take a genius to realize that Willow Price was no housekeeper, she was a slob. Immediately Sam had second thoughts about asking her to look after Lady Gaga. Would Gaga end up like her fish? Dead on arrival?

"Can I get you a drink?" Willow offered.

"It's kind of early."

"Stop being such a tight-ass," she said, giggling before adding a flippant, "Just f-ing with you. What's the favor?"

"Have you ever had a dog?" Sam inquired.

"Oh yeah," Willow answered enthusiastically. "There was this one dude who —"

"I mean an animal," he interrupted.

"Trust me," she said, rolling her eyes. "This guy was a *total* animal. He —"

"A puppy," Sam said, interrupting her again. "A real live puppy."

"What?" Willow said blankly.

"I'm asking if you can look after a puppy for me. I have a meeting in San Francisco. I'll be gone until late tonight. I'll pick her up tomorrow morning."

Willow was no slouch in the one favor deserves another department. She thought for a moment, then said, "If you drop off your script so I can take a read, it's a done deal. Oh yes, and the puppy better be cute."

Sam hesitated. He had no desire to get into

business with the likes of Willow Price, even though she *had* made him a very tempting offer. His script. He could direct. A million bucks. No agent or studio involved. What could be wrong with that? A small interesting detour from his career path. A vanity project in which he would have full control. The money did not tempt him. The full control did.

"Fine," he said. "I'll get you my script."

"Today, before you go."

"Okay."

"Where's the puppy?" she asked.

"In my car."

"Bring it in, then," Willow said, concealing a satisfied smile.

With Sam's script in hand, they were about to be in business. Alejandro should be kissing her ass.

Alejandro was not kissing anyone's ass. He was involved in a verbal skirmish with Rafael, who'd come storming into his living room at noon demanding to know why he'd woken up naked in Alejandro's guest bedroom.

"You were drunk, my man," Alejandro informed him. "You were out of your head. I couldn't allow you to drive, so I brought you here. You should be thanking me instead of screaming."

"Who removed my clothes?" Rafael demanded.

"How the fuck would I know," Alejandro responded, relishing the fact that he'd finally got something over on Rafael.

"Surely you're not saying that I did it myself?"

"Let's hope not," Alejandro said with a knowing sneer. "Let's hope that for once you got laid instead of saving yourself for that *puta* back in Colombia."

"Do not call Elizabetta names," Rafael spat. "She is a fine woman. The mother of my son. And one day she will be my wife."

"I doubt it," Alejandro sneered.

"Why do you say that? Are you jealous of what we have because you surround yourself with women who use you for what they can get out of you? Money, drugs, mindless sex — you are incapable of having a real relationship. I feel pity for you, Alejandro. You will never know true love."

"Ah," Alejandro sighed, raising his eyebrows. "True love. How romantic. You have that with Elizabetta, do you?"

"You know I do," Rafael said.

A snarky smile crossed Alejandro's face. "I will show you true love," he offered. "I will show you a man so enamored of his woman that he would never touch another."

"What are you talking about?"

"Be patient," Alejandro said, reaching for the remote control to switch on the large flat-screen TV that covered one wall of the room.

"I am not interested in watching one of your porno movies," Rafael said, shaking his head in disgust. "You should be thinking of getting yourself out of here before that DA nails your dumb ass."

"*My* dumb ass? I will show you whose ass is dumb," Alejandro said, his eyes glittering venom as he activated the TV screen, whereupon an image emerged of Rafael lying on a bed, with Willow straddling him.

Rafael let out a snort of disbelief. "What is this?" he demanded, an angry flush rising from his neck.

"What does it look like?" Alejandro responded with an obsequious smile. "To me it looks like you could be enjoying yourself for once."

"I . . . I don't understand," Rafael stammered as the film continued. "It is not possible. . . ."

"Ah, but it is very possible," Alejandro said, enjoying every second of Rafael's discomfort. "Look at you, loving the sex, loving the pussy. You can't get enough. We are not so different after all. Perhaps we *are* brothers. . . ."

Rafael glared at him. Alejandro got off on pulling this shit — hinting that they might be brothers, then denying it, although he had to know it was true.

On the screen, Rafael watched himself flip the girl over and begin to make love to her. He was sickened by what he saw and heard.

The sex sounds, the groans, flesh against flesh, then his anguished shout — *"Elizabetta! Elizabetta!"*

"Turn it off," he said harshly.

"Surely you want to see everything?" Alejandro taunted.

Snatching the remote from Alejandro's hand, Rafael hurled it across the room. The TV screen went blank.

"Too bad," Alejandro said. "The climax is the best part."

"What do you want?" Rafael said flatly.

"Why would you think I want anything?"

"Cut the shit and tell me what it is."

"Something simple," Alejandro said, a malevolent gleam in his eyes. "I want you to convince my father to give me twenty million dollars. I am about to become a very famous Hollywood filmmaker, and *you* are going to help me do it."

CHAPTER THIRTY-FIVE

Receiving the news about Bobby hit Lucky hard. She could barely take it in, it was so shocking. Not that she believed for one moment that her son was guilty of such a crime. Still . . . Bobby had been arrested. He was locked up in jail, which explained why he hadn't returned her calls.

She was desperate to speak to him, yet she knew that flying to Chicago was premature until she discovered exactly what was going on.

After listening to Bobby's urgent message, she'd immediately contacted an old acquaintance, Beverly Villiers. Way back, Beverly — who was now a prominent defense attorney in Chicago — had dated her half brother, Steven. Lucky always kept tabs on people — where they were and what they were doing. It often paid off, and Beverly's reputation was stellar.

"Don't worry about a thing," Beverly had assured her over the phone. "I'll get right on it."

Lucky trusted Beverly to find out exactly what was going on, then she would decide what her next move should be.

Palm Springs beckoned, although it occurred to her that there was nothing to do there except sit around the house with Paige, and the thought of spending time with her stepmother disgusted her. Paige had turned out to be an unfeeling bitch, and Lucky hated the way she was behaving.

She called Detective Allan.

Big surprise, he had no news.

"As soon as you release Gino's body, let me know," she instructed the detective. "I'll be flying him to Vegas for the funeral."

"You do know there'll have to be an autopsy," Detective Allan warned her.

"I understand," she said, trying not to think about her father's lifeless body lying on a cold slab in the morgue waiting to be carved up. It was simply too much to contemplate. "How soon can that happen?"

"We're making it a priority," Detective Allan assured her.

"Keep me informed," she said, all business. "And if you come up with any new leads," her voice faltered for a moment. "Anything at all —"

Detective Allan promised he would be in daily contact.

His words were hardly encouraging. It was time to get serious about finding out who had executed Gino. There was a murderous son of a bitch out there, and Lucky had every intention of tracking him down.

She needed help, so she contacted Chris Warwick, a private investigator who'd done work for her in the past at the Keys.

Chris was the real deal. Before setting up his own one-man practice as a PI, he'd completed two tours of duty in Afghanistan, and also worked as private security for a construction company in the Middle East. He was tough and smart, plus he excelled at his job. Over the years, he'd never failed her — whether it be tracking someone's cheating husband or persuading a gambler on a losing streak to pay up, he always got the job done.

Within the hour, he arrived at the Malibu house.

Chris looked nothing like people expected a PI to look like. He was tall and well built, with honest brown eyes and sandy hair. In his early forties, he had an unthreatening, easygoing stance that worked well for his job. Upon meeting Chris, everybody trusted him — which sometimes led to their downfall, because behind the cheery façade lurked a wily mind and a body of steel well versed in martial arts.

Sitting down with Chris, Lucky told him everything she knew about Gino's murder. "The cops have come up with nothing," she said. "And I have a strong suspicion that's the way it'll stay."

She showed him the note card with the one printed word: VENGEANCE.

"I'll look into it," Chris said. "In the meantime, I should take a trip to Palm Springs, find out if there's anything the cops missed."

Lucky agreed.

Shortly after Chris left, Gino Junior and Leo arrived at the house. Lucky grabbed the boys in a bear hug, happy to see them. She'd always treated both boys the same, even though Leo was the result of a one-night mistake Lennie had had with an Italian girl, now deceased. Leo was a Lennie look-alike, and Lucky had accepted him into the family when he was very young. Gino Junior, the son she'd had with Lennie, was now a teenager, and resembled a much taller version of his grandfather.

The boys were upset by the news; they clamored for answers that neither she nor Lennie were able to supply. She told them nothing about Bobby — what was the point in drowning them with more bad news? After a while, they drifted off to their rooms, texting friends and playing video games. Later, Lennie took them out for lunch, while Lucky sat down with Danny and began planning Gino's funeral service. She'd already decided that it had to be a huge and memorable event. A day so special that everyone would remember Gino with nothing but love in their hearts.

First she had to work on the guest list. Apart from immediate family, there were so many people who would expect to be invited. Gino had made plenty of friends in high places over the years. Famous, rich, political — Gino had known them all.

Second, she had to decide who she would ask to speak. Steven, of course, and Bobby. Lennie would want to contribute, director Alex Woods, and perhaps talk-show host Jack Python, legendary movie star Charlie Dollar, maybe even Nick Angel, and certainly Venus and Gina Germaine, for Gino would relish plenty of sexy famous women saying wonderful things about him. Important and powerful men too. Why not? This was going to be a party to remember.

The Magiriano Hotel — built by Gino and Lucky way back with love and affection — was where it would all take place. It was the perfect venue. Lucky still owned the hotel, and a management company ran it for her.

At the back of the hotel were beautiful gardens filled with lush greenery and a profusion of flowers. An elaborate fountain stood at the center. Behind the fountain was the Santangelo family mausoleum, where Maria, Dario, and one of the true loves of her life, Marco, had been laid to rest.

Lucky knew for sure that this was where

Gino would want to be — next to his beloved wife, his casket forever locked into the cool marble walls of the mausoleum.

To Lucky, the Magiriano would always be a special place. She would never sell it, even though she'd had many offers.

Danny was busy. He'd hired security guards to be at the house — per Lennie's instructions — and also three assistants to help out. The phone was ringing nonstop. Lucky had instructed him to take messages unless it was close family, so when Denver, Bobby's girlfriend, called, he wasn't sure how to handle it. He put Denver on hold and consulted with Lucky, who agreed to take the call.

Lucky appreciated the fact that Bobby had hooked up with a strong woman, not some sexy wannabe model or actress. Not that Denver wasn't sexy — in her own way she was extremely attractive, with a great body. But there was more to her than simply good looks. Denver was supersmart, and Lucky identified with smart women.

"I'm so sorry for your loss," Denver said, realizing that her words were a cliché. But what else could one say at a time like this? "It must be devastating for you. Is there anything I can do?"

"No. Thanks for asking, though," Lucky replied. "We've got everything covered."

"You're sure?"

289

"Absolutely."

"Um . . . I can't seem to contact Bobby," Denver ventured. "I thought he might be with you?"

Oh God! Lucky thought. *She doesn't know. And I guess I'm the one who's supposed to fill her in.* "Listen, Denver," she said evenly. "I hate to be the one to tell you."

"Tell me what?" Denver asked, experiencing a surge of alarm.

"Bobby is still in Chicago. Actually, he's stuck in jail."

"Excuse me?" Denver exclaimed, her heart skipping a beat. "Are you *serious*? What happened?"

The last thing Lucky felt like doing was informing Bobby's girlfriend that he'd been arrested for murder. "I'm sorry but I can't get into it now," she said quickly. "There's so much going on here. I have a lawyer friend who's dealing with the situation. Danny will give you her number."

Handing the phone over to Danny, she left it with him. Then she called Beverly to get an update.

"I'm on my way to meet with the DA right now," Beverly said. "It looks like a setup to me. I'm hoping to get the charges dropped altogether. If not that, at least a fast bail hearing."

"Tell me exactly what this is about," Lucky said.

Beverly obliged, repeating everything Bobby had told her.

"Jesus *Christ!*" Lucky exclaimed, and, like Bobby, it immediately occurred to her that the two things could be connected. Gino's murder, and Bobby getting set up. Lennie was right; the entire family needed protection. "How's he doing?" she asked.

"He's holding up," Beverly replied. "I'm afraid I had to tell him about Gino."

"Oh God!" Lucky sighed, filled with sadness at the thought of Bobby locked up and alone, hearing about Gino with no one to turn to. "You've got to get him out of there, Bev. He needs to be here with me and the family."

"I'm trying," Beverly assured her.

"If you think it will help, I can get on a plane," Lucky offered. "I can be there in a few hours."

"It's better if I keep you informed. There's nothing you can do here."

"Okay, I guess. If you say so. Please tell Bobby that we're all thinking of him."

"Will do."

Lucky put down her phone, angry and puzzled. What was going on? Why were terrible things happening? And wasn't it true that bad things always happened in threes? Was there something else to come?

A shudder of apprehension enveloped her. Where was Max?

Oh yes, Max had mentioned she was on her way to Saint-Tropez. But why hadn't she replied to her phone calls?

Once more Lucky picked up her cell.

CHAPTER THIRTY-SIX

"I want to use only my first name," Max announced, having already decided that there was no way she was going to trade on either of her parents' fame, and the best way to do that was to lose the surnames.

"Ah, but Max Golden is such a pretty combination," Gabriella trilled. "Santangelo too."

"I prefer just Max," she insisted, determined to get her own way, especially as she was feeling pretty confident that she was indeed the chosen one. It was about time she started calling the shots.

They were sitting on one of the luxurious leather couches going over the Dolcezza press release that was about to be sent out to all media before the press conference the next day.

"If that is what you wish — no Golden, no Santangelo," Gabriella sighed, making notes with a fancy pen. "I will inform our press office."

"And another thing," Max said boldly. "I really hate this outfit they've made me wear. It's way too big for me, and who wears jumpsuits, anyway? It's so eighties."

"Jumpsuits are making — how you say — a big comeback," Gabriella said, twirling a heavy gold bracelet on her chubby wrist. "The one you have on is part of the new Dolcezza collection. Although I must admit that it does seem a little big on you."

"A little big!" Max huffed indignantly. "Can't you see that I'm like totally swimming in it?"

"Scusi?"

"Well, not exactly swimming, more like it's *so* not my style."

Gabriella bobbed her head and wondered why she had been put in charge of the American girl. Where were Natalia and Dante when she needed them? The two of them were supposed to be the creative force of Dolcezza, although in Gabriella's eyes they were both useless. Natalia was obsessed with her womanizing photographer fiancé, and Dante was a dangerous drunk. Surely Alfredo should have considered putting *her* adult children in positions of power? But no, he'd favored his own offspring, giving them the important titles, while *her* three children did all the real work behind the scenes.

"So you agree?" Max said.

Gabriella wasn't sure what she'd agreed to.

This young American girl was quite bossy, unlike the former face of Dolcezza, a voluptuous Swedish model who'd had little to say about anything and jumped into bed with any man who asked. Gabriella nodded anyway.

"Cool," Max said. "I can't wait to get out of this outfit. It sucks."

"Ah yes," Gabriella said, finally realizing what she'd agreed to. "My assistant, Giulia, will take you to the sample room." Gabriella gestured toward Giulia, a sour-faced girl lurking in the background, and fired off a stream of Italian.

"Can I pick out anything I like to wear for the photo session?" Max asked, her confidence rising.

"As long as it is from our new collection," Gabriella said, "I see no problem."

"Got it," Max said, deciding that Gabriella was going to be easy to manipulate. Thank goodness she was dealing with her and not the other sister, who seemed far more formidable.

"Off you go, then," Gabriella said, relieved to relinquish responsibility. "I will see you later."

"Thanks," Max said, skipping out of the room.

After making several phone calls and discovering everything she could about Bobby's arrest, Denver took an Uber cab to the airport.

Maybe Lucky felt it wasn't necessary to fly to Chicago, but Denver had no hesitation. Being with Bobby was the right thing to do.

She'd had an unsatisfactory conversation with Beverly Villiers over the phone before speaking with an assistant DA in Chicago whom she happened to know. The news was so ominous, it sent a chill through her. Bobby, *her* Bobby, arrested for murder. How was that even possible?

Apparently the news had hit the Internet and the newspapers. Bobby Santangelo Stanislopoulos was making headlines. Handsome, rich, murderer of a beautiful woman. What more could the press ask for?

Before boarding her flight, she connected with M.J., who promised he'd meet her at the airport in Chicago.

"You gotta know that Bobby did nothing wrong," M.J. assured her. "This is a full-on setup. Somebody's out to get him."

"You're *sure* about that?"

"I was with him, Denver. I took him to the emergency room. He was drugged out. The doctor mentioned something about he could've died."

Denver felt her throat constrict. "Who was the girl?" she couldn't stop herself from asking.

"I'm gonna fill you in when you get here," M.J. said.

Denver attempted to remain calm; she had

to hear all the facts before she jumped to conclusions. She was well aware that there were always two sides to every story, although obviously Bobby had known the murdered woman — he'd even gone to her hotel room. The thought of Bobby with another woman was driving her crazy, and even though she knew she was being irrational, she couldn't help herself.

So . . . what *was* Bobby's side? That's what she was desperate to find out. And until she did, she couldn't rest easy.

A familiar face at last! Max experienced a surge of joy, even if the familiar face was that of Carlo, the photographer who'd felt it perfectly reasonable to spend a drunken night camped out in her bed after their photo session in London. According to Athena, he was totally into sleeping with his models.

"Ciao, *bella*!" Carlo greeted her, moving in for an intimate hug.

"Ciao right back atcha," she managed, pleased to see him, and forced to admit that there was something about him that she found wickedly hot. He was no Billy Melina, but he certainly had it going on in a low-down bad-boy kind of way. And who didn't like bad boys?

They were now in the Dolcezza photo studio, a state-of-the-art airy space at the top of the building. Earlier she'd perused the sample clothes room and come up with a skimpy white crop top and crotch-hugging blue-jean shorts. It was kind of a Miley Cyrus look. She'd added a studded low-slung belt, a cluster of bangles, a statement necklace, and a pair of insane leopard-print Prada heels. Oh yes, this was a far better look for her — no more stupid jumpsuit to get lost in. Athena would definitely approve.

Lorenzo was standing by, and so was Giulia, who'd been instructed to stick around.

The hair and makeup team from that morning were gathered on one side of the studio, glaring at her with aghast expressions on their faces. Who did she think she was? Changing everything they'd done. It was sacrilege.

They muttered among themselves until the makeup woman in her tightly belted zebra-print coat approached Carlo, who was busy instructing one of his assistants to set up the background for his first shot. There followed a fiery exchange in rapid Italian, with the woman shooting contemptuous looks and gestures toward Max, while Carlo casually shrugged and acted unconcerned.

Max loved him for that. Maybe he wasn't such an asshole. After all, it was because of him that she'd gotten this job, and he was obviously cool with the outfit she'd put together.

The zebra-print woman stalked back to her

group and took out her cell phone with an angry flourish.

Unperturbed, Carlo motioned for Max to take her position in front of the camera. She did so, and the shoot began.

Gangsta rap blared from the speakers, so loud that Max could barely hear Carlo as he issued instructions about what he wanted her to do. First he required her to stare straight into the camera, hands tucked into the pockets of her shorts, head down, expression sexy. Next he requested that she lean against the plain backdrop, shoulders arched, one leg slightly bent, expression wistful.

They had a great working chemistry and they both felt it. Every so often Carlo would stop and check out the images he was capturing on a nearby computer screen. He muttered to himself, liking what he saw, winking at Max but not offering to show her anything. Then everything came to an abrupt halt with the entry of Natalia and Dante Dolcezza.

Zebra-print makeup woman raced toward them, relaying her annoyance. She was closely followed by the hair person and the clothes stylist, all of them waving their arms in the air and venting their frustration.

Carlo ordered one of his assistants to turn off the music, then he approached the twins. It was apparent to Max that they knew each other well, for Natalia was all over Carlo, smothering him with kisses, while Dante gave him an offhand nod.

"Who are they?" she asked Lorenzo.

"Natalia and Dante," Lorenzo replied. "The Dolcezza twins."

Max checked them out. She figured them to be in their late twenties. Natalia was tall and big-boned with dark skin, a strong face, and a longish nose. Not unattractive, she carried herself as if she were the most beautiful movie star on the planet. Dante was nothing like his sister. He was shorter and scarily thin, with a deathly pale complexion and small, hooded eyes. He wore a black studded leather jacket that Max immediately coveted.

Between Carlo, the twins, and the Italian glam squad, there was a definite cluster fuck of complaints going on. Obviously it was all about her refusal to look like someone she wasn't. *Too bad,* she thought. *I've made a stand and I'm sticking to it.*

As the arguing continued, she wondered if now was the time to call Lucky back. Then she decided no — too much going on. Later would be better.

"What are they saying?" she whispered to Lorenzo.

"Complaining about you," he said with a casual shrug.

"It might be polite for them to come over and say hello," she grumbled. "It's like they're kind of ignoring me."

"Better to keep a distance," Lorenzo

300

warned. "Natalia is very jealous."

"Of me?"

"Of any girl Carlo photographs."

"How come?"

"They are engaged."

"Engaged?" Max exclaimed, caught off guard. "Are you *serious*?"

"For two years now. When it comes to making plans for a wedding, Carlo drags his feet. It does not please Natalia."

"Wow!" Max exclaimed, thinking back to the night Carlo spent in her bed. That wouldn't go down well with Natalia.

"Be careful," Lorenzo said, lowering his voice. "The prince of darkness approaches."

And suddenly Dante was standing directly in front of her, hooded eyes staring right through her. Creepy eyes. Creepy smile. Yellow teeth.

"Buon giorno," he said quite pleasantly before changing his tone. "Now, may I suggest that you get yourself into the makeup chair and stop believing you can do whatever you want," he added sharply. "Dolcezza tells you what you *can* or *cannot* do. I suggest that you read your contract, and start behaving like a professional. Am I making myself clear?"

Oh yes, he was making himself abundantly clear.

Max took a step back. Perhaps this was not going to be as easy as she'd thought.

301

CHAPTER THIRTY-SEVEN

Married or not, men were all the same. Blow jobs ruled their world, especially the kind of blow jobs Willow had perfected. Ah yes . . . although most men said there was no such thing as a bad blow job, Willow knew better. She'd been instructed by the best, a bisexual drag queen who'd taught her all the intricacies of doing it just right. She'd been fourteen at the time and working on a movie about a young runaway (her) who finds herself befriended by the drag queen. They'd become quite close on and off the screen, and she'd been happy to learn a trick or two. Tricks that had certainly enhanced her reputation among the male power players in Hollywood, plus a female executive or two.

Eddie Falcon was no exception. He might be married. His wife might be pregnant. But who was he to say no to a freebie? And since getting hitched to his Hollywood princess, Eddie had discovered that blow jobs were not high up on Annabelle's list of things to do.

The truth was that they seemed to have fallen off the menu altogether. So when Willow called and said she wanted to see him, he'd thought, *Why not? What's a quick blow job between an agent and his former client?* And when he'd run into her at the Polo Lounge, she'd been looking hot in a Hollywood slut kind of way. So naturally, he'd remembered all the wild times they'd once shared, and what was the harm in wanting more?

Of course, if Annabelle ever found out, she wouldn't be a happy camper. But Eddie was confident that there was no way she could find out, for rather than be seen in public with Willow, he'd instructed her to come to his office at six P.M. and to use his private elevator — which would bring her right into his spacious office with a mind-blowing view of Century City. That way she wouldn't have to pass by anyone because he'd given her the direct access code.

Ah . . . he could expect a world-class blow job in his future, and Eddie got off on anticipating.

Meanwhile, Willow had a puppy to deal with, and while it was cute enough, she was so not used to caring for animals — especially an untrained puppy.

True to his promise, Sam had dropped off his precious script, and after scanning it quickly, she'd decided it was definitely not the movie Alejandro or she would want to make. No sex. No violence. Mucho conversations between a man and his inner self. Boring and *so* uncommercial. It was hardly a surprise that no studio had picked it up. The script was Sam's inflated ego trip, the movie *he* wanted to make, and nobody else would give a shit.

Damn it! What was a girl to do?

Blow Eddie Falcon and ask his advice, for if anyone knew the ins and outs of Hollywood, it was Eddie.

After shutting the cute little puppy in her bedroom, she left to meet with Eddie.

Arriving at his office, she was dressed for action in slinky satin wide-legged pants — sans underwear — and a sheer top, nipples on alert. With her new earrings and exceptionally high heels, her look was complete. Sexy with a touch of class.

Stepping out of Eddie's private elevator into his well-appointed office, she was greeted by the man himself in nothing more than his underwear and a crisp white shirt, his hard-on standing at full attention poking hopefully through his shorts.

This did not surprise Willow; she was used to the sexual predilections of powerful and famous men. One studio head she'd serviced had worn a lacy ladies' thong and a plunging bra under his severe business suit. A top industry lawyer had insisted that she draw a smiley face on his penis with a felt-tip pen. And a very well-loved family star had made her trample all over his back wearing spiked hiking boots and nothing else.

Who was she to judge? She was merely a girl — an actress — trying to keep her name above the title.

"Hey, sexy tits," Eddie said with a smile as he released what he referred to as the big ride.

It was not big, it was average — but Willow always oohed and aahed as though it were the most exciting piece of real estate she'd ever seen.

"Somebody's pleased to see me," she purred. "And since you're a married man now, I guess the wife is not putting out."

Eddie's smile vanished. His hard-on didn't. "No mention of the wife," he said sternly. "She's off-limits."

"Fine with me," Willow murmured. Cheating husbands *never* wanted to talk about their wives, unless it was to complain about what a bitch they were. Annabelle Falcon *was* a bitch, according to Frankie Romano, Alejandro's drinking buddy who'd recently gotten himself arrested for drug trafficking. And Frankie should know — he was Annabelle's ex-boyfriend.

"Enough with the small talk," Eddie said, gesturing toward his crotch. "Whyn't you take a look at how much I've missed you."

"Aren't you going to offer me a drink first?"

she asked coyly, attempting to ignore his erection, which was still pointing directly at her.

"C'mon, sexy tits," Eddie said with an agonized groan. "Let's get this show started."

"Okay, okay," she said, realizing that this meeting was going nowhere until she'd given him what he was begging for. "But after we're finished, we talk. Right?"

"You got it."

Willow fell to her knees on the plush carpet. *If I wasn't so ambitious, I would've made a fantastic hooker,* she thought as he jammed himself into her mouth.

Then it was on.

Willow took great pride in being the best little cocksucker in town.

Rafael spent a restless day going over how he was supposed to handle this new circumstance that had arisen. He was being blackmailed, pure and simple. Blackmailed by the idiot Alejandro, who now fancied himself a movie producer. What a moron Alejandro was. Did he honestly believe that money could buy him anything he desired? And how was he, Rafael, supposed to persuade Pablo Fernandez Diego that making a movie was a legitimate venture for the Diegos to become involved in?

Rafael was sickened by it all. He'd been had. Plied with liquor and God knew what kind of drugs to make him think he was making love to his precious Elizabetta. How could he have allowed this to take place?

Perhaps it was punishment for the girl in Chicago. Rafael had thought he'd hired a professional who knew what he was being paid to do, but the man had killed the girl instead of beating her up. It was not the result Rafael had wanted, although according to his informant in the DA's office, it had gotten Denver Jones out of town, running to her boyfriend's side.

He still had a bad feeling about what had taken place, and now he was paying for it. Not that he was a religious man, but his mother was, and she'd instilled a certain amount of guilt in him, guilt he'd learned to brush aside because he was in the drug business. He was involved in importing all kinds of drugs into America and consequently ruining people's lives. It was not a profession he'd chosen, it was simply his lot in life.

These were the facts he usually chose to ignore. Only today was different — today he was being punished for his bad deeds. He felt it in his bones.

Alejandro was his problem, and there was nothing he could do about it, for if any harm came to Alejandro, Pablo would surely have Rafael killed. Rafael knew that for a fact.

He swallowed hard as he paced around his small office at Club Luna. There had to be an answer, and yet he was at a loss to know what that answer might be.

"Hey," a fully satisfied Eddie Falcon said, tucking his dick back into his pants. "You haven't lost your touch, babe. You always were the best."

Willow emerged from his private bathroom, dabbing her lips with a tissue. "Thank you, kind sir," she responded with a sly smile. "Positive reviews are always welcome."

"We should get together more often," Eddie noted with a pleased smirk. "Gotta say I missed your magic skills."

At least he appreciates me, Willow thought. *Now he can listen to me.*

"Eddie," she said, dropping into an ultra-modern steel-and-chrome chair. "I have a proposition you're gonna *love.*"

Eddie did not sit. Eddie was too busy getting dressed.

"Make it fast, babe," he said, shrugging on his Armani jacket. "I got a dinner to go to."

"I'll make it fast, all right," Willow responded, fumbling in her purse for a cigarette. "How does a million bucks cash — straight into your pocket — sound?"

And so Eddie listened.

Chapter Thirty-Eight

"As soon as Lennie gets back from lunch with the boys, tell him I had to go out," Lucky informed Danny, who was already hard at work making arrangements for the funeral service and the party that would follow.

"Should I come with you?" Danny asked, anxious to take a break since he was snowed under with everything he had to organize. "Or should I get one of the guards to accompany you?"

"Not necessary," Lucky replied briskly. She had things to take care of, things that did not involve anyone except herself, and she certainly didn't want security or Danny tagging along.

Danny was longing to ask where she was off to, even though he was well aware that his boss did not appreciate being questioned. "Will we be going back to Palm Springs later?" he inquired, wondering if he could bring Buff, his significant other.

Lucky was already striding toward the front

door. "No," she called over her shoulder. "Put together plans to set everything up in Vegas. We'll be making that our next stop."

Outside, her red Ferrari was parked in the driveway.

For a moment she paused before getting into the driver's seat and revving the engine. She had things to take care of, and now was the time.

Chris Warwick considered himself an expert at his job. Dealing with people was his thing — sussing them out, gauging their reactions, figuring out whether they were telling the truth or not. He always knew; he had a finely tuned antenna for bullshit.

After arriving in Palm Springs, he went straight to work — checking out the street where Gino had met his end, observing that the area was no longer roped off with police tape. The sidewalk had been power-cleaned and showed no sign of the violent crime that had taken place. The affluent neighborhood was back to normal. Palm trees softly swaying, a slight breeze, bright sunlight, birds singing in the trees. A perfect Palm Springs day.

Nice place to live, Chris thought. *That's if you don't end up with a bullet in the back of your head.*

With watchful eyes he surveyed the area, noting exactly which houses might have had a view of the crime scene — because in spite of the long driveways, there were plenty of landscape windows through which someone could have seen something.

Lucky had informed him that all the houses had been canvassed by a team of cops. However, they were both aware that cops were not always as thorough as they should be.

After a while, Chris zeroed in on two houses, noting that they both had a clear view of the crime scene.

He approached house number one — a fifties-style structure with a circular driveway and no menacing gates.

An older man wearing khaki knee-length shorts and a colorful Hawaiian shirt answered the door. Chris immediately recognized him as a once well-known crooner from the Sinatra era. His name was Bud something or other — Chris couldn't quite recall his surname.

Bud something or other was fit and tanned, and except for a row of glistening overly white false teeth and badly dyed orange hair, he looked okay for a dude who had to be fast approaching eighty.

Adopting a detective stance, Chris flashed the phony badge he'd gotten off the Internet. He looked so accommodating and honest, nobody ever doubted him.

"Saw nothing," Bud something or other

said in answer to Chris's question about the shooting. "Heard a pop, thought it was a car backfiring. Next thing I know, cops are swarming everywhere. It was like a movie happening on my own doorstep."

"Must've been quite a shock when you found out what had taken place," Chris remarked. "A brutal murder right on the street where you live."

Bud something or other bobbed his head. "You can bet on that."

"All you heard was a pop, right?"

"That's it."

Chris leaned forward. "Did you know Mr. Santangelo?" he asked.

"Sure I knew him. We played poker a coupla times a week."

"How about his wife? Did you know her too?"

Bud something or other clicked his false teeth and looked perplexed. "What's with the questions again? I told 'em yesterday I never saw nothin'."

"Understood," Chris said calmly. "We're following up."

"Well, go follow up somewhere else. I got a golf game to get to."

"Thanks for your help, Mr. . . . ?"

"Pappas. Bud Pappas." With a sneaky grin, he added, "Don't tell me you didn't get laid playin' my songs when you were in high school."

Chris laughed. "Who didn't?" he lied. "I was a big, big fan."

Bud Pappas preened, suddenly forgetting all about his golf game. "Wanna come in, grab a cuppa java?" he said with a jovial chuckle. "I got stories that'll make your cock-a-doodle-doo so hard, you'll think you died and went to Viagra heaven!"

And so Chris walked into the fifties-style house with its mud-brown shag carpets and multiple frames hanging on the wall filled with photos of an era long past.

When he left an hour later, he had found out plenty. According to Bud Pappas, everyone had loved Gino Santangelo, whereas his wife, Paige, was not so popular. The consensus was that she was a conniving, cheating, snobbish bitch on wheels. And nobody would be surprised if it turned out that she'd paid to have Gino taken out.

Interesting. Suspect number one: Paige Santangelo.

Lucky would eat this information up.

The security room at the bank was located in the basement. Gino had taken Lucky there once so that she could sign in if she ever had to. Now that time had come. He'd used a different identity — smart — so nobody could put a hold on his safe-deposit boxes should anything ever happen to him.

A heavyset woman with graying hair and a

name tag that read MRS. CRISP pinned to her blouse was sitting behind a desk. After an exchange of information, she asked Lucky to sign in and produce her key. Lucky did so, whereupon Mrs. Crisp got up, said, "Follow me," and activated the automatic lock on the steel-barred gates leading to the inner sanctum.

They entered together and proceeded to the numbered slot where Gino's safe-deposit boxes were. Mrs. Crisp inserted her key and Lucky did the same. The steel door opened, and Lucky slid the two boxes out.

"Do you require a private room?" Mrs. Crisp asked.

Lucky nodded. Mrs. Crisp escorted her to a small cubicle, where Lucky placed the two boxes on a table and waited for the woman to leave.

As soon as she was alone, her heart began to pound. She was nervous, not sure what secrets the boxes would reveal. Years ago, in Vegas when she was a teenager, she'd managed to get into Gino's bedroom safe hidden behind a Picasso. She'd been shocked by what she'd found. Apart from photos of Gino with Maria, a couple of handguns, some jewelry, a collection of expensive watches, stacks of cash, gold coins, and pornographic photos of movie star Marabelle Blue, there was an envelope marked THE RICHMOND FILE. In the envelope, she'd discovered incriminating photos of Marabelle in bed with Senator Peter Richmond, the father of Craven, the man Gino had forced her to marry at sixteen.

She flashed back on how sick she'd felt discovering the photos that Gino had obviously used as a blackmail tool to facilitate her teenage marriage to the Richmonds' dull son.

Now here she was again, faced with even more secrets.

After visiting with Bud Pappas, Chris noticed that the other house he'd targeted had an outdoor camera. According to the police report Lucky had gotten hold of, the owner of the house had stated that the camera was not operational on the day of Gino's murder.

Chris approached the house, pressed the buzzer on the iron gates, and waited. After a few minutes, a female voice came through a speakerphone demanding to know who he was and what he wanted.

"Detective Warwick, ma'am. I simply require a few moments of your time. It's about the unfortunate incident that took place yesterday."

"Oh my God!" the woman exclaimed. "I've already spoken to the police. What now?"

"Can we speak in person?"

"This is most inconvenient," she huffed, pressing the buzzer anyway, allowing him to enter the property.

He strolled up the driveway to the front door, where he was greeted by an attractive dark-haired woman with a slight accent.

"Mrs. Yassan?" he questioned.

She looked him over, liking what she saw. "You can call me Christi," she said.

"Thanks, uh, Christi," he replied, fixing her with his honest brown eyes.

"I was just making coffee. Would you care for a cup?"

"That would be very nice," he said, following her into the tastefully decorated house.

They exchanged a few pleasantries before Chris began questioning her about the malfunctioning camera. Immediately, he sensed she was lying. Her eyes refused to meet his, and her skin began to flush a dull red from the neck up. She was definitely hiding something.

"Is your husband around?" he asked.

Her eyes darted nervously around the room. "My husband is away on a business trip," she said at last.

Chris's intuition kicked in. Husband away. Perhaps a lover visits. It was no wonder she'd claimed the camera had malfunctioned; she didn't want anyone seeing the tape.

"Mrs. Yassan — Christi," he said, keeping his voice low and even. "I think there is something you should show me. And please trust me — whatever is on the tape will remain between you and me. That's a promise."

Did she really want to find out what was in these two boxes? Would the Richmond file still be in there? The pornographic photos of Marabelle Blue?

Lucky sighed. She didn't want to know, yet she had to. What if there was something connected to Gino's murder?

Her hands began to tremble — which was ridiculous, because she was so not a hands trembling kind of woman. Yet at this very moment, she felt vulnerable and apprehensive about what she might discover.

Gino and his fucking secrets. Who knew what he had hidden away.

Just as she was about to open box number one, her phone buzzed. The ID read "Unknown caller."

Should she answer? Or get on with opening the safe-deposit boxes?

A distraction would be good. Maybe it was Beverly Villiers or Detective Allan with up-to-date information.

"Hello," she said into the phone.

"Mom? It's me, Max. And have I got news for you!"

Chapter Thirty-Nine

"Is something the matter?" Lorenzo asked, reentering the small dressing room adjacent to the photo studio where he and Max had been waiting for Carlo and Dante to finish arguing about what Max should wear and how she should look in the photos. He'd left the room when Max had decided to make a call to her mother, and now he could see that she was upset. "Is it Dante?" he continued. "I warned you about him. He's a mean one. Do not let him upset you."

Max had just gotten off the phone with Lucky, and her head was in a whirl. The news she'd heard was devastating. Her grandfather had been shot to death. Her brother had been arrested in Chicago. Now Lorenzo was asking her if anything was wrong.

Yes, something was wrong, and it sure as hell wasn't creepy Dante with his yellow teeth and hooded eyes. She could deal with him, but how was she supposed to deal with the shocking news from home?

Tears started rolling down her cheeks, tears of grief because she'd loved Gino so much. They'd shared a special bond, and the one thing she'd been sure of was that any time she needed her grandfather, he'd be there for her.

Now he was gone. It was an unexpected blow.

As for Bobby, what the heck? He'd been arrested, for *what*? Lucky had refused to say; she'd merely told her not to believe anything she might read or see on the Internet, and that it was all a big mistake.

"I'll get the next plane home," she'd cried out to her mom.

"No," Lucky had said. "Stay where you are. You're safer there."

Safer? What did *that* mean?

Then Lucky had gone on to tell her that she should come home for the big funeral service, and not before.

Lorenzo awkwardly placed an arm around her shoulders, attempting to comfort her. "What is it?" he asked. "Is it Dante? Because if it is, we can go above him. We can go to Gabriella."

"It's not Dante," she managed to blurt out. "It's my grandfather. I just heard that he . . . he died."

"I am so sorry," Lorenzo said, hurriedly handing her a tissue. "What can I do for you?"

319

"Nothing," Max replied, dabbing her eyes. "He was very old . . . but I always expected him to be around."

"Of course," Lorenzo said.

"I think I have to fly home."

"We should tell Gabriella. She will understand."

"Gabriella will understand *what*?" Dante demanded, appearing in the doorway, a belligerent sneer on his sallow face.

Lorenzo quickly explained the situation in rapid Italian just as Carlo came up behind Dante.

Once again, Max wished she understood what they were saying. A lot of raised voices and angry gesturing was going on. All she wanted to do was close her eyes and be alone with her thoughts. Somehow, from the way Dante was carrying on, she knew this was not to be.

Eventually, after more explosive exchanges, Carlo shooed Dante and Lorenzo out of the room and sat down beside her. "Listen to me, *bella,*" he said in a soothing voice, his hand covering hers. "This family ordeal cannot interfere with your work. You have signed a contract, and Dante — who is a *testa di cazzo* — will force you to honor it."

"He can't *make* me do anything," she said defiantly. "Not if I don't want to."

"Ah, it is possible he can sue you," Carlo pointed out. "There is no doubt he would do that. Anyway, *bella,* this job is too important for you to walk away from. You are destined to be a star, *mio tesoro.*"

It occurred to her that Carlo was right. Becoming the face of Dolcezza was her future, her big opportunity to make it. And if she left . . . what then?

"Lorenzo tells me your mama says you should not return home until the funeral," Carlo continued. "We work around that. I speak with Gabriella, she understands."

"I . . . I don't know what to do," Max said, thinking about how Lucky had told her to stay where she was until the funeral. When would that be? Days? Weeks? No, it couldn't be weeks; it had to be soon.

She thought about Gino, her macho grandfather. What would *he* want her to do? *Hey, kid,* she could imagine him saying. *You got yourself a job — an' you'd better damn well do it. You're a Santangelo — an' Santangelos don't quit.*

Suddenly she could picture Gino — old, but still dynamic with his wicked grin and amazing zest for life. Yes. He would want her to carry on; he wouldn't expect her to sit around with a sad face.

"I guess I'll stay until the funeral," she informed Carlo. "Will you talk to Gabriella and explain?"

"*Sì, bella.* Carlo takes care of everything."

"And I don't want to do any more photos today. It's too much."

"I understand," Carlo said. "We already have what we need. You go to your hotel, you rest, and later, as you know, there is a dinner."

"I'm not sure I can manage that."

"Whatever pleases you, *mio dolce*. Although, as you know, this dinner is in your honor. Now I go discuss with Gabriella."

"Thanks," she murmured gratefully, thinking how weird it was that this cocky Italian photographer whom she initially couldn't stand had turned out to be her savior.

"Lorenzo will take you to your hotel," Carlo said. "I call you soon."

"What about Dante?" she asked anxiously.

Carlo shrugged and made a face. "Do not worry about him. He is of no consequence."

And that was that. Crisis solved.

Or so she thought.

Beverly Villiers was no slouch when it came to getting things done. She had important contacts and a team of underlings that she put to work obtaining signed statements from the doctor who had treated Bobby at the hospital; his business partner, M.J.; the doorman at the hotel; the desk clerk; the manager; and anyone else she could think of.

It was quite apparent that Bobby Santangelo Stanislopoulos had been drugged and set up, and simply because he was handsome and rich and came from a well-known family, there was no reason for him to be treated as if he were guilty of a heinous crime and refused bail.

With friends in the right places, Beverly was able to arrange an emergency bail hearing with a judge who was always available to do her a favor. Not that getting Bobby bail was a favor, although getting a fast hearing was.

Bail was set at three million dollars.

No problem. The bail money was only a phone call away.

Beverly was confident that she could get Bobby out of jail before the end of the day.

She placed a call to Lucky, and waited for the money transfer.

CHAPTER FORTY

After giving it some thought, Rafael came up with a plan that would involve both him and Alejandro making the trip to Colombia. Maybe when he got Alejandro there, he could tell Pablo what was going on, and Pablo would force his precious son to stay. Unfortunately, Alejandro did not warm to the idea at all. "You will go by yourself," he informed Rafael. "Pablo will listen to you. He always does. And do not forget that if you fail to convince him —"

"If I fail to convince him — what?" Rafael said, stifling his desire to fight back, yet at the same time knowing that the smart move was to smother his fury about the sex tape.

"You *know* what," Alejandro said, a malevolent gleam in his eyes.

Yes. Rafael knew only too well. Alejandro would relish sending the incriminating evidence to his beloved Elizabetta in Colombia. And Elizabetta would never forgive him, he knew that for sure. She would take his son and disappear, for although she was a caring and kind woman who loved him very much, she was also an unforgiving one. He would be screwed.

"What am I supposed to say to Pablo?" Rafael questioned. "How am I to get him to agree to such an investment?"

"I don't care what you say — as long as you come back with his commitment. Plus a couple of million dollars in cash."

"What?" Rafael said, quivering with anger.

"You heard. I will need start-up money."

"Even if Pablo agrees, it is not legal to bring that amount of cash into the U.S. If it was discovered, I could be deported."

With a malevolent smirk, Alejandro said, "Then you had better make sure it is not discovered, my friend. Shove it up your uptight ass. Nobody will ever suspect."

By the time Willow got home, she was feeling the need for some alone time. After she'd lured Eddie with her proposition, he'd gotten so excited that he'd said to hell with his dinner plans — then he was all up for another blow job. Naturally, she'd obliged, because Eddie was full of ideas. "Get me the cash, and I'll get your movie made," he'd promised.

Cash was the magic word. Everyone loved it.

She'd sensed it was too early to tell him that she planned on starring in it. Timing was everything. Having his attention was the most important thing.

Back at her house, she was annoyed to discover that Sam's puppy had crapped and peed in her bedroom to its heart's content. Picking up dog poop was not on her agenda, so instead she gave Lady Gaga a dish of water, petted her for a few minutes, then fell onto her couch and called Alejandro.

He sounded stoned, as usual. What else was new?

"Come on over. We'll go to the club and celebrate," he offered.

"Not tonight," she replied. "I'm dogsitting."

"You're *what*?" he snorted, as if he didn't believe her.

"When can you come up with the start-up money?" she asked, determined to keep Alejandro on track while she had Eddie's interest.

"Soon. I'm sending Rafael to Colombia. He's leaving tonight."

"Tonight?" she questioned as the puppy jumped on top of her.

"He will come back with what we require."

Willow pushed the puppy off her, while wondering if Alejandro had shown Rafael the sex tape. If so, what had Rafael's reaction been?

The way Rafael had made love to her was memorable, even if he'd imagined she was his damn girlfriend. How come she'd never taken note of him before? Now he was definitely on her radar, and as far as she was concerned, another sex session was certainly a possibility. He'd come up with moves Alejandro had never mastered. Best of all, he'd brought her to an awesome climax, something she'd only ever faked with Alejandro and most men.

Hmm . . . it occurred to her that maybe she should make a list of all the men she'd slept with. That way when she wrote her autobiography, she'd have it down.

No time for lists now, though. The only list she should be thinking of was the A-list. Getting back on it was of paramount importance.

Willow Price was making a comeback. And not a moment too soon.

With no Willow to play with, Alejandro surveyed the available talent at Club Luna. He already had two blondes sitting at his table, but they were hardly a challenge. They'd give him head under the table if that's what he told them to do. Sometimes easy was too damn easy.

A girl on the dance floor weaving around to Beyoncé was catching his attention. He'd noticed her undulating around the night before. He'd been with Willow, so he'd done nothing about her. Licking his lips, he continued to observe the girl. She had a dirty-sexy vibe going for her, a vibe he couldn't get enough of. After watching her for a while, he had Matias, his driver/bodyguard, summon her to his table.

She took her time sauntering over — all Puerto Rican ass and long curly hair. Alejandro took a closer look. She was not as pretty as J. Lo, his personal favorite, but she had major attitude. He liked what he saw. "You got a name, foxy girl?" he asked, pouring her a glass of champagne.

Sonia threw him a sultry look. Denver was right: she owned the role of party girl in a tighter-than-tight short leather dress, bare legs, and sexy ankle-strap heels. "You can call me Rita," she said, sliding in next to him. "An' you," she added boldly. "*You* got a name?"

Alejandro raised an eyebrow in surprise. "You don't know me?" he questioned, like it was impossible that she wasn't aware that he owned the club.

"If I knew who you was, why'd I ask?" she said, running a finger suggestively around the rim of her champagne glass.

The two blondes giggled nervously. Was Alejandro going to fly into a fury? They'd both experienced his short fuse, and when he lost his temper, it wasn't pretty.

But Alejandro wasn't annoyed at all. In fact, he was enjoying himself. "You got panties on under that dress?" he said, leering at Sonia.

"Whyn't you ask my boyfriend?" she responded tartly.

"You got a boyfriend?"

"No," she said scathingly, taking a gulp of champagne. "I'm makin' him up. An' for your info, this girl don't wear no panties. Not ever."

Alejandro was intrigued. "Get lost," he said, gesturing toward the blondes.

Obediently, they both rose to their feet and tottered off.

"You got a boyfriend or not?" he said, once again licking his fleshy lips as his eyes lingered on Sonia's muscled legs.

"Yeah, I got me a big macho boyfriend," Sonia said. "Only he ain't here. He sent *me* to do his business."

"Business?"

"Yeah," she answered. "I gotta take care of some things, but that don't mean I can't have myself a party."

"What things you supposed to take care of?"

"I'm on a buyin' spree. You got connections?"

Alejandro laughed out loud. Did *he* have connections? Was she shitting him? Who was this woman who seemed to have no idea who he was?

"What're you looking for?" he asked.

"The usual shit."

"Bring your boyfriend in. Maybe I can help."

"I got fifty big ones burnin' a hole in my bag."

Alejandro's eyes shifted to take in the large purse she was carrying over her shoulder. Fifty thousand dollars. And no Rafael around to warn him that this might be a trap.

Fifty thousand.

For a second or two he was tempted.

Then he thought — what would Rafael do?

Rafael would say no. He was always warning Alejandro to be ultra careful.

"Can't help you, foxy lady," he said, reminding himself that since he didn't know her, maybe he shouldn't risk it.

Sonia gave a casual shrug. "Didn't think you could," she said, downing the rest of her champagne. "Guess I'll see ya around, big boy," she added, getting to her feet.

Then she was gone, vanishing into a sea of writhing bodies on the dance floor.

Alejandro was pissed at himself. He'd turned down a deal that a month ago he would've gone for. The problem was that since Frankie's arrest, he understood — reluctantly — that he had to be more careful. The bitch DA was out to get him, and no way was he allowing that to happen.

The two blondes were hovering nearby. He gestured for them to return to his table.

They did so, giggling and nudging each other.

Two blondes were better than a hot Puerto

Rican. Or were they?

Alejandro decided it was time to find out.

CHAPTER FORTY-ONE

Secrets. So many of them. Too many to absorb. Papers, multiple contracts, a shiny black Glock, numerous family photos, jewelry, watches, stacks of cash, letters, deeds, stock certificates. Also in the box were the photographs Lucky had expected to find. The pornographic photos of Marabelle Blue. Incriminating photos of the sexy blond movie star in compromising positions with several high-powered politicians — including Peter Richmond, Lucky's ex-father-in-law, a man who had recently announced his aspirations to run for president.

Ah yes, Lucky thought — blackmail photos should Gino ever decide to use them.

Had he used the photos for his own gain? She didn't know and she never would.

There were more photos — ones she had not seen before. Among them were a series of extremely graphic nude photos of Paige, plus several more of Paige cavorting with a mix of different women and men. The photos were compromising, to say the least.

Why had Gino wanted her to have these photos? It was puzzling. Was she supposed to destroy them? Or did he expect her to keep them should *she* ever need to use them? The ones of Paige she decided to keep, just in case. Everything else she returned to the boxes to be dealt with at another time.

It was all too much, and with everything going on, she didn't care to think about it until things were calmer and she could concentrate. She had other matters to concern her. Beverly had asked her to arrange a money transfer for Bobby's bail. Chris Warwick had texted to say he was on his way back from Palm Springs with information. At least she'd spoken to Max, and that was a relief.

She buzzed Mrs. Crisp, returned the boxes to the safe-deposit wall, then got in her Ferrari and headed home.

On the way she received a text from Danny telling her that Lennie, Gino Junior, and Leo were at the house. He also mentioned that he was busy securing accommodations for everyone, plus putting together funeral services at the Magiriano and organizing a huge celebratory party, which would take place after the funeral.

Who was coming?

The family first and foremost. And there were so many friends and acquaintances who would expect to be there.

Suddenly she was overcome with a wave of emotion. Pulling her Ferrari to a stop by the side of the road, she took a few moments to reflect on everything.

Gino . . . Gino . . . Gino. Was he now reunited with Maria, the love of his life? Was he peaceful and content? Was he watching over her and his grandchildren, protecting them all from harm?

She wanted to cry, but she couldn't. Once again, she knew that she had to be strong. Above all else, she had a job to do. And that job was to find Gino's killer.

"Gotta get back to work," Lennie was quick to tell her when she returned home. "Everyone's in the editing bay except me, and it's my movie."

"How was lunch?"

"Those boys ate like a couple of cowboys coming off a weeklong fast," he joked. "They sure got big appetites."

"Glad to hear it."

"The good news is they're doing okay. They're a couple of tough little shits."

"Of course they are," she said with a soft smile.

"And you, my beautiful wife — how about you?"

She shrugged. "I guess I'm surviving," she replied, feeling the sadness envelop her like a heavy cloak.

"Always the survivor, right?"

"You got it," she said with a wry smile. "I've decided that's going to be my mantra from now on."

"How come you didn't tell me you were going out? Where'd you go?"

"I drove down the coast. Had to clear my head."

"Listen, Lucky," he said, giving her a long stern look. "Do me a favor and don't go doing that again without security. We're in a scary situation. Somebody's out to get this family, and who knows — you could be their next target."

"C'mon, Lennie," she said, summoning her strength. "Stop being so dramatic."

"Bullshit," he shot back at her. "You know I'm right."

"What you should do is get back to work," she insisted. "Everything's fine."

"In your world it always is."

"Okay," she said, determined to change the subject. "Bringing you up to date, I should tell you that I posted bail for Bobby, *and* I spoke to Max."

"About time. Is she on her way back?"

"I told her it was best if she flew home for the funeral. Right now she's in Rome doing some big-deal modeling campaign that she's all excited about."

"That's great. As long as she's happy, that's all that matters."

"She sounds as if she is."

"Okay, then, so she'll come back for the funeral. When will that be?"

"As soon as they release Gino's body I'll set a firm date. So now — please — get your ass out of here and go edit your movie. You know you want to."

"Only if you're absolutely sure you don't need me," he said, putting his arms around her.

"I don't," she said, gently pushing him away. "I can assure you that everything's under control."

"You — my beautiful, stubborn wife — are something else," he said, shaking his head as he turned to leave.

She gave a wan smile. "I know."

By the time she went looking for the boys, they'd bonded with two of the security guards. One of the guards asked if they could take the boys surfing. She gave her permission and off they all went.

How resilient the young were. Whatever life threw at them, they bobbed right back. She remembered that at sixteen she'd been exactly the same.

She called Beverly to inform her that the wire transfer had been sent. Beverly promised that she'd have Bobby out of jail within the hour.

Danny was in his makeshift office. He handed her a long list of people who'd called offering their condolences. She studied the list for a moment before deciding that the only person she felt like calling back was Venus, although there were many others she knew she should talk to. Eventually. Not now. It was too soon.

She headed for her study. It was her favorite room, filled with books, DVDs of movies she'd enjoyed, and family photos. French doors opened onto a spacious balcony overlooking the ocean. The tide was in, and the waves were breaking close to the shore.

The Malibu house was a place filled with peacefulness and love. It was her special retreat away from the craziness of Vegas.

Taking out her phone, she was happy to reach Venus.

"You do know how much I loved Gino," Venus whispered softly. "He was always my secret crush from the very first moment I met him."

"I know," Lucky replied, glad that Venus sounded like her old self. "I had to practically handcuff you to keep you away from him."

"Ah . . . if only I could've gotten rid of Paige . . ." Venus sighed.

"If only," Lucky agreed. "Although having *you* as my stepmom would not have been my lifelong dream."

"And having Paige as a stepmom was?" Venus said archly.

"Don't even go there," Lucky warned. "That woman is toxic. Her true colors are finally shining through."

"Can't wait to hear."

"The funeral service and following party will be in Vegas at the Magiriano," Lucky said, refusing to linger on the subject of Paige. "You'll be there?"

"What do *you* think?" Venus replied. "And if you need me before that, I'm around. Still shooting in Vegas. You can call me any time of the day or night."

"I might do that."

Lucky clicked off, contemplating how comforting it was to have her friend back — the Venus she knew and loved.

It occurred to her that she'd never had many close friends — plenty of acquaintances and business associates, but true loyal friends were hard to come by. Unfortunately, most people wanted something from her, and that wasn't cool.

Not that she'd missed out on anything. Lennie was her very *best* friend, and he and their family came first, then her work. Whether it was running a movie studio or building hotels, she had a passion for both. Now she was planning on combining them. She was going to build an amazing complex incorporating a grand hotel, luxurious apartments, and, most exciting of all, a magnificent state-of-the-art movie studio.

Once again she thought about how much Gino would've loved this concept. She'd so looked forward to telling him, listening to his advice and ideas.

The sad truth was that the dream was no longer possible. Gino was gone. Forever.

Danny knocked on the door. "Chris is here," he said.

"Tell him to come in," she replied, impatient to hear what Chris had come up with. He'd never let her down, and she was sure he wasn't about to start now.

It was time to find out the truth.

And when she did, it would be time to take her revenge.

CHAPTER FORTY-TWO

The desk clerk returned Bobby's belongings to him, throwing him a contemptuous look, as if to say, *You'll be back, rich boy.*

Bobby felt his jaw tighten, but he said nothing. What was the point?

Beverly was there to meet him. She was accompanied by two burly security men, and even though she'd warned him that he was all over the newspapers, he was not prepared for the onslaught of press waiting to pounce when they stepped outside. They came at him like vultures claiming their last meal.

Keeping a firm grip on his arm, Beverly instructed him not to say a word as they pushed and shoved their way to the car.

He didn't. He stared straight ahead, not even blinking as a flurry of flashbulbs blinded him while several snarky TV reporters shoved mics in his face.

Jibes about his family were thrown at him.

"Read that your gangster granddaddy just got his head blown off. Care to comment?"

"How's your mama doin'? Wasn't Lucky accused of killing someone way back?"

"Wassit like to be connected?"

"You kill that girl, Bobby?"

"Think you're gonna walk on this one?"

Beverly and security hustled him into the back of an SUV with blacked-out windows. He slumped down, feeling like shit. Over the years, he'd managed to keep a low profile. He'd never courted the press or done publicity to gain attention for his clubs. M.J. had been the public face of Mood, while he'd always stayed in the background. Occasionally he'd been mentioned on Page Six of the *New York Post* as one of the most eligible bachelors in town, but usually he flew under the radar.

This was different. This was a game changer, and he realized that he was going to have to deal with it whether he liked it or not.

It was more than upsetting considering that everything he'd achieved, he'd managed to do without any help from his family. Sure, he was privileged and came from great wealth, but so what? That didn't mean he was automatically guilty. Things had been going so well, and now this had happened.

He sat in the back of the SUV mulling over how he *should* have dealt with the girl in the red dress. Was there anything he could have done differently?

First off, why the hell had he agreed to drive her to the hotel? Why hadn't he summoned a member of the waitstaff to do so, or one of the parking attendants?

Oh yeah, deep down he knew why. Because she was hot.

Damn it, he hadn't planned on making a move, yet she'd acted so persuasive and seductive that he hadn't been able to resist driving her himself. Bad move.

Even worse, when they'd arrived at the hotel, he'd accompanied her upstairs to her suite. Why had he done that?

Because she'd fed him some pathetic story about being scared — was that why?

Shit! In the back of his mind had he been planning on fucking her?

No! Definitely not.

His inner voice piped up in his head: *You sure about that?*

"We're here," Beverly said.

"Where?" Bobby muttered.

"Your hotel. I thought you'd want to take a shower and get something to eat before we go to the airport."

"I can leave the state?" he asked, surprised.

"The state, not the country. You're going to have to surrender your passport."

"Jeez!" he said, caustically. "Just as I was planning on running off to Bora-Bora."

"Glad to see you haven't lost your sense of humor," Beverly drawled.

Bobby gave her a wry smile. "It's about all I got left right now."

The SUV pulled up in front of the hotel where he and M.J. were staying. More TV crews and photographers were gathered outside jostling for the best position.

"M.J. and your girlfriend are waiting upstairs," Beverly said. "Take an hour, then we have to leave for the airport. Lucky has arranged a private plane."

"Denver's here?" he said, startled.

"I met her for a minute. She seems like a smart woman," Beverly said.

"She's smart, all right," Bobby said ruefully. "And if I know my girl, she'll be kicking my ass big-time."

"Well," Beverly said, "the two of you will have plenty of opportunity to talk things through because she's flying back to L.A. with us. M.J. has opted to stay in Chicago to make sure the club is up and running. Negative publicity is never good for a new business."

Jesus! Not only had he ruined his own life, he'd probably ruined M.J.'s too.

Why was Denver in Chicago? Had she come to berate him? Tell him what a fuckup he was?

She shouldn't have bothered. He already knew that.

"He's on his way up," M.J. said, clicking off

his cell phone.

"Okay, then," Denver said, crossing her arms across her chest. She was not happy. In fact, she'd been furious ever since M.J. had met her at the airport and told her the whole story.

Yes, Bobby had obviously been set up. Only what kind of a moron would put himself in such a vulnerable position in the first place?

Before seeing M.J. she'd grabbed a newspaper at the airport, and on the front page was a photo of Bobby alongside a photo of the murdered woman taken outside of Mood. A beautiful Latin woman in a low-cut dress with swirls of dark hair and flashing eyes. Nadia Sharai Gómez. According to the paper, a high-end call girl.

Great! The woman Bobby had taken to her hotel was a hooker.

Bobby Santangelo Stanislopoulos. What a fool.

"You okay?" M.J. ventured.

"No, I'm not okay," she answered sharply. "I'm angry at Bobby for allowing himself to get caught in such a ridiculous situation."

"C'mon, Denver. He was drugged."

"Do me a favor and quit with the lame excuses, M.J.," she said impatiently, waving the newspaper in his face. "Look at this woman and tell me exactly *why* he was taking her to her hotel? Planning on playing chess, was he?"

"She was kinda upset," M.J. said, grimacing. "I guess Bobby felt sorry for her."

Denver shot him a withering look. "It's *me* you're talking to, so please don't think I'm buying your inane excuses for Bobby's behavior. It's insulting, and I do not need to have my intelligence insulted on top of everything else."

"Hey," M.J. said, throwing up his hands. "Don't go gettin' all up on me. This is between you an' Bobby."

"I know that."

"Then hand him a break."

"Why should I?" she demanded. "He was going to cheat on me, and you know it."

"Am I interrupting something?" Bobby said, walking in.

"Jesus, man!" M.J. exclaimed, giving him a bro hug. "I'm sure glad to see you."

Denver stood back. She didn't run to him, although she knew that's what she probably should do. After all, she was his girlfriend.

Screw it — he'd betrayed her by taking some woman to her hotel and going up to her suite. The woman had gotten murdered and Bobby had gotten himself arrested. What was she supposed to think?

"Hey," Bobby said, moving toward her. "Didn't expect to see *you* here, but I'm happy you are."

He went to embrace her. She backed away.

"I must look like shit," he said ruefully.

"Whyn't I dive in the shower an' then we can talk."

She nodded blankly. He did look like shit, although even with a stubbled chin and his dark hair awry, he was still the most handsome man she'd ever set eyes on. And he was all hers — or was he? Carolyn's words came back to haunt her. *All men cheat. You really think he doesn't play around?*

Damn it. Bobby wasn't all men. Or perhaps he was. Why would he be any different?

"Yes," she said coolly. "You should do that."

Bobby exchanged a quick look with M.J. as if to say, *What's up with her? I'm the one that's been sitting in jail accused of a crime I didn't commit.*

"Y'know," M.J. said, "I'm gonna take a walk. Let you two catch up."

"You don't have to do that," Denver said, struggling to stay calm, although all she really wanted to do was to scream at Bobby about how stupid he'd been.

"Yeah," M.J. said, "I think I do."

He left quickly, leaving them alone.

For once Denver was at a loss. Here she was with the love of her life, who'd just been released from jail, and all she could think about was the fact that he'd been planning on sleeping with somebody else. A woman who'd picked him up in the club — and with whom he'd gone, quite willingly, to her hotel.

A woman who got paid for sex.

Unfortunately, she couldn't think beyond that. All sense of reason had deserted her.

She wished she'd never gotten on a plane and flown to Chicago. Was she crazy — running out on Leon, leaving her job, and doing it without even checking in with her boss?

Yes. She was certifiable for sure.

"Do you want to talk now, or should I take a shower first?" Bobby asked, wondering why she was so damn cold. Didn't she understand what he'd gone through? What was wrong with her?

"I'm not sure I want to talk at all," she said, gritting her teeth.

"Huh?"

"You heard."

"Jesus, Denver, what's up with you?"

"What's up with *me*?" she said resentfully. "I think you know."

"No," he said, starting to lose it. "Whyn't you fill me in?"

They faced each other, both with their own agendas. All Bobby wanted was to take a shower — wash the jail experience away — and have his girlfriend show a little love. While all Denver wanted was to get the hell away from him.

"Fill you in, huh?" she said bitterly. "I'll fill you in, all right. *Why* did you take that woman to her hotel? And why did you go upstairs to her suite? What was *that* about?"

347

"For fuck's sake. I've been accused of murdering someone, and that's all you have to say?"

"I'm a prosecuting attorney, Bobby," she said stiffly. "And if I was handed this case, I'd expect a far better excuse than you being drugged."

"Are you saying you think I'm guilty?" he demanded.

"Not exactly."

A cold fury overcame him. What the fuck! She was actually thinking he could've done it. Was that how much faith she had in him? He couldn't believe it.

Wearily, he shook his head. He didn't need Denver's crap on top of everything. He didn't need his girlfriend giving him long accusatory looks.

"You know what," he said abruptly. "I'm taking a shower. You can do whatever the fuck you want."

"Great!" she retaliated. "That's exactly what I'll do."

Gathering up her purse, she stalked from the room, only to regret it the moment she was in the elevator on her way downstairs.

Why hadn't she let him tell his side of the story?

Why had she acted like a jealous girlfriend?

She'd never considered herself to be the jealous type; she'd always scoffed at girls who were. Now she'd turned into one herself, and it was driving her to act out of character, to abandon the man she loved. She'd flown to Chicago to be by his side, and now she wasn't. *Damn it!*

M.J. caught her in the lobby. "Where're you goin'?" he asked.

"Back to L.A.," she snapped. "I have a job to do."

"Thought you were flyin' with Bobby."

"You thought wrong."

"You're makin' a mistake."

"Really?" she said, shooting him an angry look — for surely he must have been aware that Bobby had left the club to screw that woman? Had M.J. known she was a call girl? Too bad that the woman had gotten herself murdered before Bobby had had a chance to seal the deal.

"Think about it, Denver," M.J. insisted. "You gotta know that Bobby is innocent."

"Thanks for the info," she answered coolly. "Oh, and the truth is, I'm over it, so do me a big favor and tell Bobby good-bye for me."

CHAPTER FORTY-THREE

Cookie, Max's BFF from high school, texted her, and so did her other best friend, Harry. Even her onetime boyfriend Ace got in touch to tell her how sorry he was to hear about Gino. All her L.A. friends were coming through, although she hadn't gotten a word from Athena.

After thinking about it for a while, she realized that Athena probably hadn't heard about Gino's demise, and if she had, it was likely that she didn't care. Why would she? Athena had never met Gino. Besides, she was probably too busy being the "It" girl of the moment in Saint-Tropez. Too caught up in partying the night away and having fun.

Still . . . Max would've appreciated hearing from her.

Back at the hotel, she wandered around feeling sad and depressed until finally it came to her that wallowing in grief was not her style. Gino was gone. There was nothing she could do about it.

Once again she thought about how he would want her to handle herself. *Get out there an' kick some ass,* he'd say. *You're a Santangelo, kid. Do it!*

Lucky had sounded strong on the phone; no tears for *her* mom. Max admired her strength, even if it did at times intimidate her. Lucky had achieved so much in life. How could Max ever hope to compete?

Well . . . for a start she could make a name for herself. And feeling miserable hanging out in a hotel room all by herself was doing nothing to achieve that.

Making a quick decision, she grabbed her phone and called Lorenzo. "What time's the dinner tonight?" she asked. "I've changed my mind — I'm going."

Piccolo Ambrosia was a candlelit restaurant filled with flowers, soft music, and the aroma of delicious food.

Lorenzo escorted Max inside, where the maître d' led them to a private room in the back of the restaurant. A long wooden table was set for twenty people. Seated around the table were the Dolcezza family, including the twins, plus Carlo and a few other people Max did not recognize. Hanging on the wall at one end of the room was a huge blowup photo of Max taken earlier that day. She stared at it in shock. There she was in her jean shorts and crop top, leaning against the plain background, one leg extended, her green eyes staring into the lens. Above the photo in fancy gold lettering was the caption DOLCEZZA — THE FACE OF THE FUTURE.

Max swallowed hard as everyone stood up and applauded her. How had this happened so fast? Carlo's photo was amazing! Was that girl in the photo actually her? Sexy and innocent and fun and freaking *badass*!

"Holy crap!" she mumbled, as Lorenzo steered her to a spot between Alfredo Dolcezza and the dreaded twin, Dante — with his evil eyes and sneery smile.

Alfredo gave her a fatherly pat on the knee. "Is *bella bella, sì*?"

"Wow!" she managed. "Do I really look like that?"

"The magic of Photoshop," Dante said with a disdainful twist of his thin lips, his leg brushing against hers under the table.

"You speak excellent English," she said, determined not to be intimidated by him. "Where did you learn?"

"America," he replied. "I attended college in Los Angeles."

"Really?" she said, trying to look as if she cared. "Where?"

"UCLA. And you, my dear?"

"I decided against college. Not my thing."

Dante raised an eyebrow, as if to say, *Ignorant girl, education is everything.*

It suddenly came to her that he reminded her of a man she'd met on the Internet who'd lured her out of town, kidnapped her, and locked her up. Fortunately, she'd managed to escape, and although it was several years later, Dante was bringing back all the bad memories.

She searched the table to see where Lorenzo was sitting. He was seated down at the far end with the people she didn't know. Across from her sat Carlo, and cuddling up next to him was Natalia, clad in a low-cut dress, her droopy boobs on display while she pawed at Carlo's neck with long scarlet fingernails, obviously marking her territory.

Apparently, after his initial rude remark about Photoshop, Dante had nothing more to say to her. He turned his back and concentrated on the woman sitting to his left. This woman was older and obviously very rich if one was to judge from the large diamonds adorning her ears, neck, and wrists. Dante failed to introduce her, so Max found herself stuck with Alfredo — whose English was sketchy.

Had she made a mistake coming?

Hell no. This dinner was in her honor, so screw the lot of them. She could play too.

Leaning across the table, she managed to attract Carlo's attention. Unfortunately, that wasn't saying much because he was on the way to being totally drunk. And when Carlo drank — as well she knew — he turned into an obnoxious fool.

"Our little Dolcezza girl wishes to speak to you, *mio amore,*" Natalia sneered, nuzzling even closer to Carlo while caressing his face.

Max had a distinct feeling that she and Natalia were not about to bond.

Staring glassy-eyed across the table, Carlo threw Max a crooked smirk. "Ciao, *bella,*" he said, his words on the verge of slurring. "You like our photo?"

"Of course she likes it," Natalia snapped. Then, staring at Max, she added a snippy, "Carlo can make anyone look *bene.* It is his special genius." And with those words she lunged at Carlo, kissing him full on the lips just in case Max hadn't realized that they were indeed a couple.

"Excuse me," Max said to no one in particular. "I'm going to the restroom." She added a silent, *And I might stay there for the rest of the night.*

Pushing her chair away from the table, she got up.

Lorenzo caught up with her at the door leading into the main restaurant. "Is everything fine?" he asked, seeming to actually care.

"Oh yeah, it's totally great," she said, her voice thick with sarcasm. "I'm stuck next to an old man who barely speaks English, and on my other side is Dante the major freako.

Things couldn't be more awesome."

"I am so sorry," Lorenzo said, genuinely upset. "I told Dante I should be seated near to you so I could translate. He informed me it wasn't necessary."

"I'm sure he did," Max said, rolling her eyes. "He *wants* me to feel left out. He hates me and I hate him."

"Understandable," Lorenzo said. "Dante is not a popular man."

"There's no way I'm letting him get to me," Max said. "When we go back to the table, I'm sitting next to you."

"I don't think that's a good —"

"Where's the restroom?" she interrupted. "I need to pee."

"Follow me," Lorenzo said, realizing that when Max set her mind on something, there was no talking her out of it.

The restroom was unisex, something Max discovered when she entered and encountered two men standing at the urinals.

Lorenzo could've warned me, she thought. *This is totally bizarre and kind of crazy.*

The men zipped up and left, barely glancing in her direction. Someone else was entering and she quickly ducked into a stall and tried to lock the door, only the lock didn't work and she wasn't about to be caught peeing by some hairy Italian man — or even worse, Dante.

Thoughts ran through her head. Lucky, the

funeral, Bobby. She missed her family and friends in L.A. Both Cookie and Harry had promised to come to the funeral. Ace? Maybe, although she'd heard he had a new girlfriend.

Sticking one leg against the door should anyone try to enter, she quickly peed and exited the stall.

A man was standing at the urinals.

Trying to avoid looking at him, she moved over to the sink and began to wash her hands.

The man finished what he was doing and turned around.

Their eyes met in the mirror above the sink.

Max gasped.

The man stopped in his tracks.

They both spoke at once —

"Max?"

"Billy?"

And for one brief second, everything was right in the world.

CHAPTER FORTY-FOUR

Alejandro had a perversion that never failed to give him a charge. And with Willow off somewhere doing her own thing and Rafael out of town, Alejandro gave Matias an order to bring him the girls.

Locked in his office above the club, he swilled vodka from the bottle while crushing up an ecstasy pill, which he proceeded to mix with a gram of coke.

He was in the mood for some entertainment. It was too bad the Puerto Rican girl hadn't stuck around. The two blondes bored him. The Puerto Rican with her sassy attitude and big ass presented far more of a challenge. He bet she would've gotten off on the show he was about to view. Yeah, she would've loved it.

Lying back on his couch, he buzzed Matias to bring in the girls.

There were two of them. Two nondescript girls who nobody would ever suspect were drug mules. One tall. One short. Not pretty.

Not ugly. Girls who transported heroin and cocaine affixed to their bodies in plastic baggies, sometimes jammed inside their bodies.

Alejandro knew them both. They had been working for him for several months, and neither of them had ever gotten caught.

Every other Monday the girls came in and did their thing. Alejandro got off on the show, and the girls got off on the money they were making.

The only other person — apart from Matias — who knew about his interaction with the girls was Frankie. Frankie had been into it just as much as he was.

"Ladies," Alejandro said, stroking his chin.

"Boss," the tall one replied. She had stringy brown hair and thin lips.

"How was your trip?" Alejandro inquired, like he gave a damn.

"Easy," the short one boasted. She had permed hair and rosy-red cheeks.

The two of them were paid excellent money. And if they were caught, they had no idea who he was. Every time Matias brought them to his office, they were blindfolded and taken upstairs through a back entrance. They only knew Alejandro as the boss.

The two girls lived deep in the Valley. Matias had recruited them — he was adept at that sort of thing. Girls trusted Matias, being that he was young and not bad-looking. After six months, he would dump these two and recruit two new girls.

"Let the show begin," Alejandro said, leaning back on his couch, his hand lingering near his crotch.

The girls knew the routine only too well. They stood in front of the boss and slowly began to disrobe. The tall one wore baggy jeans and an oversized T-shirt. The short one wore a loose dress. Under their clothes — from thighs to chest — were bags of heroin strapped to their bodies.

Alejandro ordered them to get completely naked except for the drugs. They obliged — willingly — for the money they got paid was more than they'd ever imagined.

When they were both naked, Alejandro hauled himself off the couch and approached them. His kick was removing the packets of drugs from their bodies himself — ripping away the tape, getting off on the way they squealed like two little piglets.

Two verging-on-plain naked women. And yet they gave him more of a sexual charge than all of the beautiful starlets put together.

Satisfaction guaranteed.

Sam's puppy was driving Willow nuts with its constant whining and scratching at the floorboards.

I am not a dog person, she thought, tossing around on her bed with restless abandon. *I hate dogs, and I hate Sam's script. This movie is my big comeback. Can I pull it off? Will it ever happen?*

Eddie Falcon had told her what to do. "Tell Sam you love his script," he'd instructed. "I'll have someone do a fast rewrite, an' we'll use Sam's name — which right now means something."

"I promised him he could direct," she'd informed Eddie, who'd snapped back that it was the dumbest thing he'd ever heard.

"It was the only way I could get him to commit," she'd countered, annoyed that Eddie was insinuating that she was dumb.

"Sam's a naive schmuck," Eddie had said. "All we need from him is his name. I'll get up a deal memo you'll have him sign."

"What if he wants a lawyer involved?" she'd asked, well aware that she had to trust Eddie.

"He won't," Eddie had said brusquely.

Since it was past midnight, she wondered if Sam was back. She called him on his cell. "Where are you?" she asked.

"LAX. Landed five minutes ago."

"Then get your ass in your car an' come pick up your mutt," she said impatiently. "Your little puppy is cute, but it's driving me loco. It misses you."

"Did you feed her?" Sam asked.

"With what?" she asked, frowning. "It's not as if you left me any dog food."

"Okay, okay. I'm on my way."

■ ■ ■ ■

Arriving in Colombia in the middle of the night, Rafael was tired and irritable. One of Pablo's many guards met him at the airport and drove him in a bulletproof sedan to Pablo's enormous estate outside of town.

The estate was a fortress, surrounded by high walls topped with barbed wire, mounted security cameras, guard stations, and several fierce pit bulls locked in cages — cages that could be opened by the press of a button should Pablo even suspect there was an intruder on the premises.

Pablo ruled his empire with an iron fist, instilling fear in all who worked for him. He had only one weakness, and that was women. Unlike his son, Alejandro, he truly loved them. However, his love was transient, depending on how long they satisfied him. This meant that women came and went as if they were revolving doors.

Pablo favored beauty queens. Young beautiful girls with flashing smiles, endless legs, long luxuriant hair, and taut big-breasted bodies.

"I surround myself with exquisite things, including women," he often boasted. And when there was not a woman in residence, he fucked his long-suffering housekeeper, Eugenia, Rafael's mother.

Once a beauty queen herself, Eugenia was no longer beautiful. This did not bother Pablo, for he owned her, therefore he treated her like a comfortable old couch that was always ready for him to collapse on top of whenever he was in the mood.

Unfortunately for Rafael, his mother worshipped Pablo, and refused to even contemplate leaving the drug lord's employ. This infuriated Rafael, for his dream was to take off with Elizabetta, Rafael Junior, and Eugenia, and get as far away from Pablo as possible.

In his heart he knew that his mother was serious. She would never leave Pablo, and it saddened him that his mama was a slave to such a tyrant.

Because of the late hour, Rafael realized that he would not be able to visit Elizabetta and his son until the next day. They did not live in Pablo's closely guarded compound; they resided with Elizabetta's mother in a small house a twenty-minute drive away.

Rafael was relieved that they had no immediate contact with the arrogant and dangerous drug lord. On the other hand, he was puzzled that Pablo had no wish to keep his grandson close. The truth was that if Pablo refused to acknowledge that he, Rafael, was his son, then why would he give a second thought to young Rafael Junior?

"Señor Diego will see you at the stables at

eight A.M.," the driver informed him, stopping the car outside steep marble steps that led to the massive bulletproof front door.

Rafael got out of the car and climbed the steps, and even though it was late, Eugenia was there to greet him. She opened the front door, flung her arms around him, and began whispering words of love and affection.

Eugenia was not an educated woman, but she was his mama, and in his own way, he loved her very much.

He often wondered if she would still love him back if she knew some of the things he'd done. The call girl in Chicago came to mind. The man he'd hired had never offered an explanation as to why he'd found it necessary to kill her. The man had simply collected his money via a bank transfer and vanished back into the army of faceless people who were prepared to commit heinous crimes for money.

Frankie Romano was supposed to be next. Rafael was well aware that Alejandro expected him to orchestrate Frankie's punishment in prison. So far he'd done nothing. He didn't have the stomach to arrange another beating that could so easily turn into murder.

Eugenia was carrying on about how grateful she was to have him home, asking why he couldn't visit more often.

Because I'm forced to babysit my douche of a brother, he wanted to say. *Because Pablo*

*insists that I stay by his side to watch over
Alejandro, making sure he stays out of trouble.
That's why.*

Eugenia was full of gossip about how Pablo
had recently gotten rid of his latest girlfriend
— a Colombian TV star whom Eugenia
referred to as a lowlife *puta.*

Rafael decided that this was excellent news,
for if Pablo was without a permanent female
in residence, then perhaps he'd be more open
to sampling the luscious female fruits of Los
Angeles.

Yes, Rafael thought, this was *the* way to
persuade Pablo. The lure of fresh pussy and
being around a movie set.

It was a long shot that might just work.

Willow answered her front door wearing
nothing but an oversized T-shirt bearing the
slogan *If you're gonna suck it — swallow.* The
slogan was accompanied by the image of a
cartoon girl licking a phallic-looking lollipop.

"Where's Lady Gaga?" Sam asked, insinuating himself into her house, his eyes searching for his puppy.

"She's running around somewhere," Willow
said matter-of-factly. "What do you want with
a dog anyway?"

"I like animals," Sam replied. "They can be
a lot nicer than humans. And they're loyal."

"*I'm* loyal," Willow said, pulling on the hem
of her T-shirt, which was threatening to

expose more than the top of her thighs.

Lady Gaga appeared and threw herself at Sam, barking and licking his face as he picked her up.

"I'm gonna have to get a new carpet," Willow complained, coming up behind him.

"Did you read my script?" Sam asked, trying to keep his eyes off her erect nipples, which were offering themselves up like headlights through her almost see-through T-shirt.

"Yes," she responded. "*And* I had a fantastic meeting with Eddie Falcon. He wants to fast-track this as an indie project. No studio involved. No agent. No lawyers. He's getting up a letter of intent for you to sign so we can get started immediately."

"As the director, I'm going to need six weeks' prep time," Sam said. "And casting is imperative."

"Yeah, yeah, Eddie understands all of that," Willow said dismissively. "Eddie knows how to get things done fast with no interference."

"You're sure?"

"Course I'm sure," she said with a confident smile. "This'll be a movie you'll be proud of. I'll get you the deal memo tomorrow." She stretched her arms above her head, revealing her shaved pussy in all its girlish glory.

Sam barely looked. In spite of the erect nipples and exposed pussy, Willow Price was simply not his type. Denver was his type, and he wondered what was going on with her.

One moment she was into him, the next — nothing. It was confusing.

"Since you're here, wanna have a drink?" Willow offered, thinking that it wouldn't be a bad idea to seal the deal sexually with Sam. The thing was, once they got a taste of what she had to offer, they always came back for more.

Sam demurred. "I'm tired," he said. "Long day."

"I could help you relax," she said with a suggestive wink. "We could both do with a little R and R."

"Not tonight," he said.

" 'Not tonight,' " Willow repeated, pouting. "Then when?"

"I'll wait to hear from you."

"That'll be tomorrow."

"Good," Sam said. "Because if this is going to happen, I have a lot to get organized. I'll need preproduction office space, an assistant, and an experienced line producer who can put together a budget and a top-rate crew."

"You got it," Willow said. "Like I told you — Eddie will handle everything."

"Okay, then," Sam said.

"You sure you don't want to stay a while?" she asked, giving him a provocative half smile — the kind of smile most men couldn't resist. After all, she needed him to be on her side when he got the news that she intended to star in his movie. Well, technically it wouldn't be his movie anymore because there would be a whole new script — although maybe he'd still want to direct considering his name would be on it.

"I'll take a pass, Willow," he said, heading briskly for the door.

"Why?" she said, her smile quickly replaced with a sulky frown. "You're not seeing anyone, are you?"

Sam — who had a kind heart — let her down easy. She seemed so eager, almost pathetic in a way. "I'm beat," he explained, managing a fake yawn. "Maybe another time."

"Your choice," she said, shrugging. "Although I can assure you that you have no clue what you're missing."

He had a feeling that he knew exactly what he was missing.

Before she could say another word, he and Lady Gaga were out the door.

Rafael lay on top of the bed in the guest room rehearsing in his mind what he would say to Pablo.

Your son wishes to become a movie producer.
It is an excellent way to launder money.
Your son requires millions of dollars to achieve this.

Fine. Yes, he would say these things, because if he didn't, Alejandro would send the filthy sex tape to Elizabetta. Although what he really wanted to say was:

Your son is a sex-crazed fool.

Your son is a blackmailing sick pervert.

Your son is heading toward big trouble.

You picked the wrong son to inherit your kingdom.

Unfortunately, he couldn't say those things. He was forced to eat shit and convince Pablo to hand over enough money to keep Alejandro satisfied.

Life was unfair, and nobody realized it more than Rafael.

CHAPTER FORTY-FIVE

"I can always depend on you," Lucky said, offering Chris a cold beer. "You never let me down."

"I try not to," he replied, twisting the cap off the bottle. "It's all a question of reading people. Cops don't have the time to get into it, especially when they've got dozens of houses to canvas."

"Yet you do it so easily," she said, springing open a can of 7-Up.

"I understand people," Chris said quietly. "I spot their weaknesses."

"Which is *why* you do it so well."

"Maybe."

"Now, don't go getting all modest on me," she said with a warm smile. "That's not your style."

"Put a little effort into it, and one can find out plenty," he answered, taking a swig of beer.

"So . . ." she said, eager to hear what he had to say. "What exactly *did* you find out?"

"There's something I have to show you," he said, producing a DVD.

"What's on it?" she asked, feeling a shiver of apprehension.

"You'll see. But in the meantime, I was wondering if Lennie is around?"

"Why do we need Lennie?"

" 'Cause I think you might want him with you when you view this."

"Lennie's working," she said impatiently. "And it's *me* you're talking to. I don't need Lennie or anyone else holding my hand, never have."

"If you're sure . . ."

"For God's sake," she said roughly. "What's on the goddamn DVD?"

"I got it from one of the neighbors," Chris said. "It's of the crime scene, so I don't know if —"

Gesturing toward her computer, Lucky said, "Let's get on with it, shall we?"

Chris inserted the DVD into the computer.

After a few moments, an image appeared on the screen, revealing the front area of a house and the sidewalk beyond. Blue skies. Palm trees. Perfect landscaping. Solid iron gates.

The gates slowly opened and a dark-gray repair truck drove through them.

Lucky leaned forward as an attractive woman in a short floral dress emerged from the house and ran to greet the muscular man getting out of his truck. They embraced in a very sexual way before vanishing into the house, arms entwined.

"Christi Yassan," Chris said. "Husband's out of town. Boyfriend comes to visit. Which explains why she wasn't prepared to give this to the cops."

"But she gave it to you?"

"I have a way with people."

Lucky waited, holding her breath, for she knew what was to come next.

There was a clear view of the empty sidewalk — nobody on it. Until . . . Gino and Paige came walking into the frame. Gino, so robust and alive in his tracksuit and tennis shoes. Gino. *Her* Gino. Ninety-something and still bouncing around as if he were twenty years younger. Paige strutted beside him in a bright yellow jogging outfit, wearing overly large shades, her frizzy red hair gleaming in the morning sun. It appeared that Gino was speaking, but there was no sound on the DVD. Lucky couldn't help wondering if Gino was telling Paige that he was coming to Vegas the following weekend, and that she wouldn't be accompanying him.

Then a man came into view. A medium-height man dressed all in black, with dark-lensed sunglasses, a full beard, and a baseball cap pulled low obscuring his face. Watching the screen closely, Lucky took in every detail. The man had dark skin and a barely noticeable limp. On his feet were gray Nike tennis shoes with a white stripe down the side. He didn't look American, more European. She noticed the flash of a silver wristwatch. He was heading toward Gino and Paige, passing them before walking out of the shot.

She saw that Gino glanced over his shoulder and stopped to say something to Paige.

Was he suspicious? Had there been something about the stranger that alarmed him?

She'd never know, because Paige pulled on his arm and they continued walking all the way out of the shot.

For a few seconds the screen was empty, except for a profusion of tall palm trees swaying in the breeze. Then the man in black came back onto the screen, retracing his steps.

Lucky held her breath. The inevitable was about to happen and there was nothing she could do to stop it.

Choking back a swirl of emotions, she watched as the man raised his gun and pulled the trigger before turning and walking calmly away, like killing a man was no big deal.

Everything was still for a moment, her mind refusing to compute what she had seen.

It was like a silent movie. A deadly silent movie.

"Who is he?" she muttered at last.

"I have someone working over at face recognition," Chris said. "It won't be easy identifying him. There's not much to see."

Lucky was quiet for a moment before speaking. "I . . . want . . . him . . . dead," she said at last, her voice cold as ice.

"No, you don't," Chris argued. "You want him alive so he can tell us who ordered the hit."

"And *then* I want him fucking *dead,*" Lucky said. "He shot my father, and he will pay for it with his life."

Later, after Chris had left and everyone was home, there was dinner on the terrace. Lennie barbecued steaks, while Lucky tried to put on a normal face for the boys' sake, although it seemed they were doing fine, jostling and wrestling with each other while playing games on their iPhones.

She understood that they didn't really get it. She'd tried to shield them from the truth, saying that Gino's death was the result of a robbery gone wrong. As far as the boys were concerned, death was something that happened to old people, so to them the loss of Gino was inevitable.

"Your uncle Steven gets here tomorrow," Lucky announced. "Anyone want to come to the airport with me?"

"We're goin' surfing again," Gino Junior said, quickly adding, "If that's okay, Mom?"

"Sure it is. Seems like you're having fun," Lucky replied, thinking how like his grandfather Gino Junior looked. The same unruly mop of black hair, the same features. She'd named him well. Gino Junior was pure Santangelo.

"Beats school," Gino Junior said, with a cheeky grin. "Course, I'm way better than Leo. He falls off every time."

"No freakin' way," Leo argued. "You like *stink.*"

"Get it together, boys," Lennie ordered. "The thing to remember is that it's not a competition, it's a sport. It doesn't matter who's the best."

"Oh yes it does!" Gino Junior yelled. "Leo sucks. He sucks at everything big-time."

"Okay, okay — too much noise," Lucky said. "You want security to take you for ice cream?"

"Can I drive?" Gino Junior demanded.

"You got a permit?" Lennie asked.

"Not yet."

"Then no way."

"C'mon, Dad," Gino Junior whined. "Why not? Nobody's gonna know."

"*I'll* know. That's enough. Now get your asses out of here."

The boys ran off. When she was sure they'd gone, Lucky sat down and told Lennie about the DVD.

"Did you hand it over to the cops?" he asked.

"What do *you* think?" she responded.

"I think you didn't," he said with a weary sigh, knowing exactly where this conversation was going.

"Damn right I didn't," she said, challenging him with her dark eyes. "They won't do anything with it."

"Jesus, Lucky," he groaned.

"Don't worry," she said calmly. "I'm handling this myself."

"Yeah, and that's what frightens me."

"You don't have to be involved. I can deal with it on my own."

Shaking his head, he turned away, resigned to the fact that there was nothing he could do or say. His wife was Lucky Santangelo, and like the old Sinatra song, she did it her way. There was nobody in the world who could stop her.

CHAPTER FORTY-SIX

By the time Bobby had taken a shower and changed his clothes, M.J. was back upstairs in the hotel room.

"What did I do?" Bobby raged, pacing around the room. "What *the fuck* did I do except get myself caught in a shit situation?"

"Hey, you know Denver better than anyone," M.J. said, attempting to soften the blow. "She's impulsive. She'll get over it."

"Over *what,* for crissake?" Bobby said, running a hand through his thick black hair. "Was *she* the one in jail? Is *she* the one who just lost their grandfather? Shit, M.J. Denver's not the woman I thought she was."

"You gotta give her props for flyin' to Chicago to be with you," M.J. pointed out. "That's something."

"Yeah, she flew here to fucking accuse me of God knows what," Bobby said, still steaming. "She's under the impression I was trying to get laid."

"It kinda does look that way. . . ."

"Fuck you, M.J. You *know* what happened."

"I do, 'cause I was there. The thing is, to an outsider —"

"She's not an outsider!" Bobby yelled. "She's my fucking girlfriend."

"Stay cool, my man. It's all gonna work out."

"You think?"

"We are on the road to you being vindicated of all charges," M.J. stated confidently. "This'll be over soon."

"Says you," Bobby muttered.

"Says your lawyer," M.J. said with a decisive nod. "Beverly's waiting for you in the lobby. I like her style — she knows what she's doin'."

"I hope so," Bobby said. " 'Cause being locked up is something I never want to repeat."

"An' you never will," M.J. assured him, as if he were the oracle of everything. "Beverly's got a team workin' on findin' out why this happened to you. An' I spoke to Lucky. She's sendin' that PI she works with to Chicago. He's on a plane now."

"Chris Warwick?"

"That's the dude."

"He's good."

"That's why she's sending him. We have footage from the security cameras at the club. We got images of the guy who Nadia claimed was her cousin. He shouldn't be that hard to track."

Bobby clenched his jaw. "I can't believe she was a call girl," he said.

"Yeah, she fooled both of us. An' I'm here to tell you that if you hadn't gone for her, I would've taken a shot."

"Get this straight, M.J.," Bobby said evenly. "I didn't *go* for her. I was helping out."

"Sure."

Bobby decided not to get into it with M.J. He knew what it must have looked like.

Good Samaritan or horndog?

There was no way he'd ever know.

"I should call Lucky," he said.

"Do whatever you feel like, man," M.J. said. "It's your life, an' you just got it back."

Denver flew to L.A. alone and full of regrets. She regretted losing her cool. She regretted not being more understanding. Worst of all, she hadn't even told Bobby how sorry she was about Gino, and knowing how much the old man had meant to him, that was an unforgivable mistake.

She was so mad at herself. Bobby must hate her for behaving like an unfeeling, jealous bitch.

Now what? Bobby was on his way back to L.A. Would he come to the house? Or had he had enough of her?

The overweight man sitting next to her on the plane attempted conversation. He smelled of stale cigarette smoke and cheap aftershave.

378

She politely shut him down.

Her thoughts were flying everywhere. Not only had she ruined everything with Bobby, Leon was probably pissed as hell, not to mention her boss.

You screwed up big-time, she scolded herself. *I thought you were supposed to be so damn smart.*

Yeah, smart as a fourth grader.

Arriving at LAX, she decided not to go home. Instead she took a cab to Carolyn's, thinking she might stay the night.

It was lesbian charade night, and eight pairs of female eyes stared curiously at her as Carolyn enacted a movie title in front of them.

The only person she knew was Carolyn's partner, Vanessa, who got up and beckoned her into the kitchen.

"Thank goodness you're here," Vanessa — a comely blond woman with a bountiful figure — said. "I am *so* over game night. I only suffer through it for Carolyn," she added, reaching for a half-full bottle of red wine on the kitchen counter. She filled two glasses, one of which she thrust at Denver. "Drink up," she encouraged. "You look as if you need it."

"I do?" Denver said, thinking that, yes, a drink was exactly what she needed.

"So, sweet pea," Vanessa said. "Carolyn tells me you've got a hunch that Bobby's cheating on you."

Oh my God, Denver thought. *What is wrong with Carolyn? Why is she sharing?*

"All men are pigs," Vanessa said with an affirmative nod. "You simply have to decide how much piggery you're prepared to put up with."

"Bobby is not a pig," Denver said defensively.

"Handsome men are the worst cheaters of all," Vanessa continued matter-of-factly. "They feel it's their right. And I should know — I was married to the biggest cheater of all. He didn't care if the sex was with a man or a woman. Lovely, huh?"

Denver tried to think of an exit strategy, for this was exactly the kind of conversation she did not wish to have, especially now when she was feeling so conflicted.

"I didn't mean to interrupt your game night," she said quickly.

"Like I told you — I hate game night," Vanessa complained, making a face. "And you, sweet pea, are the perfect distraction."

"Carolyn seems to be busy, so I guess I'll be going. Can you tell her I'll call her in the morning?"

"Don't go," Vanessa pleaded, leaning drunkenly across the kitchen counter and placing a warm hand over Denver's. "You and I should get to know each other better."

Denver was horrified. Was Carolyn's partner

coming on to her? It certainly felt like she was.

"Uh, I'm sorry," she said quickly, pulling her hand away. "I really have to go."

Vanessa gave her a long, meaningful look. "Have you ever crossed over?" she asked, lowering her voice. "Ever taken a walk on the wild side?"

"Excuse me?" Denver said, feigning innocence.

"Well . . ." Vanessa continued with a suggestive wink. "If you haven't, I can take you places no man has even thought of." She let out a knowing chuckle. "Multiple orgasms, here we come!"

"Uh . . . I'm not sure if this is a conversation we should be having," Denver said, placing her wineglass on the counter. "Quite frankly, I find it inappropriate and awkward. You're Carolyn's partner, and she's my best friend."

"I'm sure she's told you we're not exclusive," Vanessa revealed with another throaty chuckle. "Carolyn wouldn't mind. . . ."

"Oh for God's sake!" Denver exclaimed, making a dash for the kitchen door. "I'm out of here. Good night."

On the flight back to L.A., Bobby made a futile attempt to get some sleep. It was important that he have his wits about him. He had an urgent need to regain control of his life, for being locked up had left him feeling humiliated and helpless, a feeling he had not enjoyed. Denver hadn't helped with her fleeting visit full of accusations. She was a deputy DA, for crissake. Shouldn't she be trying to help him discover how this had happened to him? Wasn't that her job?

Instead she'd acted out *her* frustrations and to hell with how *he* felt.

Fuck Denver. Fuck women in general. He was angry and sad and there was no Gino to give him wise counsel. Gino was gone. It didn't seem possible, and yet it was true.

He'd had no time to grieve, to find out exactly how it had all gone down. All he knew was that he no longer had a grandfather, and it was a painful thought.

Soon he would be with his mom and the rest of his family. He couldn't wait to feel safe again.

CHAPTER FORTY-SEVEN

"What are *you* doing here?" Max asked, her heart racing with excitement.

"What am *I* doing here?" Billy said, staring at her. "How about *you*?"

"Washing my hands," she answered lamely, taking in every inch of his dirty-blond masculine beauty. Oh God! He was as gorgeous as ever, with his crystal blue eyes and deep surfer's tan. Six-foot-tall Billy Melina. Ex-husband of Lucky's best friend, Venus. Major movie star. Max's first real lover.

And . . . a cowardly asshole who'd dumped her on the advice of his so-called "team," who didn't think it was advantageous for his career to be hooking up with Lucky Santangelo's teenage daughter, especially in light of the scandal that had taken place at the Keys, involving a murder and a robbery during which Billy had gotten his cheek slashed.

The best plastic surgeon in L.A. had taken care of his face.

His advisers had taken care of distancing

him from Max.

"You're lookin' fantastic, Green Eyes," he said, fixing her with "the look."

The look involved his intense blue eyes gazing into hers as if she were the only girl in the world.

She knew the look well. It was the same look he used on his costars. The same look he used in photo shoots. It was the famous Billy Melina look that had women the world over fantasizing about what it would be like to make love to him. It was the classic movie-star look.

Max cleared her throat while attempting to compose herself. She was older and wiser since last they'd met. She no longer harbored a teenage crush. He'd dumped her, plain and simple, and even though she'd tried to move on, it still hurt, and she still had feelings for him. He'd broken her heart, crushed her, and now here he was again like nothing had ever happened.

Simply being in his presence was devastating, yet at the same time her heart was continuing to pound and she couldn't help flashing onto the first time they'd made love on the beach in Malibu while an out-of-control party she'd thrown while her parents were away was raging up at the house. What a night that had been. Going all the way for the first time, lying on a moonlit beach with the surf pounding, and Billy's arms around her, his body pressed tightly against hers.

It was a night she would never forget.

But she had to, didn't she?

No more heartbreak.

No more Billy.

"Thanks," she said to Billy, going for a flippant approach.

"Hey — I mean it," he said, edging closer to her, his blue eyes doing their best to draw her in.

Quickly she backed away from the sink. "All yours," she said, striving to sound as if she didn't give a damn. "I gotta get back inside."

"Who're you with?"

"Friends," she answered vaguely.

"I flew in this morning with my publicist and a couple of execs on the movie I'm about to start shooting. I was thinkin' that if I got rid of them, you and I could go for a drink."

"No. Thanks anyway," she said crisply.

"How come?" he asked, looking surprised.

"Hmm . . ." she said, tapping her chin with her index finger. "What if we were *caught* together by the paparazzi?"

"Huh?" Billy said, not getting it.

"I mean, I would *hate* to tarnish your image," she continued. "Think of all the damage it could do to your reputation." She thought about saying "precious" reputation, then she figured that might be taking it too far.

"C'mon, Max," he said, his expression

perplexed. "You gotta know I had no choice about what happened. Then when Lennie came to see me —"

"What?" she gulped, totally horrified. "Are you telling me that my *dad* visited you?"

"Yeah, the dude was all over me. Read me the freakin' riot act." A long pause. "I thought you knew."

Before she could get her head around *that* stunning piece of information, Lorenzo came into the restroom.

"Are you all right?" he asked, glancing suspiciously at Billy. "I was worried. You have been in here so long."

"Not to worry," Max said, forcing herself to sound casual. "Bumped into an old friend."

"I see," Lorenzo said.

"These unisex bathrooms are something else," Max continued. "You never know who you'll meet." She summoned a big wide grin to show Billy that she couldn't care less about him. "Anyway, Billy," she added. "Totally great running into you. Guess I'll see you around."

"Hey — wait a minute," he said, reaching for her arm.

She jerked away from him, quickly grabbing on to Lorenzo. "Gotta go," she said. "I have people waiting."

" 'People'?" Billy questioned, raising a quizzical eyebrow.

Yes, people, she wanted to yell. *You're not*

the only one with an entourage. I'm about to be famous too.

"Let's go, Lorenzo," she said, because all of a sudden Lorenzo wasn't moving. He'd recognized Billy and was gazing at him with lust in his eyes.

Not gay indeed, Max thought. *Why hide it?*

She gave Lorenzo a sharp nudge. Reluctantly he dragged his gaze away from Billy and escorted her outside.

"Was that —" he began to say.

"Yes," she said, interrupting him. "And for someone who's not gay, you certainly seemed impressed."

Lorenzo blushed.

"What?" Max demanded. "You think I didn't figure it out?"

"I . . . I . . . didn't imagine my sexual orientation was anyone's business except my own," Lorenzo stammered.

"Oh *puh-leeze,*" Max responded. "As if anyone gives a crap in this century. The closet is wide open. In fact," she added, thinking of her friend Harry, "I have the perfect person for you."

"I think I just encountered the perfect person," Lorenzo sighed, going all dreamy-eyed.

"Billy Melina is *so* not gay," Max said firmly. Then it was her turn to blush, for Billy had emerged from the restroom and was standing right behind them.

"No," Billy said, all tousled hair and blazing blue eyes. "Billy Melina is so *not* gay."

As he spoke, Max felt her reserve crumble and her stomach began performing cartwheels. He might've broken her heart into a thousand fragmented pieces, but there was no denying that she still loved him. She couldn't help herself.

Billy grinned. He knew he had her.

Shooting him a filthy look, she dragged Lorenzo back to the private room, ignoring the fact that he was desperate to be introduced to Billy.

Another time. Another place. She couldn't wait to get away.

Alfredo stood as she made her way to her seat at the table. Dante didn't, until Alfredo muttered something to him in Italian, then Dante reluctantly rose and held back her chair so she could squeeze in.

Across the table, Carlo appeared to be glassy-eyed, while Natalia was still draping herself all over him, claiming ownership.

Talk about desperate, Max thought, and for a moment she almost felt sorry for the Italian girl, because if she knew Carlo at all, she knew that there was no way he was the marrying kind.

Lorenzo was hovering at the other end of the table, not sure whether to sit or not.

"Signor Dolcezza," Max said sweetly, beckoning Lorenzo to join her, "is it okay if

Lorenzo comes and sits next to me so he can translate? It's so difficult for me not speaking Italian."

Alfredo got the gist of what she was saying. He summoned one of the waiters to bring another chair. Max made sure that the waiter squeezed the chair between her and Dante. Ha! That would show him.

Dante gave her a mean-spirited look and turned back to speak to his rich older woman.

Why does he hate me? she thought. *What have I done to him except exactly nothing?*

After the main course of medallions of veal, there was an array of delicious desserts — everything from soft, creamy panna cotta to whipped chocolate mousse and strawberry cheesecake.

Max found herself mindlessly eating every-thing in sight. Anything to take her mind off Billy.

Then Alfredo decided to make a speech. He stood up, tapped the side of his glass, gestured toward Max, and spoke glowingly in Italian.

Max knew it was a flattering speech, for Lorenzo translated everything Alfredo said into her ear. Everyone was laughing and clap-ping and toasting her with champagne, which forced her to forget about Billy for a moment as she reveled in the attention. Only for a moment, because who should walk into the private room but Billy himself. He entered the room and stood in the doorway, all six foot one of him, famous smile flashing, blue eyes seeking hers.

"Sorry to interrupt, folks," he drawled, reverting to his Midwestern roots. "The thing is, I couldn't resist congratulating my very special friend here."

As he spoke, he moved toward Max, and everyone went quiet.

Billy Melina. Famous American movie star. Every woman at the table was dumbstruck, including Max, who couldn't believe he was doing this.

She felt the color rising in her cheeks and her heartbeat quickening.

Stay cool, a voice screamed in her head. *Do not fall into his trap again. He's a user. He dumped you once, and he can do it again.*

Across the table she noted Natalia's expression of pure desire. Carlo was a distant memory as Natalia tried to decide how she could gain Billy's attention. Gabriella was beaming, and even Marcella — the stern sister — seemed to be impressed.

Billy reached her seat, bent down, and kissed her on the cheek. "Congrats, Green Eyes," he said. "Always knew you had it in you."

Had what in me? she thought, totally stunned.

"Now, if nobody minds," Billy said. "I'm whisking my girl away. Gotta hunch she needs a break."

And with that, he pulled out her chair, gripped her firmly by the arm, and before she had time to realize what was going on, he had her up and out of there.

So much for making a stand. He'd swept her up in the moment and there was no going back.

CHAPTER FORTY-EIGHT

Most mornings Willow slept late, luxuriating under the covers, reluctant to face the day. What was the point of getting up early when she had no film set to go to? Ever since she was a little kid she'd always been on call — movie role after movie role. No fun-filled childhood for Willow. She was a pint-sized worker bee — the girl with so much potential, until somehow she'd grown up and become known as the party girl. And because of her partying ways, all the worthwhile parts had dried up. She was no longer regarded as reliable — she was Willow Price, the girl with the wild lifestyle that got in the way of her once happening career.

Now with Alejandro by her side and Eddie Falcon helping, things were definitely heading in the right direction.

Today she got up early and immediately called Eddie. His uptight assistant informed her that Mr. Falcon was not available and would call back.

Not available. Really? If she were Jennifer Lawrence or Brad Pitt he'd be totally available.

Next she called Alejandro, who didn't answer.

Damn it. She was up and primed for action, so not being able to reach either of her future partners drove her a little bit nuts.

After popping a Xanax to calm down, she smoked two cigarettes in a row, took a quick shower, then started to watch her favorite DVD, *Magic Mike,* a movie that always put a smile on her face. What was not to like? Smokin' hot actors with smokin' hot bodies — could it get any better? If Billy Melina wasn't available to do her movie, how about Channing Tatum or Alex Pettyfer? Excellent choices.

She grinned to herself, thinking that she should've been a casting agent. She would've kicked ass!

Idly, she watched as Matthew McConaughey strutted his stuff on the screen, practically naked except for an extremely flimsy G-string. What a body! What a sexy dude! It was encouraging that he could do that kind of role and still move on and win an Oscar.

Willow craved winning an Oscar. It was her ultimate dream. And maybe with this movie . . . just maybe. Stranger things had happened, and everyone knew that she was a fine actress. Nobody could take away her talent.

Magic Mike finished and she tried calling Eddie again. This time the same uptight assistant informed her that Mr. Falcon had left for lunch with his wife.

Damn it! Why hadn't he called her back? She'd told him they had to get this deal together immediately or it would all fall apart. He was supposed to come up with a memo for Sam to sign, and instead he was having lunch with his wife, Annabelle Falcon — who used to be Annabelle Maestro — a privileged Hollywood princess whom Willow had never met but hated anyway. It must've been supercool growing up in Hollywood with two movie-star parents. Now Annabelle was married to Eddie Falcon — another cushy situation.

Still . . . Annabelle wasn't the one blowing her husband, Willow was. And maybe she could blow Eddie all the way to divorcing his Hollywood princess and marrying *her*.

What a power couple they'd make. Willow Price, Oscar-winning actress, married to studio head Eddie Falcon.

Of course she wasn't an Oscar-winning actress yet — that was in her future. And Eddie did not run a studio, although everyone said he was next in line.

Mr. and Mrs. Eddie Falcon.

Only one problem. He wasn't her type. Too short. Too stocky. Too full of himself. She preferred handsome — like Billy Melina.

He'd be the perfect partner.

On impulse, she called Eddie's assistant back and pretended to be Steven Spielberg's right-hand woman. "Steven needs to see Eddie urgently," she said, affecting a fake British accent. "Can you please tell me where he is lunching?"

It worked. Spago. Of course. Eddie liked going places where they knew who he was and treated him like royalty.

Willow popped an Oxy and started to get dressed.

Pablo Fernandez Diego didn't walk, he strutted, full of his own self-importance. He was a king, surrounded by serfs. He ruled his world with a steely authority and a benevolent smile. Only there was nothing benevolent about Pablo. He was a ruthless man with many enemies. He ran an empire, a drug empire.

Rafael was nervous about seeing him. He would never forget that as a young boy he'd been terrified of the man. So many brutal goings-on had taken place at the compound, many of which he'd witnessed. At the age of twelve, he'd seen Pablo order his guards to have a man who'd betrayed him tied to a tree, and he'd watched in horror as Pablo had shot the man to death with a bullet to the head.

"You see," Pablo had crowed to Rafael and Alejandro, both of who had been forced to witness the event. "*This* is how you deal with traitors." Then he'd proceeded to an outside table, where he'd gorged himself on a hearty lunch of suckling pig roasted on a spit, accompanied by mounds of fresh vegetables prepared by Eugenia. "Vegetables keep you strong," he'd announced. "Above all else, a man must preserve his strength." He'd beckoned Eugenia, who was serving the food, and crudely reached under her skirt, feeling her up, humiliating her. "Man strong, woman juicy," he'd chuckled.

It was a day Rafael would never forget.

Just before eight A.M., Rafael set off to meet Pablo at the stables. He made sure he was early, for Pablo was a stickler for punctuality.

Pablo Fernandez Diego was leaning against a stable door, petting the head of a magnificent black stallion he'd named Killer. A stablehand stood nearby holding Pablo's morning mug of coffee. Two men armed with AK-47 rifles hovered in the background.

Rafael approached tentatively. He hated that he turned into a subservient piece of shit whenever he was in Pablo's presence. He hated that there was nothing he could do about the way he felt, that it was ingrained in him.

Pablo wore pale beige jodhpurs made especially for him in India, shiny snakeskin boots, a soft cream silk shirt, and a massive leather belt. Around his neck was a huge gold medallion hanging from a thick gold chain. He was a big man, not fat, although he had a gut that overlapped his leather belt, and heavy jowls, which he attempted to disguise with a trimmed beard and full mustache. Quite vain, on formal occasions he sometimes wore a corset. Every six weeks a doctor arrived at his compound to give him Botox injections. His eyes were small — some said beady — and under his eyes were heavy black circles, which he covered with concealer.

He was not a handsome man, although like most not-so-handsome men, he thought he was.

"Ah, Rafael," Pablo said, flashing a row of pristine, extremely white false teeth. The story was that his father — a poor farmer — had knocked all of Pablo's teeth out when he was twelve years old for stealing a loaf of bread. Four years later, Pablo's father had been found in an abandoned building with his throat slit. No one had ever been accused of or indeed arrested for this brutal slaying. At that time, Pablo was working for a notorious drug lord, learning the business, until at the age of twenty-four, when his boss was mysteriously gunned down, he moved in and took over, slaughtering anyone who dared to get in his way.

The tale of Pablo Fernandez Diego's rise to power was legendary.

"It is good to see you, Señor Diego," Rafael said, bowing his head.

Yes, even though everyone suspected he was Pablo's son, he still had to call the man *Señor* Diego, as if he were nothing but a paid employee.

"And to what do I owe the pleasure of your visit?" Pablo asked, getting right to the point.

"Alejandro wishes that I speak with you about an extremely promising investment opportunity," Rafael said, experiencing an unsettling dryness in his throat.

"Investment," Pablo said with a brittle laugh. "Why would I want or indeed need another investment? We have the pharmacies, the food company, Alejandro's club."

"It is always prudent to have more opportunities to make our money legitimate," Rafael pointed out.

Pablo raised a thick black eyebrow, dyed to match his thinning hair. "*Our* money?" he spat. "Since when is it *our* money?"

"I am so sorry, Señor Diego," Rafael said apologetically. "Sometimes I use the wrong words. It is stupid of me."

"Is this an investment that Alejandro has come up with?" Pablo inquired, signaling for the stablehand to fetch him his mug of coffee. The boy did so, and Pablo took a sip before handing it back. "What is this investment?" he said, fingering his mustache.

Rafael noticed that a dribble of dark-brown

398

coffee had landed on Pablo's silk shirt. Should Pablo be aware of this, it would send him into a fury. Studiously, Rafael avoided looking at the dreaded stain.

"Alejandro has the opportunity to produce a movie," he said. "An important movie."

"A movie!" Pablo roared. "What does Alejandro know about making movies?"

Nothing, Rafael was tempted to say. Instead he said, "It is something he has wanted to do for some time. Now he has surrounded himself with top professionals who can make his dream come true. All he needs from you is the money to allow this to happen."

"Money!" Pablo snorted. "My son has plenty of money."

"He requires twenty million dollars," Rafael continued, keeping his voice low and even. "He also suggests that you come to L.A. for a visit. He says to tell you the women are very beautiful and very available. He would like you to see for yourself."

"That's a lot of money," Pablo grumbled. "A big investment."

Rafael knew for a fact that it was not a lot of money to Pablo. His drug empire brought in billions of dollars a year. Twenty million was meaningless to him.

"Alejandro wants you to know he would welcome your presence. He will make sure your visit is memorable."

"Ha!" Pablo exclaimed. "A memorable visit

with my son in California. It is tempting. But Alejandro knows that I do not care to travel."

Rafael's shoulders slumped. He was doing his best, and yet Pablo was not jumping at the idea of coming to L.A. And if Rafael couldn't persuade him to put up the money for Alejandro's "investment" — did that mean that Elizabetta would be receiving a package in the mail?

Rafael shuddered at the thought.

CHAPTER FORTY-NINE

Lucky drove herself to the airport, even though Lennie had insisted that she take one of the guards with her. She'd agreed, then she'd jumped into her red Ferrari and taken off by herself.

Sorry, Lennie. That's the way it is.

She drove the freeway as if it were a racetrack, dodging in and out of lanes with an expert flick of her wrist, Marvin Gaye and Al Green blasting away on her iPod. Nothing like old soul to temper her mood.

She couldn't get the images from the DVD Chris had shown her out of her head. The man who'd shot Gino was clear in her mind. Even though she'd barely seen his face, she remembered every other detail. His Nike running shoes. His silver watch. The way he'd calmly walked away after shooting Gino in the back of the head.

One day she would find him.

Then what?

Was she capable of killing him just like he'd

killed Gino?

Yes. She was capable of taking revenge for his unspeakable act of cowardice.

Arriving at the airport, she parked and made her way inside, heading for the arrivals area, striding through the crowds, excited about seeing Steven. The two of them shared a bond that could never be broken. Way back, Gino had spent one memorable night with Steven's mother, Carrie, and Steven was the result. It wasn't until they were both in their twenties that they'd discovered their connection.

"Hey," she called out as soon as she spotted her half brother walking toward her.

"Hey," Steven responded with a big smile. "It's little Lucky."

"Little Lucky my ass," she said, throwing herself into his arms and hugging him tightly. "It's so great to see you."

Steven Berkley — a well-respected attorney with a thriving practice in Rio, the Brazilian city he'd finally settled in. Tall. Handsome. Café-au-lait skin. Green eyes like his niece, Max. The phrase "Black is beautiful" must have been invented for Steven.

"How was your flight?" she asked, clinging on to his arm.

"Bumpy," he replied. "And way too long."

"You're here, that's all that matters."

"I wish I would've been here six months ago," he said with a rueful shrug. "You got to

402

spend time with Gino. I didn't."

"Not his fault. It was you who kept postponing your trip."

"You know how it is. Family, work."

"Gino missed you. He spoke about you often. He was really looking forward to your visit."

"Too late now," Steven said.

"Not to worry. I have this strong feeling that he's watching over us," Lucky said softly. "He knows you're here for him."

"Always the optimist," Steven said, throwing her a quizzical look.

"Let's go to the car," she said, still holding on to his arm. "Bobby's coming over, and I want to be there when he arrives."

They started making their way toward the exit.

"Still driving your Ferrari?" Steven asked.

"The best car ever," Lucky said enthusiastically.

"You do know that you're a shit driver."

"Screw you, Steven," she responded. "I'm an excellent driver, a hell of a lot better than you."

"I'll choose to ignore that."

"Wise."

"So . . ." Steven said. "What's going on with Lennie and the kids? Fill me in."

"Lennie's in post on his movie. Gino Junior is growing like a tree — he's over six feet. Leo's catching up fast. Max is doing a big modeling job in Europe. Oh yeah — and Bobby's fresh out of jail."

"Jail?" Steven exclaimed.

"I kid you not."

"Maybe you should tell me everything."

"If you're ready for a long and crazy story."

"I'm used to crazy stories. I'm a defense attorney, remember?"

"One of the best, I might say."

"Why didn't you call me?"

"Because everything happened at once," she explained. "Bobby got arrested, Gino was shot . . ." She trailed off.

"Any news on who shot Gino?"

"We do have one lead," she offered.

"What kind of lead?"

"We've got the shooter on a security camera."

"What do the cops have to say about it?"

"Christ!" she exclaimed impatiently. "You're beginning to sound exactly like Lennie. What the fuck is it with you guys and the cops?"

"You do remember the trouble you were in once before," Steven said with a stern shake of his head. "You've got to keep it legal."

"Fuck legal," she snapped. "I do things my way."

"C'mon, Lucky. You're no longer an impetuous kid," Steven said, his handsome face serious. "You're a grown-up, and it's time for you to play by grown-up rules."

"Never have," she said with a derisive laugh. "Never will."

"And she refuses to change," Steven sighed.

"Got no plans in that direction," she said flippantly.

Steven shook his head again. Like Lennie, he knew there was no arguing with Lucky when she had her mind set on something.

"Hey," he said, moving on. "Sitting on the plane, I was thinking about the first time we met."

"Oh yeah, fun times," Lucky drawled, remembering being trapped in an elevator with Steven during a big New York power outage, way before they'd discovered they were brother and sister. She would never forget the nine hours they'd spent together locked in a dark box of a prison. They'd bantered, argued, flirted, and finally been rescued.

"Neither of us knew we were related," Steven said.

"Yeah," Lucky said. "And if I recall correctly, you came on to me."

"No, lady," he objected. *"You* came on to *me."*

"Thank God we didn't fuck," she said lightly.

"Because of me," he insisted.

"You always were a bit of a prude," she joked.

"And *you* always had a filthy mouth."

"It's comforting to know we're both still following our paths in life," she said drily.

They exchanged smiles as they reached the Ferrari.

"How about I drive?" Steven suggested, standing beside the car. "After my flight I'm not in the mood to sample your death-defying skills on the road."

"Get in," Lucky ordered with a wicked grin. "I promise I won't go more than a hundred. Too much traffic."

Steven grimaced and once more shook his head.

Within minutes they were on their way to the Malibu house.

A car met Bobby and Beverly Villiers at the airport in L.A. After dropping Beverly at the Peninsula, Bobby went straight to his house in the Hollywood Hills. In spite of the fact that he was still furious with Denver, he'd kind of been hoping that she would be there waiting for him — waiting to apologize.

Too bad. No. She wasn't around.

He phoned Lucky and told her he'd come by the Malibu house the next day.

"Why not now?" she said, sounding disappointed. "I can't wait to see you, Bobby."

"Gotta detox, Mom," he responded. "Gotta figure some things out."

After speaking with Lucky, he took another shower, thought about calling Denver, decided against it, ordered a pizza, and finally fell asleep watching mindless TV.

In the morning he felt a whole lot better. Now that the jail experience was behind him, he was starting to get angry, really angry.

Someone was screwing with his life, and he didn't like it one little bit.

Someone out there had a vendetta against the Santangelos, and along with Lucky, he was determined to find out who that person was.

CHAPTER FIFTY

Leon was in a bad mood; Denver sensed it as soon as she walked into the office. He threw her a curt "Good morning," and that was it.

I deserve it, she thought. *I ran out on my job, and he's punishing me. Only please don't do it today, Leon, 'cause I'm not feeling great. I'm at a really low point. I crave love and donuts, not a cold reception.*

She'd spent the night at her parents' house trying to figure out how she could make it up to Bobby. The problem was that she couldn't get it out of her mind that he'd gone to a hotel with a call girl, and if he hadn't gotten himself drugged, what had been his plan?

To sleep with her, of course. To have sex with another woman.

Denver knew this was not something she could get over in a hurry.

In the morning she'd realized that she'd made a mistake staying at her parents'. They were full of questions she was not prepared to answer. As soon as possible, she'd gotten out of there and driven straight to the office.

"I could use a coffee," she said to Leon, hoping he might soften up.

"The machine's over there," he replied with an offhand gesture.

Great! Neither of them ever drank the office coffee; they'd made a deal that on the way into work, one of them would stop at Starbucks.

"Are you mad at me?" she ventured.

"Why'd I be mad at you?" Leon responded, raising an eyebrow. "Just 'cause you bailed on our very important case an' ran off to hold your rich boyfriend's hand — that's no reason to be mad. Right?"

It infuriated her when Leon tagged "rich" onto Bobby's name. However, she required peace, so ignoring his sarcasm, she began to apologize.

"Forget it. It doesn't matter," Leon said shortly.

"Fine," she murmured.

"I met with scumbag Frankie Romano an' his attorney without you," Leon offered. "Frankie is definitely lookin' for a deal. The attorney — not so much."

"What kind of deal does Frankie think he can make?"

"He's after a get-out-of-jail-free card. Probation. If we can get him that, he says he'll give us plenty."

"Do we have any idea of what he can offer?"

"He's talkin' about times, shipments. Accordin' to him — everythin'."

"You think he knows details?"

"He talks like he does."

"Well, that's Frankie Romano, isn't it?" Denver said, remembering the first time she'd met Frankie, when he was Annabelle's boyfriend. He'd always been a fast-talker.

"You should've been at the meet," Leon said, unable to help himself from reprimanding her. "He wanted you there. We probably could've made a deal if you'd been in the room."

"I know. I'm sorry I took off."

"I guess you had your reasons," Leon said, softening toward her. "How *was* Bobby, anyway? I've been catchin' up about him on the Internet."

"Please don't," she said sharply. "It's all lies."

"Glad to hear it. Is he back in L.A.?"

Yes, Leon, he's probably back in L.A. I can't tell you for sure because we're not speaking.

"Uh . . . yes," she said vaguely. "Can we drop the subject now? I'm more interested in finding out what Frankie has for us. We should go over everything, see what we can work out."

"You got it," Leon said. "An' Denver?"

410

"What?" she said, trying not to think about Bobby.

"I'm kinda psyched you're back."

"You are?" she said, her face brightening.

"Yup."

"Does that mean there's a decent coffee in my future?" she teased.

"Let's not get carried away."

"I'm buying."

"In that case . . ."

As far as Frankie Romano was concerned, he had a shit lawyer. Horace P. Bendon was a barf-faced, Waspy asshole, with about as much street smarts as a ten-dollar hooker on a Saturday night. The *P* definitely stood for Pisser. Rafael had hired him, assuring Frankie that Pisser was the best. But Frankie knew that Rafael had a hard-on against him — and that Rafael would like nothing more than to see him rot in jail.

Screw Rafael. Didn't he realize that he was dealing with Frankie Romano, a dude with friends in high places? Although none of them were coming through for him. Not Bobby fucking Santangelo. Or stuck-up Annabelle Maestro, his ex–partner in crime, now married to douche bag Eddie Falcon. (Did she have a clue what a whoremongering prick Eddie really was?) Not even Cookie — soul singer Gerald M.'s foxy daughter with whom he'd had a raging affair. Surely Cookie could've gotten Daddy to help out if she'd felt like it? Apparently she hadn't.

Friends. Fuck 'em and feed 'em to the fish. Frankie didn't need friends. He had himself, and he was one savvy son of a bitch.

If no one was prepared to help him, he would simply have to figure out a way to beat the system.

Yes, he'd been busted with an apartment full of drugs.

Yes, he'd been busted selling heroin and coke and an assortment of pills.

Yes, some dumb underage girl with a fake ID had overdosed on his bathroom floor.

She hadn't died, had she? And that was because he'd called the goddamn paramedics after he'd deposited her passed-out body in the lobby of his building.

Shit! If anything, he deserved a medal. He'd saved her life. He was a good Samaritan, for crissake.

So why the hell was he locked up while Alejandro — the big fucking fish — was walking around free? Alejandro was the one who should be taking the fall, not him. Alejandro was the goddamn heir apparent to one of the biggest and most feared drug cartels in the world.

Screw the prick. Frankie had heard nothing from him. It was a disappointment, because he, Frankie, was the dude who'd gotten Alejandro all set up with Club Luna. *He* was the one who'd introduced him to all his best customers. They'd been tight, really tight, and where had that gotten him? Apparently nowhere, because Alejandro had not come through for him. Instead, his dumb-fuck sidekick, Rafael, had stuck him with a lawyer who kept on telling him that making a deal was a bad idea.

"Do your time and keep your mouth shut," Pisser kept insisting.

"Who the *fuck* you working for?" Frankie had responded.

"Mr. Diego's office is picking up the tab for your troubles," Pisser had informed him. "It's essential that you listen to me."

Sure, they're picking up the tab, Frankie thought. *Which is exactly why they don't want me making a deal.*

Damn it, if a deal was getting him out of jail, he was making it, and Pisser could go screw himself.

Earlier in the day he'd met with the black dude from the DA's office — Leon something or other. He didn't trust him. What he wanted was a face-to-face with Bobby's girlfriend, Denver. She was a full-of-herself bitch, but at least he knew that if there was a deal to be made, she would keep her word.

Fuck 'em all. Frankie was ready, and if it meant giving up Alejandro, so be it.

CHAPTER FIFTY-ONE

Wearing a white Dolce & Gabbana dress, high-heeled sandals, and gold hoop earrings, her black hair wild and curly, her green eyes sparkling with excitement, Max was attending a press reception in her honor. She found it to be heady stuff as she sat behind a long table on a high platform in front of an audience of several dozen journalists. Lorenzo was hovering behind her, ready to translate. Alfredo Dolcezza was on her right, and a sour-faced Dante was on her left.

Why was she constantly stuck next to Dante?

It didn't matter. Who cared? She had her thoughts to keep her warm. And what delicious thoughts they were. Last night when Billy had kidnapped her from dinner, she'd been caught completely off guard. The speed with which he'd acted had been a total surprise. He'd whisked her off and she'd gone with him just like that, although once they were outside the restaurant she'd realized that maybe she was making a mistake.

"Like, what the hell?" she'd demanded, staring him down. "That dinner was all about me, and who are you to drag me out of there?"

"No dragging involved," Billy had said with a sly grin. "You couldn't wait to cut loose. Besides, we're in Rome. I'm gonna give you the tour."

"What tour?" she'd huffed, trying to ignore the lure of his piercing blue eyes.

"You'll see," he'd said, taking her hand and pulling her over to a car parked curbside. A driver stood in attendance.

"I'm not going anywhere with you," she'd said as the driver opened the rear door.

"Do not fight it, Green Eyes. You know you want to come with me," Billy had said, hustling her into the backseat.

"You're *so* bossy," she'd complained.

"An' you're so sweet," he'd teased, "even though you try to be a tough girl."

"I *so* do not," she'd objected.

"Yes you so do," Billy had said, touching her arm, sending chills through her body.

And so it had begun . . . a magical mystery tour of Rome at night, with a fully attentive Billy pointing out places of interest as they'd talked and laughed, until eventually they'd ended up at the Trevi Fountain, where he'd pulled her out of the car and instructed her to throw a coin in the fountain and make a wish.

"It's an old Roman tradition," he'd assured her. "Works every time."

"How do *you* know?" she'd asked suspiciously.

" 'Cause I stopped here on my way to the restaurant tonight."

"You did?"

"Yeah, an' I made a wish that I'd see you. Hey — just like that, my wish came true."

"Liar!" she'd said, trying not to smile, although she couldn't help feeling happier than she had in a long time. "You somehow or other found out where I was, then you proceeded to stalk me."

"No way."

"Way."

"Okay, Green Eyes," he'd said, laughing. "Whatever you say."

"I say that I will make my wish now, and that I'm not going to tell you what it is."

"Great," he'd said, handing her a coin. " 'Cause you're not supposed to."

At the end of the evening he'd dropped her at the front of her hotel, brushing her lips for a chaste kiss before promising he'd call her tomorrow.

It was now tomorrow, and here she was at the Dolcezza press conference, smiling like an idiot because Billy was back in her life.

Or was he?

She couldn't take anything for granted. He'd dumped her once — big-time — which meant that he was quite capable of doing it again.

Lucky would say, *Never let a boy get the better of you.*

Athena would say, *Go for it, girl. Use him like he used you.*

But who could be that cavalier when you totally loved someone?

Yes — she still loved him. Couldn't help herself. Couldn't do a damn thing about it.

Surreptitiously, she checked her phone.

No call yet. It was still early. He *would* call. He'd promised he would.

Lorenzo was muttering in her ear, repeating a question one of the gathered journalists had asked her.

Their questions were so inane.

What's it like being the new face of Dolcezza?

How do you enjoy Italian men/food/Roma/ whatever?

She answered all questions with a smile and an enthusiastic reply, until it was time to do photos for the press photographers. Alfredo, Dante, and Lorenzo escorted her outside to a flower-filled garden, where the photographers went a little bit wild — yelling her name, telling her to look this way and that, capturing her from every angle. She had to admit that she was finding the full-on attention quite addictive. For once it was all about her; in London, it was usually all about Athena.

Eventually it was over, whereupon Dante turned to her and announced that he was taking her to lunch.

"Oh!" she said, startled and not at all pleased. "Can Lorenzo come?"

"We do not need Lorenzo," Dante replied, throwing her a smarmy reptilian leer, which alarmed her even more.

"But . . . but he's my translator," she managed. "I depend on him."

"Why would you need a translator when my English is impeccable?" Dante said. "I thought I told you that I attended college in your America."

"My America?" she responded, thinking, *Who talks like this?*

"I have slept with more American girls than I care to remember," Dante boasted with a sneery smirk. "American girls are not exciting in bed. Poor girls, they try too hard, they have no real passion. They do not know how to please a man."

This conversation sucked. The last thing she wished to hear about was Dante's sex life.

"Excuse me a minute," she gulped, rushing over to Lorenzo, who was speaking to Gabrielle. "Dante is insisting that he take me to lunch," she whispered. "Can I say no?"

"You should go," Lorenzo replied. "Stay on

his good side. It would not be wise to have Dante as an enemy. He is one of your bosses, and you will need his permission to go to the States for your grandfather's funeral. Remember, you have signed a contract."

"But he hates me," she wailed.

"How could anyone possibly hate you?" Lorenzo said soothingly. "You're perfect."

Max took a moment or two to process the word *perfect.* No one had ever called her perfect before. Wild, out of control, a pain in the ass — but never perfect. She kind of liked it. What a shame that Lorenzo was gay; he might've been a fun summer fling. He was polite and caring. Better to be with someone reliable instead of chasing a dream. Billy Melina wasn't real. He was her fantasy, and there was no doubt that he'd break her heart again.

"Okay, I'll go," she said with a put-upon sigh. "Only that doesn't mean I want to."

Dante took her to an outdoor restaurant located on the Via Veneto. They were seated at a round table on a busy patio. It seemed Dante's mood toward her had improved, and she had a strong feeling that it had something to do with Billy's appearance the previous night.

Naturally, she was right. It didn't take long for Dante to bring up the subject of Billy. As soon as they'd ordered — or rather, to her annoyance, Dante had ordered for her — he said, "Is Billy Melina your boyfriend?"

"Uh . . . no," she answered carefully, although she really wanted to say, *None of your freaking business.*

"He seems to like you very much," Dante observed.

"I've known him forever," she said defensively, quickly adding, "He was married to my mom's best friend."

"It would not be such a bad thing if he *was* your boyfriend," Dante said. "The publicity for Dolcezza . . ." He trailed off before adding a determined, "I will make him an offer he cannot refuse."

"Excuse me?" Max said, startled. Did Dante imagine he was a character in *The Godfather*? What the hell kind of offer was he talking about?

"American movie stars do plenty of foreign commercials for the right price," Dante continued. "George Clooney, Matt Damon. Dolcezza can afford to pay your boyfriend top *dinero.* He will agree."

"I told you," she said, exasperated that Dante wasn't getting it. "Billy Melina is *not* my boyfriend, and I'm quite sure he doesn't need your money."

"So naive, so innocent," Dante sneered, sipping from a glass of red wine. "You will not survive in this business unless you sharpen up."

"I have no idea *what* you're talking about,"

Max said grandly, wishing she'd followed her instincts and refused to have lunch with this arrogant ass.

"I am talking about a Dolcezza commercial starring you and your boyfriend," Dante said. "Ah . . . what a publicity coup that would be."

"No way," she said, her cheeks blazing. "Billy would never do that."

"You will be surprised," Dante said. "He likes you, and if you can't see it, then you are even more naive than I thought. The Dolcezza PR people are already reaching out to his team, so we shall see."

"See *what*?" she asked, outraged and embarrassed, because what if Billy thought this was *her* idea? Oh, the humiliation!

"Do not worry that he will take the attention away from you," Dante said. "It will merely be for maximum publicity."

"I'm not worried," she said stiffly. "And I have a really bad headache, so if you don't mind, I think I'll be going back to my hotel."

Dante let loose with his disgusting yellow-toothed smile. "I will keep you informed," he promised.

Don't bother, she wanted to scream. *Billy will never do it. Of that I'm sure.*

421

CHAPTER FIFTY-TWO

Five minutes after Pablo dismissed him, Rafael borrowed a car from the compound and took off to visit Elizabetta and his son. He drove fast, in a hurry, for he hadn't seen them in over a year. This was a big day for him.

Elizabetta was an old-fashioned girl, a virgin when they'd first met. She was a girl with family values and a pure heart, unlike the *putas* he'd come across in America. The downside was that she had no desire to learn technology, which meant that even though he'd bought her a laptop, which would enable them to Skype, allowing him to see his son, she'd stubbornly refused to use it.

As he drove along the winding road, Willow came to mind.

Willow with her pale red hair and pouty lips.

Willow with her hard nipples and pulsating —

Stop, he told himself. *Stop thinking about the girl who trapped you into doing depraved and dirty things.*

He forced his mind elsewhere.

His thoughts turned to Pablo. The big man hadn't said yes and he hadn't said no. He'd ordered Rafael to join him for dinner at seven P.M., telling him that he would advise him of his decision then.

Rafael had the day ahead of him, and he was intent on making the most of it. Alejandro had warned him not to linger in Colombia. "Get the job done, and fly right back," Alejandro had said. "Otherwise . . ."

Oh yes, Rafael understood only too well what "otherwise" meant. It meant that Alejandro would send Elizabetta the depraved sex tape he'd been captured on with the American *puta.*

How could he have allowed himself to get caught in such a situation?

Because he'd been trapped, well and truly trapped.

Alejandro was nothing to him. He loathed his brother with all his being.

Spago, one of the best restaurants in Beverly Hills, was crowded, as usual.

Willow sauntered in as if she owned the place. She never had any problem getting into exclusive restaurants; everyone knew who she was.

The girls at the front desk smiled at her.

423

"Who will you be joining?" one of them asked.

"Uh . . . I have a message for Eddie Falcon," she said, tossing back her pale red hair. "Can you point me in the right direction?"

"Of course, Willow," the hostess said.

Willow did not appreciate being addressed by her first name. Surely she should be Ms. Price? Would they call Angelina Jolie Angelina? No. It would be Ms. Jolie all the way. Or maybe even Mrs. Pitt.

The hostess slipped out from behind the reception desk and said, "This way, Willow. Follow me."

Another Willow. No respect. When she won her first Oscar, things would definitely have to change.

She trailed the attractive girl (probably an out-of-work actress) to the outside patio.

Eddie was ensconced at a table for three with Annabelle and Annabelle's extremely famous action-movie-star father, Ralph.

Willow had not expected to see Ralph Maestro. He was an intimidating figure, big and macho with a weathered tan, huge hands, and a cheesy smile. Rumor had it that he'd murdered his very beautiful and equally famous wife, Gemma Summer. Naturally, he'd gotten away with it. Of course he had. He was Ralph Maestro, an action-movie hero, not a mere mortal capable of murder.

Willow hovered by their table as the hostess

took off.

"Eddie," she said, feigning surprise. "How lovely to see you."

Eddie shot her a deadly look. What the hell was *she* doing here?

"Hey, Willow," he said, aware that Annabelle was on alert, checking Willow out. A month before he and Annabelle had gotten married, she'd forced him to sign a prenup with all kinds of stupid clauses. One of them was that if either of them was caught cheating, it triggered a $250,000 penalty. He'd wanted the marriage to happen, so he'd signed. Now he regretted doing so, because cheating was part of his DNA.

"I'm lunching with Sam Slade," Willow lied, smiling prettily. "You know, the writer dude. We have much to discuss."

Ralph Maestro, a tried-and-true letch, launched into action. "Well, aren't *you* a pretty little thing," he said, cheesy smile going full force.

"Uh, everyone, this is Willow Price, a former client," Eddie said. "Willow — meet my wife, Annabelle, and her father, Ralph Maestro."

"Oh," Willow cooed. "Everyone knows who Mr. Maestro is. No introductions needed. I'm a huge fan." *Or rather, my mother is,* she thought.

Ralph responded with an even cheesier smile. "If your lunch date isn't here yet," he said, "how about joining us while you wait?"

Willow fluttered her eyelashes. Eddie glowered. Annabelle managed to look disinterested.

"Thanks," Willow said. "That's if nobody minds, 'cause I wouldn't want to interrupt."

"Sit down, sweetie," Ralph said, pulling out a chair. "You're not interrupting a thing."

Ralph Maestro was a man used to getting his own way. And today — after hearing the news that he was to become a grandfather — getting his own way meant getting laid. And fast.

Granddad was not a title Ralph Maestro relished.

Elizabetta's mother's house was located in a poor neighborhood with unpaved streets and stray dogs roaming around scrounging for food scraps. Rafael had begged her to move somewhere safer, but Elizabetta preferred to stay close to her mama.

A slender girl with a sweep of straight black hair that fell below her waist, Elizabetta had huge sad eyes in a delicate face and a pointed chin. Rafael Junior was perched on her hip. At two years of age, the child was a miniature version of his mama, with the same sad eyes and pointy chin, the same long straight black hair.

Elizabetta was standing in front of the rundown house waiting for him. Rafael pulled the car to a stop and jumped out. His gut reaction upon seeing his son was that the boy could easily be mistaken for a girl. This angered him, and without thinking he blurted, "Get this kid a haircut. What is wrong with you?"

Elizabetta took a step back. "Is that how you greet us?" she said, her sad eyes flashing signs of disappointment and anger. "Rafael Junior is a beautiful boy. He does not have to have short hair for everyone to know it."

Rafael gave her a long hard look. "If you don't cut his hair, I will," he warned, his face darkening.

Elizabetta hunched her shoulders. "What does it matter to you?" she said flatly. "You never see him anyway."

"I am here now."

"For how long?"

Was she questioning him? Surely this was not the way things were supposed to go. Surely Elizabetta should have fallen into his arms, grateful and thrilled to see him. Instead she was surly and confrontational.

"Hand me the boy," he said roughly, holding out his arms.

Rafael Junior clung on to his mama, making high-pitched whining sounds.

"What's the matter with him?" Rafael demanded.

"He doesn't know you," she responded. "You scare him."

"Doesn't know me indeed," Rafael scoffed. "What kind of nonsense it that?"

"I barely know you myself," she muttered. "You never come here. You leave me all alone with a child to raise while you do whatever it is you do in America."

"I work," he said. "I work hard to save enough money for us and our son to get away from here someday, to live a normal life."

"You're already away," she said, pointing an accusing finger at him. "You're free. You left me with a baby. You went without a thought for us."

"I *had* to go," Rafael said. "Señor Diego insisted. You know that."

"You could have said no," Elizabetta said, throwing him a resentful look.

He kept his temper in check. Was she so naive that she actually thought he could have turned down a request from Pablo Fernandez Diego? If that was the case, she was more stupid than smart. Everyone knew that turning down the feared drug lord was a sure death sentence.

"We should not fight," he said, inwardly calming himself. He had only a short time with her, so why spoil it? She was upset and frustrated by his absence; he could try to understand that.

"Come inside," she sighed. "Perhaps your son will talk to you then."

Rafael followed her into the dingy depressing house.

Soon, he thought. *Soon I will take my family away from here. And then we will be happy.*

Willow Price settled at Eddie's table like a delicate flower with her flowing pale red hair and light smattering of freckles.

Ralph Maestro inspected her from tip to toe. Very pretty, he thought. With a great pair of tits visible under her flimsy top. She would do.

He shifted his chair toward her. "And what would the little lady like to drink?" he asked.

Willow was not slow to realize that Mr. Action-Movie Star was totally into her. She was delighted, because she knew it would piss Eddie off, and it would certainly serve him right for not calling her back.

"I'd love a mojito," she said, adopting a breathy Marilyn Monroe–type voice she'd recently been trying out.

Ralph obviously liked it, for he patted her on the knee, his large hand lingering a few seconds too long. "Whatever the little lady wants," he said with a hearty guffaw.

Willow shot Eddie a sly look, making sure he noticed.

He did, although she could tell that he was trying to play it cool.

Too late, Eddie. You should've called me back. Maybe I can cut a deal with your father-in-law. He's rich, isn't he? And I bet he loves getting his big fat cock sucked.

Willow preened. For once she felt she was the one calling the shots.

CHAPTER FIFTY-THREE

Seeing Bobby gave Lucky a special kind of strength. Her son. Home at last.

Roberto Santangelo Stanislopoulos. Her firstborn. They shared a very special relationship.

Little Bobby. Son of billionaire Greek shipping magnate Dimitri Stanislopoulos, whom she'd married after Bobby was born. Had she been madly in love with Dimitri? No. However, they'd both agreed that it would be best for their son if they made it legal. Plus Dimitri put up the money for her to build a new hotel in Atlantic City. That's all she'd wanted from him. She hadn't cared that he was one of the richest men in the world. As long as Bobby was taken care of, that was all that mattered to her.

Bobby had spent his formative years living between Los Angeles and Greece. Dimitri was an untraditional father who believed in teaching his son too much too soon — and since Dimitri was a major womanizer, Bobby learned plenty at an early age. But when Dimitri lost the love of his life — famous opera singer Francesca Fern, a mistress Lucky had always known about — he'd become a recluse, refusing to leave his private Greek island.

He'd asked Lucky to stay there with him, but she'd had no intention of being stuck away on an island, and although Dimitri agreed that she could come and go as she pleased, he'd insisted that Bobby stay.

She'd acquiesced. After all, she was busy building her hotel in Atlantic City, and Bobby had his nanny, CeeCee, who was always by his side. It seemed to be a workable arrangement, especially as she visited often.

It wasn't until Dimitri died that she'd finally brought Bobby back to America. He was still a child, and it was with a great deal of pride that she'd watched him grow into the man he was today.

So many memories . . . some good, some bad.

She didn't regret any of them.

The moment he saw Lucky, Bobby felt safe for the first time in days.

"You do know I didn't do it," he blurted, frantic to make sure that she heard it directly from him.

"For God's sake," she responded. "I *know* you were set up. I knew it from the beginning. Beverly was here earlier today, and she filled me in on everything. I never doubted you, Bobby."

"Try telling that to Denver," he said with a wry shake of his head.

"What?" Lucky said, frowning. "She doesn't believe you? Because if she doesn't, then she's not the girl for you."

"She thinks I was out to get laid," he said flatly.

"Were you?" Lucky asked, giving him a long penetrating look.

"Does it make any difference?" he said. "I was accused of murder, for crissake, and all Denver's worried about is that I might've been getting my dick out. And for your information, I wasn't."

"Calm down," Lucky said. "It'll all work out."

"Hey," he said sharply. "The last thing I'm concerned about is me. What I want to find out is who shot Gino."

"We all want that information."

"Yeah, but knowing you, I bet you have more info than you're telling."

"You think so?" she said, her expression impenetrable.

"Listen to me," Bobby said tensely. "There's no way you can keep me in the dark about this, 'cause believe me, I'm after revenge just like you."

Lucky was silent for a moment before saying a slow, guarded, "What makes you think I want revenge?"

"Jeez, Mom," he exploded. "You're freakin' Lucky Santangelo. You take no prisoners. You're one kick-ass scary woman."

"Thanks for the compliment," she said drily.

"You get exactly what I mean. And whatever happens — I want in."

"Do you, now?" she said, thinking that Bobby was indeed a true Santangelo.

"Yes, I do," he persisted. "So fill me in. What have you found out?"

"Right now, nothing. I'm waiting to hear from Chris Warwick."

"Where's he?"

"Chris is currently in Chicago, working on who set *you* up."

"Are you saying that you think me being drugged and Gino getting shot are connected?"

"We don't know," Lucky said, wishing Bobby would back off. "Gino's shooter was captured on a home security camera. Chris has someone working on face recognition."

"And then?" Bobby demanded.

"I deal with it."

"No," Bobby said, his dark eyes locking with hers. "*We* deal with it."

"There's no way you can be involved," Lucky insisted. "You're in enough trouble."

"Screw that, Mom," Bobby said, his anger

bubbling up. "Don't you get it? I *am* involved. Gino was my grandfather. I'm just as vested as you in catching whoever murdered him."

"And what exactly do you think I'm going to do, Bobby?" she said, studying the face of her handsome son, realizing that it was not going to be easy shutting him out. "Do you imagine I'll catch the son of a bitch, then hand him over to the cops? Because that's not the way I handle things, and once again — I do *not* want you involved."

There was something in her voice that brooked no argument. However, Bobby was determined. He knew about his mom's checkered past, that she'd done many things to avenge and protect her family. She was resourceful and fierce.

He could be the same if need be. He *wanted* to be the same. She should understand how he felt. He was a Santangelo too.

"Come," Lucky said, eager to change subjects. "Steven's here. He can't wait to see you."

Arriving in Chicago, Chris Warwick went straight to work. First on his agenda was a visit to Mood, where M.J. met him and gave him access to all the club surveillance tapes.

"Did the detective on the case see these?" Chris asked as he checked the tapes out.

"Yeah," M.J. replied. "It's how they identified the girl. Turns out she was a high-class

435

hooker hired for the night by a dude who contacted her via the Internet."

"How do you know this?"

"It's all over the papers. She lived with another girl. The two of 'em operated via a Web site."

"Does the detective know this?"

"Hey, if *I* know it, he sure as shit does. The other girl has already made a deal to sell her story."

"No time for grieving," Chris said, shaking his head in disgust. "People just make money where they can. Whatever happened to morals?"

"I'll tell you this," M.J. said, remembering the exact moment he'd set eyes on the girl in the red dress. "Nadia was one hot, gorgeous woman. I was kinda thinkin' of makin' a move myself. Man, I'm sure glad I didn't. It coulda been *me* accused of murder."

"When she came into the club, did you get the impression that she'd targeted Bobby?" Chris asked.

"Hey, man, I was kinda tied up with a deal of my own, so like I said — it *coulda* been me."

Chris wasn't interested in stroking M.J.'s ego; he was after facts. "Did you speak to her at all?"

"I was the one who took 'em to their table, bought 'em a bottle of Cristal. Found out the guy was her cousin — or so he said."

"Tell me about him."

"Not much to tell. Latin. Short. Beard. Hard eyes. Bad temper."

"Name?"

"Didn't get it."

Chris studied the surveillance tapes again. It was quite apparent that the Latin man knew there were cameras and had tried to keep his face turned away. However, he hadn't been aware of all the cameras, and there were some clear shots of him.

It surprised Chris that the detective on the case hadn't zeroed in on him. The man most likely had a record and would not be difficult to track. It seemed that Detective Cole was happy to pin the girl's death on Bobby Santangelo Stanislopoulos. The big get.

Chris hated sloppy detective work. He'd checked out Detective Cole and discovered that he was a tough veteran detective who'd soon be put out to pasture. Not well liked, he hardly had a stellar reputation.

Within the hour, thanks to his many connections, Chris had a name and location. Pedro Albarado. Los Angeles.

Before heading back to the airport, he stopped by the apartment where Nadia had lived. After ringing the buzzer and getting no response, he waited patiently outside in a spot where he knew Nadia's roommate could see him through the peephole in her door. He'd already found out that the girl's name was

437

Yana, that she was twenty-five and originally from Ukraine.

It didn't take long for her to fling open the door and say sharply, "What you want? Why you here?"

Chris looked her over carefully. She was a dyed blonde with high cheekbones and a slender body. She appeared to be angry and a little bit afraid. Chris gave her the comforting, unthreatening look he'd perfected so well. He also flashed his phony detective badge and fixed her with his honest brown eyes.

"What you want?" she repeated, glaring at him suspiciously. "This very sad time for me. I already told cops everything I know."

"I'm aware of that," Chris said politely. "You've been extremely cooperative, and that has not gone unnoticed."

Her expression softened. Chris observed that she had mismatched eyes — one blue, one green. He wondered if she was messing with her contacts or if this was simply a freaky trick of nature.

"May I come in?" he asked. "I'm sure you don't want your neighbors spying on you."

Yana peered from left to right, trying to see if any of her neighbors were indeed spying on her.

"Okay," she said with a reluctant nod of her head. "You come in. We be quick, yes?"

I don't want sex with you, he was tempted to

say. *Just answers to a few pertinent questions.*

The apartment was small, every surface cluttered with cheap ornaments and tacky religious statues. It was apparent the girls had not entertained at home. A Mac computer stood in the middle of a table, next to a stack of what looked like seminude glamour photos. The only seating was a chair in front of the computer and a narrow bench by the window.

Chris took the bench. Yana sat in the chair. She was not dressed for work, more like for a stay-at-home day in baggy velour pants and a tightly fitted T-shirt featuring an Adam Levine image. He imagined she must be quite something when done up and ready to ply her wares.

"What I tell you?" she asked, nervously picking at a hangnail.

"I'd like to hear one more time what this john said he required from Nadia. Maybe you can repeat exactly what she told you."

Yana thought for a moment before licking her slightly puffy lips. "He say he want very beautiful girl to get this guy to go to her hotel room," she said, rubbing the tip of her nose. "He offer much money. No sex. Nadia said she could do it. Easy for her. No man ever resisted Nadia. She could get a man to do whatever she wanted."

"Until he killed her."

"Yob tvoyu mati!" Yana exclaimed, clapping

439

her hands together.

"Motherfucker," Chris said quietly.

Yana looked startled. "You speak Russian?" she said, her mismatched eyes widening.

Chris nodded.

"That is good," she said, before launching into a stream of Russian complaining about what a violent country America was, and how she couldn't wait to save enough money and head back to Ukraine before she got herself murdered like her friend.

Sure, Chris thought with a skeptical shake of his head. *No violence in Ukraine. You'll be safe there.*

He glanced at his watch and got to his feet.

Time to go.

Time to find out more about Pedro Albarado and what his game was.

Chapter Fifty-Four

"You gotta try an' keep your feelin's out of this," Leon warned Denver as they set off to meet with Frankie and his lawyer.

"For God's sake," Denver said, irritated that Leon was telling her how to behave. "If there's one thing I am, it's professional."

"I know, I know," he said. "Just don't lose your cool."

"I have no intention of doing so," she said crossly. "And kindly stop lecturing me."

They met with Frankie and his attorney in an interrogation room at the jail.

Being in the presence of Frankie Romano reminded Denver of how much she couldn't stand him. There was something about Frankie that screamed "bad news." It came off him in waves. It always amazed her that he and Bobby had once been friends. They were so different, and yet at one time — along with M.J. — they'd been very close, almost like brothers.

How was that possible? Frankie Romano

was a fast-talking piece-of-shit drug dealer who lured young girls to his apartment and then stood by while they almost overdosed. He was the lowest of the low. What could he and Bobby possibly have in common?

In spite of her feelings about Frankie, she endeavored to stay neutral as they listened to everything he had to say. He spoke fast, as usual — claiming to know plenty, then refusing to reveal any details until he got a guarantee of protection.

His attorney sat stiffly beside him saying nothing. Both Denver and Leon were well aware that Horace P. Bendon was being paid by Rafael — Alejandro Diego's business partner — and that Horace P. Bendon's loyalty would always be with the Diego family. The moment this meeting was over, Horace would report back to Rafael, and when the Diego camp heard that Frankie was willing to talk, his life would be in danger. The DA's office had already issued an order that Frankie be kept in a cell by himself, away from the general prison population.

If Frankie was bluffing and he *didn't* have the information he claimed to have, then things could get even worse for him, especially if he was put back into general. His best bet was if he came through with solid information; then he would be sequestered in a hotel with twenty-four-hour protection until they were able to indict Alejandro.

It was very complicated, and it all depended on what Frankie had to give them.

"We're gonna have to talk to the chief deputy DA," Leon said.

"Don't make me wait too long," Frankie answered, his left eye twitching. "Jail food is crap. An' oh yeah," he added, throwing a dirty look at his lawyer, "I'm firing this douche."

"Jeez!" Leon said in the car on their way back to the office. "He sure is one slippery piece of work."

"Told you," Denver said.

"You think he's gonna come up with anythin' concrete?"

"Who knows?"

"Didja get a look at the lawyer's face when he dumped him?"

"Classic," Denver said, lapsing into silence as her thoughts turned to Bobby. It would be so nice if she could discuss the Frankie deal with him. Right now it didn't seem possible, since they appeared to be on a break.

Was a break what she wanted?

As of now — yes.

Or no.

She wasn't sure.

As far as Frankie was concerned, she was torn. Was he bluffing about what information he had, and even more important, could he be trusted to deliver? Leon didn't seem to be so sure, and neither was she.

Only time would tell.

A family dinner was taking place at the Malibu house. Lucky excelled in the kitchen, making pasta and a delicious Bolognese sauce that had been Gino's favorite. She was trying to act as if nothing had taken place, and cooking for the family seemed to be the most normal activity she could think of. Not that she spent a lot of time in the kitchen, but when she did, it was major.

After everyone had helped themselves, she glanced around the table. Lennie was sitting next to Steven. Bobby and the two younger boys were chatting away. Everything was peaceful. She was thankful that the people closest to her were all assembled — everyone except Max.

Had she made a mistake not summoning her daughter home immediately?

Lennie was pissed that she hadn't commanded Max to get on the next plane. "She'll be here soon enough," Lucky had assured him.

This did not satisfy him. He wanted his daughter home, where he considered she'd be safe.

Lucky disagreed; she was convinced that Max was safer staying where she was.

What does safe *mean anyway?* she thought. *Every day is full of risks. Every time you set*

444

foot outside, anything can happen.
Gino. On his morning walk.
Gone. Shot. Killed.
Fucking brutally murdered.

She tried not to think about it, but unfortunately, she couldn't stop herself.

Earlier she'd spoken to Chris, who was on his way to the airport in Chicago. After informing her that his contact at face recognition had been unable to come up with a match on the man in the Palm Springs video, he'd added the news that they'd been successful in identifying the Latin man who'd set Bobby up. Chris had a name and a location.

Was it the same man who'd shot Gino?

Was the man a paid assassin who'd been hired to do both jobs?

Lucky shuddered when she thought about what the son of a bitch could've done to Bobby. He'd had him in his power, drugged and helpless. Anything could've happened.

Instead he'd killed the girl.

She didn't get it. Why murder the call girl when Bobby had been the obvious target?

"I'll meet you at LAX," she'd informed Chris. "I'm coming with you."

"Not a good idea," he'd replied. "It's better that I find out if this is our man, or if he's simply the hired help. It's useless for you to waste your time."

"Shouldn't I be there when you talk to him?"

"No, Lucky. I'll keep you informed."

"You'd better."

"Don't worry, I will."

After dinner the boys started talking about going down to the beach and swimming.

"No way. It's too dark and creepy," Lucky pointed out. "Who knows what's waiting out there in the ocean."

"Ew, scary!" Gino Junior said, mocking her. "Big freakin' monsters!"

"Let 'em go," Lennie said, joining in. "If they drown or get eaten, it's no big loss."

"Thanks, Dad," Leo said with an indignant scowl. "Didn't know you loved us so much."

"I'll go with them," Bobby volunteered. "I wouldn't mind taking a swim."

"I thought you were going home," Lucky said.

"I was thinking I might stay over," Bobby responded. "If that's okay with you."

"You know it is," Lucky said, thinking that he and Denver must still be on the outs. She wasn't sure how she felt about that. Before Denver, Bobby had sampled a slew of girlfriends. Since being with Denver, he'd seemed more centered. Denver was good for him. But trust was a big part of any relationship, and if his girlfriend didn't trust him . . .

Bobby jumped up. "Move it, Steven. You're

coming with us."

"You can count me out," Steven said, holding up his hand. "I don't even go in the ocean when it's bright sunlight, let alone at night."

"Lennie?" Bobby said.

"Gonna pass."

"Jeez!" Bobby exclaimed. "What a bunch of chickenshits." He turned to his brothers. "C'mon, kids, let's go."

"I'm no kid," Gino Junior complained. "I'm sixteen."

"You'll always be a kid to me," Bobby teased. "And we're goin' commando — no pants."

"Cool!" Leo chortled.

"Try not to get your little dick bitten off by a shark," Lennie joked. "The big ones come out at night, y'know, sniffing out a tasty piece of meat."

"Dad!" Leo groaned. "You're so lame."

Then they were off, running through the back of the house to the steps that led down to the beach.

"Maybe we should send one of the guards with them," Lucky suggested.

"Forget it," Lennie said. "Bobby'll watch out for them. Let 'em enjoy themselves. Nothing's going to happen."

Gino was enjoying himself when he went out for a walk, Lucky thought dourly. *Look what happened to him.*

"Okay," she said, wondering how soon she

would hear from Chris.

    She was ready for action.

    Once again, she was ready to take revenge.

CHAPTER FIFTY-FIVE

Billy didn't call. Billy didn't text. Was Max disappointed?

Yes.

Was she surprised?

No.

It was her own fault for falling back into the trap that was Billy Melina.

At least she hadn't jumped into bed with him again like some kind of lovesick teenager.

Not that he'd asked. And what was *that* about? He'd acted all into her and major romantic, so how come he hadn't made a move?

Puzzling. Annoying. What was his deal?

Back at the hotel, she called her mom to check in, and was happy to hear that Bobby was back in L.A. Lucky still had no firm date for Gino's funeral, so she instructed Max to stay where she was until there was further news.

Okay, then, Max thought. *I guess I can concentrate on being the new face of Dolcezza.*

Nothing wrong with that.

Lorenzo had assured her that soon the photos from the press conference would be everywhere and that she would be much in demand for photo spreads in magazines, while journalists would be clamoring for interviews.

Alfredo had informed her through Lorenzo that she was not to do any more press until the actual ads started to run. She'd also been told that coming up there would be full-page ads in all the most glossy and exclusive magazines, and shortly after that she and Carlo would be off to a series of exotic islands, where they would shoot the actual photos for the campaign.

If it hadn't been for the thought of flying back to L.A. for her grandfather's funeral, she would have felt a whole lot better. Billy had taken her mind off things for a while, but now her head was full of thoughts about her family and how in spite of her burgeoning career, she wished she were in L.A. with them. Yes, she'd craved her independence, but that didn't mean she couldn't miss them.

Lorenzo had spoken on her behalf to Alfredo and the Dolcezza sisters. They'd agreed that when the time came, she could return to America for the funeral, but only for a day or two.

A day or two was better than nothing. And what could they do if she decided to stay longer — kill her?

She giggled at the thought. They couldn't do anything to her except cancel her contract.

Hmm . . . that wouldn't be cool. Although with the announcements and press conference, surely she was safe? It had to be too late to replace her.

She decided to call Athena, whose tweets and Instagrams were out of control. Athena posted at least ten selfies a day of her on various beaches and luxurious yachts where she was lazing in the sun, showing off her butt in the smallest of thongs, flashing her boobs, cavorting with a series of random men and girls. Athena sure loved her bad-girl reputation.

Max picked up her iPhone and actually got through to her.

"Where the flipping hell have *you* been?" Athena demanded. "I text you, you don't reply. I summon you, you don't come. *What* is going on? We're supposed to be having delicious summer fun together."

"I'm the new Dolcezza girl," Max blurted.

"Whaaat?" Athena exclaimed. "Tell me everything."

Max explained how it had happened. Athena was silent.

"Right now I'm in freaking *Rome*!" Max said excitedly. "I had a press conference today. It's been totally crazy. The attention I'm getting is insane."

451

"I thought it was shady when you asked me if I'd heard of them. But you never mentioned you were up for the job," Athena said, sounding a tad frosty. "Why didn't you tell me? I thought we were besties."

"We are," Max replied. "Only I didn't want to jinx myself, so I didn't mention it to anyone until it was a done deal, not even my family."

"Aren't *you* the secretive one," Athena said, still sounding cold. "I hope they're paying you oodles of cash."

"Uh . . . I guess so."

"What do you mean, you guess so? You always were an idiot when it came to business."

Max did not appreciate being called an idiot by one of her supposed best friends. Shouldn't Athena be congratulating her, not criticizing?

"I'm working with Carlo," she said. "He's taking the photos."

"Ah, Carlo the stud," Athena drawled. "Have you done the dirty with him yet?"

"No way," Max said, frowning. "And even if I wanted to — which I don't — he's engaged to Natalia Dolcezza."

"Oh my God! That see-you-next-Tuesday," Athena spat. "Natalia's the jealous cow who turned *me* down. *I* should have been the face of Dolcezza. You knew that, didn't you?"

"No," Max said, quite surprised. "You

never mentioned anything about it."

"Yes, sweetie, it should've been me," Athena said grandly. "Anyway," she added, "I hear they're dreadful people to work for, so a ton of luck with that."

Max had been hoping to talk to Athena about Gino and Billy, and everything that was going on in her life, but Athena was in a foul mood and obviously couldn't wait to get off the phone, telling Max that she had a hot date with a man who owned the biggest yacht in Saint-Tropez, and that he was madly in lust with her, and was anxiously waiting to whisk her away to Sardinia. "See you, dear" were Athena's parting words.

Realizing that their friendship was probably over, Max experienced a pang of regret. She'd never imagined that Athena — queen of the European "It" girls — would be envious of her good luck. It was a shame, because they'd had so many fun times together. Obviously, Athena did not appreciate competition, and now she, Max, was the competition.

Too bad. Too sad.

"First Capri, then on to Positano," Carlo informed Max over an espresso on the terrace of an outdoor restaurant near the foot of the Spanish Steps. "Is *bene, si*?"

"Totally, Carlo," she replied, wondering if anyone had told him that she might have to fly home.

"We leave early tomorrow," Carlo continued, waving at a passing girl who blew him a kiss.

"Okay," Max said, sneaking a quick look at her iPhone to see if there was a text or any other message from Billy.

There wasn't.

"Ah, Capri," Carlo sighed, a faraway look in his eyes. *"Bellissima!"*

"Is Natalia coming?" Max asked, sipping her espresso.

"Why she come?" he questioned, wrinkling his forehead. "Why you think that?"

"Because you're engaged," Max said, stating the obvious.

"It no matter," Carlo said, running a hand through his mop of thick black hair. "We stay engaged long time. She not my *wife.*"

"She will be," Max pointed out.

"One day . . . maybe," Carlo said vaguely. "We see."

"Sounds like you're in no rush."

"Why I rush? Life is to be taken slowly," he said, leaning across the table. "Who this man come chasing you last night?"

Was it possible that Carlo was the only person in the entire restaurant who hadn't recognized Billy?

"Just a friend," she said, quickly adding, "Nobody important."

"Bene," Carlo said, satisfied with her reply.

454

" 'Cause when we shoot our photos, *I* am the only man who matter to you. Together we make our special magic. We make *you* very famous, *amore mio.*"

Why was he calling her "my love"? Shouldn't he be reserving those sentiments for Natalia?

Max was relieved that Lorenzo would be by her side for all the trips. She'd grown to depend on him; he was the only one she truly trusted. Carlo was okay when he was sober, but give him a few glasses of wine and he turned into an irascible and annoying drunk. Dante, she sensed, was pure evil. She hardly knew Natalia. And Alfredo seemed oblivious to everything except business. As for the Dolcezza sisters, they didn't seem to care much about anything.

She checked her phone again.

Nothing.

Ah . . . Billy. Playing games with her heart. It wasn't fair. It wasn't right.

What would Lucky do?

Kick him out of her life once and for all.

Max made a sudden decision, a decision she was determined to stick with.

Good-bye, Billy Melina. I'm not falling for your charismatic movie-star trip anymore.

You had your chance, and you blew it.

This is my final good-bye.

CHAPTER FIFTY-SIX

Somehow or other Willow ended up in Ralph Maestro's bed. She hadn't intended to sleep with him so quickly; it just kind of happened. After all, who was she to turn down an afternoon sexual adventure with a major movie star? Three mojitos, a surly Eddie glaring at her, and a shitload of compliments from Ralph coming her way convinced her it would be a fun thing to do. She'd had plenty of actors in her past, although never one as old or as famous as Ralph Maestro. He had to be sixty-something, but since he was a workout freak, he was still in muscular shape. Besides, maybe he could help get her a movie off the ground. He had important connections, and perhaps he'd even agree to make a cameo appearance, which would surprise everyone. Only it would have to be a brief appearance — she wouldn't want anyone stealing her spotlight.

When they'd left Spago, there were a bunch of paparazzi gathered outside. Ralph got off on the attention; he'd put his arm around her and announced, "This pretty little lady could be my new girlfriend."

TMZ, recording every word, jumped on it. Willow Price and Ralph Maestro. The tabs would eat it up.

After posing for the paps with a jovial smile, at the same time crushing Willow with his massive arm, Ralph escorted her to a white Bentley, where an alert driver jumped out and opened the rear door. The driver was a Ralph Maestro clone, only younger and uglier.

"My nephew," Ralph announced as they got in the car. "He does everything for me, don't you, Bart?"

Bart gave a half-assed grin, exhibiting teeth that were even bigger than his uncle's.

Back at Ralph's apartment on Wilshire — he'd moved out of his Beverly Hills mansion after his wife's murder — Willow wandered around inspecting shelves loaded with awards while Ralph fixed her a drink. No Oscar, but plenty of other tributes to his long career. Five Golden Globes, several People's Choice Awards, and many other trophies — quite a few from foreign countries.

Ralph's apartment was huge. Once they reached the bedroom, she couldn't say the same about his cock. For a big man, he was sadly lacking in that department. A short fat dick did not do it for her. However, she was an actress, wasn't she? And once they were in bed, she pretended it was a crown jewel to be tended to and much admired.

Ralph was not an exciting lover by any means. He was into the missionary position, which Willow had never been fond of. She tried her best to wriggle out from under his heavy body and maneuver herself on top of him. He was having none of it as he pumped and groaned and insisted that she call out his name. Then he came, and that was that.

After sex he fell asleep, snoring loudly.

Willow contemplated what she should do. She didn't care to hang around while he snored the afternoon away — she had things to accomplish. On the other hand, she didn't want to break their connection. Eventually she got dressed and wrote him a short note telling him how amazing he was — and including her cell number. She stuck it on his bathroom mirror.

On the way out, she was stopped by Bart, who blocked her by the front door as if she were a thief attempting to escape with valuable goods.

"Excuse me," she said, trying to dodge past him.

"My uncle is a very generous man," Bart said, staring at her boobs with lecherous eyes. "Did he give you money?"

What the hell did this prick think? That she was a hooker? What was wrong with him?

458

Didn't he recognize her?

"Get out of my way," she said through clenched teeth. "And if you ever dare to speak to me like that again, I'm telling your uncle, and he'll fire your stupid ass."

Bart took a step to the side. She marched through the door.

Some people were dumber than shit.

Rafael was trying hard, but nothing seemed to be working. He was sprawled on top of Elizabetta in the tiny bedroom she shared with their son. Rafael Junior was not present; he was in the care of his grandma so that Elizabetta and Rafael might have some private time.

Private time meant sex, and Grandma knew that sex was important to keep the money that Rafael sent each month coming. Grandma was a canny old bird.

Elizabetta lay stiffly beneath him. She had not bothered to disrobe, merely gathered her dress above her waist.

Rafael had removed his trousers and underwear, although he still had on his shirt.

The small room was stiflingly hot. No air-conditioning. The ragged curtains were torn, allowing the morning light to stream into the room.

Rafael couldn't help wondering what they did with the money he sent. It certainly wasn't spent on home improvements.

"Go ahead, do it," Elizabetta said sullenly, parting her legs with a weary sigh.

Was this the woman he'd left behind? The woman he'd dreamed about? The woman he'd saved himself for? In America he'd turned down countless opportunities to be unfaithful and he never had been. Except for Willow.

He couldn't get hard; his cock refused to cooperate. He was put off by the wiry bush growing between Elizabetta's legs — a virtual forest he was forced to navigate.

Flashes of Willow came to mind. Her smooth, creamy body, her long legs with no hair between them, just welcoming warmth and wetness.

How come he remembered?

He wasn't supposed to remember, and yet he did. Now he couldn't get it up for this peasant woman, the mother of his child.

It came to him in a flash.

He didn't love her anymore. It was over.

Willow made it home, where a pack of paparazzi were hanging around outside her house waiting to pounce. There were more of them than usual. Being seen with Mr. Action-Movie Star was an excellent boost for her image.

The questions flowed fast and furious.

Where's your new boyfriend?

Are you and Ralph engaged?

How long you been seeing him?
You in love, Willow?
When's the big day?

Ridiculous questions. She didn't answer any of them as she made her way into her house.

I'm hot again, she thought gleefully. *Hot and happening. Ha! Wait until they hear about my movie, then I'll really be on fire.*

Which reminded her that she should check in with Sam and assure him that he'd have his deal memo this week. Next she'd call Alejandro to find out when they could expect to have cash on hand. And finally she'd contact Eddie — who she knew would be steaming because she'd left the restaurant with Ralph.

Willow grinned. All was going as planned.

To Rafael's surprise, Pablo agreed that Alejandro becoming a Hollywood producer might be a good idea.

Really? Rafael wanted to say. *Surely you know he's a fool, and this project will be like pissing money into the wind?*

Instead he said a respectful, "You have made a wise decision, Señor Diego. Alejandro will be very happy."

A pleased-with-himself Pablo clicked his fingers for Eugenia to pour him more wine.

"Perhaps I *will* visit," Pablo said, surprising Rafael even more — for everyone knew that

461

Pablo Fernandez Diego rarely left the safety of his heavily guarded compound.

"You will?" Rafael said, not sure that he relished the thought of Pablo coming to L.A.

"Maybe," Pablo responded, clicking his false teeth. "I have a wish to meet some of the young ladies you mentioned. Beautiful sexy actresses. I have always had a yen for Cameron Diaz. I would like a meeting to be arranged. You take care of it."

Rafael almost choked at the thought of Cameron Diaz and Pablo Fernandez Diego getting together. That would *never* happen.

Eugenia served the two men platters of thick steak and an assortment of vegetables.

Pablo slapped her on the ass before cutting into his steak with a sharp knife. Blood flowed from the hefty piece of meat.

"Moron!" he screamed at Eugenia. "You know I like my steak well-done. Why are you so stupid, woman?" And with those words, he picked up his plate and flung it at her.

Rafael felt his mother's humiliation as the plate hit her full in the face.

He said nothing. He was as trapped as she was.

"I understand you visited your girlfriend today," Pablo said, turning to Rafael as if he hadn't just thrown his plate at Rafael's mother.

Rafael nodded. The last thing he wished to be reminded of was the disastrous day he'd spent with Elizabetta.

"You know," Pablo continued, twirling his fork in a not-so-playful way, "your girlfriend is fucking one of my guards. I have heard they might even marry."

Rafael experienced a sharp, stabbing pain in his gut. Was it possible that Pablo was telling the truth? Was that why Elizabetta had been so surly and indifferent toward him?

He met Pablo's gaze full on. Was the old tyrant hoping for a reaction?

Rafael refused to give him what he wanted.

"This is a fine wine, Señor Diego," he said, keeping his voice even and steady. "Might I request another glass?"

Pablo's expression changed from calm to a malicious scowl. He'd expected more from Rafael. He'd expected sniveling and whining and protestations that the information couldn't possibly be true. He'd expected to be *entertained*.

This was not to be. A shame, for there was nothing Pablo liked more than being entertained.

He rose abruptly from the table. "It is time for you to return to America," he said authoritatively. "Alejandro cannot be trusted on his own. You have to always stay by his side to protect him."

"Am I to tell him that you have agreed to finance his movie?" Rafael inquired, half hoping that Pablo would say no.

"This is so," Pablo said, fingering his beard. "I will finance his movie through you."

"Excuse me?" Rafael said.

"We both know that Alejandro can be . . . reckless at times. He is not good with responsibility. Therefore, the money will be cleaned and I shall arrange for you to open a special account that you will oversee and report to me about."

"Alejandro may not like that," Rafael ventured.

"That's the way it is," Pablo said.

"What about the cash he's asked me to bring back to the U.S.?"

"Foolish!" Pablo snorted. "There are plenty of dollars in the U.S. I will arrange delivery for the initial up-front money. He can have that, and then you will take over all finances."

Rafael was relieved. Trying to smuggle two million dollars on his person back to America was indeed a stupid idea. Alejandro had been screwing with him, as usual; he'd known Pablo would never give him the cash.

"One of my drivers will take you to the airport," Pablo said, dismissing Rafael as if he was a lowly servant. "You can leave now."

Yes, Rafael thought. *I will leave now. But one of these days, I will be back to collect my son. I make this promise to myself. It is a promise I swear I will keep.*

CHAPTER FIFTY-SEVEN

Chris Warwick had two means of transport. One was a personalized van that he used for work. The other was a fully restored 1965 silver Ford Mustang that he took out only on special occasions. Tonight he drove his van, which he'd parked in a lot at LAX before flying to Chicago.

Chris always made sure that he was prepared for anything that might happen. He carried a Glock semi-automatic pistol for which he had a license, and tucked away on different parts of his body were two five-inch folding knives always sharp and ready for action. He might look unthreatening, but with all his martial art skills, he was a lethal weapon.

It was getting late when he drove up to Pedro Albarado's door in Silver Lake, unannounced. Thanks to his many connections, he'd already found out quite a bit about Pedro. Pedro Albarado had a long history of crimes ranging from carjacking to home invasion, burglary, and receiving stolen goods. He'd done time twice, and was quite the career criminal.

Had Pedro murdered the girl in Chicago? Probably. But that wasn't Chris's problem. His intent was to find out why Bobby had been set up. And even more important — who was responsible?

A woman answered the door. A plump Mexican woman with rollers in her hair and a long-suffering expression on her sullen face. She stared at Chris with bleary eyes.

Mother? Sister? Wife? Daughter? She could be any of them, although maybe she wasn't old enough to be the mother.

Chris refrained from flashing his phony detective badge. He didn't relish the thought of Pedro leaping out a back window and making a run for it. Instead he spoke quietly in a friendly, non-threatening manner. "I have lucrative business to discuss with Mr. Albarado," he said. "Is he home?"

The woman continued to stare at him as a dog barked in the background. She had no idea what *lucrative* meant, although he could tell that she understood the word *business.*

As Chris returned her stare, his honest brown eyes luring her in, he hoped the dog wasn't a pit bull. He'd had a run-in with a vicious pit bull several years ago while rescuing a kidnap victim, and he still had the scars to prove it.

"You wait," the woman said at last. She had a heavy accent.

"Should I wait out here, or can I come in?"

Her answer was nonverbal as she slammed the door shut in his face.

Some people had no manners at all.

After what seemed like a long while, although it was only a matter of five minutes, the door opened again, and there stood a Latin man in all his stay-at-home glory. Unshaven. Floppy hair. A wifebeater T-shirt with ugly pit stains. Ill-fitting dusty-gray jogging pants — although Chris would've bet his prized Mustang that this dude had never jogged a day in his life — and a pair of scuffed sneakers.

This was hardly the dapper, sour-faced, bearded man from the security tapes. This was a slob of a man, with a brown wad of tobacco sticking to the side of his mouth and bad teeth.

"Mr. Albarado?" Chris inquired politely. "Mr. Pedro Albarado?"

The man squinted at him, a wary look on his face. "Who wants t' know?"

I do, you repugnant dumb-ass, Chris thought, inhaling a foul odor of sweat, stale cigarette smoke, and fierce garlic breath.

"I have a very tempting offer for Mr. Albarado," Chris said.

"What kinda offer?" the man said suspiciously.

"Work."

"My brother don't do no work. He's on disability."

His brother. That made sense. This one stayed at home, while Pedro took care of business.

"I do believe that Pedro should listen to what I have to say," Chris said smoothly. "It involves plenty of . . . money."

"How much?" the man asked, his eyes full of greed.

"I should discuss it with your brother. Is he home?"

"How d'you know about Pedro?"

"I know that he has a reputation for getting things done."

"Yeah?"

"Yes."

"You wanna tell me who sent you?"

"I have contacts in Chicago."

"Chicago, huh?"

A short standoff took place while Pedro's brother thought things over.

"Well?" Chris said, holding his impatience in check.

"What kinda job?"

"A job that'll pay him plenty."

"How much?"

"That's for me to discuss with Pedro."

"I'm gonna try to reach him," the man growled. "There's a diner on the corner. Be there in the back parking lot in an hour."

"Will *he* be there?"

"Mebbe he'll come," the man said noncommittally — adding a succinct, "An' if he finds out you're a fuckin' fed, he'll blow your fuckin' head off."

"Do I look like a federal agent?" Chris said mildly, although he could feel the muscles in his stomach clench.

The man gave him a mirthless laugh. "One hour. In back of the diner."

Lucky couldn't sleep. She was waiting to hear from Chris and he hadn't called. It was infuriating. He was supposed to be working for her, so she expected to be kept up to date on every move he made. He'd told her he'd tracked down the man who'd set up Bobby and that he was on his way back to L.A. to see him. Since then, silence, and silence didn't fly with her.

She'd tried to act like nothing was going on. Tried to bond with her family over dinner. But Lennie knew something was up; he had an antenna for such things.

"Anything you want to share with me?" he asked when everyone had headed down to the beach to swim and Steven had gone to bed claiming jet lag.

"Nothing," she answered vaguely.

"Nothing my ass," he responded. "You've checked your phone a dozen times."

"And I thought I was being so discreet,"

469

she said drily.

"Discreet, huh?" Lennie said with a skeptical smile. "You got a lover you're not telling me about?"

"Very funny."

"You'd better let me know what's going on," he said, turning serious. "You know you can't be doing anything foolish. You have responsibilities. You're not the same girl who took revenge for your mom's murder."

"*And* Dario's, *and* Marco's," she said with a flash of anger. "Do you honestly think I could've survived all these years without doing something about that?"

"It was a long time ago, sweetheart."

"I understand," she said coolly. "While Gino's murder wasn't."

"Promise me you won't do anything you'll regret," Lennie said, giving her an intent look. "Can you promise me that?"

"Don't worry," she said, her eyes dark and steady. "The one thing I'll have is no regrets."

Chris took his time checking out the diner on the corner. It was a small place serving the usual array of fattening dishes — everything from greasy burgers to pancakes and waffles. There was one short-order cook behind the counter, and two waitresses. All three of them looked as if they wished they were someplace else.

After inspecting the inside, he went outside

to his van and drove it into the parking lot at the back of the diner. The lot was dark and secluded, filled with overgrown shrubs and bushes. Hardly any cars. Hardly any customers in the diner.

Chris parked his van and got out. He knew exactly what would happen when Pedro turned up. The man would stick a gun in his ribs and demand to know who he was and what he wanted. He, Chris, would act scared, and Pedro would be under the misguided impression that he had him exactly where he wanted him. Maybe Pedro would bring his brother for backup. Maybe not. It didn't matter — whatever the situation, Chris was confident he'd have it under control.

He strolled back into the diner, sat down at the counter, and asked the waitress for a coffee.

"How about somethin' to eat, honey?" the waitress said, suppressing a weary yawn.

"Not hungry," he replied.

"I can have the cook fix you a tasty plate of bacon an' eggs," she suggested, thinking she wasn't about to get much of a tip on a measly cup of coffee.

Chris dug into his pocket and pulled out a twenty. "This is for the coffee," he said. "Keep the change."

Startled, she grabbed the money. "Thanks, mister," she said, her pinched face brightening. "One cuppa java comin' right up."

■ ■ ■ ■

The boys were back from their swim. Gino Junior and Leo were revved up and excited to be spending time with their big brother. Bobby was enjoying their company too.

Watching Bobby, Lucky felt a wave of relief that he was okay. He was like a little kid again as the three of them raided the kitchen, hungry for anything they could get their hands on. He didn't seem at all traumatized, although she wished that Denver had not taken this moment in time to dump on him. Foolish girl. If Denver wasn't careful, she'd lose him altogether.

"We're gonna play video games," Leo announced. "C'mon, Bobby, you gotta play too."

"Okay, okay," Bobby said, gesturing that he didn't really want to, but he'd do it for them.

"I'll see you all in the morning," Lucky said, happy that he was bonding with his brothers.

Upstairs, she shut herself in her bathroom, pulled out her phone, and sent Chris a terse text.

Where are you? Why aren't you calling me back? You'd better be dead, 'cause that's the only reason I can think of why you wouldn't reply.

After pressing Send, she felt better.

472

The moment Chris had something to tell her, she knew she'd hear from him. Chris was like that, and as irritating as it was, at least he got things done. Right now that was all that mattered.

CHAPTER FIFTY-EIGHT

After Carlo informed Gabriella Dolcezza that Max might have to leave for L.A., everything was put on an accelerated schedule. Instead of heading for Capri the next morning, Max found herself — with Lorenzo and Carlo by her side — arriving in Capri within hours.

The Dolcezza yacht was moored in the dock. The opulent white yacht was to be their base.

"Wow!" Max exclaimed, exploring the incredible hundred-foot boat with Lorenzo close behind her. "This is freaking *awesome!*"

Lorenzo was equally impressed, especially when he met the crew, a group of fit young men all dressed in tight white T-shirts with *Dolcezza* blazoned across the front.

Carlo was not so impressed. He'd been on the yacht many times before. Summer cruising with the Dolcezza family; sharing a cabin with Natalia; listening to her rant and rave about how useless Dante was, and how *she* should be in charge.

The stylist, makeup artist, and hair guru were not staying on the yacht, although they descended as if they were. Max was relieved that this was a different group from the glam squad she'd first encountered back in Rome. These people danced around her, delighted to be there. The makeup artist, a handsome gay man, made her face look summery and glowing. Max loved it. Then she had to strip down for an allover spray tan — which was kind of embarrassing, but she gritted her teeth and tried not to act like a prude.

The hair guru styled her hair with soft beachy waves framing her face, while the clothes stylist came up with a rack of assorted bikinis, tops, shorts, and cute skimpy dresses.

Carlo gave his approval as she slipped on one of the dresses, adding gold sandals, her favorite gold hoop earrings, multiple bangles, rings, and toe rings.

She'd never felt so pampered and carefree as she posed on the top deck of the luxurious yacht.

"You look like a golden princess," Lorenzo told her, full of admiration, while Carlo snapped away capturing image after image.

The Dolcezza girl. She was proud to represent.

Later, when work was done, they all gathered at a popular restaurant called the Lemon Tree, a very romantic spot, with tables set out in a beautiful garden surrounded by lemon trees.

The scent of the lemons was intoxicating, and for one brief moment, Max imagined what it might be like to be sitting at a table for two under the trees with Billy.

It was not a thought she allowed to linger.

During dinner Carlo was all over her, pawing at her skirt, whispering in her ear, attempting to kiss her neck. He'd had too much wine, as usual.

She managed to push him away, turning her attention to the entertainment steward from the yacht, Ross, a husky young Australian with whom she'd felt an immediate rapport. Why not? There was nothing and no one to hold her back from embarking on a new adventure.

When dinner was finished, they all went to an open-air club, where Ross began to kiss her while they were on the dance floor moving together under the stars. He was into long exploratory kisses that made her toes tingle.

Carlo was furious when he noticed what was going on. He complained loudly.

"You're engaged," she reminded him. "Whyn't you try keeping it in your pants?"

This infuriated him even more. He scowled at her and began coming on to a braless blond American tourist who was twirling around the dance floor. The girl obviously enjoyed drunken fumes being breathed into her face, for after a while, they vanished, and Carlo did not return to the yacht until the following morning.

Lucky Natalia, Max thought. *She's got herself a real winner.*

Rather than going back to her parents' house, Denver headed for Carolyn's, hoping that Vanessa wasn't around.

She wasn't, but Carolyn seemed distant and cool, and not that interested in listening to her carry on about Bobby and what his intentions might've been.

Denver wondered if Vanessa had been making up stories about her. She hoped not; the last thing she needed was an awkward relationship with one of her best friends.

"Let me get this straight," Carolyn said over a glass of white wine. "You're not concerned that it's possible Bobby could've *killed* a girl. You're not worried about that, because you're more concerned that he might've been planning to *screw* her."

"No, no, you're getting it all wrong," Denver protested, becoming flustered.

"Get over yourself," Carolyn said sharply. "Your man needs you, and you're acting like a jealous bimbo. Run your ass back home where it belongs. Bobby requires love and attention, and if *you* don't give it to him, I'm sure there are plenty of girls who will."

Carolyn was correct. It was about time she

made things right with Bobby.

She left Carolyn's and drove to the house, rehearsing in her mind what she would say when she got there.

I'm sorry. I love you. I'm here for you. Please forgive me.

Then they would make love. Slow, sensuous love.

By the time she pulled into their driveway, she was sure that everything would be all right.

And it would've been if Bobby had been home. But he wasn't.

She prowled around the house becoming more frustrated and angry at herself. Had she allowed things to go too far? Did Bobby hate her? Had he moved out?

Panicking, she ran upstairs and checked his closet. Everything was in its place. His suits, his sports clothes, his collection of expensive watches. Yes, Bobby was still in residence.

She felt like a fool. How could she have doubted him? He was probably with Lucky and the rest of his family.

Was he missing her? If he was, he certainly wasn't blowing up the phone lines to reach out.

She wondered if she should call him. Then she decided that no, she had to make up with him in person. Bobby was a one-on-one kind of guy.

CHAPTER FIFTY-NINE

"Weren't things supposed to be happening this week?" Sam said over the phone.

He sounded uptight. Willow didn't blame him; she too had thought everything was about to fall into place. Eddie had promised that he'd fast-track their movie as soon as she presented the cash to him, followed by the rest of the up-front money to get things moving.

The problem was that *she* wasn't responsible for getting the money, Alejandro was, and it appeared he was doing jack shit about coming up with it.

"If nothing comes together today, then I'm out," Sam threatened.

She hung up on Sam and called Alejandro. Matias informed her that his boss had been out all night and was still sleeping.

Out all night doing what? Fucking his brains out and snorting blow? It was late afternoon, for crissake. He'd better get it together or this deal was going away. She'd certainly done her part. She'd gotten them the services of a known screenwriter *and* solicited Eddie Falcon to represent them. It was disappointing, because if Alejandro didn't come through, they were on a fast track to nowhere.

She took a shower, vigorously scrubbing off all traces of Ralph Maestro's sickeningly sweet aftershave. When she was finished, she called Eddie on his private line — the line his assistant/agent-in-training did not listen in on.

"Bad move," Eddie growled.

"Bad move what?" she asked innocently.

"You know what," he snapped.

"I didn't fuck him," she lied.

"Yes you did," Eddie said accusingly.

"What if I did?" she said defiantly. After all, it wasn't as if she had to answer to Eddie Falcon. He was a married man.

"It's not right, Willow," he said, sounding uptight.

"Could be if he helps out with our movie," she said flippantly.

"Don't you get it?" Eddie blustered. "He's my fucking *father-in-law,* for crissake. He's family."

"So?"

"So you should've taken that into account."

"Why?"

"Jesus Christ, you're a real pain in my ass."

"One of these days I could be your

stepmother-in-law," she announced, teasing him. "Wouldn't *that* be a blast. Imagine what holidays would be like. Christmas Day — you and me in the bathroom, me sucking you off, while Annabelle and Ralph bond like a father and daughter should."

"You're sick, you know that?"

"Oh yes, and you're so perfect," she said, knowing that she was turning him on.

After a long pause, he said, "You coming over?"

"When did you have in mind?"

"Later — after everyone's gone."

"Why do I always have to wait till everyone's out of there?" she complained.

"Because I say so."

"Seems you're forgetting that I'm a legitimate client again."

"Premature."

"Excuse me?"

"Forget it," Eddie said gruffly. "Be here at six. Use my private elevator."

"And we'll discuss our project?"

"Sure."

"Anything else you'd like from me, Mr. Big Shot Falcon?" she asked coyly.

"I'd like you to stop fucking my father-in-law," he said with a surly grunt.

"I'll take it under consideration," she said, clicking off her phone and grinning to herself.

Eddie was jealous. Good. It would force him to pay attention. And if there was one

481

thing that Willow loved, it was attention.

Alejandro surfaced late in the afternoon. Matias gave him his messages — including one from Rafael saying he was on his way back to L.A. Summoning his housekeeper, Alejandro ordered coffee and an omelet, then he reflected on the previous night's activities. He pictured the two plain Valley girls standing in front of him wearing nothing except the plastic baggies of drugs taped to their imperfect bodies. Then he pictured himself ripping the baggies off the girls, listening to them squeal with pain as the tape tore at their skin.

Thinking about it gave him an immediate erection, which pleased him. He'd been taking so much Viagra lately that he wasn't sure if he could get it up without the little blue pill.

It wasn't that he needed Viagra like some decrepit old man. No, he simply enjoyed the explosive effect. In his mind, Viagra was heroin for his cock.

Sitting up in bed, he reached for the remote and tuned into afternoon television. He really enjoyed the talk shows with their dyke hosts and needy audiences. So many women seeking love advice. Who *wouldn't* enjoy imagining them naked — all different shapes and sizes — all searching for a man who could satisfy them?

The women in the audiences reminded him of the two girls, his obedient drug mules. Girls who would do anything for money.

Thinking of money reminded him of Willow. Matias had mentioned she'd called, so he reached for his cell and called her back.

"Where's the money?" she said, sounding shrill. "We can't get anything started without the cash."

"Rafael's on his way back. He'll have everything."

"He only just left," Willow pointed out.

"What difference does that make?" Alejandro said, watching a female on *The Daytona Rich Show* burst into tears because her boyfriend had cheated on her. She exhibited no shame in front of millions of people.

"Does this mean you'll have the cash tomorrow?" Willow asked impatiently.

"Maybe," Alejandro said, opening his nightstand drawer and reaching for a small glassine packet of coke, which he proceeded to tip out onto the top of the nightstand.

"I hope so, 'cause I've got everyone on hold," Willow said.

"Keep 'em there," Alejandro said, leaning over to snort a line.

"Should I come by later?"

"Not tonight," Alejandro said, thinking that if the Puerto Rican with the juicy ass returned, she was going to be all his.

Willow couldn't make up her mind whether

she was relieved or pissed off. Relieved won out — because how many cocks could she service in one day? First the afternoon fling with Ralph. Then later she knew Eddie would expect oral — he always did. So dealing with Alejandro might've been one cock too many.

"Then tomorrow for sure?" she said. "I'll come over around noon to pick up the cash. We can work on an announcement for the trades, and maybe discuss hiring a top PR. Publicity is king, and it's essential that we hire the best."

Alejandro snorted another line. "Okay," he mumbled.

They both clicked off at the same time.

Settling back into his bed, Alejandro continued watching TV.

Willow went into her bathroom and started getting ready for her meeting with Eddie.

Soon their movie would be set to go.

Both of them envisioned a place for themselves in the Hollywood sun.

CHAPTER SIXTY

Persuasion is a funny thing. Sometimes it takes money. Sometimes it takes violence. Chris was adept at either, depending on what the situation called for.

Pedro, it turned out, was the scruffy and unkempt brother Chris had encountered earlier — except now he'd cleaned himself up and he actually resembled the man from the security tape. Chris suddenly realized that he *was* the man.

Exactly as Chris had expected, Pedro came up behind him in the parking lot, stuck a gun in his ribs, and muttered, "Who t' fuck send you t' me, mothafucker?"

This was not the first time Chris had experienced a gun in his ribs, and it probably wasn't going to be the last. It didn't faze him. In fact, it didn't bother him at all, for he knew that whenever he felt like it, he could disarm this ass-wipe and take control.

Timing was everything.

"You killed a girl in Chicago," Chris said

evenly. "Why'd you do it?"

"Who're you, her husband?" Pedro sneered.

"Nope. I'm simply an interested party."

Pedro dug him hard with the gun, not understanding why the *pedazo de mierda* wasn't shaking in his boots. "I ain't askin' again — where'd you hear 'bout me?" he snarled.

"Tell me what happened in Chicago," Chris countered.

"Listen t' me, mothafucker —"

Enough, Chris thought. *I don't have the time to be standing here going around in circles.*

With one swift move that Pedro didn't see coming, he disarmed the man — sticking Pedro's own gun in his stomach. "I'm asking nicely. It's up to you, because if you don't care to answer, we'll be here until you do."

"What t' fuck —" Pedro fumed, trying to figure out what had just taken place. He was not used to being the victim.

"Yeah, what the fuck is right," Chris said. "Glad that you're finally getting it, 'cause I don't have the time nor the inclination to hang around waiting for you to tell me something that you *will* tell me, whether it be now or hours from now. Your choice. Now, who hired you to go to Chicago?"

There was something in Chris's tone that convinced Pedro he meant business. But Pedro was canny enough to realize that if this big lug wanted information, then why

486

shouldn't he get paid for it?

"How much?" he muttered.

"How much what?" Chris responded.

"How much you gonna pay me for the info I got?"

It's never easy, Chris thought with a weary sigh. *How come I always have to end up hurting someone before they give it up? And this ass-wipe will eventually give it up, whether he wants to or not.*

Of course he *could* pay him. But why would he pay a piece of shit murderer? No. He'd get the information he required, then he'd do Detective Cole's job for him and point the detective in the direction of the real killer, because he had no doubt that's who Pedro was.

Jamming the gun in Pedro's stomach, he began moving him toward his van.

"Okay, okay," Pedro muttered. "We stay out here. I tell you what you wanna know."

And with that he jerked his knee up — making a vain attempt to throw Chris off balance. Chris saw it coming and swiftly side-stepped, jamming the gun even harder into Pedro's soft gut.

"You want me to shoot you?" Chris threatened. "How do you feel about a bullet in your belly? 'Cause one more move like that, an' I'll do it."

Pedro grunted.

They reached the van. Chris shoved him roughly into the back. It was time to get some answers.

A couple of hours later, Lucky felt the phone she had tucked under her pillow vibrate.

Rolling over in bed, she glanced quickly at Lennie. He was sleeping soundly. Grabbing her phone, she hurried downstairs to the kitchen.

Chris had texted her. *Pedro A involved with Bobby setup. No connection to Gino. Call me a.m.*

Did he honestly think she was waiting until the morning to call him? No way.

Grabbing a 7-Up from the fridge, she made her way into her study, shutting the door behind her. Popping open the can, she called Chris.

"I thought you'd be asleep," he said.

"And *I* thought I'd hear from you earlier."

"I got held up. Had to deal with some uh . . . dental work."

"Dental work?"

"Don't ask."

"So . . . tell me everything."

"Not over the phone, Lucky. I'll meet you for breakfast."

"It's not a good idea for you to come to the house. Bobby's starting to make noise about getting involved, and that's the last thing I need. I want Bobby kept out of this."

"Where, then?"

"There's a breakfast truck parked above Zuma beach. I'll see you there at seven."

"Got it."

At six-thirty A.M. Lucky managed to exit the house undetected. Lennie was a heavy sleeper, and the boys were sleeping too, having played video games until three A.M.

She informed the security guard at the front of the house that she was taking a drive.

"Should I come with you, Mrs. Golden?" the guard asked, edging toward her.

"No thanks," she said.

"Mr. Golden told us —"

"Yes, I know," she said impatiently. "He told you I should have company, and *you* can tell Mr. Golden that you tried, okay?"

"Yes, ma'am."

Hmm . . . since when had she become "ma'am"?

She'd left Lennie a note on the bathroom mirror. *Meeting Chris for breakfast. Will call you later.*

He'd be pissed, but so what? She didn't have to answer to him. Truth was, she didn't have to answer to anyone. And the same went for him. Their marriage worked because they gave each other the freedom to do whatever they wanted. Unfortunately, Gino's murder had freaked Lennie out, and that was because he knew what she was capable of, and he didn't want her putting herself in danger. Lennie didn't understand what revenge meant. He did not share the same mind-set on that subject.

The Pacific Coast Highway was clear, no traffic. Lucky raced her Ferrari down the winding stretch of road, impatient to hear what Chris would have to say.

She arrived at Zuma early and spotted Chris's van already there, parked near the food truck.

It occurred to her that although she and Chris shared a great working relationship, she actually knew nothing about his personal life. Was he married? Did he have kids? Or maybe just a girlfriend?

Who knew? Not she. For Gino had taught her that it wasn't wise to pry into people's personal lives, not unless they offered up the information.

Chris was not offering.

She was not asking.

Chris had seen her drive onto the spacious open lot and was already approaching her. "Morning," he said.

"Hard night?" she asked, noticing that he looked tired.

"Flying in and out of Chicago in one day wasn't the greatest. I'm here, though," he said with a casual shrug.

"Let's get coffee," she said, striding toward the food truck as a couple of early-morning

490

surfers passed by all suited up and ready for action.

They both got Styrofoam cups of black coffee and sat down at a wooden picnic table overlooking the ocean.

"I used to come here with Dario when we could escape the Bel Air mausoleum," Lucky reflected, gazing at the breaking waves.

"Your brother?" Chris asked.

"Yeah, Dario was a great kid. Artistic. While all I wanted to do was take over Gino's business."

"That you did."

"Oh yes, I certainly did," she said, sipping her coffee.

"I'm sure Gino was very proud of you."

"Eventually."

"It's going to be another hot one today," Chris said, squinting at the sun.

"Okay," Lucky said. "We're not here to discuss my personal life or the weather. What's the story about Bobby getting set up?"

"You're going to find it hard to believe."

"Try me."

Chris began to explain. "This Pedro dude was hired to go to Bobby's club with a girl as bait to get Bobby to go back to the hotel with her. Then she was to drug him — which she did — and the girl was to get a beating, something Pedro omitted to tell her. The beating was to be blamed on Bobby, so that he'd get arrested and his DA girlfriend would fly to Chicago — taking her mind off the drug kingpin she's working to take down."

"Denver?"

"Is that his girlfriend?"

"Yes. She's part of a drug task force."

"Targeting who?"

"I don't know the details. Bobby does."

"Okay."

"I'm confused," Lucky said, frowning. "Exactly *how* did this so-called plan turn into a murder?"

"Like I said, the call girl they hired — Nadia — was not warned about the beating. When Pedro started doing his thing, she fought back, he got carried away, and there you go. One dead call girl."

"That's pretty fucked up."

"I told you."

"And you're certain it has nothing to do with Gino's murder?"

"No. We're still at square one on that."

"Who hired this Pedro guy?"

"I can find out if you think it matters. Pedro's story was that he was hired over the phone. Money was paid via bank transfer. I've contacted Detective Cole in Chicago with a full rundown on Pedro. And here's the kicker. I recorded everything. Got a full confession from the douche."

"You must be very persuasive."

"I have certain skills."

"Where's Pedro now?"

"Probably running his sorry ass over the border. I let him go. The shit-bag's not our problem. Bobby's in the clear. I've already alerted Beverly to take care of the details. The case against Bobby will be dismissed."

"That's great."

"You want me to follow up on who hired Pedro?"

"No. You're correct, it doesn't matter. It's done," she said restlessly. "Right now we need to concentrate on Gino's killer. You have to help me with this, Chris. I can't go on not knowing. Somebody has to pay for what they did."

"I understand."

"There must be *something* to lead us in the right direction."

"I've still got my guy at face recognition working on it. Now that Bobby's in the clear, I can give it my all."

"Thanks, Chris."

"Not to worry. We'll find him. That's a promise."

"And when we do," she said, her eyes black and deadly, "I'll deal with him. Me and nobody else. Do you understand?"

"Only too well."

CHAPTER SIXTY-ONE

As soon as her meeting with Chris was finished, Lucky drove back to the Malibu house, sat down with Bobby, and gave him the news that he would soon be vindicated. She filled him in on everything, including the information that it had all taken place because of the drug kingpin Denver was so intent on locking up.

For a moment Bobby felt numb. Denver was involved. *His* Denver.

Only she wasn't his Denver anymore, was she?

Because of Denver's stubborn determination to take down Alejandro Diego, a girl had gotten herself murdered. A beautiful girl. The girl in the red dress. Nadia. And he'd been targeted due to Denver's stupid obsession. He was furious.

After listening to everything Lucky had to say, he decided it was time to go home and confront Denver. Not that it was her fault directly, but because of everything that had

taken place, he couldn't help blaming her —
even though he realized that he was being
unreasonable. She couldn't have known to
what lengths Alejandro Diego would go.

The sad truth was that something terrible
had taken place. A girl had been murdered,
and if Denver hadn't been so fixated on
bringing down Alejandro, it wouldn't have
happened.

He said good-bye to Lennie and Steven.
Gino Junior and Leo were loathe to see him
go; they hung on to him, demanding to know
when he'd be back.

"Soon," he assured them.

At least he'd gotten to spend time with his
family. He felt refreshed, invigorated, and
ready to have it out with Denver. What would
she have to say when he told her the whole
sordid story?

I could've died, he thought for the hun-
dredth time. *And all she was worried about
was if I was thinking of getting laid.*

He was still angry that she hadn't trusted
him. She'd done nothing to help, and she
hadn't even mentioned Gino's demise when
she'd flown into Chicago to accuse him.

The more he thought about her actions,
the angrier he became. Once again he realized that she was not the girl he'd thought
she was.

By the time he reached their house in the
Hollywood Hills it was still early. Her car was

in the driveway. No time like the present to deal with the situation.

He entered the house, and when he couldn't find her downstairs, he headed upstairs.

The shower was running. Damn it. The last thing he wanted was a confrontation with Denver while she was naked. He knew exactly where that would lead, and sex was the furthest thing from his mind.

Or was it?

Maybe sex would solve their problems. Perhaps a roll around their king-sized bed would make all the bad things go away. He could certainly do with some loving.

No! A voice screamed in his head. *You gotta get things straight first.*

Making his way back downstairs, he went into the kitchen and put on coffee.

Then he sat at the kitchen table and waited.

Ross was a diversion that Max felt she deserved. Nothing serious. No falling in love, simply a lighthearted distraction from thinking about Billy, the man who'd led her on once again.

What was Billy Melina's romantic crap all about? A tour of Rome at night. Throwing a coin in the fountain and making a wish. Long, lingering looks.

I'll call you tomorrow, Green Eyes.

Sure. And I can sell you a condo in Alaska!

She wasn't mad at him for not calling or texting. She was mad at herself for believing he would.

How naive. If Athena had taught her one thing, it was not to believe a word any man said. *They're all liars,* Athena had assured her. *The trick is to out-lie them.*

Or have fun with someone else, Max thought. And that's exactly what she was doing, until Dante turned up on the yacht and ruined everything.

Dante arrived on the second day of shooting the campaign. He immediately attempted to take control, ordering a change of outfits, demanding new locations, claiming he didn't like her hair and that the photos weren't sexy enough.

Carlo argued that the photos were supposed to picture the Dolcezza girl as young and fresh. Dante retaliated by saying that she looked *too* innocent. They fought bitterly. Eventually Carlo got on the phone and summoned Natalia — who arrived hours later with six pieces of Louis Vuitton luggage and a superior smirk.

Shooting stopped for the day, and Max seized the opportunity to take off with Ross. He got one of the stewards to fill in for him, then they ran from the yacht without anyone seeing them go. She was determined to push Billy out of her mind for once, and Ross was just the man to help out. He was a true

Australian hunk with hard abs and a great body. She was definitely into his arresting accent and his stubbled chin. What was not to like? He was a Chris Hemsworth clone.

"You wanna hit the beach?" he suggested. "Get a beer, chill out. You've been workin' hard. Couldn't stop eyeballin' you."

"Really?" she said, flattered.

"Yeah, really."

"So the beach it is," she said, taking a deep breath.

They headed for a nearby beach, where Ross suggested that they rent a pedal boat and take it out to sea.

"I'm not a great swimmer," she murmured.

"No worries," Ross said, grinning. "Promise I'll save you."

"Promise?" she said, feeling the excitement that something was about to happen.

The sea was calm, and Ross was doing all the pedaling, taking them a good distance from the shore.

After a while he stopped pedaling and they rocked gently on the surface of the sea.

"You do know you're a beaut," Ross said, leaning in for a kiss.

She responded, playing tongue twisters, lost in the moment.

Suddenly he was all hands, unclipping her bikini top, caressing her breasts with his manly hands, tweaking her nipples until she began gasping with pleasure. Then he took her hand and guided it to his very impressive hard-on.

The moment of truth was upon her. Did she want to go all the way?

Maybe. Billy was out there somewhere, no doubt screwing his movie-star ass off.

Ross was busy maneuvering himself out of his shorts.

Oh God! What was she supposed to do? She liked Ross, but just liking someone wasn't enough to do the deed. And she doubted Ross had a condom stashed away.

It was decision time.

Without giving it any more thought, she began stroking his erect penis until he came with a long satisfied groan.

"Jesus Christ!" he mumbled. "Bloody hell, where'd you learn to do that?"

"Was it good?"

"Bloody ace."

"We should get back," she said, reaching for her bikini top.

"Not until I've done somethin' for you," he said. "How about I go down on you?"

"How about you owe me one?"

"You're somethin' else."

"So I've been told."

They grinned at each other, perfectly at ease. Then they headed for the shore, stopping for an ice cream on their way back to the yacht.

Dante was waiting on deck with his usual

dour expression. He promptly fired Ross on the spot, whereupon Max threw a fit. She couldn't believe Dante could be so mean and nasty. She locked herself in her cabin and refused to come out.

This was not turning out to be the spectacular job she'd envisioned.

Denver jumped out of the shower and grabbed her buzzing phone. It was Leon, telling her to get to the office as fast as possible. Apparently, Eric, the chief deputy, was ready to make a decision about Frankie Romano, and he wanted to see them both immediately.

"I'm on my way," she assured Leon, quickly throwing on her clothes, then tying her long wet hair back into a ponytail.

No time for primping; this was too exciting.

Racing downstairs, she immediately spotted Bobby at the kitchen table. "Damn it!" she muttered under her breath, for much as she was anxious to see him, the timing couldn't be worse.

"You're home," she gasped.

"Yeah," Bobby said, not getting up. "Looks like I am, and we need to talk."

"I know we do," she said, hovering in the doorway. "Unfortunately, my job calls. It'll have to wait until later."

Bobby stared at his girlfriend, his smart, beautiful, hardworking girlfriend — who apparently didn't give a rat's ass that he was back.

"What do you mean, 'later'?" he said abruptly.

"I've been summoned to an emergency meeting at the office," she explained. "They need me to be there like ten minutes ago."

"How about if *I* need you?" Bobby said, watching her closely. "Does that make any difference?"

"Of course it does," she said quickly. "And I dropped everything to fly to Chicago."

"Did you now?"

"Yes, Bobby, I did. And I know we have to talk, which we will — only later."

"Jesus, Denver," he said, not even angry anymore, merely disappointed. "Do you care at all about what I've been going through?"

"Yes, Bobby," she said, attempting to curb her impatience. "And I'll be home as soon as I can."

"That might not be soon enough," he said, his tone tinged with a wry bitterness.

"Please understand," she begged, thinking that this conversation was going nowhere. "We'll straighten everything out, I promise."

"It's already straightened out, thanks to the people who actually care about me," he said shortly.

She had no idea what he was talking about, and right now the clock was ticking.

She turned to leave.

501

He didn't try to stop her.

It'll all work out, she assured herself as she hurried out the front door. *He's angry now, but later I can get him to understand. I know he will.*

Bobby waited until he heard her car leave. His mind was buzzing with so many thoughts. He had things to take care of, and a girlfriend who was more interested in her job than in him. After his harrowing ordeal, it didn't seem right. The doubts he'd been feeling about Denver were multiplying. She didn't care about him. He'd seen it in Chicago when she'd accused him of wanting to get laid, and now he'd seen it again when she put her job first. He'd gotten nothing from her. No *What's happening? Are you all right? I'm so sorry about Gino. What can I do?*

This was not the girl he'd fallen in love with. This was not *his* Denver.

He went upstairs, grabbed a suitcase, opened his closet, and began throwing his clothes into the open case.

She could have the house. It was all hers. A good-bye present. He'd had enough.

Lucky was right: if Denver didn't believe him, there was no future for them.

Chapter Sixty-Two

Eddie was in a questioning mood. He required details about everything sexual that had taken place between Willow and Ralph Maestro. He wanted size, shape, technique, length of time.

"You're such a filthy old pervert," Willow teased, secretly thrilled that he cared enough to be jealous. "What's it to you anyway?"

"Didja blow him?" Eddie asked, pacing around his office. " 'Cause I dunno if I wanna put my cock someplace where Ralph Maestro's been."

"Then don't," Willow responded, wondering what it would be like to be married to a man like Eddie, a powerful man with all the right contacts.

"Whaddya mean, *don't*?" Eddie said. He was already sporting a serious hard-on — quite obvious through his tailored custom-made pants.

"I'm here on business," Willow said, giving him her best serious expression. "Did you find us someone to rewrite Sam's script?"

"Did *you* come up with my money?"

"You know I will. Alejandro's promised I'll get it tomorrow."

"Alejandro this, Alejandro that," Eddie complained. "The dude's a sleazy drug dealer. How d'you know you can trust him?"

"I trust him because he wants this as much as I do," she said tartly. "And for your information, he's not a sleazy drug dealer. He runs a legitimate nightclub, and he's always treated me like a princess."

"Yeah, that's so he can be photographed with you," Eddie sneered. "Don't you get it? The dude's a fame whore."

"And you're not?" she said, throwing him a knowing look. "As far as I can tell, your whole agenting deal depends on kissing clients' asses."

"I'll be running a studio soon," Eddie assured her. "When that happens, they'll all be kissing *my* ass."

"And *I'll* be starring in all your movies," she said with a gleeful grin.

"Let's see what kinda talent you got before I make any promises," Eddie said.

"You *know* I'm talented," Willow insisted. "You've seen me act. I've been in movies ever since I was a kid. I just gotta get another chance to show everyone in Hollywood what I can do."

"Yeah, babe," Eddie said, unzipping his

504

pants. "In the meantime, how about showing *me* what you can do?"

"I'm not sure I should indulge you now that I've met your wife," Willow said with a prim shrug. "She seems so . . . perfect."

"Perfect my ass," Eddie snorted, dropping his pants around his ankles. "She'd have my balls for breakfast if she ever caught me. Anyway, she's not going to, is she, sweet tits? 'Cause you an' I, we got an understanding, right?"

"We do?" Willow said, not sure what he meant.

"Y'know we do," Eddie responded, thrusting his penis toward her mouth. She dropped to her knees and took it in, deep-throating him the way she knew he liked.

He groaned his pleasure, pressing both hands down hard on the top of her head, forcing himself even deeper into her mouth.

Willow experienced a surge of power, something she felt whenever she had a man's precious member in her mouth. Whoever the poor guy was, he imagined he was in control, but no, *she* was the one in control — *she* was the one with the sharp teeth who might easily ruin his life forever. One bite and it could all be over.

Unable to hold back, Eddie came almost immediately. Hearing about Ralph and the things his wife's movie-star father had done to Willow in bed had turned him on big-time, besides he had a meeting to get to, then dinner at Craig's Restaurant with Annabelle and another power couple. No time to waste. Eddie was a big believer in getting things done fast.

As soon as Eddie was finished, Willow hurried into his private bathroom, rinsed her mouth, fluffed out her hair, applied fresh lipstick, and returned to Eddie's office, only to discover that he was already dressed. He was standing there with an impatient look on his face, which didn't suit her at all. She was tired of Eddie making a run for it as soon as she'd finished blowing him. It was major dick behavior.

"I gotta take off, sugar tits," he said, adjusting his shirt collar. "Business calls."

"I'm sure it does," she answered evenly. "That's why we should discuss our project and what's happening."

"Nothing to discuss until I see the cash," Eddie responded, determined to make a fast getaway.

"I've told you, the money will be here tomorrow."

"Then we'll talk. Same time. Same place."

Willow considered his attitude to be crap, but since he was her only real option, she couldn't argue.

On the way out of his office, she checked her phone. There was a voice mail from Ralph Maestro, her new admirer.

Where'd you run off to, little lady? his voice boomed. *Wanna take you to the premiere of my latest movie tomorrow night. Call me.*

Oh yes, she would call him, all right. Appearing on Ralph Maestro's arm at a big important star-studded premiere would ensure maximum publicity. And right now she was soaking in all she could get.

By the time Rafael arrived back in L.A., he was exhausted. His flight had been bumpy and crowded, filled with crying babies and harassed flight attendants. He drank too much — something he didn't usually do — and after downing several shots of vodka, he slept badly. Later he awoke with a massive hangover and a sour taste in his mouth.

He was not the same Rafael who'd left L.A. twenty-four hours earlier. This Rafael was a bitter and disillusioned man whose thoughts of a future with Elizabetta and Rafael Junior had been well and truly shattered. Angrily, he kept on imagining Elizabetta in bed with one of Pablo's hired men, experiencing all the things she should've been doing with him.

Whore!

Puta!

He hated her.

And yet . . . he had to control his hate, for she was in possession of his precious son, and the most important thing on his mind was getting the boy away from her.

507

He had no more worries about Elizabetta seeing the sex tape Alejandro was holding over his head. Let Alejandro send it to her. What did he care? Elizabetta could watch him make love to a real woman. An American woman. A *famous* American woman.

He got in his car, which he'd left in a parking structure at the airport, and checked his phone. There was a voice mail from Alejandro's lawyer, Horace Bendon. It was short and to the point. "Your client fired me. You'd better get on it. I think Frankie's about to make a deal."

Normally, Rafael would've panicked. Today he couldn't have cared less.

A plan was forming in his head. An excellent plan.

CHAPTER SIXTY-THREE

Finally, the call came that Lucky had been waiting for. "We're releasing your father's body," Detective Allan informed her.

She was overcome with a feeling of enormous relief mixed with a rush of pure sadness. "I'll make immediate arrangements to send a plane," she said.

"You'd better do it fast," Detective Allan warned. "Mrs. Santangelo is making noises that the body is hers. And since she's his legal spouse — or was —"

"I get it," Lucky said, her sadness turning to anger that Paige would have the balls to try to take control. How *dare* she. Didn't the bitch understand who she was dealing with?

Apparently not.

The moment she hung up on Detective Allan, she instructed Danny to get her a plane and to fast-track the funeral, which she'd quickly decided would take place in three days. Then she called Paige. They had not spoken since Lucky had left Palm Springs;

there'd been no need to.

"Paige," she said, determined to keep her cool.

"Hello, dear," Paige said, sounding sassy and full of herself.

"Just to let you know, I will be flying in to collect my father's body later today."

"That won't be necessary."

"Excuse me?"

"Although I am aware that you were thinking of having the funeral in Vegas, I have decided that a funeral in Palm Springs is far more appropriate. All of Gino's friends are here. I am making arrangements now. Naturally, you'll be welcome to attend."

Was she kidding? "Welcome to attend." What the fuck?

"Uh, Paige," Lucky said, attempting to remain calm, "I'm not quite sure that you understood me when I told you that Gino will be put to rest and celebrated in Las Vegas. The family mausoleum is there, and that's where he will end his days."

"Yes, I understood," Paige said airily, as if anything Lucky had to say didn't matter. "However, things change, and as Gino's widow, *I* am the one who has the final decision about where he is laid to rest."

"Is that so?" Lucky said, her tone icy.

"I should also inform you," Paige continued, sounding even more sure of herself, "that my lawyer has told me that I have every

510

legal right to do whatever I wish with my husband's body."

Her lawyer. The bitch was bringing her *lawyer* to the table. Tough shit, because Lucky didn't give a damn about her fucking lawyer.

"I have a strong suspicion you're not hearing me, Paige," Lucky said. "So I do suggest that you listen carefully, because although I didn't plan on bringing this up, sadly you leave me no choice."

"I knew you'd be upset, dear. It's just that you simply have to realize that I —"

"Why don't you just shut the fuck up and listen," Lucky interrupted.

"No need for language," Paige said with a testy sigh.

"Jesus!" Lucky exclaimed. "Coming from you that's a laugh."

"Excuse me?"

"Here's the deal," Lucky said. "How would you like me to post an extremely intimate series of photos of you online? How do you think *that'll* go down with your friends at the country club? Gino Santangelo's widow, naked, having sex with men *and* women. What do you think *that'll* do to your reputation?"

"You're bluffing," Paige said, her voice faltering. "There *are* no photos."

"Bluffing?" Lucky questioned. "You think? I'm a Santangelo, a *true* Santangelo. And we don't bluff."

There was a long silence before Paige said in a low voice, "I cannot believe that you would actually stoop to blackmailing me. Gino always said that you had no morals, that —"

"Don't you *dare* talk about what Gino said about me," Lucky exploded. "You got what you wanted out of your marriage to him, but now he's gone, and as far as I'm concerned, so are you. Although naturally," she added sarcastically, "you'll be welcome to attend the funeral."

"Why are you treating me like this?" Paige cried out. "What have I ever done to you?"

You took Gino away, Lucky thought. *You cloistered him in Palm Springs, where you allowed him to get himself shot. And I never liked you and your money-grabbing ways. You were always a bitch.*

"We're clear, then?" Lucky said coldly.

"You're giving me no choice," Paige muttered.

"That's the whole idea, because *I* make the choices now," Lucky said. "Gino is to be buried in Vegas. My assistant, Danny, will be in touch. Oh — and those friends of Gino's you mentioned, they're welcome to fly to Vegas to pay their respects. Just give Danny the list."

"The photos?" Paige said tightly. "When do

I get them?"

"After the funeral," Lucky said. "They're all yours." She clicked off and buzzed Danny. "Is everything on point?"

"Yes, Lucky," Danny replied. "There'll be a plane waiting for you at Van Nuys Airport."

"Call Max, get her back from Europe. And you'd better bring Lennie up to date. Try him at his editing bay, and tell him we'll all meet in Vegas. And make sure everyone we've already contacted knows the date it's actually happening."

Danny was overwhelmed with all that he had to organize. Fortunately, he'd hired even more assistants to help out, plus his partner, Buff, was also around. Danny set them all to work finalizing the arrangements he'd already put in place.

Gino Santangelo's funeral service was destined to be a magnificent affair. A celebration of a life well lived.

Danny would make sure that Lucky was proud.

■ ■ ■ ■

BOOK THREE

■ ■ ■ ■

"I wish to meet Britney Spears, Katy Perry, Willow Price, and Lindsay Lohan," thirteen-year-old Tariq announced to his grandfather King Emir Amin Mohamed Jordan. "Kindly have someone arrange it."

"I will have whoever you wish flown to Akramshar for your next birthday," King Emir assured him. "We will enjoy a big celebration."

"Why can't I meet them here?" Tariq said, his voice turning into a whine. "You're a king, and I'm a prince. Surely I can have whatever I want?"

"You can, my grandson, when I say so," King Emir replied, doting on the boy, his only connection to his son Armand.

Tariq was a fine-looking boy, tall and athletic, with his dear departed father's strong features.

The king never stopped thinking about Armand, the only son among his many sons that King Emir had truly admired. Armand had left Akramshar and traveled to America with his ex-showgirl American mother at a young age. After

517

attending college in the United States, and with the help of his mother's new husband, he'd risen to become a real estate titan. Every year, he'd dutifully returned to Akramshar to celebrate the king's birthday, and to visit Soraya, the wife the king had arranged for him to marry, and the several children Soraya had given birth to. One day Armand had made a solemn promise to his father that when the king passed, he would return to Akramshar permanently, and he would rule the country as was King Emir's wish.

Unfortunately, that day would never come to pass, for Armand had been brutally assassinated in America, gunned down at the Keys hotel, a property he had been negotiating to buy. And as King Emir had eventually learned, it was all the fault of a woman — a mere woman who'd refused to make the deal with Armand.

Lucky Santangelo. She was the responsible one.

It had taken almost a year involving much planning for King Emir to plot his revenge. Now the time for vengeance was near, and the king was running out of patience with a teenage boy desperate to meet a few celebrity whores. He knew it was time to teach Tariq that women were the cause of all the troubles in the world. In Akramshar they knew their place and they stayed in it or faced dire punishment. King Emir should know, for he had six wives and countless children. None of them had ever dared to disobey him.

King Emir did not love his wives. They were simply there for his convenience when he desired sex, or to act as broodmares giving birth to his many children. Women were vessels to be used and discarded when he felt like it. Women were weak, inferior beings, and it shocked him how they were allowed so much freedom in the Western world, whoring themselves out on TV and in the movies. Showing everyone their breasts and big buttocks like prize cows.

When Armand's American mother had left Akramshar and returned to the United States, he'd been pleased to see her go — she was hardly a good influence on his other wives, outspoken and not respectful enough. However, she'd certainly given him a son to be proud of. Armand. So handsome. So smart.

Lucky Santangelo had taken that son away from him, and for that she would be severely punished.

King Emir savored contemplating what would happen next.

Oh, how the infidels would fall. Finally, justice would be his.

CHAPTER SIXTY-FOUR

"I will be accompanying you," Dante announced when Max received the news of Gino's funeral date.

"W-what?" Max stuttered, almost speechless. "That's *so* not going to happen."

"Ah, but it is," Dante said with a snakelike smile — yellow teeth front and center. "Contractually, we should not allow you to go. However, since it is a family funeral, we have decided to excuse your absence."

Max simply stared at his deathly pale face. Why was she about to get stuck with this sicko when she was quite capable of flying to America by herself?

The last few days had been something of a nightmare. After firing Ross, Dante had come to her cabin on the yacht and tried to force himself on her, threatening that if she wasn't nicer to him, her job would be in jeopardy. He'd actually started to unzip his pants before she'd managed to kick him in the balls — her signature move — and lock him out of her cabin. He hadn't been pleased. He'd screamed a litany of insults at her in Italian and finally limped away.

Carlo was no help. It seemed that whenever Natalia was around, he had nothing to say — he simply drank himself into a stupor.

"When we are done with the funeral in Las Vegas, there are magazine editors in L.A. Alfredo wishes you to meet," Dante continued. "It is important for the Dolcezza image to become known in America, and with you as the face of Dolcezza, this is perfect timing."

Perfect timing indeed. Her grandfather's funeral. What a disaster! She didn't care to have Dante following her around; it wasn't going to happen.

"I shall be making all travel arrangements," Dante said. "We fly tomorrow."

"Will that get us there in time?" Max asked, resigning herself to the fact that she had no choice.

"Certainly," Dante said. "Tonight we leave the yacht. A helicopter will be waiting to take us to Rome, and from there we catch a flight to L.A."

"Gino's funeral is in Las Vegas," she pointed out.

"I shall arrange a helicopter to meet us in L.A. to take us there."

"Us"? Had he just said "us"? This was turning into a freaking nightmare. He was acting as if he was her significant other, and nothing could be further from the truth. The very thought. *Ugh, gross!*

"There's no need for you to come to the funeral," she said flatly. "You can't anyway. It's a close-friends-and-family-only affair."

"I have spoken to your mother," Dante said. "She will be happy to welcome me."

He'd spoken to Lucky? How was *that* possible?

"Whatever," Max muttered, determined that when they arrived in Vegas, she would distance herself from hateful Dante big-time. She'd warn Bobby what a douche Dante was — and even though he was her so-called boss at Dolcezza, she wanted nothing to do with him. Bobby would understand; he'd always been extremely protective of her. Besides, she couldn't wait to hang with Cookie and Harry. She was really looking forward to catching up with all her old friends, even though she would've preferred it to be under different circumstances.

If only Lorenzo were coming with her instead of Dante, that would've been major. She could've fixed him up with Harry, and maybe Lorenzo and Harry would've lived happily ever after.

Hmm . . . happily ever after. Was there such a thing?

No. Billy had proved that to her. She hadn't heard a word from him.

Too bad. His loss.

She was the new face of Dolcezza.

Soon she'd be famous too.

The last couple of days were a blur for Denver. They'd sprung Frankie Romano from jail and he was currently under police protection in a hotel, spewing information that, if it turned out to be accurate, would definitely put Alejandro Diego behind bars.

Denver was exhilarated to think that they almost had him.

Leon was all about going out and celebrating, but Denver was not in a celebratory mood. Bobby was gone. He'd walked out on her. Packed up and left.

In a way she was devastated. On the other hand she considered that maybe it was for the best. She'd loved Bobby, but she'd never loved his lifestyle. He was a man who had everything — and even though he didn't flaunt it, it was always there, hovering between them. Bobby was heir to an incredible fortune. He could — if he so desired — have anything he wanted. But that wasn't his particular style. He rarely used the Stanislopoulos family plane. He'd never touched his inheritance. He'd never traded on his infamous mother's name, or on his stepfather's stellar reputation as an extremely talented filmmaker. He'd forged his own way with his successful chain of clubs. And until Chicago, she'd always imagined he was faithful.

Then came Chicago, and like a fool she hadn't trusted him. Because of her suspicions, she'd sent their relationship into a spin that neither of them could struggle out of. It was over, and as sad as she was, there was something about not being with Bobby that set her free.

Instead of celebrating with Leon, she'd called Sam. "I want Lady Gaga," she'd said. "Can you bring her over?"

"She's all yours," a delighted Sam had replied.

And it occurred to her that maybe it was Sam she should've been with all along.

Newspapers were not into writing retractions. They'd labeled Bobby Santangelo Stanislopoulos a murderer, and they were reluctant to print a correction. A few lines of copy hidden in the depths of the paper admitted their mistake. Nobody read it.

Bobby realized that the story would always be out there thanks to the Internet. He was sage enough to know there was nothing he could do about it — except try to forget and move on. The Chicago incident had changed his life. No more Mr. Nice Guy — he was smarter and wiser, less trustful of people, and now he was on his own with no girlfriend. Denver had failed to stand by him, and he couldn't help feeling that a weight had been lifted from his shoulders. He'd definitely loved her, but he was beginning to realize that sometimes love is not enough to save a relationship.

After thinking about it, he called Beverly and informed her that he wished to cover all funeral expenses for Nadia. Even though she'd lured him up to her suite, then drugged him, surely she hadn't expected to be murdered.

Beverly assured him she would take care of it.

M.J. flew back from Chicago with news that Mood was packed every night.

"Hey, man, at least your notoriety was hot for business," M.J. joked.

"Thanks a lot," Bobby answered drily. "That really makes me feel it was all worth it."

As soon as he'd left the house he shared with Denver, he'd checked into a hotel for the night. When M.J. heard about the breakup, he'd made it clear to Bobby that he was to stay with him at his L.A. apartment, no argument, so Bobby had checked out of the hotel and moved in.

He wasn't quite sure when to mention to M.J. that he was intent on selling the Chicago club. He couldn't care less if he ever visited Chicago again. Too many bad memories. M.J. wouldn't be happy; they'd put a great deal of work into building an amazing venue. He could only hope that M.J. would understand.

Over the next couple of days, they'd spent a lot of time sitting around talking about women and sports and their future as entrepreneurs. Both were on the same track, with ambitions to achieve bigger and better things. Bobby was into the idea of building a series of boutique hotels, and M.J. was on board all the way.

"We should make a pact," Bobby said. "No more live-in girlfriends for the next couple of years."

"You got it!" M.J. responded. "Work bros — no hoes."

Laughter followed. But Bobby knew for sure that before anything, he had to find out who'd assassinated Gino. Like Lucky, he was not giving up.

Someone had to know something, and he was determined to chase the truth.

CHAPTER SIXTY-FIVE

Willow was flying high. Attending a glamorous premiere in Westwood with Ralph Maestro had upped her profile from the girl who used to have a promising career to Ralph Maestro's latest girlfriend. She'd stood beside him in a sleek designer dress lent to her for the occasion while he was interviewed by *Access Hollywood* and *Extra* and *ET.* The on-camera hosts had actually asked *her* questions. Mario Lopez had given her his irresistible dimpled grin and told her she looked beautiful — while Billy Bush had cocked an eyebrow and congratulated Ralph on his choice of date.

Needless to say, the next day photos of her clinging on to Ralph's arm were everywhere.

Willow was thrilled. She'd loved every minute of being out and about with a bona fide star. Well . . . more of an old-school movie star, and yes, she'd sooner have been on the arm of Billy Melina or Nick Angel — but that would happen as soon as Alejandro came up with the money for their movie. Unfortunately, this was not taking place as fast as she'd hoped, and Eddie was doing nothing until he saw the cash that would go straight into his pocket. He hadn't even gotten up a deal memo for Sam, and speaking with Sam on the phone, she'd noticed that he was definitely cooling off on the project, telling her that if he didn't get something in writing within the next twenty-four hours he was moving on.

Some people were so ungrateful. Here she was, giving Sam the opportunity of a lifetime, and he was talking about moving on. Most writers would *kill* for full control.

Who cared anyway? The moment she gave Eddie the money, he'd come up with a better writer who would tailor a script especially for her.

When the photos of her and Ralph hit the magazines and Internet, both Alejandro and Eddie were majorly pissed.

"You're *my* girlfriend," Alejandro had raged. "How do you think this makes me look? My friends are laughing at me."

What friends? she'd wanted to say. *You don't have any friends.*

Instead, she'd tried to smooth things over, telling him that it was all for the sake of their movie, and that a huge star such as Ralph Maestro might even agree to make a cameo appearance.

As for Eddie, he was just plain jealous, and she loved that she could get to him.

Days were passing and still no money. Alejandro blamed Rafael, while he kept on assuring Willow that they would be wallowing in cash any moment.

Like Sam, her patience was running thin.

It hadn't taken long for Alejandro to realize that Rafael was not the same man who'd gone to Colombia on a mission to get movie funding from his father. No, somehow along the way Rafael seemed to have acquired a set of balls.

"Where's the cash?" Alejandro had demanded upon Rafael's return. "I told you to bring back cash."

Rafael remained calm. "Pablo has agreed to finance your movie. He is making arrangements."

Alejandro's face had imploded with a dark flash of fury. "That wasn't supposed to be the deal," he'd yelled. "I ordered you to come back with cash. What kind of moron are you?"

Rafael had shrugged. "This is Pablo's decision, and neither of us argues with Pablo. He wants to slide the money through certain channels before you get it, legitimate channels. So I suggest that instead of worrying about the money, you should be worrying about Frankie shooting his mouth to the DA, the woman who's trying to lock you up."

"Are you telling me you didn't take care of Frankie?" Alejandro steamed, his eyes popping.

"You sent me to Colombia, remember? And while I was there, I convinced Pablo you could become a movie producer. Isn't that enough?"

"You dumb-ass!" Alejandro screamed. "I'm sending the sex tape to your *puta* girlfriend. She deserves to see who you really are."

"Go ahead."

Alejandro had stopped screaming and shaken his head, perplexed. Surely he couldn't be hearing right. What was going on with Rafael? Why was he acting as if nothing mattered?

"You'd better take care of Frankie," he'd snarled. "Then maybe I won't send the tape to Elizabetta."

"The DA has Frankie Romano sequestered," Rafael had replied, stone-faced. "He's under strict guard."

"Then *pay* someone to get to him," Alejandro had rasped. "You're capable of doing that, aren't you?"

"Sure, Alejandro," Rafael had replied, while thinking, *Why would I do that? The money is coming and it's going straight to me. Alejandro will soon be arrested and when he is, I'm taking off.*

Karma was a sneaky bitch.

CHAPTER SIXTY-SIX

The day before Gino's funeral, Lucky awoke in her penthouse at the Keys with a peaceful feeling. Her father was to be laid to rest in Las Vegas, scene of his greatest triumphs, a fitting place to celebrate his life.

Everyone he'd loved was either there or on their way. Max was flying in from Europe, the boys were already present with Steven and Lennie. Bobby and M.J. were driving from L.A. And Brigette and her girlfriend had arrived from Sweden. Gino's old-time cronies — the ones who were still alive — had all made it. Also present were close friends of the family, among them Venus; Max's closest friends from high school, Cookie and Harry; movie director Alex Woods; a scattering of beautiful movie stars; and several politicians, including Lucky's ex-husband, Craven, and his politically pushy parents, Senator and Mrs. Peter Richmond. It was certainly a mixed group.

Paige had announced that she would be

coming with guests. She'd spoken directly to Danny, and imperiously demanded that he send a plane for her convenience. Danny had checked with Lucky, who'd said, "Do it."

Accommodations were at the Keys. Luxury rooms for everyone. Danny had attempted to book some of the guests into the Magiriano, but the hotel's penthouse suites were all booked. Apparently some Middle Eastern king and his enormous entourage had taken over the two top floors. Danny didn't bother Lucky with the details; instead, he put the overflow of guests from the Keys into a neighboring hotel — the Cavendish, a hotel owned by two lesbians who were friends of Lucky's.

Chris Warwick conferred with Danny about security; with so many high-profile guests due to attend, it was imperative that everything run smoothly. Danny had imported the guards from the Malibu house to Vegas, while Chris had hired his own team of crack ex–Israeli army security. In Chris's opinion, there was no such thing as being too careful.

It occurred to Lucky that she'd better do something for all the early arrivals, so she put together a special dinner in one of the banquet rooms at the Keys for everyone who was already there. There were a lot of people catching up, reminiscing about Gino, telling stories about his nefarious past.

Wearing a simple black dress and flashing

emerald drop earrings — a gift from Gino — Lucky flitted from table to table, not lingering, experiencing waves of nostalgia as she encountered so many faces from Gino's past. The old cronies table was the best — former tough guys now rocking thick glasses and heavy canes. Some of them were attached to oxygen drips, although all of them had a smile on their wizened faces as they talked about Gino the Ram, and what a formidable character he'd been.

Yes, Lucky thought with pride. *My father the character, a street-smart kid who came to America at thirteen and rose to conquer all. A man of the people.*

I will miss him forever.

She'd made up her mind to get through the next twenty-four hours with strength and dignity. It was what Gino would've expected of her.

"Where's the helicopter?" Max asked when their plane landed at LAX.

"Change of plans," Dante answered smoothly as a VIP escort met them at customs. "We are now driving to Vegas."

"What?" Max said, surprised and frustrated. "There's no time to drive. The funeral's at noon tomorrow."

"That gives us plenty of time," Dante responded, creepy smile and yellow teeth going full force. "My friend from college, Alejandro Diego, has offered to drive us. He owns a VIP club in L.A. and is happy I am here. We stop by his club, later we drive to Vegas with Alejandro and his girlfriend."

"Oh my *God*!" Max exclaimed. "This is a freaking *nightmare*. I'm not driving to Vegas with someone I don't know. I'm taking a plane."

"No," Dante said. "You're not. Alejandro is interested in investing in our company, he is most anxious to meet you, and Alfredo *in-sisted* you see him. This will be advantageous for you too."

Max shook her head. Her family was already in Vegas, or she would've gone straight to the Malibu house. She'd come this far with the despicable Dante by her side; what was she supposed to do?

Get to Vegas, that's what.

Tired and confused, she realized that the only option seemed to be to stick with Dante. At least she wouldn't be alone with him, and that was something.

Suck it up, she told herself. *Suck it up and once you get there, have Lucky deal with this douche.*

Gino Junior and Leo were sitting with Max's high school friends Cookie and Harry. Lucky strolled over and joined them. She'd known

Cookie and Harry since they were little kids, and she'd always liked them. Both of them had been loyal friends to Max.

"I'm so glad you could make it," she said.

"I just got a text from Max," Cookie volunteered. "She's landed in L.A. She'll be here soon."

"Great," Lucky said. "I spoke to her boss yesterday. He's arranged for a helicopter to get them here."

"The whole Dolcezza gig sounds awesome," Cookie said, her pretty face glowing. "Our girl's gonna be famous."

"Fame isn't everything," Lucky mused. "I hope she realizes that."

" 'Course she does," Cookie said confidently. "Y'know our Max. She's gonna love it, an' she's not gonna take it too seriously."

"Well . . ." Lucky said. "She's following her dreams — that's what everyone should do."

"Yeah," Cookie said enthusiastically. "I'm thinkin' of becoming a rapper like Iggy Azalea."

Harry almost choked on his drink. "Since when did you ever rap?" he demanded.

"Since I decided to follow *my* dream, asshole," Cookie responded, throwing him a snarky look.

Spotting Venus across the room, Lucky got up. "See you later, guys," she said, heading in Venus's direction.

Wearing a sleek burgundy pantsuit with

nothing underneath the jacket, major cleavage on show, her platinum hair swept up into a tight topknot, Venus was back to her beautiful and very sexual self, which could be because there was no Venezuelan director clinging protectively on to her arm.

"Hey," Lucky said, embracing her friend. "No Hugo?"

Venus gave a thin smile. "Hugo who?"

"It's over?"

"Done. The movie too. We wrapped two days ago and it occurred to me that as a director he's a genius, as a man — not so much. I'm seeking fresh young blood."

"And she's back," Lucky said, grinning.

"Oh, you can bet she is," Venus agreed.

"Hmm . . ." Lucky mused. "She's on the loose, so — warning — stay away from Bobby."

"Where *is* your delicious son?" Venus inquired, downing a lychee martini.

"He's on his way. But I'm not kidding. Stay away."

"Oh my God, you're so bossy," Venus said, laughing softly. "Bobby and I would make a divine couple."

"Don't even think about it," Lucky warned. "Bobby is off-limits."

"So was my ex, Billy," Venus said caustically. "However, that sure didn't stop little Max from having fun with him, did it?"

"I knew nothing about what was going on,"

Lucky said quickly. "You know if I had I would've never allowed it to happen. Billy took advantage of Max. She's only a kid, and he moved right in on her. You've got to admit that for a teenager, Billy is a hard act to resist."

"Okay, okay, I get it. I'll back off," Venus said, her eyes lingering on a hovering waiter who resembled a young Channing Tatum. "I'm sure there's plenty of talent around here to keep me happy."

"How about going manless for a day or two?" Lucky suggested. "Ever thought of doing *that*?"

"Excuse me," Venus drawled. "It's *me* you're talking to."

Alejandro zeroed in on Max as if she were the dish of the day. Max could not believe that now she was stuck with a pair of double douches — for she loathed Alejandro on sight. He had that *I-am-so-smooth-and-rich-and-irresistible* attitude with his stupid mustache and greased-back hair. It was no wonder that he and Dante were friends. Two of a kind. And his sleazy club was more like a drug den than a cool hangout. Club Luna was filled with all the dregs who didn't have a chance of getting into Mood. Sinister-looking guys with ragged ponytails and ludicrous outfits. Girls with ultratight skirts that barely covered their asses, and an abundance of fake tits. Bottle service was five thousand dollars a table. What a freaking rip-off.

Max was tempted to boast about her big brother and his awesome chain of clubs, but she decided against it.

Where was Alejandro's girlfriend? She was in need of female company, and there was no girlfriend in sight. After a couple of glasses of champagne, all she wanted to do was sleep. The flight from Europe had left her feeling exhausted.

"What time are we leaving?" she muttered to Dante, who'd been trying to give Alejandro the impression that they were a couple. How gross was *that*?

"Soon," Dante said. "Alejandro's driver says with no traffic it'll take us less than three hours."

Three hours of sleep, that's what she craved. Three hours of sleep and then she'd finally be with her family.

CHAPTER SIXTY-SEVEN

After spending time with Venus, Lucky continued to circulate from table to table. There were so many people present who'd loved Gino, so many faces from both their past lives. It was crazy trying to talk to everyone when all she really wanted was to be with close family only.

She was happy to see talk-show host Jack Python, and after chatting with him for a few minutes she turned away to find Craven Richmond looming in front of her. Craven, the son of Senator Peter Richmond, the idiot Gino had married her off to when she was sixteen. Ah yes, fond memories — a baby married off to an awkward jerk. What a pair of losers!

Poor Craven; he hadn't changed. He stood before her older and no wiser, with a sad-sack expression and a plump wife by his side.

"Y-You look . . . uh . . . beautiful," he stuttered.

Totally inappropriate, Lucky thought. *Still an*

idiot. How about saying, "I'm sorry for your loss"? Or maybe introducing me to your wife?

She noted that he was losing his hair and immediately felt sorry for him. It wasn't his fault he'd been born into such a messed-up family. Peter Richmond, the philanderer, and his frozen-faced hard-ass wife, Betty, who had about as much compassion as an ant. No parenting skills between those two.

Remembering her time in Washington, Lucky shuddered. Nonstop games of golf and tennis, endless fund-raising parties, dinners, and plenty of mindless bullshit. A life in limbo while she waited desperately for an opportunity to escape. And when that opportunity had come around, she'd taken it and never looked back.

"Nice to see you, Craven," she said, trying to sound as if she meant it. "And this must be your lovely wife."

The plump woman smiled, a gummy, ingratiating smile. "We're pregnant," the woman said with a proud smirk.

"Congratulations," Lucky said, swiftly moving on to the movie-star table, where Nick Angel was busy holding court.

"Where the fuck are you?" Alejandro yelled to Willow on his cell. "My friends are already here and we're waiting to leave. You're embarrassing me. Get your ass to the club."

"I'm on my way, had a slight setback,"

541

Willow said, staring crossly at her mom, who'd turned up on her doorstep bitching and moaning that Willow had not sent her the check she'd promised, and that perhaps she should speak to the nice men with cameras gathered outside Willow's house and tell them what a cheap little monkey her darling daughter was.

Oh shit, Willow thought. *This is exactly what I don't need.*

Furiously, she realized that it was her own fault because what with all the excitement of trying to put a movie together, she'd forgotten about sending her mom a check. Now Pammy — verging on drunk — was in her living room, while *she* was supposed to be going to Vegas with Alejandro. He'd assured her they would be picking up the start-up cash they needed, so finally their movie could get on track. What was a girl to do?

A disgruntled Pammy placed both hands on her hips and glared at her daughter. "I saw you in the magazines with that man who's old enough to be your grandfather," she said accusingly. "What were you thinking?"

"Ralph Maestro is not a man," Willow answered grandly. "Ralph Maestro is a big movie star."

"He's a murderer too," Pammy muttered ominously. "Everyone knows he killed that lovely wife of his. Shot her in the head. The

Enquirer is *still* investigating, an' you can bet that's a paper who knows a thing or two, you'll read nothing except the truth there."

"I'm writing you a check," Willow said, running out of time and patience. "If I give it to you, will you leave and please not talk to the photographers outside?"

"Leave?" Pammy exclaimed as if it was the most ridiculous thing she'd ever heard. "It's eleven at night an' I might've had a drink or two. Can't get home until tomorrow. No, little lady, I'm staying with you."

"That's impossible," Willow blurted.

"Why's that impossible?" Pammy wished to know, her faded blue eyes darting around the living room, taking in her daughter's chaos, seeing if she could spot a bottle of vodka or scotch.

" 'Cause I told you — I have to go," Willow said, swooping up her purse. "I've got an important date. I'm already late."

"With the old man?" Pammy said knowingly.

"No," Willow snapped back. "It's none of your business who it's with."

"None of my business indeed," Pammy sniffed belligerently. "After all I've done for you, it's none of my business. When're you gonna realize that if it wasn't for me, you'd be nothing. I paid for everything so you could have a career. Singing, dancing, acting lessons. And —"

"Okay, Mom," Willow interrupted, rolling her eyes. "I know, I know, you're a saint. Saint Pammy."

Once again Pammy glared at her daughter. Willow glared back.

"I have to go," Willow repeated, adding a reluctant, "You can sleep on the couch. Don't touch anything and don't answer the door or talk to the paps — sometimes they sit out there all night."

"While *you're* out whoring your body."

Willow bit down hard on her lower lip to stop herself from getting involved in a battle of words. Pammy was an expert at never letting anything go, and she could out-argue anyone.

Opening her purse, Willow took out her checkbook and was about to scribble a check when Pammy cleared her throat and said a crafty, "Make it double what I asked for."

"Excuse me?" Willow said, shocked.

"You heard," Pammy said, spotting a bottle of vodka and heading unsteadily toward it. "Double, or I give an interview to those nice men outside."

"First of all, they are not nice men," Willow said, exasperated. "And secondly, I don't think there's enough in my checking account to cover that amount of money."

"Then whyn't you ask one of your rich boyfriends?" Pammy said, pouring herself a shot. "They got plenty of money to spare."

"I thought you didn't approve of my rich boyfriends," Willow countered.

"Gimme the check," Pammy snapped. "You owe me big-time, young lady."

I don't owe you anything, Willow thought. She wrote the check anyway, handed it to her mom, and made a quick exit, for once ignoring the gathered paps who yelled out her name.

Her future was waiting. And if the check bounced, it was Pammy's fault for being so damn greedy.

"Where's Max?" Lennie wanted to know, coming up to Lucky between tables.

"On her way," Lucky assured him. "Cookie got a text that she's landed in L.A. and will be here soon by helicopter."

"How're *you* doing?" Lennie asked, catching her by the arm.

Tossing back her mane of jet-black hair, she shrugged. "I'm fine," she said. "The turnout is impressive, don't you think? And thanks for working as a team, Lennie. It's not easy trying to say hello to everyone while making them all feel as if they're special. Couldn't do it without you."

"Sure you could," he said with a smile.

"Yes, sure I could," she said, smiling back. "But I'd sooner do it with you anytime."

"So . . ." Lennie inquired with a caustic tilt of an eyebrow. "Have you made your boyfriend feel special yet?"

"My boyfriend?"

"Alex Woods. He hasn't stopped watching you all night."

"Oh, c'*mon,*" she said, laughing softly. "Let it go."

"Hey, don't spoil my fun — I get off on spying on other men who lust after you, especially when they haven't got a chance in hell."

"Alex is an old friend," she admonished, thinking about Alex for a moment. He was an Oscar-winning filmmaker who'd always had a thing for her. "You *do* know that? Right?"

"Yeah, *old* is the operative word," Lennie said with a cynical laugh. "Way too old for the twenty-something Asian girl he's hanging on to."

"Jealous?" Lucky teased.

"Huh?"

"How would *you* like to be with a cute little twenty-something?"

"Are you *crazy*?"

"Well?"

"Stop f-ing with me Lucky, and go put your boyfriend out of his misery."

"Come with."

"And ruin his night?" Lennie said, laughing. "No way. You're on your own, sweetheart."

"Thanks for your loyal support."

"Anytime."

Shaking her head, Lucky made her way toward Alex and his young date. Somehow or other, she had a feeling that it was going to be a long night.

The one thing Willow did not appreciate was competition, and the moment she met Max she was aware of competition staring her straight in the face. Max was younger, prettier, and about to be a very well-known face — as her yellow-toothed, shady, foreign boyfriend couldn't wait to inform her.

Alejandro was all hyped up, and Willow could tell that he fancied the dark-haired brat, although she was hardly his type. Too young. Too wild. Dante had shown him some of the photos from the Capri shoot on his iPad, and now Alejandro was acting as if Max were the next coming of Gisele.

Settling into Alejandro's usual booth, Willow picked up a glass of champagne. She noticed Rafael lurking near the bar, which was unusual because he rarely spent time in the club — he was always upstairs in the office. She chose to ignore him, although she couldn't help remembering how talented he was in bed. Hmm . . . maybe sometime in the future, she'd revisit that stellar action. Why not? When she was a big star again, she could do anything she wanted.

"I'm investing in Dante's company," a

stoned Alejandro informed her, leaning in. "Dante and I have discussed how Dolcezza can work with us on the movie. Max has to be in it. We will have a part specially written for her."

Willow remained cool and in control, even though she was ready to rant and rave about how dumb Alejandro was. The truth was that she'd always known he was dumb, only this crap took his dumbness to new heights. "We could do that," she said, trying not to grit her teeth. "Can she act?"

"Who cares?" Alejandro chortled. "Look at her."

She looks like a sulky little teenager to me, Willow thought. *Selena Gomez with a splash of Mila Kunis.*

Willow managed a smile and bobbed her head as if she agreed with him. If Alejandro was about to develop a crush on this little nobody, then maybe she should pay some attention to his shady foreign friend.

"So," she purred, flinging back her pale red hair and turning to Dante. "Tell me all about what you and Alejandro got up to in college. I bet you were a couple of real super-studs, ready to do anything."

Dante zeroed in on Alejandro's girlfriend. He was getting nowhere with Max, and it seemed to him that this one had potential.

"There is nothing Alejandro and I didn't do," he said, removing her clothes with his small evil eyes. "In Vegas you and I should experience everything. Do you agree?"

Willow smiled politely. There was something about this dude that was a total turnoff, and she had no intention of experiencing anything with him.

"When are we leaving?" she whispered, grabbing Alejandro's arm.

"One more drink," he promised. "Then we will be on our way."

One more drink. In Alejandro's world it was always one more drink.

CHAPTER SIXTY-EIGHT

Denver was in the mood to let it all out, and Sam was the perfect listener. On the day he'd dropped off Lady Gaga, she hadn't invited him in. Now it was a couple of days later — the night before Gino's funeral — and she was feeling vulnerable and alone, so she called him and invited him over.

Before she made the call, a thought came to her that maybe she should attend Gino's funeral to pay her respects. She'd texted Bobby to ask him if she should — it was the first time they'd been in contact since the split. His answer was short and to the point. "Not a good idea," he'd texted back. And that was it.

Yes, they were definitely over.

The day before, she'd received a call from his business manager, who'd informed her that Bobby would like her to keep the house as a gift. "No thank you," she'd said. "I'll be moving out next week."

Ah, Bobby . . . generous as usual.

She didn't need his house as some kind of payoff. She didn't need anything from him.

Sam arrived carrying two bottles of wine and a pizza.

Lady Gaga jumped to attention, frantically attempting to hump his leg.

"How's my favorite district attorney?" he asked, fending off the rambunctious puppy with a gentle shove.

"I'm okay, actually. Especially since I think I see pizza in my future. Your instincts are so right on."

Sam grinned, displaying his crooked teeth.

"I know you live in L.A. now," Denver remarked, checking out his smile. "Only promise me that you'll never get your teeth fixed."

Sam's grin widened. "What makes you think I'd ever do that?"

" 'Cause L.A. is the city of perfection."

"In that case you're perfect enough for both of us," he said, following her into the kitchen.

"No compliments. Please," she said, immediately feeling vulnerable.

"Howszatt?"

"I'm not in the mood."

"Ah, but *she* is in the mood for pizza and wine," he said, still grinning. "Such a gourmet combination."

"Yet somehow you knew it's exactly what I wanted."

"I don't only write scripts, I read minds too."

Denver gave a wan smile. Sam had a habit of making things seem normal.

"Okay," he said, reaching for an opener. "I'll open the wine while you micro the pizza. After that we'll sit down and you can tell me everything."

"Everything?"

"Whatever you feel like, Denver. I'm an excellent listener."

"What kinda girl you lookin' for?" M.J. questioned as he raced his Maserati down the highway heading for Vegas.

"Who's looking?" Bobby replied, leaning back in the passenger seat. "I'm done with being tied down."

"You enjoyed it while it was happenin'," M.J. pointed out, shooting him a knowing look.

"That's not the kind of tied down I was talking about," Bobby quipped.

"Funny."

"How about you? You ever miss being with one woman?"

"No way, man," M.J. said, vigorously shaking his head. "Freedom is where it's at. There's a whole world of pussy out there, an' I'm takin' my time."

"Yeah. I guess," Bobby said, gazing thoughtfully out the side window. Days had passed and he'd almost come to terms with breaking up with Denver. Unfortunately, there was always that lingering doubt when a relationship ended. Were they making the right decision? Because it wasn't just him; obviously Denver had reached the same conclusion.

He had to admit that he missed her laugh, and the way she snuggled up to him in bed, wrapping her long legs around him, making him feel safe and secure. He missed their conversations; she was a girl who actually knew what was going on in the world and could converse on any subject. He missed the smell of her hair when she'd just washed it, and the way she always seemed to know exactly what she was doing.

He did not miss her work ethic — pursuing the son of a dangerous drug lord was all she'd talked about for the last few months. Things had finally come to a head when she'd arrested Frankie Romano. Oh sure, he'd known that Frankie was a bad boy, but Denver hadn't been prepared to cut Frankie any slack. She was all about locking him up. They'd argued furiously about it, then Bobby had taken off for Chicago and things had imploded.

He'd truly thought Denver was the girl he was going to marry — he'd even bought an engagement ring to give her when the time was right.

Now it was over. No more a couple.

He gave a wry laugh.

"Wassup?" M.J. asked.

"I was just thinking," Bobby said. "You know anyone who's in the market for a secondhand engagement ring?"

M.J. burst out laughing. "You're gonna be okay, bro," he said. "We need t' get you laid, an' somehow I gotta hunch that's not gonna be a problem."

Denver wasn't sure whether she wanted Sam to stay the night. She'd just broken up with Bobby, and surely starting things up with another man wasn't the coolest move in the world?

Yet Sam was there, he was understanding, he made no demands. He didn't even complain when she spent half an hour on the phone with Leon, planning their next move as far as Alejandro Diego was concerned.

Once Frankie had started talking, he'd unleashed a whole lot of information. They had more than enough to put Alejandro away, but catching him in the act of accepting a shipment or selling drugs on his premises was imperative to their case.

Sonia, their undercover agent, had not managed to hook up with Alejandro himself, although over the last few days she'd spent enough time at Club Luna to be able to report on Alejandro's movements. She'd gotten friendly with one of the bartenders, and according to him, Alejandro had taken off to Vegas for the night — which gave her the opportunity to nose around even more. Leon told her it would be a big bonus if she could get the layout of Alejandro's private office and take photos. "I'll try," she'd said.

Currently Sonia was still at the club, and she'd assured Leon that she would check in with him later. Leon had relayed this information to Denver, who was now trying to relax and make the most of her time with Sam.

"You always ply me with too much wine," Denver murmured.

"I'm not *forcing* you to drink it," Sam said, amused. "*You're* the one chugging it down."

"I'm hardly chugging it down," she said indignantly.

"One and a half bottles later — of course you're not."

"Oh, and I suppose *you* haven't drunk anything?"

"One glass. My deal is staying in control."

"*I'm* the prosecutor," she said, realizing that she'd probably drunk far too much and that wasn't cool. "*I'm* the one in control," she added grandly.

"Sure you are," he replied with a good-natured grin.

"I think you're right," she muttered, falling back against the soft cushions on the couch. "I might've had a tiny bit too much wine, and that's okay, 'cause I'm finally celebrating."

"And the celebration would be about you and Bobby breaking up?" Sam asked hopefully.

"No, silly. It's 'cause next week we finally get to nail Alejandro Diego."

"You do?"

"I shouldn't be telling you this, but we have everything in place to nail him good."

"That's a coup, right?"

"It sure is. One more sleazebag off the streets."

"How'd this happen?"

"Can't tell you. Privileged information," she mumbled, suppressing a ladylike hiccough. "I've told you more than I should."

"I'm still writing that script about the smart, feisty DA," Sam said. "Any inside information is more than welcome."

"Well, you're not getting anything out of me," she said, making a sudden attempt to stand. And when she did, the room began to spin, and she found herself reaching out to Sam for support.

He caught her before she tripped and fell.

"I think it's time for you to go to bed," he said, as Lady Gaga barked excitedly.

"And . . . I think . . ." she said softly, leaning close to him, "that's only gonna happen if you care to join me."

"That's what you think, huh?"

"That's what I know."

"You're sure?"

"Stop stalling. I'm quite sure."

They made it into the bedroom, where Denver collapsed on the bed.

"You've had too much to drink," Sam pointed out. "I'm not taking advantage of you."

"And he's such a good guy," Denver sighed, kicking off her shoes. "Come here, good guy, before I change my mind."

"I'm only human," Sam groaned.

"Yes," Denver agreed. "And so am I."

Within moments he was on top of her and they were rolling around locked in a passionate embrace. Denver was well aware that she'd had too much wine, but she didn't care. She needed Sam. She needed him to fill her up with unconditional love.

Sam was her future, and she was with him all the way.

The lights of Vegas glittered in the distance.

"This," Bobby said, staring straight ahead, "is why I always prefer driving to Vegas. Gotta love the view."

"I get it," M.J. said, nodding his agreement. "From a freakin' barren desert straight into the mouth of the neon city. Can't beat it."

"The first time I saw Vegas at night, I was a kid asleep in the back of my mom's Ferrari," Bobby reminisced. "Lucky pulled over to the side of the road and woke me up. 'Take a look, kiddo. It's a sight you'll never forget,' she told me. And yeah — she was so right."

"Lucky's the greatest," M.J. enthused. "She never changes. She's always on top of everything, always relevant."

"Don't I know it," Bobby responded.

"Guess she's gonna miss Gino big-time."

"That goes for everyone," Bobby said, once more thinking about Gino's murder, and the son of a bitch who'd raised his gun and blown Gino away.

He would track the bastard down with or without Lucky. It was a given.

CHAPTER SIXTY-NINE

"You've been avoiding me," Alex Woods said accusingly, standing up as Lucky approached his table.

"Avoiding you how?" she asked, plucking a glass of champagne from a passing waiter's tray.

"Ever since Gino's murder, I haven't been able to reach you."

"It's nothing personal," she said quietly. "I've hardly spoken to anyone."

"I'm not just anyone," Alex said gruffly, remembering the one time they'd been together when Lennie was missing and she'd thought her husband was dead. It was a memory he could never erase.

"I know," she said softly. "I did receive your flowers and your messages. Much appreciated."

"C'mon, Lucky," he said, fixing her with a penetrating look. "It's me, Alex. We've shared too much in the past for you to shut me out when I know you need me."

"I *need* you to be my friend," she said, wishing he'd let it go. "Nothing else."

"Yeah, that's 'cause you've got Lennie," Alex said with a resentful scowl. "It's always about Lennie."

"Could be because he's my husband," she answered coolly.

"Anyway," Alex said, giving her another long meaningful look. "How're you really doing? Help me out here, 'cause I'm one of the few who care enough to hear the truth."

"I'm getting through it," she said, meeting his intent gaze. "Staying strong. It's what Gino would've expected of me."

"Gino couldn't've loved you more."

"It took him a while to tell me, but yes, I do know that."

"Gino was quite the guy. He was a man's man."

"So tell me about you," she said, quickly moving on. "Still working your ass off?"

"Making movies isn't work, it's my passion."

She wondered if she should share her idea to incorporate a movie studio into the new complex. Then she decided this wasn't the appropriate moment. Besides, Lennie might not be thrilled if she involved Alex in any way. Lennie claimed he wasn't jealous, but she suspected he was.

"Isn't it time you thought about settling down and marrying one of your girlfriends?"

she suggested.

"Like Ling?" Alex said sarcastically. "You gotta remember Ling. She was that insane bitch who attempted to shoot you."

"I was kind of thinking of someone a little more together," Lucky said, indicating the exquisite Asian girl sitting at the table patiently waiting for Alex to return to her side. "This one looks to be a likely candidate."

"I think not," Alex said, vigorously shaking his head.

"How come?"

"Maybe 'cause she's the biggest porn star in Asia," he said, cracking a sly smile. "They call her the Asian Open."

Lucky started to laugh. Only Alex could make her laugh at a time like this.

"I still don't understand why we can't fly to Vegas," Max muttered to Dante as they made their way to Club Luna's underground garage in Alejandro's private elevator.

"I told you," Dante answered, tightly gripping her arm. "It's possible we do business with Alejandro. He is about to make an important movie, and we might partner up for a big advertising campaign. Besides, he wishes to drive his new car."

"I thought you told me he had a driver?" Max said, pulling her arm away.

"He does. Tonight he chooses to drive himself."

"He's been drinking," Max stated, wishing she was somewhere else and not caught up in this predicament.

"Stop being such a baby," Dante admonished. "When we were roommates in college we drove to Vegas every weekend stoned out of our heads. Alejandro can do the drive with his eyes closed."

"Awesome," Max said in a low voice, shooting Willow a wary look. She'd already decided that the redhead wasn't the most friendly of girls, although it was obvious that Willow considered herself a star. A couple of years back, Max remembered seeing her in a movie with Billy. She couldn't help wondering if they'd slept together.

Had Billy climbed into bed with the slender actress?

Had he made love to her?

Willow was pretty enough in a Hollywood starlet kind of way, and she was definitely into flaunting her assets — nipples on display under a floaty top, her ass barely covered by an ultrashort leather skirt.

Max attempted a couple of friendly overtures. Willow immediately shut her down with a blank stare.

Great, Max thought. *Stuck in a car with this piece of work for the next few hours. Fun times.*

She swallowed hard, suppressing a desire to make a run for it, to just take off and find her own way to Vegas.

But how could she? Getting there was of prime importance, and right now sticking with the group seemed like her only option.

She took out her phone and texted Cookie again. *On our way. Driving. Don't wait up. Breakfast in the a.m. Can't wait to catch up.*

Extracting herself from Alex's lustful gaze, Lucky made it over to the family table, where Steven was talking to Brigette and her Swedish girlfriend. Since changing tracks and moving to Sweden, Brigette seemed much happier. She'd had a difficult life, always hooking up with losers who'd treated her badly, even marrying one of them. She'd once had a successful modeling career, which she'd given up. Now she painted, wrote poetry, and lived a simple life — even though as Dimitri Stanislopoulos's granddaughter, like Bobby, she was heir to a great fortune.

Lucky gave her a hug and told her that Bobby was on his way.

"Uncle Bobby," Brigette said, with a big smile. It was their private joke that even though Bobby was much younger than she was, as Dimitri's son, he was indeed her uncle. "I'm dying to see him. It's been a while."

"He recently broke up with his girlfriend," Lucky said, lowering her voice. "So do me a favor and watch out for Venus. She's always had a thing for Bobby, and I don't want her pouncing on him."

"Of course, Madame Lucky," Brigette said, mock-saluting. "I will be happy to act as the Bobby police."

Steven got to his feet. "Don't know about everyone else, but I'm going to bed," he announced. "Gotta think about what I'm going to say tomorrow."

"I wish I could take off," Lucky said wistfully, thinking how much she couldn't wait to collapse into bed.

"You can," Lennie said, coming up behind her. "Tomorrow's the big day, so you should go get a good night's sleep. I'll take care of everyone."

"You're the best," she said gratefully. "Bobby should be here any minute and Max is on her way."

"No worries. I'm around for them. You go, sweetheart. I'll catch up with you later."

With Alejandro on his way out of town — even if it was only overnight — Rafael imagined he was the boss for once as he sat in Alejandro's reserved booth at Club Luna, drinking champagne while contemplating his future.

Things were working out nicely. At first Alejandro had insisted that he go to Vegas to pick up the cash Pablo had arranged. Then things had changed when a friend of Alejandro's arrived in town, and Alejandro had decided to take his new Bentley and drive to Vegas himself.

This suited Rafael, as he continued to work on his exit strategy. Pablo Fernandez Diego was about to deposit several million dollars into a bank account, giving Rafael full control. Pablo trusted him.

How nice. How dumb. Because Rafael had been busy making his own arrangements. Over the past few days he'd gotten a new passport in a different name. He'd opened an untraceable bank account in the Cayman Islands, where he would transfer the money, and he'd booked a one-way ticket to Perth, Australia — a place so far away that Pablo would never think of looking for him there. After six or seven months, he would put into action plans to get his son out of Colombia.

Screw the Diego family. For once he was looking out for himself.

King Emir's orders were sharp and concise.

"The family leaves in the early morning," he informed Faisal, his trusted consort.

"I will make sure everything is in place," Faisal assured him.

"They have to all be gone before the . . . event."

"The plane is waiting," Faisal said. "What about Tariq? Does he go with the family or does he stay with you?"

"Tariq stays. Tariq will become a man as he helps to avenge his father's death. When it is done, we will leave immediately."

"Yes, my king."

"Now I wish to give an audience to my loyal citizens who have waited many months for this very special time. My two brave warriors."

"I will bring them to you."

King Emir sighed. "Soon it shall be over. It is God's will. Tomorrow the infidels will die, and my dear son shall finally be avenged."

CHAPTER SEVENTY

"This motherfucker goes from zero to sixty in 4.3 seconds," Alejandro boasted, standing next to his latest purchase — a gleaming custom-made purple Bentley Flying Spur W12 Mulliner, with special wheels and a one-of-a-kind purple leather interior featuring expensive gold trim. "I can take it up to two hundred miles per hour anytime I feel the urge."

"Really? And where would that be? On a racetrack?" Willow drawled, not thrilled that he'd purchased such an expensive car and hadn't even mentioned it to her. Surely if he had money to throw around, he should've thrown some in her direction?

She was more than irritated. Of *course* he had money to throw around. His stupid club was a front for drugs, so he was probably rolling in cash. Yet he was stalling on giving her a million measly bucks — an amount that meant nothing to him.

What Willow didn't know was that Pablo

kept strict control over what money came Alejandro's way. Pablo had people who handled all his finances, and he'd instructed Rafael to watch over whatever money Alejandro was able to get his hands on. His son received a generous allowance, and that was it. The new car was a birthday present.

Willow had questions. Was Alejandro serious about producing a movie? Or was he simply stringing her along?

Vegas would answer those questions. He'd assured her he was picking up a shitload of cash there. Finally, she could give Eddie his money, and then he would immediately get their project going.

"I like this car," Dante rasped. "I should buy one."

"Get in line," Alejandro said. "Took me eight months to get mine. Everything custom. One of a kind."

"I have many connections," Dante said with a dictatorial smirk. "I can probably get one quicker."

"I doubt it," Alejandro snapped.

In college, he and Dante — although supposedly friends — had always been in vicious competition with each other. Who drove the fastest car? Who banged the prettiest girls? Who threw the wildest, most out-of-control parties?

They both had rich daddies to finance their

lifestyles, so money had never been a problem.

Now, as adults, nothing had changed. Dante was determined to screw Alejandro's redheaded girlfriend simply because he knew he could. She had that available look of a girl who'd do anything if it suited her purpose.

While Alejandro had plans to hit on Max — even though she was not his type, why not try something new?

"Get in," Alejandro ordered. "Girls in the back. Dante, you ride up front with me."

"Why should I sit in the back?" Willow complained. "I get carsick on long rides. I want to be up front with you."

Alejandro tossed her a look — a look that screamed, *Shut the fuck up and do what I tell you.*

Willow sighed and did as he said.

Sometimes it wasn't worth arguing with Alejandro. Not when they were so close to picking up the money.

Walking into an outpouring of unwanted attention was not what Bobby wanted or expected. Apparently his recent arrest and following vindication had not gone unnoticed. He wasn't used to this much attention; usually he preferred to keep it low-key. Today was different, though. Today congratulations that he was a free man with no stigma attached to his name seemed to be the topic

569

of the night.

Yeah, he thought bitterly, *no stigma indeed. The whole Chicago debacle is all over the Internet. It'll never go away.*

After doing the rounds of greeting people, he sought out Lennie and asked where Lucky was.

"Gone to bed," Lennie replied. "It's the big day tomorrow, and she needs to get as much sleep as she can."

"And Max?"

"On her way."

Bobby nodded, and moved over to the table where Brigette and her girlfriend were sitting.

"Hiya, *uncle,*" Brigette said with an artful grin. "I hear you've been knee deep in big bad trouble."

"Everything's cool," Bobby said. "And do me a favor: stop calling me uncle. Makes me feel ancient."

"It's not *my* fault Granddad knocked your mom up," Brigette teased. "You *are* my uncle."

"Jeez, Brig, you make it sound so tawdry. Let me remind you that Dimitri and Lucky were *married.* It was a legit relationship."

"I know, I know," Brigette said with a beguiling smile. "I'm just f-ing with you. We're off to bed anyway. Oh yes, and if you get stalked by Venus, I'm supposed to advise you to steer clear."

"Huh?" Bobby said, frowning. "What's *that* about?"

"You heard," Brigette said, getting up from the table. "No screwing around with Mom's best friend. Lucky's orders."

"Got another text from Max," Cookie informed Harry. "They're just leaving, so that means she won't get here for hours."

"That's a bummer," Harry complained.

"And guess what?" Cookie added.

"What?"

"Willow Price is with them."

"Crazy Willow Price. How come?"

"She's apparently the girlfriend of Max's boss's friend."

"Sounds like a party."

"Yeah, an' talkin' of parties, instead of hanging around waiting, we should go hit a club," Cookie suggested.

"Why'd we wanna do that?" Harry asked.

"To have fun," Cookie replied, fishing out a hand mirror from her Birkin purse — a present from Daddy — and inspecting her pretty face. "We're totally capable of gettin' trashed without her, aren't we?"

"Sure, 'cause you just wanna go somewhere to pick up some random dude and get laid," Harry said accusingly.

"Don't *you*?" Cookie questioned. "We're in Vegas. We gotta totally go for it."

"I can go for it on Grindr, thankyouverymuch," Harry reminded her. "Best app *ever.*"

"Does that mean I've gotta make do with Tinder?" Cookie groaned. "That's *so* loser city."

"Better than a club. At least you know you're getting a sure thing."

"You're such a *perv.*"

"Oh," Harry said. "An' I suppose you're not?"

They both giggled. For their generation, getting laid was so damn easy.

With a throaty "Bobby," there she was. His boyhood crush. His mom's best friend. The delectable, gorgeous, ageless, sexy Venus.

"Hey," he managed, remembering the things he'd done staring at her photos in magazines when he was just a kid.

Auntie Venus. Superstar. Lounging by the pool in a barely there bikini when he was fourteen.

Auntie Venus taking it all off for *Playboy* and showing just enough to make a teenage boy never forget.

Auntie Venus onstage in Vegas cavorting half naked with the best-looking male backup dancers ever to grace the stage.

Eventually he'd grown up and dropped the Auntie, and they'd become casual friends, running into each other at family events, always polite. She'd usually been with a boy toy or a husband. Never alone.

Now here was Venus on the night before Gino's funeral looking like a million bucks, and she was indeed alone. And so was he. No more Denver. No more commitments. He was a free agent and so, apparently, was she.

"I'm not supposed to talk to you," Venus said with a wicked glint in her eye. "You're off-limits."

"So I heard," Bobby replied, grinning.

"From whom?"

"From Brigette, who was put in charge of keeping us apart."

"She was, huh?"

"Apparently so."

"Where is dear Brigette?"

"Gone to bed, like everyone else around here," he said, indicating the banquet room, which was emptying out fast. "How come you're still here?"

"I was having a drink with Charlie Dollar. That man talks a blue streak until he's just too stoned to go on."

"What happened to him?"

"He fell asleep in a booth."

"You're kidding. And you left him there?"

"Oh, someone will mop him up," she said with a casual wave of her manicured hand. "Old movie stars are hardly my responsibility."

"Okay, then."

Her startling blue eyes met his. "Okay,

573

then," she said, gently mimicking him. "Are you up for a drink?"

"Where?" he asked cautiously.

"My suite."

"The last time I accepted a drink in a woman's suite, I got roofied."

"Yes, I read about that," she said with a slight smile. "Does that mean that if I promise not to roofie you, we're on?"

"Depends what 'we're on' means."

Leaning toward him, she lightly touched his arm. "You're a big boy now, Bobby. No explanations needed."

He experienced a sharp jolt of electricity mixed with unforgettable memories of his horny teenage years.

Venus was his fantasy. And he was about to step into fantasyland.

At last they were off, Alejandro roaring out of the underground garage as if he were being chased by a dozen police cars, bragging about how much speed he could summon from his new toy in less than six seconds. Gangsta rap blared from the multiple speakers.

Max curled up on the backseat and shut her eyes, willing herself to fall asleep. But sleep refused to come; her mind was too full of random thoughts.

Would she ever see Billy again?

Why was Dante such a miserable pain?

What were Cookie and Harry up to?

Did Athena even miss her?

How was Lucky dealing with Gino's murder?

Eventually she fell into a half sleep, waking when they hit the freeway and she felt her phone vibrating.

Retrieving it from the pocket of her jacket, she noted that it was Lennie.

"Daddy," she whispered tentatively. "Can't wait to see you."

"Where the hell are you?" Lennie demanded.

"On my way."

"What? By horse and carriage?"

"By car. I'm with my boss from Dolcezza."

"Your boss, huh?" Lennie said, frustrated. "That would be the asshole who was supposed to get you here by helicopter. What happened to *that* plan?"

"I dunno."

"I'll be speaking to him when you finally arrive."

Great, she thought. *You can tell him what a dick he is.*

"What's all that noise?" Lennie growled. "Sounds like a party."

"It's just car music," she said lamely.

"Well, take it easy."

"Yes, Daddy."

"See you soon, sweetie."

Up in her suite, Venus offered Bobby a drink.

575

He declined.

"You still think I might drug you?" she murmured teasingly.

"I thought we covered that," he said.

"Oh yes, we did, didn't we?" she drawled. "Why don't *you* open us a bottle of champagne."

She was treating him as if he was one of her fans, and he didn't like it. She was toying with him, probably wondering what kind of move he was about to make.

"I didn't come up here for a drink," he said.

"No? What did you come up for?"

As if she didn't know. Auntie Venus. Famous. Beautiful. Talented. Sexy. A tease.

He refused to let her intimidate him.

"Come here," he commanded.

"Excuse me?"

"You heard."

"I don't take kindly to orders."

He'd had enough. Years of lusting after her propelled him into action. He wanted her. He wanted all of her. And he wasn't waiting any longer.

"You wanna fuck or you wanna play games?" he said.

"My oh my, the little boy has a mouth on him."

He strode across the room and grabbed her hard, ripping the revealing jacket off her.

She wore nothing underneath.

He cupped her breasts, pushing them

together, shoving her up against the wall, bending to suck on her nipples until she cried out.

Within seconds they were in the bedroom, clothes falling off along the way.

Then he was rolling around with Mommy's best friend, and he didn't give a damn about upsetting Lucky. Some things were bound to happen, and this was one of them.

Venus. All soft blond curves, sweet-smelling and succulent. Naked, she did not disappoint. Pilates and daily workouts had kept her body in pristine shape. Being in bed with her was like taking a luxury trip to heaven.

"To think I knew you when you were a little boy," she purred, her long, manicured fingers raking his chest. "Now look at you, all grown up."

"Cut the shit, Venus," he said, climbing on top of her and spreading her golden thighs. "Do you have any idea how long I've wanted to do this?"

"Why don't you tell me?"

"It might take too long."

And as he spoke, he plunged inside her, reliving every lustful teenage memory.

Denver was forgotten. Denver was yesterday's news.

He was a man with no ties, and he could do exactly as he liked.

CHAPTER SEVENTY-ONE

Dave Riggio was tired. He was tired of his nagging wife, his stripper girlfriend who had her own line of nagging, and his two teenage brats — both into drugs and partying. He worked like a fucking dog while they all played. On *his* money. The money he made driving a fucking big rig back and forth across the country — sometimes working a twenty-hour shift with no sleep.

Tonight was one of those nights, and all he wanted was a decent night's rest. However, that was not about to happen, because he was on the road from Vegas to L.A. carrying a full load of fruit that had to be in L.A. early in the morning in time for market, and it was already three A.M.

Sitting next to him in the rig was a young girl — a runaway, no doubt. She wore ripped jeans and a T-shirt featuring the slogan *Freaks rule*! She had frizzy brown hair framing a thin face, and buckteeth. He'd picked her up at a well-known truck stop, and in exchange for a blow job, he'd offered her a ride to L.A., thinking — mistakenly — that she'd entertain him with some kind of inane chatter.

This was not to be. The girl was silent and sulky, huddled in the passenger seat, and the blow job she'd given him was not worth the ride.

"Fuck it," he muttered under his breath.

"What?" the girl said, suddenly coming to life.

"You ever given a blow job before?"

"Course I have," she said, rubbing her eyes.

"Didn't seem like it," he said gruffly.

"I could do it again," she said, sensing that he might be planning on dropping her off, even though they had a deal.

Dave took one hand off the steering wheel and patted his crotch. He might be tired, but he was still horny.

"It'll be better the second time," the girl promised.

"Gonna pull over at the next exit," Dave said, although he realized that he was pressed for time and every minute counted.

"You don't have to," the girl said. "I can do you while you're driving."

Dave salivated. He liked a girl with fresh ideas.

"Why not?" he said, patting his crotch again. "An' this time try t' pretend you're enjoying it."

CHAPTER SEVENTY-TWO

While Alejandro settled behind the wheel of his latest acquisition, testing how fast his car could go as they hurtled through the desert, Willow found her mind wandering. She'd been reluctant to leave her mom alone in her house, but Pammy hadn't given her much choice. Right now Mother Dearest was no doubt nosing through her possessions. She'd never given Willow one inch of privacy when Willow was growing up, and now she must be in heaven checking out her house.

Willow could just imagine the scene. Pammy laid out on *her* bed snorting cocaine from *her* secret supply, downing vodka from *her* bottle, and probably watching porn on *her* TV.

"Motherfucker!" Willow muttered, cringing at the thought. Her house was all she had, and she didn't want it tainted with her mom's presence. She bet Pammy would still be in residence when she returned from Vegas, which meant she'd be forced to throw her out.

Pammy was an embarrassment she did not need in her life, especially with all that would soon happen.

Willow Price was about to regain her place at the top of the tree, and before she did, Pammy had to go.

Her thoughts moved on to Ralph Maestro. Ralph had left her several voice mails demanding to know where she was. It delighted her that a big movie star was hot to keep playing, although getting her hands on the money came first, because once she gave Eddie his million bucks, all she had to do was sit back and watch everything fall into place.

That was her plan. She'd worry about Pammy and Ralph when it was done.

Back at Club Luna, Sonia — who'd been busy working on the bartender — had noticed Rafael, Alejandro's business partner, shooting her sly looks.

She knew who he was; his photo was on the pin-board at the office right up there next to Alejandro's. Usually Rafael did not hang out at the club, but tonight, with Alejandro gone, he was settled in a booth chugging champagne.

Sonia was not one to miss an opportunity. Her job was to gain access and take photos of Alejandro's private office, and she had a far better chance of doing that with Rafael than with the bartender.

The music playing was loud and sexy —
strident beats that allowed her to shake her
assets in front of Rafael's booth.

He was staring, his watchful eyes taking in
every inch of her.

She'd heard he was a tight-ass, not a player
like Alejandro. Tonight he seemed like a
player.

She undulated toward him. He continued
to stare.

Flopping down next to him, she began fanning herself with her hand. "Too hot!" she
exclaimed. "This girl needs a drink."

Rafael said nothing.

"Gonna buy me one?" she asked, touching
his arm. "Gonna make a girl happy?"

Rafael thought about Elizabetta with anger
in his heart. Which one of Pablo's guards was
she fucking? Then his thoughts turned to
Willow and how she'd ignored him earlier.

Puta!

They were all *putas.*

Perhaps this one was different?

It didn't matter. He would fuck her and
send her on her way.

Rafael was a changed man.

Sometimes the sex is so hot that neither party
wishes it to end.

Bobby felt it, and so did Venus. She was
caught up in the way he made love to her. So
strong and sure of himself. Her Venezuelan

boyfriend had been a boorish lover, thinking only of his own climax. Before him there had been many, but none like Bobby. Their chemistry sizzled. He touched her in ways she felt she'd never been touched before. His cock was a thing of beauty, and she couldn't get enough.

Bobby felt the chemistry too. Sex with Denver had been great at first, but then their passion had kind of fizzled, and maybe he *had* been thinking of making out with Nadia. Yes, he was finally admitting it to himself.

Making love to Venus was pure animal lust. He inhaled her skin, her hair, everything about her.

"I want us to come together," she whispered. "Make me come, Bobby, because I'm ready."

And so she got her wish.

Stretching luxuriously, Venus was beginning to realize that Bobby was everything she'd imagined he'd be in bed and more. Usually very handsome men were selfish lovers, but not Bobby. He knew how to please a woman and then some.

How unfortunate that he happened to be Lucky's son, because she knew full well that a steamy affair between her and Bobby would enrage Lucky. Liberal as Lucky was about most things, her best friend screwing her son would *definitely* not fly.

Bobby jumped off the bed.

"Planning on leaving?" Venus inquired, licking her lips as she admired his ripped body.

Flexing his muscles, he grinned, feeling as if he'd just conquered Everest. "Is that what you want me to do?" he asked.

"What do *you* think?" she murmured.

"I think you want me to stay," he said confidently.

"Well," she said, her voice a husky drawl. "We may as well take advantage of tonight due to the fact that this might never happen again."

"Does that mean you're shutting me out?"

"Yes, 'cause in case you forgot, your mom happens to be my best friend."

"You really think she'd be pissed?"

"C'*mon,* Bobby, do you *know* Lucky?"

"Yeah," he was forced to admit. "I guess she wouldn't exactly be thrilled."

"Of course, there *is* another way," Venus offered, her voice full of seductive promise. "We could always get together on the down-low."

Bobby burst out laughing. "Sure, me and one of the most famous women on the planet screwing on the down-low, that'd work. Nobody would ever suspect."

"I have a variety of disguises."

"You do?"

"Oh, yes, I certainly do," Venus purred, licking her full lips.

"In that case —"

"Come back to bed, Bobby. Once is never enough."

He did not need to be asked twice.

Max wished that Dante and his greasy friend Alejandro would turn the music down — if you could call hard-core gangsta rap music. She was into the beat, but sometimes the blatantly sexist and downright hostile lyrics toward women got to her. And what was with the big-butt syndrome? Half-naked singing divas thrusting their enhanced bottoms at everyone was totally gross. In every video, there they were — diva singers shoving their big fat asses right in your face. So how come all the male stars managed to stay fully clothed? It was a mystery.

She yawned and shot a glance at Willow, who seemed happy to ignore her. The redhead would no doubt change her attitude when they got to Vegas and she realized that Max's mom was Lucky Santangelo and her dad was Lennie Golden.

Too late, mean girl. It'll be my turn to ignore you.

Checking her phone, she noticed there was a text message she hadn't looked at. It was probably Cookie bitching because she wasn't there yet. Clicking on it, she read the message.

Hey. Where are you? Can't find you. Want to. Need to talk. Hear me out even though you gotta think I'm a major prick. Call me. Billy.

She attempted to stay cool.

Billy! Was he kidding?

What did he want with her?

Why was he screwing with her?

What was his deal?

She didn't know and she didn't care.

Or did she?

Maybe.

Maybe not.

Billy Melina. Unfortunately, he was the love of her young life.

When it came to sex, Venus was not adverse to adventure. She traveled with her toys, and if a man failed to satisfy her, she put them to good use.

No sex toys needed with Bobby. He had every move down.

"What did you do, go to training camp for lovers?" she gasped as he spread her legs and went down on her for the third time.

Bobby didn't reply; he was too busy living the fantasy, thrusting his tongue deep inside her until she could take it no more.

Shuddering from head to toe, she reached an earth-shattering climax.

The Puerto Rican whore was all over him and Rafael did not object. Since Willow had ignored him, made him feel like he was less than nothing, he decided it was time to boost

586

his confidence.

"I'm Rita," Sonia confided, pretending to guzzle champagne. "Who're you?"

"Rafael," he muttered.

"Cool name," she said, leaning provocatively toward him, full cleavage on show. "It got some kinda ring to it. You the manager or what?"

"I own this club," Rafael said, deciding that playing the boss had its advantages. "This is my place."

"I thought Alejandro —"

"You thought wrong."

"You gotta be important, then," Sonia said, widening her eyes as if she was impressed. "You gotta be the big boy around here."

"I certainly am," Rafael boasted, the champagne loosening his tongue.

"If you're the boss you must have a private office, a place we could maybe have ourselves a fun time."

Yes, Rafael thought. *Fun.* Exactly what he needed before he took off with Pablo Fernandez Diego's money.

Sonia could tell she had him — this one was easier than she'd thought. "What we waitin' for, big boy?" she said. "Whyn't we go get ourselves some privacy?"

Rafael did not need to be asked twice. This girl was offering herself to him, and he was accepting.

He stood up and was surprised to discover

that he wasn't quite steady on his feet. It was the champagne. He wasn't used to it. No more drinking after tonight. No more women either. This one was his final fling.

CHAPTER SEVENTY-THREE

None of them saw it coming.

Not Alejandro, who was showing off the enormous speed his new toy could achieve.

Not Dante, who was smoking a joint and imagining what he would do to the redhead in the backseat when they arrived in Vegas.

Not Willow, who was daydreaming about her career comeback.

And certainly not Max, who was thinking about the text she'd received from Billy and what it all meant.

Further down the desert highway, barreling along in the opposite direction toward L.A., Dave Riggio was enjoying the ministrations of the young runaway who was determined to show him that she was worthy of the ride as she buried her head in his lap, sucking his dick and gasping for breath, not letting go for a second.

A second was all it took as Dave Riggio shut his eyes for one brief moment, causing his heavy rig to veer across the highway into the oncoming lane. And even though Alejandro — driving 150 miles per hour — saw the rig bearing down on them, it was too late. There was nothing he could do.

It was a fiery crash of major proportions. The impact so strong that the Bentley was demolished and both vehicles were immediately engulfed in flames.

Metal against metal.

Deadly.

Fatal.

The night sky lit up like one huge firework.

CHAPTER SEVENTY-FOUR

Chris Warwick was angry. Why hadn't anyone thought to warn him that the main lobby of the Magiriano was going to be filled with a milling crowd of Middle Eastern women wearing long black abayas and face veils, their mascaraed eyes staring out at the world? The women were surrounded by mountains of luggage, and a plethora of shopping bags from Chanel, Vuitton, and Cartier. Unruly children abounded, racing around the lobby yelling and laughing like packs of wild hyenas.

Chris summoned Ian Simmons, the general manager. "What the hell is going on?" he demanded to know. "This is unacceptable."

Ian, a tall, thin import from England, was embarrassed. "It wasn't supposed to happen this way," he said. "King Emir and his entourage were not due to check out for another ten days."

"It sure looks like *that* all changed," Chris huffed. "We have many VIPs arriving for the funeral service at noon, and I expect the

591

lobby to be clear of all this chaos as they walk through to the outside. I thought this was made clear."

"There is a fleet of limos arriving any moment to pick everyone up," Ian assured him. "We're doing our best."

"Your best won't be good enough for Ms. Santangelo if she sees what's going on here," Chris threatened. "You'd better get this lobby clear and soon."

"I understand," Ian said, somewhat resentful that this security person was speaking to him in such a dismissive way. "Although I should point out that during his stay, the king has racked up a bill of over three million dollars. I'm sure Ms. Santangelo wouldn't object to that."

Unimpressed, Chris said, "Who is this king anyway?"

"King Emir Amin Mohamed Jordan."

"From where?"

"Akramshar. It's a small country rich in oil. These women are all his wives."

Akramshar. The name sounded familiar, but why?

Taking out his phone, Chris called Danny. "You ever heard of a Middle Eastern country called Akramshar?" he asked brusquely.

"Why?" Danny ventured.

"Have you or have you not?" Chris said, in no mood to play games.

"Uh . . . yes. Last year there was a shooting

incident at the Keys. A man was shot —
Armand Jordan. He was originally from
Akramshar, one of the king's sons."

Chris had been abroad at the time, but now
Danny had jogged his memory. As far as he
could recall, the story was that Armand Jordan had been trying to negotiate with Lucky
to buy her hotel, she'd refused, and Armand
had been assassinated by — as the cops put
it — a professional. No arrests had ever taken
place.

Chris experienced a feeling that all was not
right. Why was King Emir in Vegas? And why
was he checking out on the day of Gino's
funeral?

He was mad at himself that there had been
no early security checks on the king and his
entourage. Wasn't Danny supposed to be in
charge of that? It pissed him off when people
didn't do their job properly. Surely Danny
should have connected the dots?

Too late now. Anyway, it was probably a coincidence — rich Saudis were always in Vegas,
indulging in big-stakes gambling while their
women shopped for ridiculous shoes, expensive jewelry, and designer clothes they would
never dare to wear in their home country.

They were leaving, which was a good thing.

Still . . . Chris couldn't shake the feeling
that all was not right.

Her cell was ringing, and Denver was not

inclined to answer it since she was in the middle of a dream that had her floating on a raft in the ocean. It was a peaceful dream.

Reluctantly, she stretched out her arm for her phone, whereupon she encountered a body lying next to her. For a moment she was disoriented, until she realized that the man asleep beside her was Sam.

Damn it! She'd slept with Sam. In Bobby's bed. Well, technically it wasn't Bobby's bed; they'd chosen it together. Still, she immediately felt overwhelmed with guilt and she was furious with herself for drinking too much the night before.

Grabbing her phone, she muttered a quick, "Hello."

"Where were you last night?" Leon asked, sounding put out. "I told you I'd be calling you back. We're on a job here, Denver."

"I guess I fell asleep," she admitted sheepishly. "What time did you call?"

"Three A.M. Couldn't reach you, so I met with Sonia myself."

Now she was really pissed. While she'd been busy screwing Sam — although she couldn't remember the details — Leon had been working the case without her, and that wasn't right.

"What did Sonia come up with?" she asked, struggling to sit up.

"The entire layout of Alejandro's private office. She got the photos on her phone."

"Really?"

"Told you she was the shit," Leon boasted.

"I'm on my way in," Denver said, trying to navigate her way out of bed without waking Sam.

"Make it fast. We're payin' another visit to Frankie."

"We are?"

"You bet we are. He says he has more for us. Somethin' that'll nail Alejandro's ass for sure."

"I'm excited."

"Me too."

"See you in a minute," she said, clicking off her phone.

"Hey," Sam said, rolling over with a big smile on his face and a massive hard-on. "How about me? I'm excited too."

"Not now," Denver said, pulling away, her feet hitting the floor. "Gotta go to work."

"Where the hell is Max?" Lennie grumbled, walking in on Lucky as she sat in front of her makeup table. "I stayed up half the night waiting for her to arrive."

"You did?"

"Yes, I did. I can't wait to ream that so-called boss of hers a new asshole. What was he thinking? Driving when they were supposed to get a helicopter."

"Calm down," Lucky replied, applying a smoky brown shadow to her eyes. "She's no doubt having breakfast with Cookie and Harry."

"We don't see her for months," Lennie steamed, standing behind his wife. "Then she gets here, and all she wants to do is hang out with her friends. I'm pissed."

"That's the way it goes with teenagers," Lucky pointed out, remembering her own wild teenage years. "You'd better stop behaving like the ogre father or you'll drive her away."

"Drive her away? She's fucking living in Europe as it is. How much farther can she go?"

"Who knows?"

"Max and I used to have a very special bond."

"I know that," Lucky said, putting down her makeup brush. "We'll see her soon, so what you *should* do is get dressed and stop complaining."

"Who's complaining?" Lennie said, frowning. "I'd like to spend time with my daughter. Is that a crime?"

"Jeez!" Lucky said, suddenly losing patience. "Aren't *we* the dramatic one."

"Not dramatic, merely concerned."

"Okay, okay. I get it."

There was a short silence before Lennie said, "Bobby's here. I saw him last night."

"What time did *he* arrive?"

"Late. I don't know why Max couldn't've

come with him."

"You should call her," Lucky said, standing up.

"I have. Her phone doesn't seem to be working."

"Then go downstairs and find her. I'm telling you she'll be with Cookie. When you see her, ask her to come up. I need to know what she's planning on wearing."

"For crissake," Lennie snapped. "This isn't a fashion show."

Lucky gave him a long dark stare. When it came to Max, he was way too protective and sometimes it was too much — especially today of all days. "I'm well aware of that," she said coolly. "And since it's my father's funeral, I'd appreciate it if you'd take your pissy attitude and dump it elsewhere. I'm not in the mood."

Realizing that he was being unreasonable, Lennie paused by the door. "Sorry, sweetheart," he said. "I understand how difficult this day is for you."

"No shit?" she said with a sarcastic drawl.

"Hey — we're all on edge, but we'll get through it together," he promised. "We always do."

"I guess so," she said, thinking that this was no time to start a fight.

"Okay, I'll go find Max and bring her up."

"You do that."

After Lennie left, Lucky went into her

closet and tried to decide what to wear. Everyone would probably be dressed in black or muted colors, but she had in mind Gino's favorite, a simple white outfit.

Screw it if people thought it wasn't suitable. She was Lucky Santangelo. She could wear whatever she liked.

"Gotta go," Bobby said, barely moving from the warmth of Venus's embrace.

"Who's stopping you?" Venus drawled, tiptoeing her fingers across his bare chest. "I'm certainly not."

"Yeah, you are," he said with a rakish grin. "You're making it very difficult for me to get up."

"And that would be because?" she asked, her voice early-morning husky.

"As if you don't know," he chided.

"God!" she exclaimed, sneaking her hand under the covers. "Aren't *you* the insatiable one."

"Can I help it if I find you irresistible?"

Slithering her body down his, she began flicking her tongue around his erect penis, causing him to groan.

Arching his back, he let her do her thing.

"I always knew you'd taste delicious," she murmured, nonchalantly taking him into her mouth.

The world stopped still for a moment as he reveled in the sensation. Then he pulled away, and moving on top, he thrust himself deeply inside her.

Morning sex. Something Denver had never been into.

Venus positioned her long legs around his waist and began moaning with pleasure.

It occurred to Bobby that this was not a rebound thing. This was something special, and with or without Lucky's approval, he was in no way ready for it to end. After all, it had only just begun.

Chapter Seventy-Five

The initial impact of the big rig and the Bentley was so fast and devastating that the back passenger doors were flung violently open, propelling Willow and Max out into the barren desert. Then came an enormous explosion. Everything happened within seconds.

Trapped in the two front seats, Alejandro and Dante had no chance. They were incinerated along with the car, as were Dave Riggio and his pathetic little runaway.

The flames roared high into the sky — burning brightly.

Both sides of the highway were deserted, no other vehicles in sight. The silence was broken by the sounds of the flames cackling and roaring — devouring metal and human flesh.

Willow lay facedown in the desert, her left leg twisted in a grotesque position beneath her body. She was unconscious.

Nearby, Max was half wedged under a jagged rock. She was also unconscious.

Although hot and steamy during the day, at night and during the early-morning hours the desert was cold — a brisk wind fanning the flames of the fiery collision.

Two coyotes slouched toward the crash site, hypnotized by the flames.

A large snake slithered across the top of the rock where Max lay trapped.

Finally, when the flames died down, silence prevailed.

A deathly silence.

CHAPTER SEVENTY-SIX

"I feel like dog crap," Harry groaned, dunking a croissant into a mug of steaming coffee and taking a bite.

"Me too," Cookie agreed, toying with her sunglasses. "Two hours' sleep like in no way cuts it."

"Morning, kids," Lennie said, approaching their table.

Cookie summoned a weak smile. She'd always liked older men, and Max's dad was totally hot. "Hello, Mr. G.," she said, trying not to look as if she hadn't drunk half the bar at the club the night before.

"I'm wondering where Max is," Lennie stated. "Either of you seen her?"

"Don't think she's up yet," Harry said.

"Or she might be with Bobby," Cookie offered, taking a gulp of strong black coffee. "You know how she gets when they're together. She like follows him everywhere. Sisterly love an' all that crap."

"Her phone's not working," Lennie said

brusquely. "If you see her, tell her it would be nice if she checked in with her parents."

"Speaking of parents," Cookie said. "Did my dad arrive yet? He was flying in on his plane with his latest conquest." She pulled a face. "Can't *wait* to see the new love of his life. Got a hunch it's another Russian hooker with enormous fake boobs."

"Sorry, Cookie, I have no idea. Ask Lucky's assistant — Danny."

"Where can I find him?"

"He's around somewhere."

"This place is so freakin' big it's impossible to find anyone," Harry complained.

"You kids should go get changed," Lennie said. "The service is at noon."

"We're on it," Cookie said. "If you see Max first you can tell her we're pissed. We came here to support her."

"Yeah," Harry agreed.

"I'll be glad to tell her," Lennie said. "That's if I ever discover where she is."

And with those words he took off.

Chris decided that he'd better inform Lucky that King Emir Amin Mohamed Jordan and his entourage were at the Magiriano, where Gino's funeral service was due to take place, so he took the private elevator to her penthouse apartment at the Keys and reported the news.

"Are you serious?" Lucky said, her dark

eyes filled with fury. "How come you're only just finding this out?"

"They're leaving," Chris informed her.

"That's not the point," she said, eyes still flashing. "Why were they here in the first place? How come nobody told me?"

"I wasn't in town when the Armand killing went down," Chris said. "It didn't happen on my watch."

"Danny was," she said sharply. "Surely he checked out the guest list at the Magiriano?"

"He's not security, so I guess not."

Lucky was furious that this complication had arisen. She'd had nothing to do with Armand Jordan's murder. He'd been shot — not by her or anyone she knew. It just happened that he'd gotten shot in her hotel. The man was a pig; he'd no doubt had a shitload of enemies. The investigating detectives had said it looked like a professional hit, an execution. After a couple of months they'd written it off as a cold case.

An execution. A professional hit. Which is exactly what had befallen Gino.

So why was Armand's father in Vegas? Was he seeking revenge? Because if he was, he was seeking it in the wrong place.

She consulted her watch. Time was passing quickly. Should she go see this so-called king and try to find out what he was doing in Vegas?

No. There wasn't time for that. The king

and his entourage were leaving anyway. It all had to be one big unfortunate coincidence.

"I'm not happy about this," she said to Chris. "You'd better make sure that your team double-checks everything."

"My men are on it."

After leaving Cookie and Harry, Lennie made his way up to the family floor and spoke to the concierge, who was stationed behind a desk in front of the elevators.

"What time did Max check in?" he asked.

The concierge told him that he had only been on duty for an hour. "I'll look in the book, Mr. Golden," he said, opening a desk drawer and taking out the guest book, which was supposed to be signed by everyone when they arrived.

Lennie glanced at his watch. It was coming up on eleven, and the funeral service over at the Magiriano was due to take place at noon. Where the hell was his errant daughter?

"It seems that Max has yet to check in," the concierge said.

"You're sure?"

"Well, yes, unless she forgot to sign the book."

"Give me the passkey to her room," Lennie said. "She got into Vegas very late. She's probably still sleeping."

"Certainly, sir."

The Puerto Rican girl was a tease. Rafael was mad at himself for not realizing it earlier. The previous night he'd taken her up to Alejandro's private office expecting sex, and all he'd gotten was a list of excuses — everything from it was her time of the month to she had a jealous boyfriend who could turn up at any moment. She'd even taken out her phone and walked around making calls, while he'd simmered with fury and considered whether he should rape her or not. There was no one to stop him. They were alone together. Alejandro's office was soundproof, so nobody would hear her if she screamed.

No. Making trouble for himself was not on his agenda. Soon he would be leaving America, and he had to be careful, so he'd finally escorted her out and left her downstairs in the club. Then he'd driven home alone.

Now it was morning and he was proud of himself for not giving in to his basic instincts.

Today he would continue planning his exit strategy. That was far more important than getting laid by some club tramp.

Rafael was looking forward to an exciting new life, and nothing was going to stop him. When the money from Pablo came through, he was on his way to freedom. Not a moment too soon.

Forcing himself to make a supreme effort, Bobby began pulling himself away from the comfort of Venus's arms and everything else she had to offer. It wasn't easy, but it had to be done, for Lucky would be expecting him to stand by her side and he fully intended to do so. Right now he had to get back to his suite, shower, and put on a suit. He also had to give some thought to what he was going to say about Gino.

Venus placed her soft arms around his neck, pulled him closer, and kissed him long and hard, tempting him to stay.

Much as he wanted to, there was no way he could let Lucky down, so after a few minutes, he reluctantly untangled himself. "Gotta go," he said. "And you should be getting dressed."

"I thought you preferred me undressed," she purred.

"Later," he promised.

On the way to his suite on the family floor, he bumped into M.J. emerging from his room. M.J. was accompanied by an exotic-looking Asian girl with silky black hair and a slim body. She was the kind of girl Bobby would've expected to see on Alex Woods's arm, but it seemed M.J. had gotten there first.

M.J. threw him a sheepish grin. "Meet Tia," he said.

"Hey, Tia," Bobby said.

"Hard day's night," M.J. said with a jaunty wink. "We're gonna grab some breakfast. Need the energy. See you at the service."

Bobby made it to his suite, his mind still buzzing about Venus. She was an amazing woman. What did it matter that she was quite a few years older than him? They were magical together, and after all he'd been through, he could do with a touch of magic in his life. He decided that if Venus was up for it, they'd present a united front and tell Lucky together. What could she do? Exactly nothing. It wasn't as if he was Max, running around with Venus's ex, Billy Melina. That had been a ridiculous situation. Lennie had put a stop to it, and rightfully so.

Thinking about Max made Bobby realize that he missed her — even though she could be an annoying pain in the ass. Since she'd moved to Europe, he hadn't seen her in months. Lucky had told him that little sis had gotten herself a big advertising campaign that was shooting in Italy. He was happy for her, and he hoped she was behaving herself. Max had a wild streak — it ran in the family.

He'd always considered himself to be the sane one. Perhaps not so much now. What was so interesting about being sane? He was enjoying his newfound freedom. No more Mr. Good Guy.

Things had definitely changed.

CHAPTER SEVENTY-SEVEN

Norma and Willy Rockwell and their three boisterous children were driving along the highway in their rental moving truck when one of the kids, an acne-ridden thirteen-year-old, spotted the wreckage up ahead, plumes of smoke still rising.

"Look, Dad!" the boy shouted, wriggling in his seat. "Somebody's had an accident."

By this time, Willy Rockwell had also seen the debris spilled across the highway, and he was already carefully steering the rental truck to the side of the road. It was five A.M. and just beginning to get light.

"This don't look good," Willy said, sharing his voice with a hacking cough.

"No, it don't," Norma agreed, pulling her woolen cardigan close across her chest.

"Whatcha gonna do, Dad?" the thirteen-year-old asked. "Shouldn't we go take a peek?"

"No," Norma said sharply. "It's best not to get involved in this sorta thing. Somebody

609

else'll come along. Leave it to them."

"Your ma's right," Willy said, starting his engine. "Never shove your nose in where it don't belong."

The thirteen-year-old did not agree with either of them. What if there were survivors they could help? Shouldn't they at least call the highway patrol?

He began to say something, but to no avail. Both his parents ignored him, and once again they were on their way.

Ten minutes later a BMW crammed with a bunch of drunken teenagers — four boys and two girls — roared down the highway heading toward L.A. The driver, a baby-faced sixteen-year-old, had yet to score his driving license. What he *had* managed to score was his stepdad's BMW, and he'd gathered up a group of friends for a wild night in Vegas. Now they were hell-bent on getting back to L.A. in time for school.

Loud music blared from someone's iPod, and all six kids were in a take-no-prisoners mood, smoking grass and chugging Red Bulls, when the BMW hit a large chunk of metal debris spread across the highway. The BMW careened out of control, left the highway, and flipped over four times before shuddering to a sickening stop.

This time there was no fire, but the screams of the teenagers trapped in the car could be heard from quite a distance away.

One of the girls crawled from the wreckage, blood streaming down her face from a deep cut above her eye. She was crying and hysterical as she reached for her cell phone in her jeans pocket and managed to dial 911.

Help would soon be on the way.

CHAPTER SEVENTY-EIGHT

The lobby of the Magiriano was cleared. King Emir's entourage was long gone, much to the relief of Ian Simmons, who thought it best not to mention that the king himself and a small group of his men and bodyguards were still in residence. Chris Warwick made the hotel manager nervous — Chris might look friendly enough, but there was something about him that announced he was not a man to be crossed. Besides, it was highly unlikely that King Emir would emerge from his penthouse. Ian had sent a messenger to his suite with a polite letter explaining the funeral situation, and asking that the lobby please be kept clear for the mourners to pass through. In return the king had one of his men personally deliver a handwritten note card thanking him for a pleasant stay. The note was accompanied by a jewelry box containing a gold Rolex.

Although gifts from satisfied guests were not unusual, a gold Rolex was quite a treat.

Ian was surprised and delighted. It proved to him that he was doing his job well. He deserved to be rewarded.

"Where are you?" Lucky asked, calling Lennie on his cell.

"I'm the one tracking our daughter, remember?" he said irritably. "I just discovered her room hasn't been slept in."

"You should come up and get changed," Lucky said, feeling apprehensive about what lay ahead, which wasn't like her at all. Her mind was full of Gino. She had to do him proud; she had to make this a day to remember.

"You're not concerned that Max seems to be on the missing list?" Lennie asked.

"Yes, I'm concerned, but there's nothing you can do now, and we have to leave in ten minutes."

"For your information, she never checked in last night."

"You know what Max is like," Lucky said, exasperated. "She probably went with her boss to the Four Seasons — that's exactly the kind of thing she'd do, especially if they got into Vegas late."

"If you think so. What's her boss's name again? I'll check out the Four Seasons."

"Ask Danny. He knows. And have Danny chase her, because I need you to be with me. So please . . . get here fast."

It wasn't often that Lucky said she needed him, and he couldn't help but note the urgency in her voice. Lucky was strong, but she wasn't superwoman, and today was putting her to the test.

"I'm on my way," he assured her.

The arrival of Paige caused quite a commotion. She and her entourage of six people had been whisked from the airport straight to the Magiriano, where Danny had arranged a hospitality suite for them to use while they were in Vegas. Paige had already informed him that she would not be staying the night. After the service and the celebratory party, she expected a plane to be waiting to take her and her friends back to Palm Springs.

Her entourage consisted of Bud Pappas, resplendent in a bright yellow suit (an outfit he was known for in his heyday); Paige's other neighbors, the Yassans; Darlene, a tall, broad-shouldered woman who was at the house with Paige the day Gino was shot; and an attractive married couple, John and Mary Lou Area, who lived nearby in Palm Springs.

Clad in a tightly fitted black dress, a perky hat complete with veil, and a tad too many ostentatious diamonds, Paige was playing the Widow Santangelo to the hilt, and enjoying every moment of the attention coming her way. As she walked through the lobby of the Magiriano, early-comers to the service stopped her to pay their respects. She accepted their good wishes with a forlorn expression and a barely audible "Thank you so much for being here. It means the world to me."

"You look so chic," her friend Darlene whispered in her ear. "I can't wait until we're alone together. Ah . . . the things I plan to do to you."

"Shh . . ." Paige said, glancing around. "Someone might hear you."

"What if they do?" Darlene said boldly. "You're a free woman now. You can do what you like — what *we* like."

"You're being inappropriate," Paige said, pretending to be cross, although there was nothing she liked better than Darlene fawning over her. Their affair had been going on for almost a year, and Paige had managed to keep it on the down-low. Now, with Gino gone, Darlene seemed to think it was time to bring it out into the open. Paige had no intention of doing so. She had a reputation to protect, not to mention a Palm Springs social life. She was not prepared to come out — not yet anyway. And certainly not at Gino's funeral service.

With his full security team in place, Chris was satisfied that the Magiriano was on lockdown, which meant that unless you were an invited guest with a numbered pass, you were not getting in. All hotel guests had been alerted that an important event was taking place and that they had to steer clear of certain areas of the hotel, which were now roped off and secure. As compensation, they were offered a free night's stay.

Too many famous people in one place was always a challenge, but Chris was confident that so far everything was running smoothly. He did not anticipate any problems. What he didn't like were the personal security teams some of the high-profile guests traveled with. They always seemed to cause problems, especially the ones attached to politicians. It was almost like a game of who's looking after the most famous and important of them all.

The random security teams made dumb demands, such as which celebrity should arrive last, because celebrities did not appreciate sitting around. And where would *their* celebrity be sitting? It had to be up front in a prime position or else trouble would ensue.

Yeah. Sure. Chris put Danny in charge of seating. He couldn't care less about who sat where. Keeping everything and everyone safe and on track was his main concern.

Assholes.

Chris hated assholes.

Back in L.A., Frankie Romano was reveling in his newfound freedom. Well, not freedom, exactly, for he was under strict guard in a hotel with a couple of armed cops on watch duty. The place he was sequestered in was hardly a four-star luxury hotel, and other than his stint in prison, Frankie was used to the best.

Prison was the pits. No place for a man like Frankie Romano.

He'd come up with exactly how they could trap Alejandro. Every week, Matias brought two girls to Alejandro's office at Club Luna. Two pathetic drug mules that Alejandro liked to play with for his own amusement. Frankie was the only one who knew about Alejandro's predilection — apart from Matias, and he didn't count. Catching Alejandro with the girls and the drugs should be more than enough to put him away. And once Alejandro was arrested and locked up, Frankie was under the false impression that he'd be free. He didn't realize that they'd keep him under wraps until he testified at Alejandro's trial, telling him that it was for his own protection.

He ordered room service breakfast while waiting impatiently for the two deputy DAs to turn up. Denver Jones, whom he would never forgive for treating him like a lowlife drug dealer when they were once friends. And Leon, the black dude who considered himself one smart son of a bitch.

Nobody was smarter than Frankie Romano. He would emerge from this fuckup un-scathed.

He was Frankie Romano. He always came out on top.

CHAPTER SEVENTY-NINE

"Where am I?" Willow muttered, opening her eyes, before vaguely realizing that she was trapped in a hospital bed with her left leg held aloft in a splint, while an IV was attached to her arm. She felt completely disoriented. "Where am I?" she repeated, because she had no idea *why* she was in a hospital bed or how she'd gotten there. Her mind was one big blank.

A nurse stood by her bed, a stout black woman with a kindly smile and a name tag that identified her as Shaquita.

"There you are," the nurse said cheerfully. "I knew it wouldn't take you long. The moment they brought you in, I said to myself, *Shaquita, this one'll be up an' at 'em before you know it,* even though you got a mild concussion an' you're all bruised up, poor baby. You're lucky you survived. From what I hear, it was a fiery crash."

"Brought me in . . . from where?" Willow asked, confused.

"You were in a car accident, hon. Don't you remember?"

An image of her mom flashed in front of Willow's eyes. She saw a faded blonde waving a check. *Was* it her mom? She thought it probably was, but she couldn't be sure. Then the image faded.

"What's your name, honey?" Shaquita asked. "The police were here earlier to question you, only Dr. Ferris wasn't havin' it. Our Doc Ferris is a tough one. Nobody messes with his patients."

Name? Did she have a name? Because if she did, she sure as hell had no idea what it was.

Dr. Ferris, an older man with a hangdog expression and thick spectacles balanced on the end of his aquiline nose, entered the room and approached her bed.

"Well, well," he said in a loud voice. "You were right, Nurse. This one's a fighter." He bent down close to Willow and spoke softly. "What's your name, dear?"

Why did everyone want to know her goddamn name?

"My head hurts," she muttered, clenching her teeth. "Maybe my mom should take a look at it. Can you call her?"

"That's an excellent idea," Dr. Ferris said, straightening up. "And her name is?"

Closing her eyes, Willow began drifting off. These people were batshit crazy. All they could think about was finding out people's names.

Surely they knew who she was?

After all, she was famous . . . wasn't she?

Across the hall in the intensive care unit, Max was attached to a variety of tubes. She lay motionless in a deep coma, her green eyes closed, her complexion deathly pale.

She and Willow and the teenage girl who'd survived the BMW crash had all been brought to a hospital near Barstow. The teenager had given a statement to the police, tearfully telling them that she had no idea who the other girls were. Two of her friends had died in the BMW crash, one of them being her best girlfriend, the other her brother. She was sobbing uncontrollably, waiting for her parents to drive in from L.A.

The police had quite a job ahead of them. The initial crash of the big rig and the other car had destroyed all evidence. They were combing through the burned-out wreckage searching for clues as to whom the car belonged to.

A detective was at the hospital waiting to question Willow, who seemed to be their only hope of discovering the identity of the victims. Two bodies had been found in the car that had crashed with the big rig, their bodies burned beyond recognition.

Who were they? Willow was the only one who could answer that question.

CHAPTER EIGHTY

A sleek black limousine with an armed driver and a follow-up car close behind drove Lucky, Lennie, Bobby, and Chris to the Magiriano. The two younger boys had gone on ahead with Brigette and Steven.

"I'm thinking this is overkill," Lucky remarked, tapping her fingers impatiently on the leather seat as she gazed out the window.

"No," Chris replied, ever alert. "It's called being careful."

"Listen," Lucky said with an irritable shake of her head. "If somebody wanted to get to me, they'd have done it by now."

"Chris is right to take precautions," Lennie said, always the voice of reason. "We're heading for a high-profile event, and let's not forget that you're the star."

"Star!" Lucky exploded. "What do you think this is — a fucking movie premiere?"

"Okay, okay. Calm down everyone," Bobby interjected. "We're all on edge. This is Granddad's day, and he sure as hell wouldn't want anyone fighting."

"You're right," Lucky said, imagining Gino saying, *What the fuck's wrong with you people? For crissake, get it together.*

"When we arrive at the hotel, I'm putting you in the manager's office until all guests are seated," Chris announced.

"Is that necessary?" Lucky asked.

"Yes, unless you want random guests stopping you and trying to grab your attention on your way to your seats," Chris pointed out. "The plan is to wait until everyone's seated, then I'll take you straight out to the podium and the ceremony can begin."

"Sounds sensible enough," Lennie agreed.

Leaning back in the limo, Lucky began thinking about what she was going to say. She hadn't written a speech — too formal. She wanted her words to come straight from the heart.

Gino. Father. Fighter. Ladies' man. Tough guy. Business titan. Man of the world.

Gino the Ram.

How could she ever hope to capture the essence of Gino with mere words? It was impossible.

Taking a quick glance over at Bobby, she wondered if he'd written anything to honor his grandfather. Should she ask him? He looked as if he hadn't slept all night. Oh God, the strain was getting to all of them. He was probably missing Denver too. Bad timing for a breakup.

And Max — where *was* she? Although she realized that Lennie was concerned, she was also aware that Max was quite capable of looking out for herself. Knowing her daughter so well, Lucky wouldn't put it past her to be screwing with Lennie because she was mad at him for calling a stop to her fling with Billy Melina.

Still . . . Max had better show her face at Gino's service or else.

"We're almost there," Lennie said.

Taking a long deep breath, Lucky attempted to compose herself.

Stay strong, she told herself. *Hold it together. And tomorrow you can get down to the serious business of tracking Gino's killer.*

People mingled. From movie stars to politicians, TV personalities and many acquaintances, everyone was there to remember their old friend Gino Santangelo. They filled the lobby of the Magiriano, moving slowly to the outside area where rows of chairs faced a specially erected podium with a center dais where the speakers would stand in front of a microphone to honor the memory of Gino. The podium was covered in an array of lavish floral tributes, and a single blowup photo of Gino and Maria on their wedding day. It was Lucky's favorite photo.

The atmosphere was festive, exactly as

Lucky had planned. Sunshine and flowers, smiles and friendship. No religious ceremony, as Gino — a lapsed Catholic — had not believed in religion. He blamed religion and people's differences for all the troubles in the world. Lucky had always agreed with him.

Paige and her entourage marched toward the front seats full of entitlement. Danny had to tell her that were only two seats for her in the reserved section, and that her other guests would have to sit further back. She did not take the news well. Glaring at Danny, she chose Bud Pappas to accompany her to the front row.

Now it was Darlene's turn to be annoyed as she was forced to find seats further back with the rest of Paige's entourage. She threw Paige a furious look.

People jockeyed for position. Danny was beside himself, as he was the one who had to protect the several rows of reserved seats — seats where most of the important guests expected to be seated.

Charlie Dollar rolled in with Venus, Alex Woods, and Alex's Asian girlfriend. Awkward, as there were only reserved seats for Charlie, Venus, and Alex — no seat for Alex's girlfriend. Charlie Dollar was one movie star who frightened the crap out of Danny, so he made an executive decision and decided not to argue the point.

The Richmond family came through, followed by talk-show host Jack Python; a gaggle of gorgeous blondes; Cookie's dad, soul singer Gerald M., with a very tall model; and Eddie and Annabelle Falcon.

Although Eddie had met Gino only a couple of times, he considered this to be an important event not to be missed, so he'd persuaded one of his star clients, Jack Python, to score him an invite. Now here he was, ready to conduct business at the after party. A good agent never lets a funeral get in the way of networking.

The reserved seats were filling up quickly. Steven, Brigette, her girlfriend, Gino Junior, and Leo were all seated in the front row. Only four more seats were available, for Lucky, Lennie, Max, and Bobby.

Danny told his significant other, Buff — who was helping out — to guard those seats with his life.

Refreshments were served by pretty girls and attractive waiters offering trays of still and sparkling water.

The crowd was beginning to settle. Soon the service would begin.

Pacing impatiently around Ian Simmons's office, Lucky recalled the time it had once been her office, and even though it had been refurbished, being there brought back so many amazing memories. Nothing was the same, yet it was as if nothing had really changed. She remembered sitting behind her desk in this very room, running the place, giving orders, relishing every minute of being in charge.

"I guess I'll go take my seat," Bobby said, wondering where Venus was sitting, and if he could position himself near to her. "We don't want to march in like a parade. It should be just you and Lennie."

"We'll see you out there," Lennie said. "And you can tell your sister when you see her that she's in deep trouble."

"I'll do that," Bobby said, leaving the room.

Chris had already gone to check on everything, assuring them he would be back soon. Lucky moved over to Ian's desk and sat behind it, observing that at least the view was the same. Lush greenery and a profusion of swaying palm trees. She remembered the day she'd ordered the trees to be planted. They'd been quite small then, but now they were tall and majestic.

"How d'you feel?" Lennie asked.

"How do you think?" she responded.

"You're gonna do great, sweetheart," he assured her. "You'll make Gino proud."

That's all she'd wanted as a kid, to make her daddy proud. It had been a struggle, but over the years she'd gotten there. Gino had finally accepted her as the strong woman she'd become.

Ian Simmons kept a pristine desk. There

was a neat stack of papers ready to be dealt with, and two Mac computers containing files on important guests and high rollers. In pride of place stood a framed photo of a woman and two young children — obviously his wife and family. Propped against the frame was a note card with an embossed gold trim around the edge. Reaching out, Lucky picked up the note card. Immediately an image flashed before her eyes. VENGEANCE. A word that had been printed on a note card identical to this one, the note card she'd discovered locked in Gino's desk.

Coincidence or not?

Hurriedly, she read the neat script.

King Emir Amin Mohamed Jordan thanks you for a pleasant stay, and hopes you will accept this gift as a small token of his appreciation.

A rush of adrenaline hit her hard. The stationery matched. The note cards were identical.

Her mind began racing. Had King Emir come to Las Vegas to take his revenge for the murder of his son? Was that possible?

Yes. That had to be it.

King Emir Amin Mohamed Jordan had somehow or other arranged Gino's assassination, and now the son of a bitch was here on the day of the funeral to gloat.

But was that all? Or could there be more?

Vengeance. The son of a bitch wanted vengeance for something she'd had nothing to do with.

Had he put other plans in place?

Was something bad about to happen?

"Get Chris," she said urgently, turning to Lennie. "Get Chris right away."

CHAPTER EIGHTY-ONE

Student nurse Felicity Lever, a plain, over-weight girl with mousy-brown hair and a pronounced overbite, was twenty years old and bored by her job. She'd wanted to be a model, only God had not given her the gifts to achieve that dream. She'd thought about becoming an actress, but how was it possible for that to happen unless a Hollywood producer discovered her? Instead she was a student nurse who would eventually become a registered nurse, and, according to her parents, that was her lot in life.

Felicity was a keen follower of popular culture, and the moment she entered Willow's hospital room, it struck her that there was something very familiar about the girl lying in the bed. Edging closer, she attempted to get a better look.

The girl had long pale red hair and pretty features. She was all beaten up. Apart from a broken leg, she had a swollen black eye and coagulated blood bruises down one side of her face. Even so, Felicity was sure she was someone.

Without warning, Willow suddenly opened her eyes. "I'm thirsty," she mumbled.

"I'll get you some water," Felicity said, still trying to figure out who the girl was.

"Why'm I here?" Willow asked, her eyelids fluttering.

" 'Cause you was in an accident," Felicity said.

"What accident?"

"A bad one," Felicity said. Then, just like that, it came to her. The girl was Willow Price. *The* Willow Price. The young actress with a shady track record who'd made many a headline in her time — from being voted the most popular newcomer in *People* magazine to a series of DUIs and accusations of shoplifting, plus a slew of very public fights with unsuitable boyfriends.

Felicity experienced a tingle of excitement. This was big, very big.

She rushed outside to the nurses' station, where Shaquita was stuffing her face with a brownie. "Guess what?" she crowed.

"What, child?" Shaquita responded, chewing contentedly.

"The girl in room six is famous."

"Famous?"

"Yes," Felicity boasted. "And I'm the only one who recognized her."

Shaquita put down her brownie and

squinted at Felicity. "Who is she, then?"

"Willow Price."

"Willow who?"

"Willow Price. Go ahead and google her. I'm telling you, she's famous."

"You sure about this?"

"Positive," Felicity said with a triumphant smirk. "Do you think it's okay if I ask for her autograph?"

"Certainly not," Shaquita said sternly. "Right now the poor dear doesn't even know her own name. She has a mild concussion, so it might take time before she remembers anything. We should inform Dr. Ferris an' the police, so they can go about finding a relative or a husband."

"Don't think she's married," Felicity stated, wondering if she dared to take a selfie with the famous girl. "I'll go check Wikipedia and find out."

Shaquita frowned. "Wiki what?"

"It's a place on the Internet where you can discover everything about anyone," Felicity explained, thinking, *Old people. They know nothing.* "I might even be able to find her address or contact info."

"Leave it to the police," Shaquita admonished. "It's not our job."

Well, it might not be your job, Felicity thought. *But why shouldn't I make some money out of this?*

An avid consumer of the tabloids, Felicity had often read about how they offered money for inside information, and what was Willow Price lying in a hospital bed in Barstow if not information?

Shaquita had no clue what a coup this was, and Felicity was determined to take full advantage of the situation. After a few moments she slipped away from the older nurse, who was now paging Dr. Ferris, and returned to Willow's room with a paper cup of water and a straw.

Willow was attempting to struggle into a sitting position and not having much luck. "What's wrong with my leg?" she whined. "What happened to me?"

"It's broken," Felicity said matter-of-factly, feeding her some water through the straw. "No biggie. Better a broken leg than dead."

Willow's eyes filled with tears. "Where's my mom? I want my mom."

"I guess you must've been driving?" Felicity said, probing for information.

"What?"

"Like I bet you were coming from some wild Hollywood party," Felicity said, her eyes sparkling with the excitement of it all. "A party chock-full of movie stars."

"Huh?" Willow mumbled.

"Do you know Justin Bieber?" Felicity continued. "I've read he's supposed to be trouble, but it doesn't matter to me. I like him anyway. Do you think he'll ever get back with Selena?"

"My head hurts," Willow said, pushing the straw away.

Abandoning the cup of water, Felicity decided it was time to whip out her cell phone. Switching it to camera mode, she began snapping a few random shots.

Willow raised up her hand to shield her face. "What're you *doing*?" she cried out.

"We need photos," Felicity said with an authoritative nod of her head as she moved in and took a couple of selfies next to Willow.

"For what?"

"For . . . um . . . the doctors."

"Doctors," Willow murmured, and once more she shut her eyes and drifted off to sleep.

Time to make a phone call, Felicity thought.

There was nothing Jeff Williams liked better than a scoop. And Willow Price languishing in a hospital near Barstow was definitely a fresh story, which nobody else had. After getting the call from some young nurse, he'd thoroughly checked the Internet to see if anything had broken. Nothing. *Nada.* The Willow Price story was all his.

He called the nurse back. She e-mailed him the photos of Willow lying in a hospital bed. After seeing the photos, he'd offered her five hundred dollars not to talk to anyone else.

635

She'd been so thrilled that he realized he could've gotten away with offering her two hundred.

I'm too freaking generous, he thought. *Mustn't make the same mistake again.*

Pammy was luxuriating in Willow's bed when the house phone rang. Most people didn't have house phones anymore, but when Willow had rented the place it was there, so she'd kept it as a backup for when she forgot to charge her cell.

Pammy picked up and said a cautious "Hello."

A male voice came back with "Who am I speaking to?"

Pammy considered the question. Could the voice belong to movie star Ralph Maestro? If it *was* him, as Willow's mom, shouldn't she tell him off for sleeping with her daughter? The age difference between them was disgusting. Surely he'd be more comfortable with a woman like her? A sexually mature woman with plenty of life experience.

"This is Willow Price's mother," Pammy said, putting on her best posh voice. "To whom am *I* speaking?"

Instead of announcing himself as movie star Ralph Maestro, the man said, "Jeff Williams from *Truth and Fact.*"

Truth and Fact magazine was Pammy's bible. She read it from cover to cover every week. Was there anything better than devouring stories about celebrities who'd had horrible plastic surgery, and cheating spouses readying themselves for multimillion-dollar divorces?

"Oh," she said.

"Hello, Willow's mom," he said.

"What can I help you with, Mr. Williams?" she said, still with the posh voice.

"We've received a report that Willow was in a bad car accident," Jeff said. "I'm leaving for the hospital right now and I was thinking that you might wanna come along with me so's we can run an exclusive family story."

Car crash. Hospital. Exclusive family story. Pammy's mouth dropped open. "Is . . . is she all right?"

"Banged up a bit, from the photos I've seen. Nothing life-threatening." He paused, then said, "Of course we're gonna pay you." After another pause, he added, "You on?"

Pammy was already out of bed. "How much?" she asked.

And so a deal was made.

CHAPTER EIGHTY-TWO

Everything was under control, and yet everything wasn't. Lucky felt it, and she hoped Chris did too, for her intuition had never failed her.

She told Lennie about the matching note card. He didn't seem at all concerned. "It's gotta be a coincidence," he said. "Besides, we've got security up the ass. According to Chris, this place is on lockdown. Nobody's getting in without a pass, so no worries."

"Maybe you're right," she said, forcing herself to sound calm, but filled with uncertainty because she had such a strong hunch that this two-bit king from a foreign country was in some way responsible for Gino's murder. "Anyway," she added. "Do me a favor and go be with the kids while I check on a couple of things."

"What things?" Lennie asked, exasperated. "You know it's time to get the service started. We can't keep everyone waiting."

"I'll be right there," she said, remaining

calm, but seething inside.

Lennie left and Ian arrived — having been summoned by Chris.

Ian took one look at their severe faces and realized that something was up.

"Shouldn't the service be starting now?" Ian said. "I am informed that all the guests are seated and everything is ready to go."

"What time did King Emir leave the hotel?" Chris asked curtly.

Ian hesitated for a moment, sensing trouble ahead. He should've informed Chris that the king was still in residence, only it hadn't seemed that important.

"The . . . uh . . . king and a few of his people decided to stay," Ian said, nervously clearing his throat. "However, not to worry. His man, Faisal, assured me that they will not be leaving their accommodations. The king understands that a private funeral is taking place. He will not disturb us."

"A private funeral of which he has a bird's-eye view," Lucky pointed out. "I'm sure you're aware that the penthouse suites overlook the gardens where the service is taking place. Did he request those rooms?" she added sharply.

Ian tried to remember. As the general manager, he didn't usually deal with normal bookings, but yes — he did recall that the king's travel representative had been very explicit about the king and his entourage occupying the penthouse floors.

"Yes. His man, Faisal, was here ahead of time to make sure the accommodations were exactly what King Emir required," Ian said.

Lucky experienced a shudder of apprehension. "What date did they arrive?" she asked, although she was pretty sure that she already knew the answer.

Ian checked his computer and told her the date. It was the same day Gino was shot. Of course it was, and she didn't have to look it up to know that Gino's murder had taken place exactly one year after Armand had met his end in her hotel.

Why hadn't she thought about this before? Why hadn't she put King fucking Emir on Gino's enemy list?

Because there was no reason for her to have done that. She wasn't responsible for Armand's death; he'd been targeted by someone else.

Only the king didn't know that, and now it seemed that he held *her* responsible, which is why he could've ordered Gino's murder — to punish her, although surely *she* should have been the target?

Perhaps she still was. Something was coming. What devious plan had been put into motion?

She turned to Chris, certain that she was on the right track. "It might be smart to get everybody out of here," she said, her voice low and steady.

"That's impossible," Chris replied. "There are four hundred of your guests on the premises. What's the threat? Tell me and I'll take care of it."

"If I knew, I'd tell you. But Chris, something's about to go down. Something big. I can feel it. We should try to move everybody."

"Move them where?"

"Anywhere away from here."

"People will panic. You know that."

"They'll panic even more if anything happens."

"Like *what*?"

"I'm sure this king person has something planned."

"You really think so?"

"Yes, I do."

"Then I suggest we pay the man a visit and find out exactly what it is."

Lucky nodded, her face grim. "Let's go."

King Emir Amin Mohamed Jordan was comfortably seated on the penthouse terrace overlooking the sea of people gathered below. His grandson Tariq sat beside him. On a glass table between them sat a two-way radio device and a cell phone. The king had ordered Tariq to touch neither of them.

It was a beautiful day — a perfect day, in fact, and as soon as the ceremony began it would be even better.

Tariq was an impatient boy. He asked too many questions. He wanted to know why he couldn't have left with the others. He wanted to know what they were waiting for.

"You will see," King Emir said, resplendent in a flowing headdress and a floor-length white robe, the hem decorated with intricate gold and silver embroidery. "You will understand."

"Understand *what*?" Tariq argued.

"You will finally understand the meaning of retribution."

Tariq didn't understand at all. He was anxious to return to Akramshar and show off his new toys to his friends. He had in his possession the latest iPads and iPhones, and stacks of CDs, DVDs, and video games, plus all his downloaded music. American car magazines, American girlie magazines, and suitcases packed full of the hottest running shoes, sweatshirts, hoodies, and baggy pants. It was only on formal occasions at the palace that he had to wear the traditional long robe — other than at those times, he much preferred to run around in Western clothes. Tariq had fallen in love with America, and he had thoughts to persuade his grandfather to allow him to attend an American college. His father, Armand, had been hugely successful in the United States, and Tariq wished to follow in his father's footsteps. Even better, his grandmother was American, so he could live with her.

"Why are we still here when everybody else has left?" Tariq asked for the third time.

The king was getting tired of the boy's questions. Way below him he could see all the guests assembled for Gino Santangelo's funeral ceremony. He beckoned Faisal and asked why there was a delay, why things weren't starting.

Faisal shrugged. He didn't know why. "Soon, my king," he said, bowing slightly. "Very soon."

The two young men, Nazeem and Salman, had been working in the kitchen at the Magiriano for the past nine months. Both in their early twenties, they were polite and extremely hard workers — unlike some of the other kitchen help who were constantly moaning and groaning about anything and everything.

Nazeem and Salman kept to themselves; they did not mix. Occasionally one of their coworkers would attempt to lure them out with promises of girls, booze, and strippers. Partying did not interest either of them. They had let it be known that it was against their religion to smoke, drink, or fornicate, unless the sex was with a woman who was their wife. According to them, they were in America to save money until they had enough to return to their homeland, where they both claimed

643

to have a fiancée waiting.

Executive chef Kurt Schaefer, originally from Switzerland, was pleased that he had a couple of dedicated workers in his kitchen. He found most of the American help to be lazy and slapdash. He preferred hiring foreigners, who never complained about the long hours they were asked to work.

They'd started out as general kitchen help, but Chef Kurt had soon promoted Nazeem and Salman. They appreciated their promotions, working twice as hard as anyone else. Chef Kurt had grown to trust and depend on them.

Now, today of all days, with the funeral service taking place, followed by an elaborate party, they were late.

Chef Kurt was livid. This was no day for them to let him down when they were both supposed to be on duty — helping with the hors d'oeuvres and buffet tables in the grand ballroom.

Chef Kurt stomped around his kitchen and hoped they would turn up soon, for when they did, he had a few choice words waiting.

CHAPTER EIGHTY-THREE

On the way up to the penthouse suites in the elevator with Chris and an agitated Ian, Lucky called Lennie.

"What's going on?" he asked, sounding annoyed. "The crowd is getting antsy. They're not used to sitting around waiting. Everyone's expecting you, Lucky. We gotta get the service started."

"I told you — I'm looking into something," she said. "And I was thinking you might want to get the kids out of there."

"You can't be serious," he said. "Do you really expect me to get up and walk the family out of here for no reason?"

"Why not?"

"Come on, Lucky, you're being paranoid. And for your information, Max is not here, and Danny tells me that she and her boss never checked into the Four Seasons last night. So if you want to look into something — look into that."

"I'll call you back," she said abruptly as the

elevator stopped at the penthouse floor.

Now she had something else to worry about. Max really was on the missing list, and that wasn't good. Could this be part of King Emir's plan? Because she was now absolutely positive that he had one.

If anything happened to Max . . .

Two security guards were stationed outside the doors to the main Presidential suite, both dark-skinned men with full beards. They wore formal suits and stony expressions.

"We're here to see King Emir," Chris said, flashing his detective badge as he approached them.

The two men exchanged glances before the taller one stepped forward and said, "Our king is not receiving."

"I don't give a fuck about what your king is doing," Chris responded, his friendly demeanor long gone. "This is urgent hotel business."

A nervous Ian hovered behind him while Lucky assessed the situation. Were the guards armed? Possibly. Were they prepared to use their weapons? Possibly not. If they were in their own country, they wouldn't hesitate, but here in America they would think twice.

She moved toward the door. One of the guards put his hand on her shoulder, pushing her back.

She spun around, eyes dark and deadly. "Don't you *dare* touch me," she spat. "I own this hotel, and I can have you all thrown out. I am here to speak to King Emir about his son Armand, so let me through or you will live to regret it."

For a woman to speak to them in such a way was a disgrace. If she was in Akramshar, she would be stoned to death for speaking so boldly.

But this wasn't Akramshar, this was America, and they had been warned to be polite and stay out of trouble.

Lucky moved toward the door of the presidential suite again, and this time nobody tried to stop her.

"What is going on?" Senator Richmond snapped at his security detail. "Why isn't this service progressing? I'm getting goddamn tired of sitting around."

"I'm sorry, Senator," the man replied. "The word is they're waiting for Ms. Santangelo."

Lucky Santangelo, Senator Richmond thought. *Of course it's her holding everything up. It would be.*

How he loathed his former daughter-in-law. She'd never conformed to what he'd expected of her. From the moment she'd married Craven and moved into their house in Washington, she'd been nothing but trouble. Damn Gino Santangelo for forcing the little bitch into their lives. Gino had wanted to get rid of her, and Peter Richmond soon understood why. Teenage Lucky was willful and full of big ideas; she'd had no intention of settling down and giving Craven a family. The divorce had been a blessing as far as Peter was concerned.

Today Gino was gone, and Peter's big worry was the whereabouts of the incriminating photos Gino had held over him all these years. Did Lucky have them? Would she use them if it served her purpose?

He was in Las Vegas — a city he hated — at Gino's memorial service because he had to find out. He was ready to make a deal with Lucky to retrieve the photos, and this had seemed like the perfect opportunity to talk to her.

Now she was keeping everyone waiting. Showing all the important people who was the boss.

All these years later nothing had changed. She was *still* a little bitch.

Paige was busy being social. There was nothing she liked better. And not having to share the limelight with Lucky was a definite plus. The downside was the blowup photo of Gino and Maria up on the podium for all to see. Damn Lucky for doing that. She, Paige, was Gino's widow. It should have been *her* with Gino, not his long-dead wife.

Lucky was a conniving cow, and Paige hated her.

Hovering beside Paige, Bud Pappas was in his element. His star might be long past, but everyone remembered him with great fondness. He was very happy to be there.

Venus bent down to kiss Bud on the cheek, telling him that she'd grown up listening to his music because her mom had been such a big fan. Venus's scent was so seductive that poor old Bud almost keeled over.

Eddie Falcon had moved in on Nick Angel in the hope of scoring him as a client, while Annabelle chatted with Bobby about how excited she was to be pregnant.

Harry flirted with Danny. Cookie flirted with Charlie Dollar, who in spite of being old enough to be her grandfather still had it going on.

Forty-something Gerald M. entertained his twenty-something Russian girlfriend with promises of all the important people she would get to meet at the party following the service. His girlfriend, a model, bared her large white teeth and gave a knowing smirk. She'd already spotted Jack Python, and as far as she was concerned, *he* would be the man of her future.

Lennie cornered Bobby, rescuing him from Annabelle. "Your mom's on a crazy trip," he muttered. "She seems to think something's about to go down."

"Hey," Bobby replied. "If we don't get this thing started soon, something *will* go down.

In case you haven't noticed, the natives are getting restless."

"I can see that," Lennie said. "She wants me to get the kids out of here."

"Why would she want you to do that?"

"Who knows with Lucky."

"That's true."

"I'm more worried about Max," Lennie continued, shaking his head. "Where the hell is she?"

"You checked her phone?"

"It's dead."

"How about her boss? You reached him?"

"As soon as we get out of here, I'm on it."

"Maybe she ran off and got married," Bobby said lightly. "After all, this is Vegas, and you know our Max — she's a little Lucky. They're two of a kind."

Lennie threw him a deadly look. "This is no joke, Bobby."

"Yeah, yeah, sure," Bobby said quickly. "Don't worry, we'll find her."

"In the meantime, maybe you can chase Lucky and insist she get her ass out here."

"Now?"

"No," Lennie said drily. "How about tomorrow morning?"

"I'm on my way," Bobby said, noticing that Venus was in a close conversation with Charlie Dollar.

Curbing the urge to go over and intervene, he realized that this wasn't the time or the place to act like a jealous boyfriend. And the truth was, he had no boyfriend status — not yet, anyway.

Moving briskly, he started to head back inside.

CHAPTER EIGHTY-FOUR

Pammy flung open the door of Willow's house and was confronted with Jeff Williams. She'd borrowed one of Willow's dresses, put on an expensive pair of her daughter's Louboutins, and applied far too much makeup. She was feeling rather full of herself.

"You ready to go?" Jeff Williams asked, standing on the doorstep impatiently cracking his knuckles.

He was older than Pammy had expected. She'd been hoping he would turn out to be a young stud — instead she'd gotten a leathery-faced man with squinty eyes, a burgeoning gut, and a gray crew cut.

"We gotta get goin'," Jeff said, a cigarette dangling from the side of his mouth.

"I'm ready," Pammy said, stepping outside and shutting the front door behind her.

His car was parked in front of the house; it was a beat-up old Chevrolet with blacked-out windows. Pammy took one look and wondered if she should be going with him at all. Maybe this was a bizarre kidnap attempt, and she was the victim. She wouldn't put it past Willow to try to get rid of her.

She hesitated before getting in his car.

"Whassamatter?" Jeff said, puffing smoke and crinkling his eyes.

"How do I know you're who you say you are?" Pammy ventured, wishing she'd taken a shot of vodka before leaving the house.

"You don't," Jeff replied with a dry chuckle. "Gotta trust me if you wanna see your daughter. Oh yeah, an' let's not forget there's a check in your future, right?"

"I'd prefer cash," Pammy said, pursing her lips.

"Then cash it is," Jeff said. "Now get in the friggin' car an' let's get this show started before anyone else finds out what's goin' on."

Pammy did as she was asked.

"I made a mistake," Felicity informed Shaquita.

"What kind of mistake would that be?" Shaquita said sternly.

"I . . . I don't think it's her," Felicity stammered.

"Who?"

"The girl in room six. I was wrong. She's not famous."

Shaquita made a clucking sound with her teeth. "For God's sake, child, why you makin' these things up?"

"Sorry," Felicity mumbled, hoping and praying that Willow's memory wouldn't resurface before Jeff Williams arrived. Felicity couldn't wait to meet him. Jeff Williams was a proper journalist bringing her money and fame — for surely she'd get credit for discovering the girl was Willow Price?

I could be famous too, she thought. *I could be discovered.*

"Now I gotta tell the doc we *still* don't know who the girl is," Shaquita grumbled with a put-upon sigh.

"Sorry," Felicity said again, before returning to Willow's room to check on her cash cow.

After making sure that the famous girl was sleeping soundly, she decided that she'd better take a look at the other girl, the one who'd been brought in with Willow, so she headed for the ICU, where she greeted the desk nurse on duty outside with a brisk "Nurse Shaquita asked me to check on a patient. Okay if I go in?"

The desk nurse bobbed her head, and went back to reading the latest copy of Oprah's magazine.

The girl in the ICU was still in a deep coma. Felicity considered the fact that this girl could turn out to be famous too. What a coup *that* would be. Two for the price of one.

The ICU gave her the creeps; it was always so grim and silent, except for the ticking machines keeping the patients alive.

Felicity hovered over the bed and took a long look at Willow's friend, a dark-haired beauty who didn't seem to have a scratch on her. Felicity didn't recognize her as she lay there in a coma. Unlike Willow, this girl was not about to wake up anytime soon.

Felicity decided that the girl wasn't famous. It was disappointing, but she snapped a couple of photos anyway, just in case.

Now all she had to do was wait for Jeff Williams to put in an appearance.

Pammy did not appreciate the way the seat belt squashed her tits. "Do I have to wear this?" she grumbled.

"Yeah," Jeff said, stubbing out his cigarette in an overflowing ashtray. "Gotta follow the law, an' I'm not gettin' a ticket on your account."

"The belt is too tight. I'm uncomfortable," Pammy complained.

"Too bad," Jeff said, immediately lighting another cigarette before informing Pammy that they were on their way to the hospital in Barstow.

"What the heck is Willow doing in Barstow?" Pammy exclaimed.

"Barstow's on the road to Vegas," Jeff said. "I reckon she coulda been headin' there. You got any clue who she was with?"

Pammy bit down hard on her lower lip. Why

hadn't Willow told her she was going to Vegas? What was the big secret? How come Willow was so intent on shutting her out?

"I dunno," she admitted. "She's been seeing that old movie star Ralph Maestro. Could be they were together."

"Yeah," Jeff snorted. "I know about her and Ralphie — who doesn't? The two of 'em were all over the Internet. What I want from you is stuff I *don't* know." He took his hand off the steering wheel and flicked on a recording device. "It's time for you to get talkin', Willow's mom," he said, blowing smoke in her face. "You gotta gimme the *real* inside Willow Price story, 'cause that's what I'm payin' you for."

Thrilled to be the center of attention, that's exactly what Pammy did, revealing much more than she ever should have.

CHAPTER EIGHTY-FIVE

"What is the meaning of this intrusion of privacy?" Faisal demanded, glaring at Ian, who was desperately wishing he were someplace else. As far as Ian was concerned, this was an embarrassment of mammoth proportions. Lucky Santangelo might own hotels and be a big shot, but in his mind, the woman was obviously deranged.

Chris didn't give Ian a chance to reply. "Where's your boss?" he said to Faisal.

Faisal's lip curled. "If you mean the king, he is not receiving visitors, especially not common people who are here to violate his private space."

Ian felt obliged to say something; after all, he was the one with the relationship with these people. King Emir had spent millions of dollars during his stay. Surely the king had a right to privacy? Ian began muttering an inane apology.

Chris turned on him. "You can go," he said sharply.

Ian didn't need to be asked twice. He scuttled from the room without looking back.

Lucky was busy staring at Faisal, a nondescript dark-skinned man of medium height and build with a full beard wearing a traditional long robe. She was sure he would do anything for his king.

Her black eyes studied him from head to toe as he argued with Chris, who was insisting they talk to King Emir immediately.

Faisal wasn't budging.

Upon hearing raised voices, the two guards entered the room.

The situation was getting tense. Chris was not giving up, in spite of the guards who had taken up threatening positions. "We have to see King Emir immediately," he insisted.

"No!" Faisal yelled, his voice choked with anger. "I tell you no and you must listen. My king does not receive infidels. You go. You go now."

Lucky fixed him with her eyes — black and deadly. "Infidels?" she said. "Is that what you think? So tell me, why are you here? Why are you in our country if you hate us so much? What the fuck are you doing here?"

A crafty expression crossed Faisal's face. "You will see," he sneered. "Everyone will see."

And that was the moment when Lucky knew she was right. Something terrible was about to happen, and somehow or other she had to stop it.

Outside on the terrace, King Emir was becoming restless.

"Go see who is making noise," he said to his grandson. "It is disturbing me."

Tariq got to his feet. "Can we leave soon?" he whined. "I'm bored."

King Emir fingered his thick beard. "The time is almost upon us. You will see justice as it should be done. You will witness retribution for your dear father's death. Only then will we leave this place."

Tariq threw him a sulky look. Sometimes he didn't understand a word his grandfather said. What was with justice and retribution and all the things the old man carried on about? What did retribution even *mean*? None of it made any sense to him.

Nazeem and Salman stood side by side in a rarely used narrow passageway that led outside to where all the guests were gathered. Nazeem and Salman wore long black robes and their faces were expressionless. For many, many months they'd been living a life they'd refused to embrace. American culture was not for them. It was crass and degrading. They'd managed to blend in as much as they could, and the previous night their loyalty had been justly rewarded, for King Emir Amin Mohamed Jordan had granted them an audience.

The two of them had stood before him in awe while their king had told them how proud he was of them, and how the people of Akramshar would be forever grateful for the act of sacrifice they were soon to commit.

"You will be heroes," King Emir had promised. "Your families and many other of your relatives will be revered because of your brave and loyal acts. Money will flow toward them, and the memory of your courage will never die."

They both had courage, although they were also filled with a deep fear of the unknown. They shivered beneath their heavy robes, painfully aware of the suicide vests strapped to their chests. Vests that could be detonated only by a cell-phone device in the hands of their king.

They feared discovery as they hovered near the opening. If that happened, the king would detonate early. He had the power; they didn't. It was all right, though, because King Emir was their ruler, and therefore, he had to be obeyed at all times.

Still . . . this didn't stop their feeling of dread.

Soon it would be all over, and so would they.

It was inevitable. It was their king's desire.

Chapter Eighty-Six

Driving down the freeway listening to Pammy carrying on, Jeff Williams couldn't help reflecting on his life. He lived alone in a one-bedroom apartment in Silver Lake. He had two ex-wives and a kid that he never saw. Work was his pleasure. Unearthing stories he could headline in *Truth and Fact* or on his very popular Web site, The Truth with Jeff, was really all he was interested in — that and a full bottle of scotch to start the evening. Jeff Williams was a man used to getting his own way. He had a press pass and a macho attitude, plus plenty of cash to hand out if needed. There was no way he was looking to get involved with anyone. Whenever he felt horny he simply summoned an available call girl, who'd come by his place and satisfy him.

So why was he suddenly experiencing an attraction to Willow Price's mom?

It shouldn't be happening. She'd obviously been around the block one time too many, and she had to be over forty. Not that age mattered anymore; most of the actresses who were hanging in there were way past forty. Jennifer Aniston, Gwyneth Paltrow, Cameron Diaz. Yeah, forty was the new shit.

He shot a sidelong glance at Pammy. Nice tits. Pretty face. Must have been a knockout when she was younger, just like her bad-girl daughter. And oh boy, was she spilling about Willow — he was getting a load of stuff, much more than he'd expected, for once Pammy started talking, she couldn't stop. A lot of the crap she was coming out with was all about her, and how she'd struggled and sacrificed to give Willow everything she could, but along the way there were a few hidden gems such as Willow's abortions and affairs with powerful married executives.

Jeff reckoned he was going to end up with one hell of a juicy story. And maybe he'd even end up with the mom. Stranger things had happened.

So far all was going smoothly. Felicity hovered near Willow's room, occasionally peeking in to make sure she was still sleeping. Soon Jeff Williams would be arriving, and that was the time for Willow to wake up and hopefully remember who she was. Then Jeff would get his story, she'd get her money, and all would be well — as long as Shaquita didn't interfere. Fortunately, a couple of gunshot victims had recently been admitted, and Shaquita was all over them. She'd instructed Felicity to keep an eye on the girl in room six, and that suited Felicity just fine.

Jeff Williams had told her he would call her the moment he arrived, and she couldn't wait. She ran to the restroom to check out her appearance. This was her big day; she had to look her best.

"We're here," Jeff announced, pulling his car into the parking lot of the hospital.

"About time," Pammy said, releasing her squashed tits from the confines of the seat belt. "I'm parched," she ventured. "I sure could use a drink before we go in."

"I'm guessin' you don't mean water?" Jeff said, scratching his stubbled chin.

"You're guessing right," Pammy replied with a coquettish tilt of her head.

"Well, Willow's mom, this has gotta be your lucky day," he said, leaning across her to reach into the glove compartment, his arm surreptitiously grazing her breasts. " 'Cause I got a bottle of scotch stashed right here with your sweet name written all over it."

"Ohh . . ." Pammy sighed, fluttering her over-mascaraed eyelashes. "You're my kind of man."

A few minutes later, they were heading in to the lobby of the hospital, both duly fortified with a couple of swigs of scotch.

"Remember," Jeff told her, taking a firm

grip on her arm. "We're a married couple. I'm Willow's dad an' you're the mom."

"But I *am* her mom," Pammy said, confused.

"Yeah, yeah, I know. Only hand these fuckers an ounce of authority, an' they might try t' gimme a hard time if they get a sniff I'm not a relative."

"I understand," Pammy said, changing her first opinion of Jeff Williams. It occurred to her that she might have been slightly off; he had a strong macho personality that went a long way to making up for the leathery skin and burgeoning paunch. She also suspected that he was into her.

She wondered if he had money — not a fortune; enough to make her happy would do.

Mrs. Jeff Williams. It had quite a pleasant ring to it.

Felicity's phone buzzed.

"We're downstairs in the lobby," Jeff said. "You wanna come an' get us?"

"Us"? Who was "us"? He hadn't mentioned that he would be bringing someone. Could it be his photographer? She wished she'd washed her hair; she was sure they'd want to photograph her.

Bypassing Shaquita, who was on the phone at the nurses' desk, Felicity took the elevator downstairs. She immediately spotted the couple. Jeff Williams was hard to miss in his red shirt and crumpled blue jacket. The woman with him was also quite a sight in a too-tight yellow flowered dress and exceptionally high heels. Felicity approached them. "Jeff?" she questioned.

"That's me," he said, winking at her.

"I'm Felicity."

"Yes you are," Jeff said with a genial smile. "Bonus points," he added, indicating Pammy. "This is Willow's mom."

"Oh," Felicity said, disappointed. "I thought she might be your photographer. I don't mind having my photo taken." A pause. "That's if you want to."

"Sure," Jeff said, used to dealing with what he called "civilians." "Maybe later, 'cause right now we gotta go see our little girl." Another wink. "I'm playin' Daddy, get it?"

No. Felicity didn't get it. Full of even more disappointment, she led them toward the elevator, getting a noseful of stale cigarette smoke and booze.

This was not how she'd imagined it would be.

Should she ask him for her money now? Or was it best to wait?

She couldn't decide.

CHAPTER EIGHTY-SEVEN

Unaware of a room filled with tension, Tariq walked in and was surprised to see that Faisal had visitors.

"Grandfather says you're making too much noise," he muttered to Faisal. "It disturbs him."

Lucky took one look at the teenage boy, and the image of Armand Jordan came rushing into her head. The boy looked exactly like him; he had the slightly hooded eyes, the sharp nose, the same features. This had to be the son of Armand Jordan — the man who'd been shot to death in her hotel, the man who'd tried to buy the Keys and failed, the man who'd said to her as he'd marched from her office in a fury, "I can assure you, *bitch,* this is not the end. It is merely the beginning of a battle you will eventually lose. So get off your high horse and run back into the bedroom where you belong."

Armand Jordan. She'd never forgotten his ignorant words. He'd been a delusional,

666

pathetic man who'd spent his time in Vegas ordering up hookers that he'd refused to pay, gambling, drinking, and drugging. Now his son was here. And the son's grandfather was King Emir.

On impulse she grabbed the boy's arm in a steely grip. "Take me to your grandfather," she commanded. "Take me right now."

Startled, Tariq looked to Faisal. Faisal attempted to move toward them. Chris blocked him.

One of the guards stepped forward. "Back off," Chris growled, pushing back his jacket to reveal a gun stuck in his belt.

"Let's go, kid," Lucky said to the boy.

Tariq's eyes were wide with anticipation. This was more exciting than sitting beside his grandfather being bored to death.

After checking Ian's office and not finding Lucky, Bobby headed back to the lobby, where he ran into a pale-faced Ian emerging from the penthouse elevator.

"Have you seen Lucky?" he asked.

"She's up in the penthouse suite," Ian replied, thinking it was definitely time he moved back to England. These people were insane with their out-of-control accusations. He didn't care to work for them anymore.

"What's she doing there?"

"Harassing the king of Akramshar, who just spent millions of dollars at this hotel."

"Why's she doing that when everyone's waiting for her?"

"Your *mother,*" Ian said tightly, "seems to be under the false impression that King Emir is involved in a ridiculous plot to create some sort of havoc during the ceremony."

"What plot?"

"There *is* no plot," Ian said testily. "I'm afraid this is out of my hands. I cannot believe this is happening. Your mother has an extremely fertile imagination."

"My *mother,*" Bobby said sharply, "is not a woman to be messed with. And you seem to be forgetting that you work for her, so I suggest you think before you speak."

Ian threw Bobby a spiteful look. "What's it like to live in Lucky Santangelo's shadow?" he asked.

"Fuck you," Bobby retorted.

"Most eloquent," Ian sneered, already planning his letter of resignation.

Bobby ignored him and pressed the button for the elevator. He didn't have time to exchange barbs with an uptight prick like Ian Simmons. He had other things on his mind, and that was to find Lucky and get her outside to the ceremony.

Tariq wondered what his grandfather was going to say when he appeared with this woman who was so unlike the women of Akramshar. This woman was strong and determined. She was also very beautiful — even though she was older. He wanted to ask her why she was here. He wanted to know her name. She had clouds of black hair and she smelled of jasmine and peaches. Her eyes were darker than night.

The man with her had produced a gun. Tariq had a gun too, but his gun was back in Akramshar. His grandfather had taught him to shoot on his twelfth birthday, then later he'd presented him with a solid gold gun. It was one of his most prized possessions.

Tariq's mouth was dry. He'd witnessed the king's wrath before, and when King Emir was approached by this woman, surely it would be bad? He only hoped that he would not get the blame.

"Who . . . who are you?" he stammered as they approached the outside terrace. "What do you want with my grandfather?"

"This is a joke," Senator Peter Richmond steamed. "We've been sitting out here in the heat for almost half an hour. I've had enough."

"What did you expect?" his wife, Betty, scoffed. "May I remind you that this is a Lucky Santangelo event. Tasteless and flashy — exactly like the woman herself. I do not know why you insisted we attend."

"I have my reasons," Peter responded, thinking of the incriminating photos he was desperate to get his hands on.

Betty threw him a venomous look. She knew exactly why they were there; nothing got past Betty.

"I need to use the restroom," Peter said, standing up. "Craven, you come with me."

Craven jumped up. Obeying his father was always number one on his list of things to do.

A few seats away, Annabelle complained to Eddie that she felt sick. "I can't take sitting out here sweating my ass off," she said with a petulant sigh. "Don't they realize there's a pregnant woman present? Why isn't this thing starting?"

"Like *I* would know," Eddie responded. He was as irritated as his wife, although he was also determined to see it through. After all, there were important people everywhere, and networking was his life.

"Whyn't we take a walk and get high?" Cookie suggested to Harry.

"Thought you'd never ask," Harry said, getting up.

The two of them headed for the interior of the hotel.

Paige stamped her foot impatiently. Had she been in charge, things would be moving at a much brisker pace. She suspected that this holdup was a devious plan for Lucky to get even more attention when she finally made her entrance.

Bud was driving her mad with his incessant chatter about his glory days. Who gave a damn? It wasn't as if he'd been in the Dean Martin/Sinatra league. He was a long-forgotten has-been, and Paige wished she'd given Darlene the honor of sitting with her. But she hadn't, and it was too late now.

Next to Brigette and her Swedish girlfriend, Steven was pleased to have reconnected with Beverly Villiers, who'd flown in from Chicago for the ceremony. Beverly and he had had quite a thing going years earlier, and she was still looking damn good. Plus she was a successful lawyer, and nothing turned Steven on more than a smart woman.

Steven didn't mind that Lucky was keeping everyone waiting, since it gave him more of a chance to catch up with Beverly.

"I need me a Jack on the rocks," Charlie Dollar mumbled to Venus. "Gino an' I used to sit around an' knock 'em back like real men. You wanna go get me one, doll?"

"Do I bear any resemblance to a cocktail waitress?" Venus retorted, shooting him a disparaging look.

Charlie chuckled. "You always had balls, just like Lucky. I admire that in a woman."

"You just admire women," Venus said

sagely. "Any shape, size, age, or color. If it's female and breathing, you'll fuck it."

"You got that right," Charlie said with another ribald chuckle.

"I know," Venus said smiling.

"Hey," Charlie said. "Isn't it about time t' get this damn show on the road?"

"It certainly is," she agreed, fanning herself with the program and wondering where Bobby had vanished to.

"Why're we just sitting here?" Gino Junior asked Lennie. "This is stupid. Where's Mom?"

"Bobby's gone to get her," Lennie said, and for a moment it occurred to him that Lucky might be right. Could it be that something bad *was* about to take place? Should he get the boys out of there like she'd asked?

No. Now he was being paranoid. Lucky was taking her time because saying good-bye to Gino was not easy. This would be her final good-bye, and he felt her grief and sorrow.

After today, things would be better. Life would go on, and the good news was that Lucky was a true survivor. She would get over Gino's death, and when she did, she could start to celebrate her father's spectacular life. It was time.

CHAPTER EIGHTY-EIGHT

"Kitten!" Pammy crooned, leaning over Willow's bed in full caring mom mode.

Willow's eyes snapped open.

"My poor baby kitten. Tell Mommy exactly what happened to you."

And just like that it all came back to her. Club Luna. Alejandro and his creepy friend. The dark-haired girl with a boy's name. Alejandro's new car.

We're on our way to Vegas!

Then crash, bang, hurtling through darkness, followed by pain and blackness.

"Oh . . . my . . . God," Willow muttered. "Am I alive?"

"Silly girl," Pammy singsonged. "Course you're alive."

"What . . . what are *you* doing here? How did you find me?"

"I came as soon as I heard."

"Where's Alejandro?"

"Who?"

"Alejandro, my boyfriend," Willow said,

panicking. "Where is he? Is he okay?"

Standing back, Felicity decided it was time for her to intervene.

"Willow is suffering from a slight concussion," Felicity said in her most authoritative nurse's voice. "Best that she doesn't get too agitated."

Now it was Jeff's turn to step forward. "You're lookin' good, Willow," he said as if they were old friends. "So how's about you tell me who was in the car with you. This Alejandro dude got a surname?"

"Alejandro Diego," Willow murmured. "We're making a movie, getting the start-up money . . ." She trailed off and fixed her eyes on Jeff. "Who're you?" she asked.

"A movie, huh?" Jeff said, his mind automatically drifting toward porno, because he sure as hell knew who Alejandro Diego was — the lowlife son of Colombian drug lord Pablo Fernandez Diego. He also knew from one of his informants that the car crash had incinerated the two males sitting up front. Only Willow and another girl had survived. He needed information on the other girl.

"I want a mirror," Willow said.

"No you don't," Pammy said.

"Do I look that bad?" Willow wailed.

"Who else was in the car?" Jeff asked, thinking that he had to get this up on his Web site as quickly as possible before the news leaked.

Willow was about to answer when Shaquita

674

bustled into the room. "What's goin' on here?" Shaquita demanded, throwing Felicity a furious look. "Who are these people?"

"We're her parents," Jeff said, turning on his own brand of smarmy charm. "An' *you* gotta be the lovely nurse who's been takin' care of our little baby."

Willow began to say something. Pammy quickly stopped her with a whispered, "Play along. We're makin' money an' you'll be gettin' some front-page publicity. Pretend he's your daddy for now."

Pammy was up to something, and Willow was too weak to argue. "Where's Alejandro?" she repeated.

Dead, Felicity wanted to say. *Your boyfriend is dead.* Only she remained silent, because it wasn't up to her to be the bearer of such devastating news.

Shaquita was busy glaring at everyone; she couldn't quite understand what was happening. One minute Felicity had told her the girl in room six was famous, then she'd changed her mind and said she wasn't. So who were these people? How had they received the news that their daughter was in the hospital? And was the girl famous or not?

Confusion ruled. "I'm fetching Dr. Ferris," Shaquita said, hurrying from the room.

Jeff took the opportunity to zero in on Willow. "Listen, hon," he said, "this is important stuff. Who else was in the car with you?"

675

Willow attempted to sit. Her head hurt, but her thoughts were clearing. "Alejandro," she muttered. "And a girl — Max something. Also Alejandro's Italian friend, Dante Agnelli. Is everyone all right?"

Bingo! Jeff had names. He could run with his story. The fucker was all his.

He reached for his cell phone and quickly googled Dante Agnelli, discovering that Dante was part of the well-known, ultra-rich Dolcezza fashion dynasty in Italy. As for the other girl . . . "Who's Max?" he asked, craving a cigarette.

"I still don't know who *you* are," Willow said, frowning. "Why should I tell you anything?"

"He's Jeff Williams," Pammy said, as if his name meant something. "He's our friend who's trying to help."

"Help *what*?" Willow said. "Where's Alejandro? How did you find me?"

Felicity was getting fed up with being relegated to the background. After all, *she* was the one who'd discovered that the famous Willow Price was in the hospital. Surely Jeff Williams should be paying more attention to *her*?

"I can take you to the other girl," Felicity said, edging closer to Jeff. "She's a nobody."

"Wait a minute," Jeff said, still checking out google and the Dolcezza family. "Did you say the girl's name was Max?"

676

Willow nodded.

"She's the latest model for Dolcezza," Jeff muttered, almost to himself.

"For what?" Pammy said, wishing she'd taken another shot of scotch. She didn't relish sitting around a hospital; it gave her the creeps. Willow was fine. Jeff had his story. Couldn't they leave?

Jeff turned to Felicity. "Okay," he said. "Take me to the other girl."

"She's in the ICU," Felicity said. "You won't be allowed in."

"Try me," Jeff said confidently, grabbing her arm and guiding her to the door.

"Where're you going?" Pammy asked, getting more flustered by the minute.

"Hold the fort. I'll be right back," Jeff said, leaving Willow and Pammy alone together.

A half hour later, Jeff was sitting in the lobby posting his story. He'd found out that Max was a Santangelo, and the girl was in a coma, which made his story even more strong and dramatic.

Jeff was psyched. He had an exclusive on four young people — all well known in their own particular way. The bad-girl movie starlet. The lowlife son of a drug czar. The daughter of two major players. And the Italian playboy, heir to the Dolcezza fortune.

Jeff was first out of the gate with this one,

and he couldn't have been more pleased with
himself.

CHAPTER EIGHTY-NINE

The boy had asked her what she wanted with his grandfather. Lucky didn't know *what* she wanted as she sent Tariq away and headed for the man sitting serenely on the terrace high above where the ceremony would soon take place.

The man — the king — or whoever the fuck he was had his back to her, and the only thing she knew for sure was that she had to find out what devious plan he had in place. It was obviously something he cared to witness, for why else would he have gotten his family to leave while he remained behind?

Had he arranged for a gunman to run riot among the crowd below, randomly shooting people?

Or maybe there was a bomb placed somewhere.

She shuddered at the thought.

Her entire family was present and SOMETHING BAD WAS ABOUT TO HAPPEN.

She surprised him with her presence, moving in front of him, her dark eyes blazing.

King Emir was taken aback; he had not expected to be confronted by this lowly female creature. Where was Faisal? Where were his guards? This intrusion was unforgiveable.

"Who are you?" he growled, his voice thick with contempt.

"I think you know who I am," Lucky answered, fearless and determined.

"I do not take kindly to a woman daring to speak with me without my permission," the king said, with an imperious glare. "You will leave now. Immediately. It is an order."

"I'm not going anywhere," Lucky responded, thinking, *Like father, like son.* They both hated women. "I want you to be aware that I am not responsible for Armand's death. But you — you *are* responsible for arranging the execution of my father, isn't that so?"

"How dare you presume to speak to me directly? Do you not understand that I am a king, a monarch? I am royal, majestic, and you are nothing but an odious female whose only use in this world is to be there for a man's sexual pleasure and to bear his offspring."

"God!" she exclaimed. "You really do have one foot in the Stone Age."

"Shut your filthy mouth."

"Why are you here?" Lucky said, staring him down. "What do you have planned?"

"Ah," he said, a crafty expression crossing his swarthy face. "That is for you to find out, for in my country we punish sinners. We relish the death of infidels who have violated our laws."

"Your so-called laws mean nothing here," Lucky said scathingly. "You're in America now, not some tin-pot monarchy that nobody's ever heard of and that you think you rule. Don't you get it? If anything goes down, I will have you arrested and thrown into jail."

The king gave a disdainful sneer as his hand hovered over the cell phone placed on the table beside him.

With a sudden flash of clarity, Lucky knew. The cell phone. It had to be the detonator. The cell phone was the key to what was about to take place.

Instinctively she flung herself forward, desperate to stop him from reaching the phone.

Shocked that he was being attacked, he roared his displeasure as she grabbed his wrist, attempting to wrest his hand away.

"You American *whore,*" he screamed, struggling to free his hand. "You dare to touch a *king* — you will *die* for your impudence."

"Screw you, old man," Lucky said breathlessly. "You're stone-cold crazy, and I *know* what you're trying to do. I *know* your plan."

"You know nothing. Do you hear me — nothing."

They battled it out, both resolute in their quest to win. Lucky was strong. The king was stronger. With an animalistic roar of fury, he managed to shove her away, giving him just enough time to press the trigger button on his cell.

There was a moment of silence, then they both heard the explosion from way below.

The king gave an evil laugh. "It's a shame you are not down there," he said. "It will suffice that your loved ones are, for they deserved to be punished, exactly like your dog of a father. Yes, you are quite right. I arranged for his execution, and I can assure you that it was my profound pleasure to do so. I knew you would bury him here, so I made sure that I would be in attendance. I think it is true that you suffer more when it's your relatives and friends who die because of you."

"You sick *motherfucker.*"

"Unfortunately for you, there is nothing you can do to me," he continued, rising to his feet. "I have diplomatic immunity in your country." With a vile smile of triumph, he added, "I am a king, and you are no more than a useless woman. I will leave now. I shall return to my country, where women know their place."

A black fury came over her. A fury so strong that she could not control it.

She flew at this monster of a man, ready to gouge his eyes out. She raged against him with all her strength, clawing at his face with her nails, spitting at him, kicking him.

He reeled back from her attack, falling hard against the railings of the terrace, tripping on his long robe. He attempted to regain his balance, leaning his full weight against the railings, and to his surprise he found himself falling . . . falling . . . into the chaos forty stories below.

CHAPTER NINETY

There was nothing Lucky could do. Nothing she wanted to do. She couldn't save King Emir, and even if it had been possible for her to do so, she would've allowed him to fall. He'd ordered the cold-blooded assassination of Gino, and for that he was being duly punished.

Justice ruled.

Santangelo justice.

She ran from the terrace into the living room, where Chris still held Faisal and the two guards at bay.

"We've got to go," she said tersely, aware of what would take place when they discovered that their precious king was no longer with them.

Chris didn't need to be asked twice. He'd heard the explosion, and he dreaded what they would find when they got downstairs.

The elevator doors opened. Bobby was standing inside. "Jesus, Mom —" he began to say.

Lucky stepped into the elevator with Chris close behind her. "We have to find the kids," she said, her voice choking up.

And as the elevator door closed, they all heard the wails of despair coming from the penthouse.

King Emir Amin Mohamed Jordan was dead.

So be it.

Nazeem and Salman were hunched in the narrow passageway when King Emir detonated the suicide vest attached to Salman's chest. Salman was hovering behind Nazeem as they waited for the signal that would send them out among the many guests, for only then were the bombs supposed to be detonated. Both men had received explicit instructions. On the king's signal, Nazeem was to head toward the podium as soon as Lucky Santangelo began to speak, while Salman was to make his way to the center aisle.

However, thanks to Lucky, none of this took place, although the explosion was still lethal enough to do plenty of damage.

Chaos reigned. Everyone was panicking, running and screaming. Acrid smoke filled the air. There were injuries, mostly to the people who had been sitting at the back near the passageway. Things could have been worse had Nazeem and Salman emerged from the passageway before the bombs detonated.

On their way to the men's room, Senator Richmond and his son, Craven, were caught in the mayhem — pieces of flying debris hit Peter on the head, rendering him unconscious. His security detail dragged him away to a safer spot, while Craven stood there, stunned — even more so when King Emir's body came hurtling down from above, landing only a couple of feet away from him.

Craven sank to the ground and began crying like a baby.

Meanwhile, Lennie was busy trying to get everybody away from the mayhem to a safer place behind the mausoleum. None of the family and close friends were injured, although everyone was reeling in shock.

Lennie couldn't help wondering if there was more to come. Lucky had been right; she was always right. Why hadn't he listened to her?

He tried to stay calm and in control. Where was Lucky? And Max? Was it possible that Max had been kidnapped? Could her abduction be part of a plot to destroy the Santangelos?

He ushered Gino Junior and Leo toward Steven, who was helping to move everyone. "Watch out for them," he said urgently. "I'm going to find Lucky."

"You do that," Steven said, grabbing both boys.

"I want to go help," Gino Junior insisted, skipping free of his uncle.

"It's too dangerous," Steven said tersely. "There could be another bomb about to go off. Nobody knows what's happening."

"I don't care," Gino Junior replied, his young face full of sincerity. "There are people who need my help."

Before Steven could stop him, he ran off.

Adrenaline pumping, Lucky raced outside, Bobby close behind her. She didn't know what to expect; her heart was beating out of her chest. What if her kids were injured or even worse? And Lennie, was he okay? She prayed that he was.

The carnage was bad, but not as bad as she'd expected. Later she learned that by tackling King Emir, she'd forced him into detonating the bombs while the two suicide bombers were still in the passageway — and that had saved many lives.

People were running everywhere, and there was blood and wreckage.

Lucky began searching desperately for her family, finally spotting Gino Junior, who was tending to a woman with blood pouring down her face. He'd torn off his jacket and was trying to stem the flow.

"Hey, Mom!" he shouted. "Over here."

"Where are Lennie and Leo?" she asked, bending down to tell the woman that help was on the way and that she'd be all right.

"They're okay, Mom," Gino Junior assured her. "Dad's looking for you."

The woman moaned. Lucky recognized her. It was Darlene, Paige's friend.

Nearby a man was crouched on the ground in a dazed state; it was apparent that his leg had been severed below the knee.

Lucky experienced a flash of deep fury that such a devastating act had taken place at her hotel. Could she have stopped it?

No. How could you stop something when you had no idea it was going to happen?

Someone must have called 911 the moment the bombs went off, for police and paramedics were already swarming. *Thank God for that,* she thought.

Bobby was helping the injured, and so was Chris.

Why? she wanted to scream. *Why would someone plan such a heinous act?*

Suddenly Lennie was by her side, holding on to her, moving her away from the danger zone, although she wanted to stay and help.

"There's nothing you can do," he insisted. "The paramedics have it under control."

"The bastard is dead," she said flatly. "Dead and gone."

"What happened?"

"I'll tell you later. Where are Leo and Brigette and Steven? Are they okay?"

"Everyone's fine." He was silent for a moment. "You didn't —"

"Didn't what?"

"You know what."

"No, Lennie, I didn't. But I wished I had."

CHAPTER NINETY-ONE

Denver was packing the last of her things from the house she'd shared with Bobby when Leon called her with the news of Alejandro's demise. Apparently it was all over the Web. She was shocked when she heard about the car wreck. Should she be upset or relieved that a scumbag like Alejandro Diego had been taken off the streets in such a horrific way?

Leon sounded quite cavalier about it. "Less work for us," he joked. "Now we can move on."

To what? she wanted to say. *It's not as if the whole Diego drug operation is about to come to a stop. Somebody will take over; it's inevitable.*

"Check out The Truth with Jeff on the Internet," Leon said. "There are other people involved in the crash. Bobby's sister is one of them."

"Max?"

"Some dude posted a story from the hospital. According to him, she's in a coma."

"Oh my *God*!" Denver gasped, thinking first Gino, now Max. Bobby had to be wrecked.

She didn't know what to do about that. Bobby and she weren't together — he wasn't her concern anymore, yet she felt she had to do *something*.

After hanging up on Leon, she rushed to her computer to read the full story. Before she could get to it, there was a news flash about two suicide bombers in Las Vegas at the Magiriano hotel.

Wasn't that Lucky's hotel?

Denver felt sick. This was all too much.

Plans were made to be broken. Things happened in mysterious ways. Always expect the unexpected. When Rafael heard about Alejandro's fiery demise, he realized that an opportunity had opened up for him that he had not thought would ever take place.

Alejandro was gone. Pablo had no other heir, so surely he, Rafael, would be recognized at last?

Unfortunately, it was he who had to inform Pablo by phone of Alejandro's death, and Pablo did not take the news well. At first he refused to believe what Rafael was telling him, then he turned his grief and anger against Rafael, as if it were *his* fault.

"I'm sorry," Rafael kept on saying. "It was a terrible accident."

"Why weren't you with him?" Pablo roared, his voice a steely blast. "You should have been protecting him. That was your *job*, you sniveling coward. *You* are the one that should be dead, not Alejandro."

At that moment, Rafael realized that Pablo was never going to recognize him as his son. He would never be respected, and Pablo would forever blame him for Alejandro's death.

It was time to move on after all.

Rafael knew what he had to do. He didn't hesitate.

Billy Melina was on the set of his movie, sitting in his trailer checking out various sites on his laptop when a story about the Santangelo family popped up. And what a story it was. A murder in Chicago. An assassination in Palm Springs. A lethal car crash. Suicide bombers in Vegas.

The story was more violent than any movie script. And Max, sweet young Max, was caught in the middle of it all. It was no wonder she had not answered his text. According to the story he read online, she'd survived the deadly car crash and was now in a coma.

He found it hard to believe, yet it was true, and here he was, stuck in Rome, thousands of miles away, making a movie.

He'd had his chance with Max and he'd

blown it.

Why? Could it be because he was shit-scared of making a commitment to a girl who he knew was not going to be a casual fling?

He'd bailed on her once, then after their magical reunion in Rome, he'd gotten the proverbial cold feet and bailed again.

One morning, after a night out with two hot girls who'd meant nothing to him, he'd woken up and thought, *What the fuck. I love Max. I want her back in my life, and I don't give a crap about what anyone thinks.*

He'd immediately sent her a text, to which she hadn't responded, and now he knew why.

Was it too late to do anything?

For Billy it was never too late.

CHAPTER NINETY-TWO

Fury abounded that such a despicable terrorist act had taken place at the Magiriano.

A cluster fuck of police officers, detectives, FBI agents, and members of the bomb squad had descended. Shortly after, the media started arriving in hungry droves, desperate to capture everything.

There were questions, statements, and police reports. Lucky gave her version of exactly what had taken place on the penthouse terrace. Nobody doubted her account of the events. Nobody except Faisal, who was arrested yelling and screaming that his king had been brutally murdered and that he demanded justice. He also demanded to be immediately released due to the fact that he and his people — including a terrified and traumatized Tariq — were all supposed to have diplomatic immunity.

Lucky had many connections; most of the major city officials plus the mayor of Vegas and the governor of Nevada had been present to honor Gino. The governor's wife had been injured — not badly, but enough to make the governor realize how fortunate they were. Three people had died, and two dozen were injured. It could have been so much worse.

Once Lucky heard the news about Max, she and Lennie had taken a helicopter to the hospital in Barstow. Her heart broke when she saw Max lying there in a deep coma. She immediately got to work, summoning the best doctors in L.A. and arranging to have Max transported by air ambulance to Cedars.

And there she lay in a deep coma.

Lucky questioned the doctors relentlessly, hungry for anything they could tell her. Unfortunately, they could give no definitive answers about Max's condition. Their prognosis was that she could wake up tomorrow and be perfectly fine, or she could linger in a coma for months.

The grim alternative was that she would not wake up at all.

The family kept a steady vigil by her bedside. Every day Lucky held her daughter's hand and told her stories; Lennie talked about the movie he was working on and how he couldn't wait for her to wake up and visit him on the set; Bobby played audiotapes of books he knew she liked, while Gino Junior and Leo blasted all her favorite music.

Nothing had any effect. She lay very still in

her hospital bed, serene, her eyes closed as if she were sleeping peacefully.

A week passed and nothing changed, until one day while sitting in the hospital, Lennie got a call from Billy Melina.

"I'm comin' to see her," Billy said.

"Not possible," Lennie replied.

"Why?"

"You know damn well why."

"You're being a fuckin' dick," Billy exploded. "Whether you like it or not, you *know* she cares for me, and believe me — it's mutual."

"I'm not allowing it," Lennie responded, and clicked off.

"Who was that?" Lucky asked, glancing at her husband.

"You'll never guess."

Lucky threw him a steely look. "I'm so not into guessing games right now," she said.

"Okay, it was Billy Melina, if you must know."

Was it her imagination, or did Max imperceptibly squeeze her hand?

Yes, she was sure that she did.

"What did he want?" she asked.

"What do you think?" Lennie said, frowning. "The dumbass wants to see her."

"When?"

"Are you fucking kidding me? Never."

Lucky took a moment before saying, "Lennie, sometimes you're right and sometimes you're wrong. I have a strong feeling that we should say yes."

"Why's that?"

"Because . . ."

"Jeez, Lucky," he groaned. "You and your strong feelings."

"Call him back."

"*You* do it."

"I will."

"Oh yeah, I *know* you will."

Later that night, Billy came to the hospital. Visiting hours were over, but for Billy Melina exceptions were made. The nurses were all excited to catch a glimpse of such a famous and sexy movie star.

The family had left for the night; only Lucky remained. Sometimes she stayed all night, sleeping on the couch.

When Billy arrived, she found herself hugging him, finding comfort in his embrace. She'd always enjoyed his company, especially when he was married to Venus. She'd had fun teasing him about being Venus's "boy toy." He'd taken it in good spirits. Then the divorce had happened, and later, when he'd gotten together with Max, Lennie had gone nuts. "That son of a bitch is taking advantage of my teenage daughter," he'd fumed. "And that's going to stop right *now.*"

Nothing Lucky could say had calmed him down.

"How's she doin'?" Billy asked, moving over to the bed.

"Unresponsive," Lucky replied.

"What do the doctors say?"

"It's a crapshoot, Billy," she sighed, weary from spending days at the hospital. "She'll either snap out of it or she won't. Nobody knows anything."

"Yeah," Billy said, giving Lucky a long penetrating look. "You should go home. You look exhausted."

"Thanks," she said drily.

"I'm telling you — go home. Let me stay here."

"Why would I do that, Billy?"

" 'Cause I think I can help. Me and Max, we got a special connection."

Lucky was willing to give it a try. She had nothing to lose, and Billy seemed to be genuinely concerned. Maybe he *could* help. Maybe he was exactly what Max needed.

After a while, she said good night and took off, knowing that Lennie would be furious if he found out that she'd left their daughter alone with Billy. She was too tired to care. Besides, she could hear Gino's voice echoing in her head — *Give it a shot, kiddo. It's all gonna work out.*

Billy perched on the side of Max's bed. He reached for her hand and began stroking it. Then he leaned close to her and began talk-

698

ing, reminiscing about when they'd first gotten together on the beach in Malibu, making jokes, telling her what an asshole he'd been and how he wanted to make it up to her.

He kept on talking until he had nothing left to say, then finally he gave up and dropped off to sleep at the end of her bed.

It was four A.M. when something woke him — a noise, a gasp. He sat up abruptly and moved closer to Max. Her eyes were fluttering open. She gazed up at him.

"Hey," he managed. "Is that you, Green Eyes?"

"Billy!" she mumbled, her voice barely audible.

She recognized him! Holy crap! This had to be a good sign.

"Where . . . am . . . I?" she whispered.

"You're coming back to life, babe. You're gonna be okay."

Feebly, she reached for the tube attached to her arm, making an attempt to wrench it out.

"Stop!" Billy yelled, frantically ringing for the nurse.

"Wow," Max murmured. "I guess you really do care."

Then she closed her eyes again, a peaceful smile on her lips.

The phone call in the early hours of the morning is the phone call one dreads. It is rarely good news. When Lucky's cell rang at a few minutes past four A.M., she answered with a shaky "Yes?"

"Hey, Lucky. It's Billy."

"Is everything okay?"

"Better than okay," Billy said, hardly able to contain his excitement. "She's back with us, an' here's the kicker — she's weak and exhausted, but other than that she seems totally herself. She recognized me immediately."

"Oh my God! This is fantastic! We're on our way," Lucky said, overcome with relief. She jumped out of bed and shook Lennie awake.

"Wassup?" he mumbled.

"It's all good," she said excitedly. "Get dressed. We're going to the hospital."

Once again Gino's voice echoed in her head. *Told ya, kiddo. Told you it was all gonna work out.*

A huge smile crossed her face. Somehow she knew that her father would never leave her. Gino would always be around to protect and look out for them. All of them.

The Santangelos.

What a family!

EPILOGUE

Faisal, King Emir's loyal consort, was held in jail on a charge of conspiracy to commit a terrorist act. Therefore, he was not granted diplomatic immunity.

He pleaded no knowledge of what had taken place, while continuing to scream about the murder of his king.

Eventually, after his country intervened, he was released and sent back to Akramshar in disgrace.

Faisal lived with vengeance in his heart.

Traumatized and scared, Tariq was claimed by Peggy, his American grandmother.

"You are never returning to Akramshar," she informed him. "America is now your permanent home. You will become an extremely successful businessman, exactly like your father. You must abolish all memories of Akramshar."

Tariq was delighted to do so. As far as he was concerned, America was it, and never returning to Akramshar was no hardship.

Rafael put his plan into action, ending up in
Perth, Australia, with a new identity and
plenty of money stashed away. Unfortunately,
he did not know a soul, so being in Perth was
an unwelcome change from his life in L.A.

Much as he'd thought he'd hated Alejandro,
he found himself at odds without his imperious, strutting brother ordering him around.
He actually missed the hustle of Club Luna,
the financial dealings, even the women.

Now he was stuck in a city he did not love
with no family and no doubt a considerable
bounty on his head, for Pablo Fernandez
Diego would not take his absconding with
millions of dollars lightly.

Rafael continued to lay low. He had no
other choice.

Disappointed, student nurse Felicity Lever
did not become a worldwide celebrity. Stuck
at the hospital in Barstow, she had only her
selfies with Willow Price and Max Golden to
remind her of the day she almost became
famous.

But she did have a plan. One of these days,
she was going to take a trip to Hollywood
and look up Willow Price.

Surely there would be a job waiting for her;
she'd make a great personal assistant.

Felicity had her dreams, and they kept her going.

Chris Warwick decided that he needed a change of scene. While he was fine working for Lucky, Vegas did not offer him the kind of lifestyle he relished. He'd seen too much, done too much, chased down too many sleazebags. It was time for a shake-up.

One morning, he woke up, sold his van, stored his classic Mustang with a friend, headed to the airport by cab, and booked a ticket on the first flight to Hawaii. It took him all the way to Maui.

On the plane, he'd hooked up with a mysterious Hawaiian woman who'd invited him to stay with her. It turned out she was rich. Very rich.

Chris did not need her money, but he did enjoy her company. Eventually he'd moved into her oceanfront mansion.

After a few weeks, he was surprised to discover that she had an ex-jailbird husband she'd failed to mention, and that they were in the middle of an acrimonious divorce.

Was it his imagination, or did she keep dropping hints that if her husband were to have a deadly accident, their life would be so much easier?

Chris had the distinct feeling it was time to move on.

■ ■ ■ ■

A baby girl was born to Annabelle and Eddie Falcon. They named her Princess Angel.

Eddie was not involving himself in any Daddy duties, nor was Annabelle prepared to be a stay-at-home-up-in-the-middle-of-the-night mom. They hired two baby nurses and visited little Princess Angel once a day in her designer nursery. They were both too busy to see her more often than that. Annabelle was intent on getting her figure back, while Eddie was negotiating a lucrative deal to run Cameron Studios.

Everything was working out well for the Falcons.

Pammy and Jeff Williams got married in Vegas. Where else would such a classy couple celebrate their nuptials? An Elvis impersonator officiated. Pammy had always had a thing for Elvis; she was under the mistaken impression that she might have even dated him once.

To celebrate the occasion of their wedding they headed to a sleazy strip club, followed by a night of binge drinking and gambling at a downtown casino, where Jeff won six thousand dollars playing craps.

The money was rolling in. Jeff had already negotiated a deal with a New York publisher for them to write a book about the trials and tribulations of Willow Price.

Pammy was ecstatic. Had she finally hooked up with the man of her dreams? Or would Jeff turn out to be a loser, like every other man she'd been with?

Only time would tell.

Willow refused to attend her mom's wedding. She was furious that Pammy and Jeff were collaborating on a tell-all book about her life to be called *Poor Little Bad Girl.* It was disappointing enough that her dreams of producing and starring in her own movie were off the table. Alejandro was dead, and quite frankly — crass as he'd been — she actually missed him. He'd been generous to her in his own way. He'd bought her expensive presents, supplied her with the drugs of her choice, and promised her a comeback movie.

Now everything was gone, and all she had left was old movie-star Ralph Maestro, a man who was tighter than a virgin when it came to his considerable fortune.

She had to admit that he had come through when she'd needed him. He'd sent a car and driver to pick her up from the hospital in Barstow.

The big drag was that he'd expected a blow job in exchange for his good deed, even though she had a broken leg.

Men! Disgusting pigs!

She'd obliged, because she was an obliging

kind of girl. And although Ralph was kind of old to still consider himself an action-movie star, he had no intention of quitting. There were — according to him — many more big-budget movies in his future. Movies that it was possible he might even think of putting her in.

Willow always veered toward the sunny side. It wasn't too late. She still had so much to accomplish. And with Ralph by her side, who knew what her future held?

It was quite simple for Paige to walk away from Darlene. Her lesbian friend was damaged goods, and unfortunate physical disabilities did not appeal to Paige. Darlene had lost the sight in one of her eyes due to the suicide bombers' attack, and after visiting her in the hospital once or twice, Paige had cut off all contact.

Being a free woman, she wished to explore other possibilities. There was no one to keep her in check. No Gino. No Darlene.

Within weeks she headed for Europe with Bud Pappas in tow. Bud was the perfect traveling companion. He was a once famous old man who had nothing to say about what she got up to. And she got up to plenty, living out all her sexual fantasies.

Unluckily for her, one cold night in Paris she ended up in a dungeon of pain with a dominatrix who took things too far. Paige choked to death after indulging in a session of ligotage where she was tied up with leather restraints for her erotic pleasure.

Paige died in the throes of an orgasm.

Forgetting about Bobby was not easy for Denver, although moving in with Sam softened the blow. Sam adored her; he would never cheat on her; he was successful, an amazing cook, and an extremely attentive lover.

He was not Bobby.

Nobody would ever be Bobby. Denver had resigned herself to that fact.

Bobby Santangelo Stanislopoulos. The onetime love of her life.

Now it was all about Sam, and the truth was, she had no regrets.

Venus and Bobby made a mutual decision that it was wise to keep their affair on the down-low. Who needed the attention it would bring if they appeared publicly as a couple? They would be dogged by the paparazzi, trailed by TMZ, written about on all the blogs. Yes, keeping things under wraps was definitely the way to go, especially as neither of them were that anxious to come out to Lucky.

Their arrangement worked well. Venus was gearing up for a very hectic awards season, promoting her performance in the movie she'd made with her Venezuelan ex-boyfriend, Hugo Santos. There was talk in the press of an Oscar nomination. Meanwhile, Bobby and M.J. had nailed Miami as their next location for Mood, and they were also talking about building an ultramodern hotel in Dubai.

Venus and Bobby were two work-oriented people. But work didn't stop them from getting together, and when they did, it was as exciting as the first time.

The sex was where it was at. Mind-blowing, passionate, incredible sex. They couldn't get enough of each other.

And the fact that nobody knew what was going on made it all the more exhilarating.

The house in Tuscany was perfect for a newly engaged couple. It was not a glamorous retreat, more like a cozy nest for two people who wished to stay out of the limelight.

Max was happier than she'd ever been. The Dolcezza campaign had fallen by the wayside — the family in Italy had canceled the campaign out of respect for Dante — but Max couldn't care less about not being the face of Dolcezza.

Billy was back in her life with a vengeance, and she *did* care about Billy. And this time he seemed to care about her.

Coming out of the coma, she'd felt weak and disoriented, but otherwise she'd been miraculously back to her normal self. The doctors had said that she was very, very fortunate. They'd done a battery of tests and discovered no brain damage, no impairments. However, they'd insisted that she remain in the hospital for observation.

While she was recovering, Billy had visited her every day, bringing books, magazines, and movies on his iPad that they watched together. He was self-deprecating and funny and she'd fallen in love with him all over again, although she couldn't help herself from thinking that one day he might not turn up, once more breaking her heart.

"You're not a nice person," she'd told him from her hospital bed.

"Hey," Billy had replied, grinning. "*Some* people like me."

"You think you can play me like a violin," she'd sighed.

"And the girl is sounding smart," he'd responded.

"I *am* smart. Smart enough to know that I should stay away from you."

"I'm here, aren't I?" he'd said, giving her the famous Billy Melina look. "I left the set in Italy to be with you. The studio's threatening to sue my ass."

"Too bad."

"Yeah, too bad, 'cause who cares? You needed me, an' here I am."

"Yes, here you are."

"I like having you exactly where I want you."

"And where would that be?"

"Helplessly lying there," he'd said, still grinning.

"I am *so* not helpless," she'd said indignantly. "I'll be out of here any day now."

"Then I'm not letting you out of my sight."

"Seriously?"

"Yeah, seriously, Green Eyes. Get used to it. I want us to be together all the time."

They'd gotten engaged a few weeks after Max was released from the hospital. A secret engagement that only the family was privy to.

Currently they were in paparazzi-free Tuscany, lazing around and enjoying each other's company.

Max had an unbreakable feeling that she'd found her soul mate. Billy was it, and even though she was still young, she knew for sure that this time it was all going to work out.

Lennie wasn't thrilled that Billy was back with Max; he did not view him as a suitable boyfriend for his teenage daughter.

It took her a while, but Lucky had managed to talk him down. "If it wasn't for Billy, Max might still be in a coma," she'd pointed out. "We should be thanking him."

"Bullshit," Lennie had growled, until finally he'd been forced to accept the situation because it was what Max wanted.

The day they'd announced their engagement, Lennie had freaked all over again. "She's too young," he'd bemoaned.

"She's nineteen," Lucky had responded. "Let's not forget that I was married at sixteen."

"Okay, okay," Lennie had said, shaking his head. "I'll shut the fuck up."

"You do that."

All was peaceful at the Malibu house. Lennie had finished postproduction on his movie, and Lucky was busy working with her team of architects to create the perfect plans for her new hotel complex.

Lennie wandered out onto the deck overlooking the ocean and handed her a drink. "How're you feeling?" he asked.

"You've got to stop asking me that," she responded. "It's over."

"Can't help it."

"I guess I feel . . . vindicated," she said thoughtfully.

"Hey, all is good in the world. Max is happy, Bobby's working, the boys are doing fine, the son of a bitch who arranged the hit on Gino is dead — and not by your hand, thank God, because that would've opened up a shitload of trouble."

"You know something, Lennie? I would've preferred to have put a bullet in the back of his head," Lucky said calmly, meaning every word.

"Now you *really* sound like Gino."

"I'm glad, because Gino did things his way, and that's exactly how it should be. Let me tell you about the Santangelo philosophy: if somebody screws you, screw them back. An eye for an eye. Street justice rules. I'm a believer."

"Not to mention a badass."

"Yes, and don't you love it?" she teased.

"Wouldn't have it any other way," he said, stroking the back of her neck. "You're *my* badass, and that's all I care about."

"Really?"

"You know it."

They exchanged smiles, for they knew that whatever came their way they could handle it. Together.

They had each other, and that was all that really mattered.

ABOUT THE AUTHOR

There have been many imitators, but only **Jackie Collins** can tell you what really goes on in the fastest lane of all. From Beverly Hills bedrooms to a raunchy prowl along the streets of Hollywood; from glittering rock parties and concerts to stretch limos and the mansions of power brokers — Jackie Collins chronicles the real truth from the inside looking out. With over 400 million copies of her books sold in more than forty countries, and with some twenty-seven *New York Times* bestsellers to her credit, Ms. Collins is one of the world's top-selling novelists. She is known for giving her readers an unrivalled insider's knowledge of Hollywood and the glamorous lives and loves of the rich, famous, and infamous. Ms. Collins books include *Poor Little Bitch Girl, A Santangelo Story* and *Drop Dead Beautiful.* Jackie Collins was awarded an OBE by Queen Elizabeth II in 2013. She lives in Los Angeles, CA.

The employees of Thorndike Press hope you have enjoyed this Large Print book. All our Thorndike, Wheeler, and Kennebec Large Print titles are designed for easy reading, and all our books are made to last. Other Thorndike Press Large Print books are available at your library, through selected bookstores, or directly from us.

For information about titles, please call:
  (800) 223-1244

or visit our Web site at:
  http://gale.cengage.com/thorndike

To share your comments, please write:
  Publisher
  Thorndike Press
  10 Water St., Suite 310
  Waterville, ME 04901